P9-CKJ-953

# THE GONE WORLD

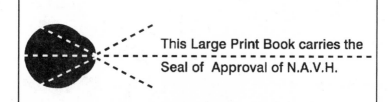

This Large Print Book carries the
Seal of Approval of N.A.V.H.

# THE GONE WORLD

# TOM SWETERLITSCH

**THORNDIKE PRESS**
A part of Gale, a Cengage Company

Farmington Hills, Mich • San Francisco • New York • Waterville, Maine
Meriden, Conn • Mason, Ohio • Chicago

LIBRARY OF CONGRESS CIP DATA ON FILE.
CATALOGUING IN PUBLICATION FOR THIS BOOK
IS AVAILABLE FROM THE LIBRARY OF CONGRESS

ISBN-13: 978-1-4328-5337-2 (hardcover)

Published in 2018 by arrangement with G. P. Putnam's Sons, an imprint of Penguin Publishing Group, a division of Penguin Random House LLC

Printed in the United States of America
1 2 3 4 5 6 7 22 21 20 19 18

FOR SONJA AND GENEVIEVE

If I have heard correctly, all of you
can see ahead to what the future
holds but your knowledge of the
present is not clear.

— DANTE, *Inferno,* Canto X

# PROLOGUE

*2199*

She had been warned she would see things her mind wouldn't understand. In a dead forest, in winter — never-ending winter, the trees blackened from old fire and coated with ice, several trunks toppled, a lattice of charred sticks. Climbing across the field of dead pines for hours, but her space suit kept her warm, a thin-profile suit that allowed her a range of motion to keep moving. The space suit was orange, the color for trainees: this was her first excursion to a far-future Earth. Everywhere she looked, in every direction, she saw the frost-blanched sky and the snowy ground crosshatched by fallen trees. There were two suns — the pale disk of the sun she knew and the garish white radiance of the phenomenon her instructor had called the White Hole. This was once West Virginia.

She had ranged far from base camp and

grew worried about finding her way back to the Quad-lander in time for extraction. A dosimeter measured her amount of radiation exposure, a color blotch that had dimmed over the past few hours from bright green to a green the color of pond scum. She had become infected by this place, the air and soil here polluted by a vapor of metal, particles minuscule enough to pass through her suit, into her body. QTNs, her instructor had called them — quantum-tunneling nanoparticles, he had said. She had asked her instructor if QTNs were like a swarm of robots, but he said to think of them more like cancer — that they'd house within the microtubules of her cells, and once enough of them had taken residence within her, she would be lost. Not death, he elaborated, not exactly — he told her that she would see what QTNs do with human bodies, but that her intuition might reject what she was seeing, that she might be filled with revulsion, that she might feel a violent need to *unsee.*

One of the burnt trees still stood, a barren pine whitened by a skin of ash — and when she passed the burnt-white tree, the landscape changed around her. She was still in the forest, in winter, but the trees were no longer burned, fallen. The pines were lush now, green, though snow-covered. Ice bent the boughs of distant pines vague through the scrim of snow. *How did I get here?* She looked behind her: no tracks, not even her own. *I'm lost.* She pushed through branches and needles, exhausted from the effort of lifting her steps from the drifts. She passed another burnt white tree identical to the first she had seen — dead, its ashen branches skeletal. Or was it the same tree she had passed? *I'm turned around,* she thought. Clambering over roots and stones, sliding down snow, trying to find something familiar, some land feature she could recognize, she pushed through a gap between pines and came to a clearing, to the shore of a black river. She screamed when she saw the crucified woman.

The woman had been crucified upside down, but there was no cross; she was suspended midair, hovering above the black water. Fire burned at her wrists, her ankles. The woman's rib cage was stretched, protruding, her body diminished, thinned to the point of starvation; her legs were striated black with gangrene. Her face was livid, purple, a pooling of blood, and her hair, pale blond, dangled low enough to touch the surface of the water. She recognized herself as the crucified woman and she fell to her knees on the shore of the black river.

*A trick of the QTNs,* she thought. It was repugnant, this absurdity. *They're inside me, making me see these things —*

Panic lurched within her at the thought of QTNs accumulating in her cells, her brain — but even so she realized this was no hallucination, that the crucified woman was real, as real as she was, as real as the river and the ice and trees. She thought to cut the woman down but was horrified to touch her.

Her meter changed from green to mustard yellow and she ran, activating her retrieval beacon, trying to remember her extraction point — but the forest surrounding the river was unfamiliar, and she was lost. She backtracked the way she thought she had come, buffeted by icy wind, slipping in snow. She passed another white tree, identical to the others — *or no, it must be the same . . .* a burnt pine, its bark a carapace of ash. The yellow of her meter had darkened to the shade of reddish clay. *No, no, no,* she thought, running again, ducking through a clutch of branches. The meter flashed brilliant red. Nausea swept over her and she collapsed, brought down by the heaviness in her blood. She crawled forward through a break in the trees and found that she had arrived again at the clearing by the shore of the black river, to the scene of her crucifixion, but there were innumerable crucifixions now, thousands of bodies hovering upside down along the length of the river, nude men and women screaming in the light of two suns.

"What is happening?" she said out loud, to no one.

Her vision dimmed, she gasped for breath. When she saw flashing lights in the sky, she thought she might be losing consciousness, but they were the lights of one of the Quad-landers, a module named *Theseus. The retrieval beacon,* she thought — *I'm saved.* The Quad-lander bounced in the clearing before settling onto the ice.

"Here," she said, her voice weak. She tried to scream: "I'm over here."

Two men in slim olive space suits worn by the Navy scrambled out of the hatch, and she saw them approach the river. "I'm here," she said, but the men were too far away to hear her. She tried to crawl from the tree line, she wanted to run to them, but she lacked the strength to stand. She saw the two men wade into the river, hip-deep, and saw them pull the crucified woman from the air, cradle her. They wrapped the woman in heavy blankets.

"No, I'm here, I'm *here,*" she said, but watched them carry the crucified woman, that other version of herself, on board the lander.

"I'm here," she said, "please." Her meter darkened to muddy brown, the next color would be the lethal shade of black. She closed her eyes, waiting.

The mule kick of the thrusters shocked her into consciousness, and she recognized where she was — she was in one of the Quad-lander's pods, she realized, her wrists and ankles strapped to the cot, her head and neck secured in a padded block. She was numb, shivering, covered in blankets that were tied down at the edges. The g-force of their liftoff abated, and she felt weightlessness.

"Please," she said, "go back. I'm down there, please go *back,* don't leave me —"

"You're all right, we've got you now," said her instructor, floating through the pod to her bedside. He was a much older man, with silvery hair, though his blue eyes seemed young. His hands were leather-soft when he checked her pulse. "Your wrists and ankles will be in considerable pain," he said. "I don't know how you were bound, but you suffered burns. You suffered from the exposure, extensive frostbite. Hypothermia."

"You have the wrong body," she said, remembering that she had somehow seen herself in the orange trainee space suit crawling along the tree line. "You have to believe me, please. I'm still down there. Please don't leave me —"

"No — you're back on *Theseus*," said her instructor. "We found you in the woods." He wore blue athletic shorts and white socks pulled to his knees, an NCIS T-shirt, gray. "You're confused," he said. "The QTNs are confusing you. They're in your blood. You have dangerous levels of them inside you."

"I don't understand," she said, trying to remember, but her mind was sluggish. "What's inside of me? I don't know what QTNs are." Her teeth chattered, her body shook. Excruciating pain raked her limbs, bright shoots of nerve pain, but her fingers were deadened, and her toes. She remembered stepping from her space suit by the river, shedding her clothes. She remembered ice burning her shoulders, blistering her. She remembered fire at her wrists and ankles. She remembered that she had hung upside down over that rushing black water for hours, for days maybe. She had been praying to die when she'd seen herself appear through the pines. "I don't understand," she said, crying against the pain.

"Our main concern right now is your hypothermia and frostbite," said her instructor, floating nearer to her feet and peeling back the corner of the blanket to check on her. "Oh, Shannon," he said. "Oh —"

She lifted her head and saw that her feet were purple-black and swollen, the surrounding skin flaky and yellowed. "God, no. Oh, God, no," she said, and in her shock almost felt like these feet belonged to someone else, that they were anyone's but her own. Someone had placed pieces of cotton between her toes. Violet lines stretched up her left leg. Her instructor rubbed her feet with a damp washcloth, but she couldn't feel the water even as it slid from the cloth over her toes and spun away like beads of glass through the air.

"Your mind was affected, your memory may have been affected by the hypothermia," he said. "First Lieutenant Stillwell and Petty Officer Alexis rescued you, stabilized you here. You're not there anymore, you're here. You're safe now."

"I don't know who they are," she said, their names unfamiliar. First Lieutenant

Ruddiker had piloted the Quad-lander, along with Petty Officer Lee — there was no Stillwell, as far as she knew. The bay window framed a view of Earth, distant now, marbled white with mists and ice. She wondered at her own body dying below in the wilderness, still in her space suit, but she could see that her space suit was locked in one of the pod closets, bright orange like a hunter's blaze camouflage. *What the hell is happening to me?* Although her wrists and ankles were covered with bandages that smelled of ointment, she felt her skin burning as if she had been doused with acid.

"This hurts," she said. "I hurt so much."

"We've let the medics know you're coming," said her instructor. "They'll be ready to treat you once we dock with the ship."

"What . . . what was down there? What happened to me?" she asked. "I was hanging. They all were —"

"You saw people who were crucified, along the river," he said. "I've seen them too when I've traveled to study the Terminus, many times — we call them the 'hanged men.' The QTNs crucify those people. They crucified you."

"You said they're in my blood. Get them out, get them out of me —"

"Shannon, we've been through this — we

17

can't get them out. We covered this in training. I thought you were ready. I warned you about them."

"No, you never did," she said, fighting to concentrate through the pain, the throbbing burn in her wrists. Her memories were confused, muddled . . . she remembered she had traveled to Deep Time on the USS *William McKinley* — to the year 2199, or one of an infinite number of possible 2199s, a distance of nearly two hundred years. A pale radiance hung over the Earth when they arrived, shining like a second sun — the entire crew had been astonished. No one knew what that pale light was. No one had warned her about QTNs or the hanged men. "You said you were taking me home, that's all you ever said."

"Shannon," said her instructor, helpless. He rubbed her feet again with the washcloth. "I don't know what to say. The hypothermia — it can cause amnesia. Maybe as you recover —"

"*Rendezvous with* William McKinley. *Prepare for docking,*" said a voice over the loudspeaker — a voice she didn't recognize. She remembered black water rushing beneath her. She looked again at her feet. Some color had returned to her right foot, but the toes on her left were still black, and the lines reaching up her left leg had darkened. The sight sickened her.

"What are they? What are QTNs — what's inside of me?" she asked, rebelling against her bewilderment. "I don't care if you think we've been over this before."

"We don't know where they come from, or what they want," said her instructor. "They might not want anything. Quantum-tunneling nanoparticles. We believe they are extradimensional — they come through the White Hole, that second sun you saw. Sometime in our future. They cause the event we call the Terminus."

"The crucifixions."

"The moment humanity ceases to be relevant," said her instructor. "No one is left alive. Not in the conventional sense, at any rate. There are the hanged men, but there are runners, too. Millions running in great packs until their bodies disintegrate or they run into the ocean to drown. Some dig holes and then lie down inside. Some people stand with their faces toward the sky, their mouths filled with silver liquid. On the beaches they line up and perform what look like calisthenics."

"Why?"

"We don't understand why, or to what purpose. Maybe there is no purpose."

"But this is just a version of the future," she said, imagining she could feel the QTNs like parasites in her blood. "This is just one of infinite possibilities. So there are other possibilities, other futures. The Terminus doesn't have to happen."

"The Terminus is a shadow that falls across the future of our species," said her instructor. "Every timeline we've visited ends in the Terminus. And it's moving closer. We first dated the event to 2666 — but the next travelers to witness the Terminus found that it had moved closer, to 2456. And the Terminus has moved closer still, to 2121. You see, the Terminus is like the blade of a guillotine slicing toward us. Our Navy and its fleet have been tasked to find a way out from that shadow, and our vocation is to support the Navy. Everything I'll teach you, everything you'll see, is to help our species avoid the Terminus. We have to find our way out from the shadow."

"What else will I see?"

"The end of everything."

# PART ONE

1997

# ONE

"Hello?"

"Special Agent Shannon Moss?"

She didn't recognize the man's voice, though she recognized the drawl on the vowels. He'd grown up around here, West Virginia, or Pennsylvania — rural.

"This is Moss," she said.

"A family's been killed." A quaver in his voice. "Washington County dispatch logged the 911 a little after midnight. There's a missing girl."

Two a.m., but the news was like an ice bath. She was fully awake now.

"Who am I speaking with?"

"Special Agent Philip Nestor," he said. "FBI."

She turned on her bedside lamp. Cream-colored wallpaper patterned with vines and cornflower-blue roses covered her bedroom walls. She traced the lines with her eyes, thinking.

23

"Why my involvement?" she asked.

"My understanding's that our SAC communicated with HQ and they instructed him to involve you," said Nestor. "They want NCIS assistance. Our primary is a Navy SEAL."

"Where?"

"Canonsburg, on a street called Cricketwood Court, just off Hunter's Creek," he said.

"Hunting Creek."

She knew Hunting Creek, Cricketwood Court — her best friend growing up had lived on that street, Courtney Gimm. The image of Courtney's face floated from Moss's memory like ice surfacing through water.

"How many victims are we dealing with?"

"Triple homicide," said Nestor. "It's bad. I've never —"

"Slow down."

"I'd seen some kids hit by a train once, but nothing like this," he said.

"Okay," said Moss. "You said the call came in after midnight?"

"A little later," said Nestor. "A neighbor heard commotion, finally called the police —"

"Do you have someone speaking with the neighbor?"

"One of our guys is with her now," he said. "I'll make it there in a little over an hour."

She gained her equilibrium before attempting to stand — her right leg still the lean, muscled leg of an athlete, but her left terminated in a conical mid-thigh stump, the end muscle and flesh there wrapped like a fold-over pastry. She'd lost her leg years ago when she'd been crucified in the deep winter of the Terminus — a transfemoral amputation, the Navy surgeons having cut away the part of her that had gone gangrenous. When she stood, she perched on her single foot like a long-legged shore bird, rocking on the pads of her toes for balance. Her crutches were within reach, Lofstrand crutches she kept propped in the gap between her bed and nightstand. She slipped her forearms through the cuffs and gripped the handles, propelling herself through her bedroom, a cluttered mess of clothes and magazines, loose CDs, empty jewel cases — slipping hazards her occupational therapist had warned her against.

*Cricketwood Court . . .*

A shiver passed over Moss at the thought of returning. She and Courtney had been like sisters through middle school, freshman year — closer than sisters, inseparable. Moss's memories of Courtney were the

25

sweetest essence of childhood summers — endless days spent poolside, roller coasters at Kennywood, splitting cigarettes down by Chartiers Creek. Courtney had died their sophomore year, murdered in a parking lot for the few dollars she'd had in her purse.

Headline News on the bedroom set while she dressed. She applied antiperspirant to her residual limb, then nestled her polyurethane liner against the blunt edge of her thigh, rolling it to her hip as if she were rolling on a nylon stocking. She smoothed the rubbery sleeve of any air bubbles that might have accrued against her skin. The prosthesis was an Ottobock C-Leg, a prototype — a computerized prosthesis originally designed for wounded soldiers. Moss slid her thigh into the socket and stood, the volume of her thigh forcing out air from the carbon cuff, vacuum-sealing the prosthesis. The C-Leg made her feel as if her skeleton were exposed — a steel shank instead of a shin. She wore slacks, a blouse the color of pearls. She holstered her service weapon. She wore a tailored suede jacket. A last glance at television: Dolly skulking in her hay-strewn pen, Clinton touting the newly signed human-cloning ban, promos for *NBA on NBC,* Jordan versus Ewing.

Cricketwood Court was a cul-de-sac, sirens flaring against row houses and lawns. A quarter after 3:00 a.m., neighbors would know something had happened, but they might not know what yet — if they peered from their windows they would find a confusion of patrol units, sheriff's cars and Canonsburg PD, state police cruisers, investigations a web of jurisdiction by the time federal agents were involved. Moss's cases tended to concern Naval Space Command sailors home on shore leave from "Deep Waters," the black-ops missions to Deep Space and Deep Time. Bar fights, domestic violence, drug charges, homicides. She had worked cases where NSC sailors had snapped and beaten their wives or girlfriends to death — tragic occurrences, some sailors spiraling after seeing the terrors of the Terminus or the light of alien suns. She wondered what she would find here. The county coroner's van was parked nearby. Ambulances and fire engines idled. The FBI mobile crime lab had backed over the berm into the front lawn of her old friend's house.

"Jesus Christ . . ."

The house Moss remembered from her childhood was as if superimposed over the house as it stood — two films playing concurrently, a memory and a crime scene. Courtney's family had long since moved from here, and Moss never thought she would set foot within her old friend's house again, certainly not under these circumstances. A two-story end unit, the other houses in its row lined up like mirror reflections, each with a driveway, a petite garage, each front stoop lit by a single porch light, the façades identical down the line, brick topped by white vinyl. Growing up, Moss had spent more time here than at her own house, it seemed — she still remembered the Gimms' old phone number. An oily sensation of one reality oozing into another, like a yolk pouring through a crack in its shell. She took a swig of coffee from her thermos and rubbed her eyes as if to wake herself, to convince herself that this coincidence of houses was real, that she wasn't caught dreaming. *A coincidence,* she told herself. There used to be a flowering dogwood in the front yard that had since been hacked down.

Moss slowed her pickup at a sheriff's blockade, and a deputy approached her window, a middle-aged gut and Chaplinesque mustache that would have been humorous except for the weariness weighing in his eyes. He tried to get her to turn her truck around until she rolled down her window and showed identification.

"What is that?" he asked.

"Naval Criminal Investigative Service," she said, accustomed to explaining her agency's initials. "Federal agent. We're interested in a possible military connection. How bad is it?"

"My buddy was in there earlier and told me this is the worst he's ever seen, just the goddamned worst," he said, his breath stale with coffee. "Says there's not much left of them."

"Reporters been around?"

"Not yet," he said. "We were told some news vans are on their way down from Pittsburgh. I don't think they know what they'll find. Quiet otherwise. Come on through."

A lace of police tape cordoned off the lawn and driveway, stretching from a lamppost and looping around the house's wrought-iron stoop railing. Some of the forensic technicians huddled near the garage, a smoke break. They watched Moss approach without the casual chauvinism or bald stares she sometimes encountered at scenes —

their eyes were haunted tonight, glancing her way as if they pitied her for what she was about to endure.

The doorway was draped with a plastic tarp, but the smells of the house assaulted her once she ducked through, the cloying tang of blood and bright rot and shit mingled with chemical stenches of the techs' solutions, the collection kits and ethanol. The odors seeped into her, a metallic tinge from the blood, her saliva immediately coppery as if she'd sucked on pennies. Criminalists in Tyvek crowded the foyer, busy with evidence preservation, photography. A nervous anticipation roiled Moss in the moments before her first view of a new crime scene; once she turned the corner and saw what she was dealing with, however, her nervousness dissipated, replaced by an urgent and sorrowful compulsion to reassemble the broken pieces as quickly as possible.

A boy and a woman lay on the floor, their faces smeared away in a mince of brain and blood and whorls of bone. Flannel pants on the boy, a jersey for a nightshirt — ten or eleven years old, Moss guessed. The woman's nightgown was filthy with blood, her bare legs shading to plum where lividity had discolored her. Both had voided their bowels, the floor so sopped that shit and standing blood had pooled in the uneven runnels of the carpeting. The odors gagged her. The smells of the boy and his mother degraded them, she thought, their humanity debased by sewage stink and formlessness.

Moss had long ago learned the dissociative technique of viewing bodies through different lenses, divorcing the mutilation as much as possible from the personalities they once were — seeing her colleagues around her through the lens of humanity, seeing the bodies through the lens of forensics. Moss objectified the corpses. The kill stroke for the woman had been one of two blows to her head, either to her left zygomatic or to the parietal on the same side. The woman's left pupil had dilated to a wide black saucer. Moss noticed that the boy's fingernails had been removed, all of them. And his toenails, too, it looked like. She checked the woman and found that her nails had been removed as well. Someone — a man, no doubt — had killed these people, then knelt in the gore to pluck their nails from them. Or had he taken their nails before he'd killed them? Why had he done that? One of the technicians ran lengths of thread from the blood spatter on the ceiling and walls, creating a web of thread that delineated an area of

31

convergence — it looked like the victims had been on their knees when they were struck, an execution. The room they had died in was bland, tasteless — nothing like the room Moss had once known, the comfortable, cavelike rec room kept by her best friend's family. Oatmeal tones now, track lighting. Nothing on the walls, no artwork, no photographs; the room didn't look lived in, it looked staged for resale.

"Shannon Moss?"

One of the men in Tyvek had paused in his work. Bloodshot eyes, nearly crimson, his dark skin ashen, VapoRub daubed beneath his nostrils in twin greasy streaks.

"Special agent, NCIS," she said.

He crossed the living room on stainless-steel risers the investigators used like stepping-stones over the blood. He chewed gum, said, "William Brock, Special Agent in Charge. Let's talk."

Brock led her through the narrow kitchen, the few men gathered there no longer wearing their Tyvek, their shirts and ties rumpled from hours of work, their faces wan with sleeplessness. Brock, however, seemed tireless — like he would charge bullish until this killer was caught. Angry, almost scowling as he led Moss, as if personally offended by what had happened here. He was sizeable, his voice a resonant baritone in a room of hushed voices.

"Right through here, in this little den," he said, pulling aside the flimsy accordion door of a room that branched off from the kitchen.

The rest of the house had been soullessly updated over the years, but the den remained unchanged, seemingly untouched since Moss had seen it last. The effect was unnerving — like this little patch had been forgotten when the rest of time had passed on. Faux-wood paneling, a gaudy light fixture that cast the room in amber. Even the particleboard desk and metal filing cabinets were similar, if not the same pieces left over. Courtney had once found a stash of letters in one of those cabinets that her parents had written as they were divorcing. The girls had sat on the front stoop and read them aloud to each other — Moss struck by how earnest, how almost childish a grown man's letters to his wife could be, nothing different from high-school breakup letters, she'd thought, no difference at all. Nothing changes. The human heart doesn't age.

"Do we have pictures of the victims?" asked Moss. "Anything recent? It's impossible to tell what they might have looked like."

"We have some albums," said Brock. "Fotomat receipts and negatives. We'll get them to you once they're developed. Have you had a chance to see the entire scene? Upstairs?"

"I'll need to see upstairs," said Moss.

Brock folded closed the accordion door. "I need to talk with you, clear up a few things," he said, taking a seat behind the particleboard desk. "The FBI's deputy director called me in the middle of the night, pulled me from bed. I don't receive calls from him on a regular basis. He told me there's a federal crime scene in Canonsburg, told me to lock it down."

"But that's not all he told you," said Moss.

Brock bared his teeth — meant to be a smile, an easing, but it looked like a pained expression. He wadded his gum into its silvery wrapper, replaced it with a fresh black stick. Licorice wafting on a cloud of breath. Moss noticed tooth marks on his pencil — maybe he'd quit smoking, she thought, or was trying to. Early forties, maybe mid-forties, muscular — a regular at the gym, she figured. She imagined him sparring, a boxer. She imagined him running miles on treadmills in empty exercise rooms.

"I'm struggling to understand what the

deputy director told me," said Brock. "To wrap my mind around what we've found here. He briefed me on a Special Access Program called 'Deep Waters.' " Brock spoke the words like an incantation, a shadow of fear passing over his eyes. "A Navy program — a black project. He said our primary suspect, a SEAL named Patrick Mursult, is connected with the Deep Waters program, part of the Naval Space Command. He said to include Shannon Moss in the investigation."

The scope of the possible world had opened for this man just a few hours ago, thought Moss, seeing Brock struggle to believe the unbelievable. He'd been brought into the secrecy of Deep Waters — but how much had he been trusted with? Moss remembered her first dreamlike glimpse of sunlight glaring off the hulls of the NSC fleet in space, like a spill of diamonds on black velvet — a sublimity few other people have witnessed. She imagined Brock taking the phone call at home, imagined him sitting on the edge of his bed listening to his superior describe what must have sounded like miracles.

"Mursult was . . . some kind of astronaut," said Brock, his jaw grinding his licorice. "Deep Space — I understand deep space, I can understand we've been farther in the solar system than has been reported, but I don't understand *how.* Quantum foam —"

So he'd been told about Deep Space but not Deep Time, thought Moss. Naval Space Command had a public face, had been involved in Star Wars under Reagan, line items in Department of Defense budgets along with the Air Force Space Division and NASA, but the bulk of its operations were closely guarded secrets. Moss had traveled to Deep Space, but she had also traveled to Deep Time — had time-traveled to versions of the future, not only to witness the Terminus but for her criminal investigations as well. IFTs, these futures were called, pronounced like the word "If" — inadmissible future trajectories. "Inadmissible" because the future was mercurial — the futures NSC traveled to were only possibilities stemming from the conditions of the present. She was prohibited against using evidence gleaned from a future to build a case for prosecution in the present because the future she observed might not ever occur.

"Think of me as a resource," said Moss. "That's why I'm here, that's why you were asked to call me. My division within NCIS investigates crimes relating to the Deep Waters program."

"I don't know what to believe," said Brock. "I don't know what to believe about Patrick Mursult, about a black-ops space program — it all sounds . . . I don't know how much of this I'm understanding."

"There's a missing girl," said Moss. "She's our priority."

The reminder of the missing girl focused him, the thought of something actionable. "Marian Mursult," he said. "Seventeen . . ."

"Marian," said Moss. "We'll find her. Let's start with tonight."

"Locals were first on scene," said Brock, any fog of bewilderment dissipated now, "pegged our person of interest right away as Patrick Mursult — figured he killed his own family. Once Canonsburg PD found paper-work suggesting Mursult was a sailor, they called the reserve center, to keep the Navy in the loop. They ID'd him — served in the Navy during Vietnam, he must have been just a kid."

"What else have you learned?"

"Your supervisor forwarded me a fax about Mursult from the National Personnel Records Center in St. Louis," said Brock. "Broad strokes about him, redactions. Navy SEAL in the late seventies. Served with the Naval Space Command since the early eighties. Petty officer first class, but his record stops in 1983. Turns out this guy has been living off the grid, everything under his wife's name. His official status is missing in action."

Moss thought, *A sailor living off the grid* — an NSC sailor MIA. A sailor lost to Deep Waters was a tragedy, but a sailor presumed lost suddenly appearing like this, living off the grid, was a national security threat. "We need to locate him immediately."

"Can we find out anything more definitive about this guy?" said Brock.

"I'll be working with my director, but NCIS is a civilian agency," said Moss. "I have top-secret clearance, same as you, but information about Deep Waters is on a need-to-know basis, compartmented. We can only work with what the Navy tells us."

Brock spit his gum into its wrapper, flicked the wad into the wastebasket. "Let's focus on what we know," he said. "The actor woke his victims, gathered them together in the family room before attacking them."

"With what?" asked Moss.

"An ax," said Brock.

She imagined the woman and boy kneeling — the wet thwack, pulling the ax free and swinging again. The annihilation of the family as simple as splitting wood.

"Any reason to doubt Patrick Mursult did

this?" she asked.

"None," said Brock. "But he might have had someone with him. The neighbor who called 911 mentioned a friend of his, a guy who drives a red pickup truck, West Virginia plates. We're focusing on the truck, trying to find this individual. She described him as a nuisance, often blocked her driveway. The truck's covered in bumper stickers. Let's take a look upstairs."

Moss followed Brock from the den. He ducked a line of police tape, led her upstairs, a climb she'd made countless times trailing Courtney, whose room had been the first on the right. The twisting metal railing seemed to spin against her palm, a familiar feeling. Self-conscious climbing stairs now, the movement of her prosthesis vaguely stop-motion, motorized. Brock paused at the top stair, watched Moss climb — he seemed to be spotting her, almost ready to try to catch her if she were to rock backward or fall. Moss had grown weary at these moments of awkwardness, when people first realized they were working with an amputee, trying to puzzle out how they should treat her.

"What happened up here?" she asked.

"His seven-year-old daughter, Jessica, escaped the initial attack," said Brock. "Ran in here."

Courtney's room. Brock put his hand on the doorknob. "I have two daughters," he said. "Two beautiful girls . . ."

He opened the door, let Moss through — returning to this room felt like curling back into a cocoon. She remembered coating these walls a pink called Bubblegum sixth-grade summer, slopping the roller from the tray, Courtney yelping whenever paint glopped from the ceiling into her black curls. She remembered puffing cigarette smoke through the window screen in the summer swelter, AC/DC on the turntable, *Powerage* until the record was scratched and couldn't play past the first few seconds of "What's Next to the Moon." The room was lavender now, with a white dresser and a bunk bed — the Mursult girls must have shared this room. Zeppelin and Van Halen had been replaced with DiCaprio, *Romeo + Juliet,* but the room felt the same. Jessica Mursult's body was in the corner, near where Courtney's bed had been. The girl's nightshirt was shredded, her back gouged with a deep cut between her shoulder blades that flayed out like gaping lips.

*Poor girl. Poor girl . . .*

"Are you all right?" asked Brock.

"Where are their nails?" asked Moss, her

40

focus watery but noticing that the girl's fingernails and toenails had been removed as well.

"You've gone pale," he said. "Do you need to sit down?"

"I'm all right —"

She wavered, Brock steadied her, a hand on her back. "Thank you," she said, though still unmoored. A heat of embarrassment flashed through her. *Pull it together,* she thought. "I'm . . . I don't know what's wrong," she said. "I'm sorry."

Brock shepherded her from the bedroom into the hall. "Listen," he said, shutting the bedroom door, "a scene like this is hard for anyone to take, let alone if you aren't used to it. It's all right if you're a little weak in the knees."

"I have to tell you something," she said. "This is . . . I'm having some trouble tonight, this is uncanny. I know this house."

"Go on."

"I grew up around here," said Moss. "I practically lived in this house when I was a kid. My best friend lived here. Courtney. Her name was Courtney Gimm. This was her room. I spent a lot of time in this room. Her bed was right over there."

"No shit," said Brock.

"I'm unnerved by this, but I'm all right,"

41

said Moss. "When Nestor called and said the crime scene was on Cricketwood Court . . ."

She steadied herself against the wall — touching the wall, she felt like she could tear this present world away and see her friend again, be with her friend as if no time had passed, as if she could step into the old bedroom, the gone world. Slap bracelets and jelly shoes, colored bands in Courtney's braces.

"We used to hang out in the woods behind these houses," said Moss. "We'd share cigarettes back there."

Sunbathing on lawn chairs, sharing High Life. Courtney's dad worked night shifts, so they had this place to themselves, her mom living up in Pittsburgh with her boyfriend. Pot some nights when Courtney could score, but most nights just staying up too late watching TV — school the next morning with bloodshot eyes. They partied with the other girls on the track team some nights. Neighborhood boys some nights. Some nights Courtney and Moss and whatever boys they'd picked up at the mall would get high and drink and fool around while *Letterman* played, nothing too serious, just petting and kissing and hand jobs, late nights ending with the smell of hand soap and semen.

"Christ, I lost my virginity in the room down the hall," she said. Courtney's brother, Davy Gimm — she could see his face as clearly as if she'd been with him just yesterday. A senior when she was a sophomore, when he took fistfuls of Moss's hair and kissed her, when he ran his hands under her shirt and unbuttoned his jeans and placed her hands on him. Hardening in her hands. Feeling his weight press on her and feeling him push into her. "I'm sorry, I shouldn't have said that."

"Let's get some fresh air," said Brock. "Can you make it down the stairs?"

"I'll be fine," she said. "I'll be down in a moment."

Her first night with Davy Gimm had been in the small bedroom at the end of the hall, more of a closet or nursery than a proper third bedroom. Knives that Davy Gimm had bought from flea markets, she remembered, a poster of Christie Brinkley from *Sports Illustrated.* Lying on the creaking twin bed, his eager fingers searching beneath the elastic of her shorts, his wet breath heavy on her neck. Remembering the sound of his sleeping, lying awake as moonlight crawled across the swimsuit model.

Moss waited until she heard Brock's voice

from downstairs before she opened Davy Gimm's old bedroom door — stepping into his room was like stepping into the cosmos, star clusters and the constellations of the zodiac bursting from the infinite darkness. She flipped on the light switch — maybe a part of her expected to see the swimsuit poster and the collection of knives, but she found the room of a little boy instead, walls covered with glow-in-the-dark star stickers. Foolish, regretting what she'd confessed to Brock — realizing she should have just kept her mouth shut, that she shouldn't have mentioned anything about this house at all. Unprofessional, a moment of weakness. She saw the room not as it had been but for what it was: the room of a dead child.

She found Brock outside. The lawns of Cricketwood Court were touched with frost, crystals feathering the windshields of parked cars. An upstairs light in a neighboring unit had flipped on.

"Where was Marian through all this?" she asked. "Has anyone seen her?"

"All the neighbors know who she is, but she hasn't been around," said Brock. "Not since Friday. We're waking friends and family, trying to track her down."

"You mentioned that Mursult has a friend who drives a red pickup truck," said Moss.

"No one knows this guy?"

"No one," said Brock. "Neighbors noticed the truck because it was often parked out on the street, but Mursult and his friend kept to themselves."

"I think we should go ahead and create the Amber Alert," said Moss.

"She might turn up," said Brock. "She might be at a friend's house. We're checking everywhere."

Amber Alerts were new, Moss reminded herself, not as familiar as they would become. "It will help us," she said. "Someone might have seen her."

Brock checked the illuminated dial of his watch. "Moss, your office is at CJIS, isn't that right?" he said, pronouncing the abbreviation like the name "Jesus." CJIS was the Criminal Justice Information Services building, the nerve center of the FBI — a newly minted campus, a crystalline oddity nestled in the middle-of-nowhere hills just outside Clarksburg, West Virginia. An FBI building, but without a Navy or Marine Corps installation in the region, Moss's NCIS office was colocated there. "You live out that way?" he asked. "Out near Clarksburg?"

"That's right."

"My wife Rashonda's at CJIS, in the print

45

lab. Maybe you've crossed paths."

"You're Rashonda Brock's husband?" Moss said. A few thousand with offices in the CJIS facility, but Rashonda Brock was well known, the deputy assistant director of the Laboratory Division. Moss's office was near the facility's day care, so although she had never met Brock's wife, she saw Rashonda drop her daughters off most mornings, a flurry of kisses and hugs. "I think I've seen some of your kids' paintings," she said. "Brianna and Jasmine, right? Their name tags are hanging on a corkboard near my office. Purple dinosaurs —"

"Barney," said Brock, smiling now, chuckling. "Everything's Barney the dinosaur — Brianna's room is covered with him." Moss understood how Rashonda might fit together with Brock, Rashonda always radiant, a plump woman, tall — she must feel a warm sense of satisfaction whenever she drew laughter from this serious man.

"So you drove in from Clarksburg, thereabouts? That's, what . . . an hour, an hour and a half from here?" he said, fishing out a key card from an envelope in his jacket pocket. He offered it to Moss. "We rented a block of rooms nearby — don't make the trip home to Clarksburg tonight. You'll need to be right back here tomorrow morning."

"I'll crash for a night," she said, weighing the change in Brock's demeanor. He'd softened since noticing her prosthesis, since mentioning his wife.

"Deep Waters," he said, glancing skyward, though cloud cover occluded any chance of stars. "My boyhood dream was to be an astronaut. My grandparents took me to see a rocket launch at Cape Canaveral. It was the most beautiful sight I'd ever seen until my daughters were born."

Moss had seen the flares of firelight streak across the dawn, rockets lifting and vanishing from view. "It's always beautiful, every time," she said.

"Get some sleep," said Brock. "My team will continue through the night. Progress meeting at nine a.m. with everyone involved, and then we'll do the presser."

A desire to put distance between herself and that house prickled her shoulders, her spine, as she pulled away from Cricketwood Court, from Hunting Creek. The hotel Brock had booked was a Best Western nearer to Washington, Pennsylvania, but before picking up 79 she looped through the parking lot of the Pizza Hut that edged Chartiers Creek. Courtney had been killed here, November of their sophomore year.

The Pizza Hut was as it ever was, unchanged since the last time Moss had swung through here, a brick building with a Quonset hut roof, two dumpsters around back, blue dumpsters illuminated by Moss's headlights. Courtney's body had been left between those dumpsters. Moss counted hours — nearing thirty-three since Marian Mursult had last been seen. Marian was seventeen, Courtney had been sixteen when she died. Moss drove to the hotel, thinking of her dead friend, thinking of the missing girl. Fingernails and toenails missing from the bodies of the dead. Had Patrick Mursult killed his family? Where was he now?

Moss kept her go bag in the trunk, two changes of clothes and a toiletries kit, ready to travel at a moment's notice. She undressed in her hotel room, removed her prosthesis, removed her liner — a whiff of moist, pungent sweat knocked her awake for a moment. The shower was tricky without safety bars, but once the water had warmed, she sat on the edge of the tub and swung her leg in, sliding down the porcelain to sit on the nonslip mat. Hot water streamed over her. She washed her hair, using the full complement of shampoo, tried to wash away the smells of putrescence and blood. Without her crutches or wheelchair, she hopped across the hotel carpeting before slipping between the bed's crisp sheets, bundling into the comforter. With the blinds drawn and the lights out, the room was miraculously dark. Cold. She turned over to sleep but saw the bodies of women and children unspooling in great bloody arcs and flowering wounds. A rising disgust and hopelessness burned acidic in her throat. She thought of Marian — *still alive, please still be alive* — but she didn't know what Marian looked like, so her imagination filled with the image of Courtney Gimm and her mind raced to ax blades biting through bone and wounds that opened like mouths. Clammy, tossing against the mattress and tangled in her sheets, the smell of her prosthesis liner wafting over from across the room, sour. She sat up and fumbled in the darkness for the remote control. The local channels were all reporting about the family killed in Washington County, just outside Canonsburg. Moss squinted as the growing television brightness stabbed her eyes — aerial shots of the neighborhood roofs and film of the sheriff's blockade, the deputy with the Chaplinesque mustache hitching up his pants near the sawhorses.

The Amber Alert was first broadcast nearing 5:00 a.m. *Marian Tricia Mursult, seventeen, of Canonsburg, Pennsylvania.* An image sun-kissed and freckled, cutoffs and a tank top, her straight hair the color of coal. Moss's breath caught at the similarities between her friend and the missing girl — casually beautiful, each with that long, dark hair. Moss had been trained in time travel — accustomed to reliving future events as they played out in the terra firma of the present, but this déjà vu was something else, like she'd caught the world repeating itself, the house, the girls, like she had seen something she wasn't supposed to see, the repetitive mechanics of cyclical time. Or maybe the similarity between the girls was something more rare, something like a second chance. She had lost Courtney, but she could still save Marian. Moss relaxed into bed, comforted knowing that people would be looking for the girl, that someone might already have seen her, might know where she is, safe, safe — but as she drifted off for only a few hours of sleep, Moss could almost feel the girl's body grown cold.

# Two

Listless after Courtney died, Moss just shy of sixteen. The Gimms invited her to stand with them at the funeral home, an exhausting honor — awkward next to Davy in the reception line, Courtney lily white from concealer, laid out in an approximation of sleep. Courtney had always said she'd wanted to be buried in blue jeans, but they dressed her in a crushed-velvet dress with a high lace collar, necessary to cover what the makeup couldn't hide of the slash across her neck. The stillness of the body so complete, so unnaturally still, that Moss almost expected her friend to sit up, to somehow stir or breathe.

Coming from the funeral home, Moss imagined that a version of herself had died and would be buried alongside Courtney. Despondent, isolated, uninterested in the new version of herself, the self who survived. She lived alone with her mother; her father had abandoned them when she was five. Friendly enough with her mother, but her mother was never around, either at work or at McGrogan's for happy hours that melted into long nights of drinking. Moss grew inward, every night escaping to her room alone with her expanding collection of records: the Misfits, the Clash, the Sex Pistols, the Pixies, punk albums she picked from vinyl bins in CD stores — just lying in bed with her headphones in the dark, lost in soundscapes. Utterly wasted years, those remaining years of high school — drunk on Jack and Cherry Coke or whatever alcohol someone snuck in the parking lot at lunch. Vacant in her own skin, almost failing out of school but not quite — ready to just keep living at home if she had to, ready to work at the same telemarketing firm her mother worked for, but her track-and-field coach had taken notice, pulled some strings, secured a partial scholarship for Moss to attend WVU.

Three years after she lost Courtney, Moss was called to testify against her friend's killer. She sat in the Washington County Courthouse wearing her mother's work clothes, answering questions about the night her friend had died — Courtney's parents listening to her testimony, Courtney's mother weeping, Courtney's killer listening unimpassioned. Moss never questioned her lack of empathy for the man who'd killed her best friend — a junkie, a vagrant. She'd wanted him to die, horrifically, or to serve life without parole, some sort of revenge, some sort of *justice.* She learned about the sentencing only later, the killer given twenty-eight years to life, but the sentence hadn't seemed enough. Her rage at the idea that this man would live and might someday gain his freedom sliced through the fog of grief that had been suffocating her. The first semester of her sophomore year of college, drunken weekends and dorm-room dime bags gave way to coursework. She declared her major as criminology and investigation, secured an internship at the Washington County Coroner's Office per her course requirements.

Intimidated by the internship at first, but the coroner's office was an enjoyable way to spend an afternoon — the women there grateful for the help and eager to spoil her, chatting with her about birth control and music as she scuttled on her hands and knees reorganizing their filing cabinets. Dr. Radowski, the coroner, greeted her every morning but kept a cordial distance — an alcoholic, some of the clerks had told her, a homosexual, it was generally known, and while Radowski's face was often glowing reddish when he arrived back from longer lunch hours, he was unfailingly kind. Some of her roommates had been appalled at the idea of what she was up to, squeamish at the thought of cadavers, but Moss readily scheduled classes around her internship and found she anticipated 12:20 every Thursday afternoon, when she would drive up 79 to Washington in her banana-yellow Pontiac Sunbird, to make it to the coroner's office by one o'clock.

Nervous but not fearful the first time Radowski had allowed her to assist in an autopsy, dressed in a lab coat and goggles and gloves like a child playing scientist, standing only a few feet away as Radowski prepped the body, the decedent a sixty-four-year-old woman who'd been found only when the family in the adjacent apartment had called to complain about a smell. Moss's first whiff of human putrefaction had taken root in her, a sickly-sweet pungency — but her curiosity made the leap over her disgust. The procedure had been surgical at times, scalpel slices and dissections, had been unexpectedly brutal when Radowski used hedge clippers to break through the rib cage and an industrial saw to cut through the skull, the sound a high-pitched squeal that powdered the room with dust. Radowski's assistant had irrigated the woman's viscera, running water through armfuls of colon in the sink, filling the room with the smell of feces — the same assistant cracked a joke when he found partially digested Twinkies in the woman's stomach: "They would have lasted for eternity."

Radowski allowed Moss to hold the woman's heart. She cupped it in her gloved hands carefully, more like she was holding a bird with a broken wing rather than a dead muscle. Surprised by the heft of it, how much heavier a heart was than she would have imagined. Radowski had needed to scalpel through a protective sac in the cadaver's chest to reach it, the pericardium, spilling fluid across the stainless-steel slab and onto the tile floor.

"Place the muscle here, please, so I can weigh it."

Moss had done as Radowski instructed, setting the heart in a drip pan to drain.

"Take a look here," Radowski said some time later, lifting an organ for her to see. "You're looking at what amounts to the cause of death. The liver. Notice the deeper purple coloring, the texture like crushed charcoal. A healthy liver looks like a cut of meat you might pick up from the super-market, pinkish and smooth. This is cirrhosis. She drank herself to death."

Death is an unshared intimacy, Moss would sometimes think, finding a center of calm in the science of the morgue. Death and loss close company for her, her best friend dead, her father gone. The autopsy procedure helped bring closure to her experiences with mortality — death might still be a mystery, but the entirety of people's lives could be summed up in file folders, in weights, in measurements.

Campus dorms in Morgantown, but summers she rented the upstairs unit of a Dormont duplex, commuting downtown to Pittsburgh to support herself. One of dozens in the secretarial pool at Buchanan Ingersoll, a law office in the USX Tower — her desk was cluttered with a boxy computer monitor and an electric typewriter, the steel shelves behind her a manila sea of alphabetized folders. A fashion plate back when she was twenty-one — military jackets with decorative epaulets, chunky gold earrings, glossy red lipstick, and leopard-patterned press-on nails. The older women called her "Madonna" — a compliment maybe. An hour every morning in the bathroom and several visits to the ladies' room throughout the afternoon, teasing her hair, then blasting it with Aqua Net, fluffing her mane into puffed-out curls she gathered into a scrunchie. Coworkers gave her distance on smoke breaks, fearing her head might ignite.

Forensics and criminology textbooks during her lunches in Market Square. A waxed-paper basket of fried oysters and french fries on the afternoon she was approached by a man in a sports coat and a paisley tie. He took the chair opposite without bothering to ask permission to join her. He lifted the cover of her book, *Introduction to Criminology: Theories, Methods and Criminal Behavior, 2nd Edition.*

"Have you learned why men do what they do?" he asked.

Accustomed to businessmen and lawyers from Grant Street insinuating themselves into her company, men who thought downtown secretaries existed only to serve their pleasure, she'd been dismissive until the man showed his badge — NAVAL INVESTIGATIVE SERVICE, something she'd never heard of. Even then her first thought was that something had happened with her mother on one of her benders.

"We're recruiting the best and the brightest," he said.

Moss wondered what that had to do with

her. "All right," she said. "Yeah?"

He introduced himself as Special Agent O'Connor. "One of your professors put your name forward as a possible candidate for federal law enforcement," he said. "She's been impressed with your work."

"Okay," said Moss, wondering which professor, wondering if this was some sort of scam. "Don't you have pamphlets to mail out or something?"

"I have you in mind for a specific division within NIS," said O'Connor. "I wanted to meet you personally before I made the pitch. I don't always recruit like this, but I already have reason to believe you'll make an exemplary agent — still, I have to be sure to actually recruit you."

A sales scheme maybe — give out her name and address and get hammered with junk mail and cold calls. Any minute now he'll ask for twenty bucks to "ensure space in the program" or ask for a donation.

"My record can't look that good to you," she said, trying to call the man's bluff. "I almost didn't graduate high school."

"Your past plays a role. I'm interested in your renewed focus, your dedication now. Some people wilt in high school, bloom in college — that suits me. I don't want brilliant kids who will flame out in a few years.

I read a paper you wrote about the responsibility of a strong society to defend the rights of the vulnerable, the victims of violent crime being the most vulnerable. Did you copy that from somewhere or are those your original thoughts?"

"I didn't copy anything."

"I found your paper moving," said O'Connor. "Passionate. I'm interested in that articulate passion of yours, Shannon. I think your passion might see you through what I have in mind."

"I had a friend," said Moss. "She's the reason I'm interested in criminal justice."

"As it turns out, Shannon, I do have a pamphlet to give you," said O'Connor. "You have — what, another year before graduation? By the time you apply, we'll have reorganized from NIS into NCIS. If you're still as passionate then as you are now, and if you decide to apply, send your application directly to me."

He jotted down his mailing address, *Building 200, Washington Navy Yard,* on the back of the glossy advertisement — men and women in windbreakers, sentinels on the deck of an aircraft carrier. Her father had been in the Navy, a sailor on the battleship USS *New Jersey* in the late sixties, but Moss knew little of his service.

A month before graduation, she mailed her NCIS packet along with applications to local police departments and to the district attorneys' offices in both West Virginia and Pennsylvania. O'Connor called within the week, asked her to report to Oceana, Virginia, to begin the interview process — "Clear your schedule," he'd said. Lost in daydreams of deployment aboard hulking ships cutting through steely ocean waters, imagining that her father's naval experience somehow ran in her blood, she was surprised on the appointed day to find herself passing through the gates of the Apollo Soucek Field just as a squadron of F/A-18 Hornets screamed overhead.

O'Connor had recruited a class of twelve, Moss one of only three women, and within a few days two of the men had dropped out rather than endure the physical regimen the instructors demanded of them. Moss realized she wasn't being interviewed but rather weeded out. Hours swimming in the tank wearing scuba gear over her bathing suit. Bouts of spinning in the g-force simulator bearing mounting pressure until her eyes rolled backward and she lost consciousness, only to wake and spin again. The recruits were given small meals and bunked together in a dorm with room enough only for six —

one toilet to share among them, a carton of wet wipes instead of a shower. The spartan conditions frayed some nerves, but Moss adapted well enough, her track-and-field experience having trained her for endurance, conditioned a strength of mind over body. Only seven of the recruits remained at the end of five weeks, Moss the last woman. In a ceremony held in one of their classrooms, O'Connor presented each recruit with a choice: "Report to the Navy Yard, Building 200, and be welcomed with open arms to begin a fulfilling career as a federal law-enforcement agent," he told them, "or stay seated." One of the men did stand and leave, but the others remained at their desks, perplexed and excited as O'Connor handed out forest-green T-shirts and certificates printed with their names.

A reception with coffee and sheet cake in the hallway, instructions to change into their flight suits within the hour. After nightfall the graduates boarded a jet called *Ogopogo,* a sea serpent painted along its tapering nose cone — the jet was called a Cormorant, long and sleek, the color of obsidian, it looked like an SR-71 Blackbird but larger, the size of a small airliner. O'Connor and his class strapped into their seats and the *Ogopogo* lifted from the runway. Moss was utterly delirious when the Cormorant entered an accelerated climb and pulled from the tug of gravity. A crescent shine of earthlight, the scattered diamonds of city lights on the distant globe. Moss felt the dizzy bliss of weightlessness in her chest, her hair rising around her like a blond dandelion puff until she gathered it into a bun. O'Connor had been the first to unfasten his harness and float freely, his aged features suddenly child-like, the others following his example, whooping up the free fall like children on a trampoline. Moss rose from her seat and wept openly, gleeful, but her tears glommed like sticky balls over her eyes and stung until she wiped them with her sleeve and laughed.

The moonscape was a lake of darkness. They approached the Black Vale station, the lunar outpost like a secret city built into the Daedalus crater, a crater sixty miles wide and centered in the hemisphere of the moon that never faced Earth. The downslopes from the crater's raised ridges were ter-raced, like massive stairs descending two miles to the wide basin floor. No one spoke as they caught their first glimpse of the lunar launching sites. The Black Vale was outlined with lights, the buildings and runways, the layout reminding Moss of the oil rigs of West Virginia and Pennsylvania, the flight tower a spire of steel and bright lights like the scaffolding of a derrick. Seven ships were docked at the Black Vale, massive vessels the size of Ohio-class submarines — sleek and angular, the ebony ships built as if from origami.

"Those are the TERNs," said O'Connor, pointing out each of the seven ships. "Look there —"

Their engines were the Brandt-Lomonaco Quantum-Foam Macro-Field Generators, he explained, the military technology that allowed travel to Deep Space and Deep Time.

A cloverleaf of launch and landing pads spread out from the tower, networked with roads and taxiways that led to the hangars and a scattering of white domes, the dormitories and machine shops, offices and labs. O'Connor explained that the designs for the Naval Space Command ships — the Shrikes, the Cormorants, the TERNs — had been conveyed back from a point nearly six hundred years in the future, retrofitted for the nascent industrial capabilities of the 1970s and 1980s, when most of the fleet was built — skunkworks engineering projects carried out by Boeing and McDonnell Douglas, Lockheed Martin and Northrop

Grumman. The Cormorants used enhanced Harrier engines for their reaction-control system thrusters, short bursts adjusting the ship's roll, pitch, and yaw, the *Ogopogo* settling on Pad 4 like an insect alighting on a leaf. The views from every portal were vast plains of gray dust lit by floodlights. Everything fell slowly on the moon; in the weaker gravity, Moss fell like she was dropped through water. She was twenty-two years old, overwhelmed by the secrecy and miracles of the military, the complexity of the Naval Space Command operating just beyond the realm of public knowledge.

Dreamlike, those first few weeks of continued training, lectures in the sunlamp solarium, bunking in the dormitories, finding her way through the greenhouses and corridors and learning about the ships of the fleet. Moss was assigned O'Connor's TERN battle group afloat the USS *William McKinley* and launched to Deep Waters. Within two months of her arrival in Virginia Beach, she had time-traveled to the Terminus of humanity and sailed the farthest reaches of the Andromeda Galaxy, bathed in starlight that wouldn't touch Earth for another two and a half million years.

Newsmen glutted the Canonsburg Borough

Building's central hallway, reporters begging quotes about the multiple homicides and the missing child. The mayor's office was housed in the Borough Building, as was the Canonsburg Police Department, but they seemed unprepared for the sheer amount of news interest, Moss thought, pushing past a throng of photographers. She showed her credentials to a police officer and signed her name to a printout list of authorized personnel before she was allowed through to the conference room. An older man, someone from the borough, noticed her prosthesis and stepped aside. He laid his hand on the back of her blouse as she passed, and she stiffened at the touch, too familiar, at this man's fingers lingering on the contours of her bra strap. He smiled, gesturing her to go ahead — chivalrous, he must have thought, or fatherly, but his touch remained between her shoulder blades until she managed to separate herself to the far side of the meeting room. Still a few minutes before nine. Several of the joint task force had already taken seats around a horseshoe of a half dozen banquet tables. Moss recognized faces from the night before, FBI men mostly, but their demeanors had changed, the dolor of the Mursult deaths dissipated in the light of day, replaced by fresh hair gel and changed clothes, Styrofoam cups of coffee, doughnuts from white boxes on the back table.

Someone waved to catch her attention, a man with sandy blond hair, his jaw shaded by stubble that prefaced a beard. He had a warm smile, Moss thought, a smile that softened his otherwise rugged features. Bright powder-blue eyes — hooded eyes, thoughtful.

"Are you Special Agent Moss?" he asked. "Philip Nestor. We spoke on the phone last night."

"Oh, of course," she said. "Shannon."

"I have a seat for you," he said. "Brock asked me to take care of you."

Bristling at *being taken care of* and unwilling anyway to negotiate the gaps between chair legs. "I don't want to fight my way up front."

"Oh, all right — okay, sure," said Nestor, leaning against the wall beside her. "And not like that, not 'taking care of you,' more like a liaison," he said, quick to read her tone. She remembered his voice from last night's call — disturbed, edged with sorrow. Calm now. A nice voice, she thought. "Brock says you should have full access, but since he has a lot to juggle," he said, waving at the room, "I'll be your conduit."

An outdoorsman, she guessed — he had an easy athleticism, unlike the gym rats with their burlier bodies. He wore chocolate-brown corduroys, a contrast to the gray or beige slacks his colleagues wore — shirt-sleeves rolled to his forearms, a sweater-vest, and a tie, professorial despite the FBI tags he wore on a lanyard.

"I don't remember seeing you last night," she said.

"I was there — I saw you when you came in," he said, "but I was" — gesturing to indicate a Tyvek suit — "taking photographs. You wouldn't have noticed me. I have to ask you if it's true, what Brock told me."

*Fuck,* thought Moss, wondering at what had gotten around. "That depends on what he told you."

"That you knew the family over on Cricketwood Court."

"The family that used to live there," said Moss. "My best friend lived there, years ago. I was over at that house almost every day."

Nestor sighed. "I'm sorry," he said. "That must have been a shock."

"What else did he tell you?"

Nestor raised his hand, a gentle conciliation. "Only to be respectful, said you were taking it hard."

67

The clamor of conversation silenced when Brock made his way to the lectern. His clothes were the same as from the night before, rumpled — he'd maybe splashed water in his face before this meeting, cologne, but he hadn't showered, hadn't rested. A film of exhaustion clung to him, his eyes underscored by plum-colored bags that stood out stark against his dark skin. He dimmed the room to half-light.

"Good morning," he said, switching on the overhead projector, a block of light appearing on the whiteboard behind him. "I'll keep this brief. Special Agent in Charge William Brock, FBI. My team will be working closely with Canonsburg PD and the Pennsylvania Bureau of Forensic Services in the murder investigation of the Mursult family and in the search for Marian Mursult. Our lead investigator is Special Agent Philip Nestor."

Brock's first transparency showed the image used for the Amber Alert.

"Marian Mursult," he said. "Know her face. Thirty-eight hours gone."

Brock sipped from a water bottle, paused in his talk until he registered all eyes on the image of the young woman. Silence except for the whirring fan of the projector.

"We already have significant media interest in this young woman, most likely on a national scale. She was last seen on Friday afternoon leaving her shift at Kmart in Washington, where she's a cashier. Clocked out at seven p.m., and that was the last confirmed sighting we have. We have recovered her car from the parking lot — so she left with someone, or was taken. Her shift supervisor and her coworkers don't recall anything unusual about that afternoon. She has no regular boyfriend that we know about. State police are following up with her extended network of friends."

He switched the transparency. A cropped photograph of a man wearing a zippered blue sweatshirt, his hair dusted gray. He was smiling, squinting in the sunlight.

"This is the most recent photograph we have of her father, Patrick Mursult. Petty Officer First Class, United States Navy. Born 1949, August third. Patrick Mursult is on the board as our primary suspect both for the abduction of Marian and for the murder of his family. An arrest warrant has been issued. We do not have any solid information as to his whereabouts."

Another transparency. A Polaroid, jungle fauna, Mursult in drab green, his skin tanned leathery — he looked like a child, Moss thought, despite the cigarette and the

M16 slung casually over his shoulder.

"Triple homicide," said Brock, showing a transparency of the woman's blood-slathered face.

A close-up of a hand gloved in blood.

"The actor removed the fingernails and toenails from the woman and children," said Brock. "That information is not to be given to the media. Is that understood? In case we're wrong about Mursult, we're holding this piece back to weed out false confessions that come through the tip line."

An air of disquiet simmered in the room — the missing fingernails bothered the men gathered here, pushing these deaths from common brutality to something more bizarre, with unfathomable intention.

"Are you all right?" asked Nestor, his eyes troubled.

Moss asked, "Are you?"

Brock held his press conference a half hour later, the conference room's whiteboard screened with an FBI backdrop. He focused on the only substantive lead they had, the neighbor statements about Mursult's unidentified associate, a white male, bearded, who drove a red Dodge Ram with West Virginia plates. Brock described the truck as covered with bumper stickers, including a prominent sticker of the Confederate flag. Moss joined a few cops watching on the break-room television. She filled a mug with the oily dregs from the pot while reporters from Pittsburgh and Steubenville-Wheeling peppered Brock with questions about Marian Mursult, her family's murder.

Moss drifted from the break room, found a vacant office in the downstairs bullpen. She dialed her supervisor's direct line at NCIS headquarters. O'Connor had recruited Moss to NCIS, their afternoon over fried oysters, had mentored her during the training that followed, had sailed Deep Waters with her afloat the *William McKinley* — he had accompanied her on her first space walk, the two of them floating far from their ship, tethered to the hull like spiders suspended on silken threads. O'Connor was born only a decade before Moss, but he was well traveled in Deep Waters and IFTs, had already aged while the rest of the world stood still. His hair was a thatch of white curls, his face deeply wrinkled, but his deadpan glare broke easily into the crooked grin of a mischievous child.

"O'Connor," he answered.

"This is Moss. I need information about Mursult, if you can get it for me. The information I have was redacted. He's listed as missing in action."

"I have something for you," said O'Connor. "I've been meeting with NSC through the night. Mursult turning up is a major problem, Shannon."

"What do you have?"

"Patrick Mursult was a major player when NSC was part of Star Wars, flush with cash because of Reagan," said O'Connor. "The early days, part of the broader DoD space initiative — before *Challenger* and the consolidations. Mursult participated in the air force's Manned Spaceflight Engineers program out in Los Angeles, he also had his hand in the military floor at Johnson Space Center. But, Shannon, his record ends with the Zodiac missions. Are you familiar?"

"Twelve ships, deployed from the late seventies until about 1989. Before my time. Three of the ships are still commissioned."

*"Aries, Cancer, Taurus,"* said O'Connor. "The other nine ships never returned, hundreds of lives presumed lost. Catastrophic. And the *Taurus* —"

"The *Taurus* discovered Terminus," Moss said. "They were the first." She had studied crime-scene photographs of the USS *Taurus*. The ship had launched in late 1986 but returned from a far-future IFT with a depleted crew, only a few survivors, the inside of their ship covered in crude pictures

72

of dead men and warnings written in their own blood.

"Patrick Mursult is listed as missing in action because he was a sailor aboard the USS *Libra*," said O'Connor. "The *Libra* is assumed lost, Shannon."

Lost to Deep Waters, but appearing now. "How is that possible?" she asked. Moss had observed NSC launches, had seen ships launch to Deep Waters and return within a second, nearly instantaneous — the ships merely shimmered even though the crew might have sailed galaxies and lived for several years within that time. An uncanny sensation to see a man board a ship one moment as a young man and disembark the next moment grown to retirement age. Occasionally, however, an NSC ship launched but never returned — it would simply blink out of existence altogether. Those ships that blinked were assumed lost, irretrievably. They were either torn apart by debris or cast into a burning sun or devoured by a black hole, or more likely suffered a mechanical failure that had proved catastrophic or one of any other ruins — but the ships never returned and they never appeared in another location. If a ship blinked out, then the ship was lost and the crew dead, listed as missing in action only because their

73

bodies would never be recovered. "If *Libra* was lost, then Patrick Mursult shouldn't exist," she said. "Or he was never on *Libra*. Maybe he's a deserter? Or never made his assignment?"

"We need to account for *Libra,* we need to account for Mursult," said O'Connor. "That's why you were called in. We need to apprehend Patrick Mursult, find out his story."

"Brock says the guy's been living off the grid, everything in his wife's name except for a few counterfeit IDs, a fake driver's license," said Moss. "We have witnesses who know Mursult personally — I don't think we're dealing with a false identity, or anything like that. He's been living here in Canonsburg, right out in plain sight."

"No one's been looking for him," said O'Connor. "As far as anyone knew, Patrick Mursult blinked along with everyone else on *Libra*. You can hide a long time when no one's looking."

"We have a lot of people looking for him now."

"Shannon," said O'Connor, "Special Agent Brock mentioned you have a personal connection to the crime scene —"

"Fine — I'm fine," said Moss. "A child-hood friend lived there. And the crime scene was horrific last night, but I'm all right."

"I can offer you more agents, if you think you'll need the help," said O'Connor.

"I'm handling it," she said, thinking of Jessica Mursult, the body gouged. Courtney Gimm's bedroom, where Moss had dreamed of ditching Canonsburg. No one would ever leave that room. "I'm fine," she said again. "I'm focused on Patrick Mursult."

"What's your take on this?" he asked.

She thought of the woman's hand gloved in blood, the missing nails. "Right now this seems like a domestic situation," said Moss. "I think we'll find Mursult before too long — we have his face all over the news. Whatever his military situation, whatever the complications concerning *Libra,* you know as well as I do that this probably comes down to a question of money, or maybe an affair. Something quick and brutal but common. He took their fingernails — I don't know why. Let's consider more agents when we take him into custody. You should know that the missing girl's a looker."

"I saw the Amber Alert," said O'Connor.

"I'd only expect media interest to grow once Marian's picture makes the rounds," she said, knowing that media scrutiny was anathema to NSC. "Won't be too long before someone starts asking about Mursult, who he is."

"We're already on it," said O'Connor. "FBI has been cooperative. Our directors have been talking — we have a memorandum of agreement on this investigation. They have the manpower to handle the media inquiries, lead the search for Marian."

"They're having a press conference right now," said Moss, thinking that her mother might very well be watching. *Damn,* she thought — her mother a gossipy hawk for local misery, news stories of maimed animals, house fires, familial slayings. *I should call her.* Her mother would remember Cricketwood Court — all those afternoons dropping her daughter off at her best friend's house. Once Moss hung up with O'Connor, she dialed her mother's number. The line rang twice before clicking to the answering machine.

"Mom, this is Shan," she said. "Mom, if you're there, pick up. I'll swing by the house tonight. Don't worry too much about the news. We'll talk soon."

Nestor opened the office door with a soft tap.

"Let's go," he said.

Moss flipped her cell phone closed.

76

"Where are we going?" she asked.

"We have the truck," he said. "West Virginia state patrol just called it in. Come with me."

The red Ram belonged to Elric Fleece, expired license, expired plates, an address somewhere off Barthollow Fork Branch, near Dents Run and Mannington. Local cops seemed to know him, a belligerent drunk they've had to chase away from bars, but no arrests — a Vietnam veteran, an unlicensed electrician who worked odd jobs for cash. Nestor drove Moss in an FBI Suburban, skimming past slower traffic on the interstate as shallow Pennsylvania hills gave way to the greater swells of West Virginia. Over an hour's drive, discussion of Patrick Mursult shifted to personal chatter. Nestor was from southern West Virginia, grew up poor. A freelance photographer a few years before he fell into steadier fingerprint and crime-scene work with the Phoenix, Arizona, police department. Back home to West Virginia when his father was dying. Moss was circumspect in everything she offered of herself — she was drawn to share with Nestor, an attentive listener, but she knew how easily the covers for her life and career could fray.

"I guess I'm not much of a talker," she had said.

"You're guarded," said Nestor. "I respect that."

They came up on the junction with Barthollow Fork Branch and seemed to leave the world behind, swallowed by woodland. Barthollow Fork Branch tapered as they drove, the tree line butting against the road, reedy trunks, a canopy of branches that choked out light. Moss peered through the veil of woods to houses built far from the road, isolated places. They passed a series of houses propped up on cinder blocks — pastel siding faded and streaked with water damage from rusted gutters. Yards that looked like junk sales. Moss wondered what all these trees sounded like when they swayed. The road was little more than a mud path by the time they crossed a wood-plank bridge that bounded a dry creek bed. Nestor turned down a track that split away from Barthollow Fork, just two strips of dirt through the undergrowth.

"I can't really see where I'm going," he said. Moss felt the SUV's tires run up against large stones and knots of growth, felt the SUV correct back to the furrows of the path. Branches reached across the road and slapped at the windows.

"Wait, wait, wait," said Nestor. "Here we are."

A flash of red as he brought them into a clearing — the rear hatch of the Dodge Ram. An older model, something from the eighties, but it fit the description, cherry except where rust had chewed the doors, the Confederate flag just one of dozens of worn and half-peeled stickers. THE SOUTH WILL RISE. A sticker of Calvin taking a piss on a Ford logo. A pistol, THIS TRUCK PROTECTED BY SMITH & WESSON. The gun rack a thing handmade from lumber nailed together, empty of guns but well worn.

"Look at that," said Nestor. "What *is* that?"

Moss followed where Nestor pointed. "What the fuck," she said, climbing from the SUV, spotting the skeletons in the woods. Sculptures. Stag skeletons taken apart and refashioned with wire so they looked like men with antlers, veined with copper. Four of them hung from the trees by their ankles, arms spread wide — upside-down crucifixions. *Terminus,* she thought. *This guy knows the Terminus.* The house was ramshackle, the roof sagging in like the place was melting. Moss followed Nestor up the front walk, a series of stone slabs half sunk in mud. A slew of rodents' bones near the front door — groundhogs and squirrels mostly. Deer skeletons were laid out in the grass to dry in the sun.

"You think he's here?" said Moss.

"I don't know. The truck's here," said Nestor. "He could be taking a walk."

"What's with all the bones?" said Moss.

Nestor laughed. "Hell, I don't know —"

The bright stench of rot hit Moss and Nestor like a rolling wave — *death.* Moss thought, *Marian.* She drew her weapon, Nestor did the same. The front door was a flimsy screen over a sheet of plywood, the plywood warped and crawling with flies that leapt buzzing as Moss pushed through. The smell was heavy, seemed to weigh bodily on her — coated her tongue, her sinuses, seemed to grow spongelike in her mouth. Death, wet fur, shit. Her eyes watered.

"Marian?" she called out.

The air was alive, humming — flies bumped against her, Nestor with her. A dim front room. A carpet of animal pelts covered the walls, striped raccoon hides, the slate gray of squirrel, groundhog browns — the realization lit that she was looking at a mural made of fur, of vales and hollows, the skin of white rabbits as snow-capped peaks. *Mountains — a mural of mountains made of fur.*

"Marian?" she called out, the rot-infused air pouring into her lungs as she breathed. A fly crawled across her lips — she flinched, blew it aside. She feared them, feared what the flies might mean — feared discovering Marian's body. *Not here, not here* —

"FBI," said Nestor. "Federal agents."

Moss moved through into the adjoining room, gun leveled — a larger room with a corner kitchen and a television with foil-wrapped rabbit ears. *Family Feud.* Nazi flags draped the walls and were stapled to the ceiling. Black flags, SS in white bolts. Emerald flags with white stags' heads, antlers cradling swastikas. *Lunatic,* she thought — but she was scared, like she'd found the gateway to Hell. Mountain Dew and Pabst empties covered the floor, writhing with black ants.

"Here," said Nestor. "Over here."

A hall extended to the back rooms of the house, a hall lined with mismatched mirrors hung in a random scatter. Something on the hall floor was wrapped in garbage bags, a body, the plastic so thick with slivers of white maggots and flies it looked as though the bag crawled. Nestor wrapped his hand in his sleeve, pulled at the plastic — Moss expecting Marian's pale face, but the face was covered in black fur, toothless red gums, its black eyes like glass marbles.

"Jesus," said Nestor, jumping back. "What is that? A fucking bear?"

Moss continued down the mirrored hall, her image a multitude of reflections. *What is this place?* — but on some level Moss understood the design, on some level recognition bloomed. The mirrors in the hall, her reflections — something about this place tugged at her memory, and she thought of snowy climes, hiking through drifts in her orange space suit, so cold the wind was sharded with ice. She passed a bathroom, then a bedroom — a mattress on the floor, a duffel bag at the foot of the bed. She followed the mirrors to the back bedroom, the master, and when she looked inside, she heard herself scream.

The man had hanged himself from a tree made of bones — a sculpture of a tree, bones and iron and copper wire, the walls and ceiling of the room paneled with mirrors so the hanged man's reflection was an endless recursion. He dangled from skeletal branches, his face bloated, his tongue a purple bulge. Obese, his great white body wriggling with flies. Moss stepped closer, her weapon leveled but her hands shaking, and saw herself reflected with the dead man. This place was a representation — she was overwhelmed with the sensation of *returning* — the mirrored hall and the bone tree in the mirrored room uncovered memories Moss had worked to diminish over the years, the memory of her crucifixion, the roar of the black river beneath her. These rooms, however, were like a prodding finger. She remembered ice, remembered the air around her shimmering like a panoply of mirrors. She had seen the tree when she was in the Terminus, a tree the color of blanched bones, infinitely repeated. Fleece had reconstructed the scene as if he'd pulled the landscape from her mind.

"Let's go," said Nestor, putting his hands on her shoulders, leading her from the room. "Marian's not here. Let's go."

The Brooke County sheriff blocked off the property at Barthollow Fork Branch, barred access until the FBI Mobile Crime Unit arrived. They pulled the body of the decomposed black bear from the house and dragged it to the woods before cutting down Elric Fleece, an operation for several men because of the corpse's girth. The bear had been disassembled — skinned, boned, the organs removed. The technicians documented Fleece's residence like a crime scene, but the opinion spread quickly that his death was suicide, that he'd been hanging from the bone tree at least a full day, if not longer. Moss watched the men carry Fleece's sheet-wrapped body on a gurney, load it into the back of an ambulance for transport to Charleston for the autopsy. *Everywhere I look will be turned to ice,* she thought, and it was almost as if she could feel the ice encroaching from some future time. She walked the edges of Fleece's property, out into the woods, where she followed a path that led to the four skeletons hung from branches by their ankles. They had been crafted with horrific ingenuity — the copper wire wrapping the deer bones hinting at veins and musculature. How had he known about the Terminus, the hanged men? Moss imagined Patrick Mursult haunted by the future death of the world, whispering his visions to Fleece — or maybe Fleece had seen for himself, maybe he was another sailor aboard *Libra* appearing now, an apparition. NSC sailors suffered a high rate of suicide. Moss had observed several autopsies of men who had hanged themselves or cut open their own wrists, or who had ended their lives with a self-inflicted gunshot wound, broken men who couldn't readjust to the creeping pace of normal time. O'Connor would be able to verify if

Fleece was NSC, but Moss felt increasingly certain here was another sailor whose record would read "missing in action." She heard footsteps — Nestor tromping through the underbrush, coming for her.

"Hey, are you okay?" he asked. "You disappeared out here."

"Collecting my thoughts," she said. "You ever see anything like this before?"

Nestor's forehead rippled as if the question had been a stone tossed into the lake of his thought. "That room reminded me of something my dad used to talk about," said Nestor. "This recurring dream he called the 'eternal forest.' Come on, let's get away from these statues — or whatever they are."

They walked together along the path, through the shallow woods back toward Fleece's house. "What dream?" she asked.

"We lived in Twilight, this little coal town. My dad worked the mines, always had dreams he was in the dark," said Nestor. "So he wakes up in the night screaming — I hear him get up, and he comes into my room, sits on my bed, and looks at me. I was nine or something, just hoping he would think I was asleep, but he was drunk, and he says he was caught in a cave-in and he couldn't get out through the mine, so he crawled deeper until the mine ended and he came out into a forest. He tells me about the trees like they were there in my room, like he could touch them."

"The eternal forest," said Moss.

"There are doors in the trees," said Nestor. "And when he opened a door and stepped through, he stepped into a whole new forest. He said he was lost, and he asked me to find him. I told him I would and waited until whatever dream had a hold of him started to clear and he left my bedroom. He went to the bathroom, and I heard him back down the hall. I heard him start to snore and knew he was asleep. I never went back to sleep."

"You were nine?" asked Moss, imagining the child, imagining his father.

"Sometimes he talked about this dream like it was a place you could go to, like it wasn't a dream at all, so when I saw those mirrors . . ."

She wanted to unburden herself, but she said, "Don't think about Fleece's bullshit. You don't want this in your head."

She steeled herself before reentering the house. Even though the immediate sources of putrefaction had been removed, the other odors remained: the fur walls, the festering garbage bins. The techs had pulled cardboard boxes from Fleece's front closet.

Moss wore latex gloves, picked through the contents. She found an album of yellowed photographs, of Vietnam — pictures of PBRs, the four-man river patrol boats called swift boats. *Mekong* and *Rung Sat,* labels in blue ballpoint. Navy, in Vietnam — a connection to Mursult, she thought. She wondered if Mursult and Fleece had served together. Matchboxes filled with dead spiders, beetles, one of the other techs discovered a pillowcase stuffed with dead birds. *Filth,* she thought. His "art" covered the walls, not only the large mural made of animal hides but framed pictures, photographs he had doctored. Two hung in the bathroom. A still image from the Zapruder film, the moment Kennedy was struck by the second bullet, his face fleshy pink and opened outward, like his face was a door with a hinge. Fleece had painted a halo around Kennedy, oxidized brownish blood radiating from the president's head. In the other picture, he'd painted seven halos over a photograph of the *Challenger* — the explosion puff a burst of cloud and shuttle pieces in curlicues of smoke, odd trajectories.

"We found something," said Nestor. "Over here."

Nestor had been working in the smaller of

the two bedrooms, a relatively clean room — the mattress on the floor had been made, the sheets and comforter tucked tightly at the corners. The largest of Fleece's doctored photographs hung here — she recognized an enlarged photograph of Fleece's Vietnam swift boat, but it had been coated with crescent-shaped nail clippings and the nails and claws of animals. A plumb line of sorrow dropped through her — she thought of the fingers of the Mursult family, their fingernails removed. The picture was labeled, *This is the Ship of Nails that will Carry the Bodies of the Dead.*

"We're figuring Mursult stayed here," said Nestor. "That this is his stuff."

The contents of a black duffel bag were spread out across the mattress. A few thousand dollars in stacks of twenties, clothes, toiletries, a pager. Twenty-four Polaroids were laid out in a grid — graphic in their portrayal of a woman. A black woman, thin. Her face was never shown. Her breasts were beautiful, thought Moss, her belly taut — Moss studied the smooth, dark lines of the woman's thighs, the images of her genitals, how she spread herself pink. Intimate rather than pornographic — pictures no one other than the photographer and the subject were ever meant to see. They had been taken in a cabin, it looked like, not here. A rental cabin, maybe. The walls were exposed lumber, a glimpse of a bedside table, a pad of paper, a phone.

"Can you ID the woman?" she asked.

"No."

"What makes you think Mursult?" she asked.

"The first few numbers we recovered from the pager are Mursult's home phone number," said Nestor. "I'm thinking he called himself a couple of times, made sure the pager was working."

They stepped outside. Nestor was staying to oversee the evidence collection, but he made an arrangement with one of the sheriff's deputies to ride Moss back to Canonsburg. Late afternoon, the day bleeding away from them.

"Did you catch the picture of the boat?" asked Moss.

"The fingernails? Yeah," said Nestor. "We'll have our guys test the fingernails, see if any of them are from the Mursult family — it will take a while. I don't see this guy Fleece being able to kill three people without using a gun, though, do you? Out of shape — he didn't look like he could have caught them or defend himself if any of them fought back. The wife, Damaris Mursult, was athletic. The son —"

"I'll bet the autopsy says he's been dead too long to be our guy anyway," said Moss.

"What was that he wrote on the picture? A ship of nails?"

"A ship of nails to carry the dead," said Moss. "I don't know. Jesus Christ, we've seen a lot of death today."

"Are you religious?" asked Nestor.

"What?" she said — she realized she'd blasphemed, was worried she might have offended him. Several men she'd met in law enforcement were Christians, evangelicals. "I'm sorry, I —"

"My faith is the only thing that sustains me," said Nestor. "Thinking about the boy and girl, thinking about Marian. It breaks me, but I believe in eternal life, I think of how God will care for these victims, and it helps me — it helps me stay focused. I imagine a new life for them. Do you believe in the resurrection of the body?"

Moss thought of all of humanity in a funnel leading to a singular point.

"No," she said.

# THREE

Her mother still lived in Canonsburg, in the same house Moss had grown up in, a little blue house on the steep hills northeast of East Pike, just a few blocks up from the Sarris candy factory. Her childhood had been scented with chocolate. Moss popped two wheels onto the sidewalk whenever she parked, angling the wheels, setting the brake. She made her way along the weedy path to the side door and unlocked the dead bolt with the same key she'd used since middle school.

"Mom?" she said.

"Up here," said her mother.

Surprised to find her mother home, figuring she might be at McGrogan's — almost every night after her shift at the call center, her mother changed into stone-washed jeans and a tight top and rambled downhill to the bar, walking so she wouldn't have to worry about driving home. Everyone knew

91

her mother to see her, she was always ambling about the neighborhood to find cigarettes, to find a drink, a forty-four-year-old often lit after last call, bumming in empty lots with other barflies too stoned to want to go home. A character, a regular. McGrogan's was an off-and-on bar, some nights quiet with nothing to do but watch the news on the TVs and chat up the bartenders, other nights so full you had to shuffle sideways just to get to the bathrooms. Her mother had her usual stool, at the corner of the bar where she could relax with her back to the wall and see what developed. Her hands were rippled with veins, and her natural hair had dulled to the color of wheat bread, but she could still turn heads if she wore the right outfit and the lights were dim. Moss looked at her mother and saw herself in a few years. The irony of traveling to IFTs was that Moss's body aged in these futures even if the terra firma of the present had seemed to pause, waiting for her. Chronologically, Moss was only twenty-seven, born in 1970 when her mother was seventeen. Biologically, though, Moss was almost forty, just a few years shy of her mother. Moss and her mother never mentioned their ages to each other, however, even though Moss was certain her mother must have noticed the contracting gap between them — a sibling more than a daughter, a weirdness too disturbing to discuss or even acknowledge. No intimacy had ever developed between them, though, no sense of equal footing — their experiences too divergent, their lives lived in such different places. Moss was taller, toned, serious, while her mother was brassy — people invariably figured they were sisters the rare times they went drinking together.

Her mother was at the kitchen table tonight, already in her pajamas, flipping through a *Reader's Digest.*

"Not at McGrogan's?" asked Moss.

"I saved you some chicken if you're hungry," said her mother.

"I already ate."

"Eat more," her mother said. "Shiner's been going around with that girl from . . . wherever the hell she's from — South Fayette or somewhere. I don't want to drink with them tonight. Deb wants to start going to that new place I told you about — what's it called? I tried to call you. Anyway, I made the chicken."

"I've been working," said Moss.

"Trying to find that girl? I couldn't believe it, the news made it seem like that family was killed over in Courtney Gimm's old house," said her mother.

"Yeah," said Moss.

"The same house? Is that what you're working on?"

"Looked like that family was already trying to sell the place. They couldn't have been the people who bought the house from the Gimms, right? Someone named Mursult?"

"No, no — they must have been renting," said her mother. "Her brother, what's his name?"

"Davy."

"He's the one that enlisted? I think he started renting out the place after his dad moved to Arizona. I ran into Davy — must have been a few years ago — '93 maybe? '94? I think he said he wanted to hold on to the place, draw some income if he could. I'm so nebby but can't never remember what I've nebbed about."

"They use a referral service to find housing for one another," said Moss. "Military families." She had been rattled at finding the crime scene at Courtney's house, the chilling synchronicity of her present and past braiding, but it was just a coincidence, she reminded herself. Davy Gimm had listed the house for rent, and another Navy family had moved in — a referral service.

Talking with her mom settled things, made her feel like she was rousing from an unpleasant dream to find the waking world as normal as it ever was.

"What happened?" said her mother.

"I don't know," said Moss. "Domestic abuse, I think."

"Awful," said her mother. "I've been following the missing girl's story on the news because of Courtney — made me think of Courtney."

"Marian Mursult," said Moss. "Reminded me of Courtney, too. The hair."

"I was going to mention her hair," said her mother. "Courtney had that beautiful hair, all those curls."

Growing up, Moss thought of her mother as just another Guntown drunk, a wreck, but now she saw her mother was wounded, a perspective that came with age, when everyone settled into the same slew of adulthood, when everyone was wounded and could more easily overlook the wounds of others. Moss picked at the Shake 'n Bake, tough and dry. She found rum in the liquor cupboard, mixed it with Cherry Coke. Her mother poured herself vodka.

"Anyway, I'm meeting Cheryl down at McGrogan's tomorrow night," her mother went on.

"Cheryl from work?" said Moss. "I thought you were over each other."

"I sold the most subscriptions this past month, so I promised I'd take Cheryl out with the gift certificate they're giving me, fifty bucks. By the way, I saw your subscription to *Homemaker's Companion* lapsed, so I signed you up for a renewal. Helped push me over the top."

"I hate those things."

"That ain't the point."

Her mother at the call center, pushing magazine subscriptions. Moss drank her rum and Cherry Coke in the living room, took her place on the leather love seat, her mother reclining on the full-size couch. Moss had almost gone to work for the call center — her mother had pulled some strings with the manager, but Moss had blown off the chance. That near miss of a career was one of the few true forks in the road she'd traveled. Fashionable to think of a "multiverse" consisting of infinite directions, infinite paths, but the forking paths weren't truly innumerable, she knew; there were only so many options available to most people, especially girls who grew up poor. Had she taken the job at the call center, she could have turned out just like her mother. She would have made a good alcoholic, she always thought. Call centers and bars and sleeping with whoever was willing to pay her tab for the night — sometimes she thought of that lifestyle with disgust, other times she found comfort in the daydream, wishing she could have just lived a regular life of men and stress and shit jobs. A quarto-size framed picture of Moss's father stood on the mantel above the television. His smile was more a smirk, but the glint in his eye hinted he'd keep on laughing forever, wherever he was. Moss had grown up with this strange, formal picture of her father as a young man who was younger in the photograph than her memories of him — he had been in the Navy, and in the photograph he wore his dress whites. When she thought of the call center or thought over the ways her life might have been different or wondered why she had joined NCIS, she sometimes told herself she was searching for her father — but that was a bullshit answer, she knew it. He had left the Navy before she was born; he had left the family when Moss was five.

"We can watch *The X-Files*," said her mother. "I know you like that show."

Sunday nights were Scully nights, but tonight's was a repeat — "Fallen Angel," the episode a Mulder episode, so Moss told her mother to flip channels if she wanted. Her mother a newshawk, Headline News interrupted by CNN's BREAKING STORY banner. RAPPER DEAD was blunt enough, though they followed with a headline released from the *L.A. Times:* GANGSTA RAP PERFORMER NOTORIOUS B.I.G. SLAIN. Four shots fired through the side of his SUV. A black GMC Suburban roped off by police tape. Her mother sat up. "Oh, damn," she said. "Damn it. I've got to call Shelly. She loves him."

"I think I'm heading to bed," said Moss, her mother waving good night but staring mournfully at the screen. Moss's old bedroom had been converted into her mother's junk room over the years, but the spool-turned Jenny Lind bed that had once been her grandmother's had been kept, and the bookshelves still had a few of her old books: *The Black Stallion, A Wrinkle in Time,* some Choose Your Own Adventure books with the death-scenes dog-eared. The rocking chair was covered with boxes of clothes. She turned out the lights, thinking she would fall immediately asleep, but the news of the rapper's death bothered her, mixed with the heaviness already in her heart. Moss felt like the world was dissolving. She had the sensation of constellations disappearing from the sky. "Nestor," she said, thinking of the immortality of souls, the resurrection of the body — Nestor's naïvety, the ignorance of his faith, but still trying the sound of his name, how it started on the tip of her tongue and worked its way back.

In the darkness of her bedroom, surrounded by familiar shadows, she imagined the world around her buried under snow and blizzard winds, the only warmth the pocket beneath her comforter where she lay curled. The muffled sound of the distant television, the sound of her mother's voice speaking on the kitchen telephone. Sounds from her childhood. Easy enough to convince herself she was still just a child, a little girl in her bed, that her entire life was nothing but a strange dream, and if she were to wake now, she would wake years younger, everything as it was twenty-five years ago. She felt like an interloper on her own past and so reached to touch her left thigh, run her fingers along the bumps of bone and scarred skin tissue of her stump, reminding herself of who she was now. Her mother must be calling everyone about the news she was watching. Moss loved the sound of her mother's laughter — how casually she made lasting friendships, how she gave of herself freely, unguarded. Moss too easily became entangled. She tossed in the twin bed, thinking. Thinking again of Nestor. Never able to spark casual relationships like her mother, never one for trysts — Moss's infatuations developed suddenly, her emotions came with thistles, like a bur. Once a photographer, he had mentioned, and Moss wondered at that — she wondered who he was, if he was always so pious. Anyway, annoyed at how he'd reduced the deaths of children to Christian bathos about eternity, but nevertheless she wondered at the women in his life, wondered if there was one. She tried to remember if he had worn a ring. Nestor. The glare of headlights on her ceiling, fragmented by her window, made her remember mirrored images of Elric Fleece and skeletons in the trees. A ship named *Libra* disappearing into Deep Waters, lost sailors returning. A dissected black bear swathed in maggots. A trick Moss had taught herself for falling asleep was to imagine a river of black water — she would stand naked before wading into the river, the water creeping to her knees, her thighs, black as ink against her white skin, stomach, her breasts, and soon the water would be above her head, the wavering sunlight disappearing over her, falling deeper into ever expanding darkness. When she drowned, she slept.

A telephone ringing. The tone of her cell on her nightstand.

"Hello?" she said.

"This is Brock."

Red digits hovering in the dark, 2:47.

"One of our guys just called about the pager you and Nestor recovered at Elric Fleece's residence," said Brock. "Figured something out."

"Tell me."

"We found saved pages. No phone numbers, only codes. We haven't figured out what most of the codes are, but we did find a few that repeated — 143 and 607. My guys tell me codes like these are shorthand for 'I love you' or 'I miss you,' things like that. Teenagers use them."

Mursult and the woman in the Polaroid photographs scheduling times to meet, maybe using codes learned from his daughters.

"Having an affair," said Moss. "There were twenty-four pictures of a woman."

"We checked Mursult's home-phone records against the pager and found a correlation," said Brock. "Several times when the pager received the code 22, he placed a call to the Blackwater Falls Lodge, down in

Tucker County."

Blackwater Gorge was familiar — a section of the massive Monongahela National Forest, touristy and accessible because of the stunning waterfalls like pearls on the string of the Blackwater River. Moss had once stayed for a week in the lodge, exploring the miles of trails through the gorge, grueling treks with her prosthesis over uneven terrain, searching the Red Run branch of the Dry Fork River where she had been rescued from her near death in the Terminus. She had looked for the part of the river where she had hanged, had searched for the ashen tree she remembered, the burnt-white tree that had seemed to repeat, but she never found the site of her crucifixion. She'd returned to the cabins around Blackwater Falls often in her summers, losing herself on the trails, gazing for hours at the crashing eddies and whirlpools of the Elakala Falls — reminding herself of the beauty of the world, when it was so easy for her to remember this landscape as desolation and ice.

"That lodge is a few hours from here, but would be a good place to meet someone," she said. "Romantic, remote."

"Mursult called the lodge dozens of times, twice in the last month," said Brock. "I

102

called over to the lodge, but the clerk didn't have records for anyone named Patrick Mursult. I'll call the Tucker County Sheriff's Department first thing in the morning, see if they can send someone out."

"I'll head over," said Moss, doubtful she'd be able to get back to sleep. "I'm in Canonsburg. I can make it out there. I need to head home out that way."

Her mother snoring from across the hall. Moss crept downstairs, feeling like a teenager again, sneaking out in the middle of the night — she remembered which stairs creaked, knew where to put her weight to stay silent. She brewed a pot of coffee in the kitchen, splashed water on her face to wake up. Marian Mursult was three days gone, last seen this past Friday; Monday morning would dawn in just a few hours. A bottle of aspirin above the sink — Moss took the pills with coffee. She drove the dead-hour interstates, Canonsburg to 79 South, West Virginia, allowing images to swirl in her mind, glom together, the *Challenger* in the immensity of the sky, a ship for the dead built of fingernails, the forest in winter. The interstate was a river of asphalt illuminated by streetlamp light. She was aware that the mountains grew around her, but she couldn't see them — they were gargantuan darkness, snuffing out the stars.

A serpentine cut through pinewoods that opened into a parking lot — only a sparse few cars parked here. The lodge was built like a longhouse, red-roofed, with an exposed-stone chimney stack crowning the front entrance. Moss made her way through the vacant lobby, a dropped ceiling and a cream tile floor, the front desk the color of natural cherrywood, everything bathed in garish fluorescence. Moss lingered for a few moments at the unattended front desk, peering behind the counter into an empty manager's office.

"Hello?" she said.

The murmur of a distant television. She followed the sound around to the hotel bar, where varicolored liquors lined the mirror-backed shelves. A young woman sat alone, drinking coffee, looking over a *Vogue* piece about the Spice Girls. She was willowy, in knee socks and a skirt embroidered with a forest scene, deer and rabbits, wildflowers, her lip and eyebrow pierced with silver rings, her hair voluminous save for the shaved sides, dyed a jolting shade of electric blue.

"Excuse me," said Moss.

"Sorry," said the young woman. "I should be at the desk."

"Are you in charge here?" asked Moss.

"Checking in?" she asked. "We should have rooms available."

Maybe in her early twenties, just out of college, or maybe this was a student job. Fine features and dark, lovely eyes. Moss held out her identification.

"NCIS," she said. "I'm wondering if you can answer a few questions for me, maybe help me out."

"Are you, like, a cop?" the young woman asked.

"Naval Criminal Investigative Service," said Moss. "I'm a federal agent investigating crimes relating to the Navy."

That explanation often calmed people who might otherwise have feared becoming entangled in police business — NCIS something remote, harmless-seeming to people with no connection to the armed forces.

"Like the FBI?" she asked. "Someone just called here a little bit ago."

"I'm not the FBI," said Moss.

"I'll see what I can do," said the young woman. "I can serve alcohol, if you want a drink. Or coffee. I just brewed a fresh pot."

"Coffee, thank you. I don't normally keep these hours."

"I feel like a vampire sometimes," she said, heading behind the bar to pour Moss's cup.

She set out sugar and a carton of half-and-half. "Petal, by the way."

"Petal?" said Moss. "That's beautiful. Shannon."

"Skeleton crew tonight," said Petal. "Got the lobby to myself. More staff will show up closer to breakfast."

"You work here regularly?" asked Moss.

"Most nights," said Petal. "Two nights off a week, not necessarily together. Hard to plan a life with no real weekends. And it's boring. I'm glad you showed up, gives me something to do."

"Do you know someone named Marian Mursult? Or Patrick Mursult?" asked Moss.

"They aren't familiar names," she said.

"I believe Patrick Mursult may have stayed here frequently," said Moss. "What kind of information do you keep on file about your guests?"

"Basic stuff," said Petal. "Name, how many people are checking in. That sort of thing. Credit-card number, unless they pay with cash."

"Phone calls from the room? Incidental costs, damages?"

"Sure," said Petal.

Moss showed Petal a photograph of Mursult. "Do you recognize him?" she asked.

Petal scrutinized the picture. "No," she

said. "But I don't have a lot of contact with our guests at my hours. Most people check in before I'm here, check out after I leave — and most of the time they're out through the forest, hiking. I see people occasionally at breakfast if I stick around to eat."

"I have dates this man would have stayed here over the past year or so," said Moss, "and the phone number he used to make the reservations."

"The phone number wouldn't be much help," said Petal. "The dates, though — we could try to cross-check by date."

"You can run a search like that on the computer?"

"Oh, no," said Petal. "Our computer system is nonexistent. Ever play Memory?"

They set up in the lounge on either side of a glass table, sitting by a fire that Petal had kindled in the stone fireplace, several file folders arranged between them by date. Each folder contained a stack of receipts from past occupants, some handwritten — Moss started with the lightest folder, flipping through names, credit-card numbers, room numbers — information blurring together as she read. No "Patrick Mursult."

"Read the names out loud so I can hear them," said Petal. "Or — don't bother with the names, let's stick to credit-card numbers. I have an idea. Give me the last four numbers, and I'll write them down, we'll check for duplicates."

"All right," said Moss, unaccustomed to receiving this level of engagement, but Petal seemed particularly game, readying her notebook, starting a new column next to a poem she'd been writing. Moss read out the credit-card numbers, and Petal checked each number against her list, looking for repeats. They worked for nearly forty minutes, taking a break only to refill their coffee.

"Wait, wait — can you give me that last one again?" asked Petal.

Moss repeated the number and Petal said, "Here we go. Yes. I found a match, here. Patrick Gannon."

"Patrick Gannon," said Moss.

Moss jotted down the credit-card number that "Patrick Gannon" had used to make his reservation. He hadn't reserved a room in the lodge but rather one of the cabins along the south rim of the gorge: Cabin number 22, the same number as the code on his pager. She had him. She checked all the past receipts — the number of guests was listed as two, though there was no information on the second guest.

"Anything unique about that cabin?"

Moss asked. "About the name 'Gannon'? Maybe someone you work with might have an idea about him? Might remember him?"

"I'll ask around when the morning shift clocks in," said Petal, tying her bright blue hair into a loose knot. "Let me check the file for Cabin 22, see if we've kept any notes about it."

"Are you in college?" asked Moss as Petal gathered up their paperwork.

"I'm working a few years," said Petal, "not sure if I want to go to school. I wanted to backpack across Africa, but my dad found me this job."

"Consider a career in law enforcement," said Moss. "You're a natural. You've been a help tonight."

Petal replaced the files of room receipts in the management office before stepping behind the front desk, opening up the three-ring binder labeled CABINS. She flipped to the back, scanned a series of forms. "Wasp's nest in Cabin 22 in 1983," said Petal. "Looks like it was taken care of." She opened another three-ring binder labeled CHECK-IN, said, "Oh, shit. Gannon's checked in right now. Cabin 22."

"Tonight?" said Moss. A prickle of adrenaline. She thought of Marian, wondered if she was in one of the cabins, possibly held here.

Petal checked a pegboard full of keys on the rear wall, checked again in her binder. "He made the reservation Friday night, checked in Saturday, and has the cabin through the week."

A Friday-night reservation — he'd booked his cabin just as Marian had been kidnapped. "I need to get there," said Moss, no moment to spare if she might recover Marian here, now. "I can follow one of the roads that lead from the parking lot?"

"About a mile from here," said Petal. "It's tricky in the dark, I can take you over."

Petal threw on a pea coat, brought Moss through the administrative office to the garage, where she found a golf cart spattered with mud. They left the garage and rode along the cabin path, a winding strip of concrete lit only by the dim wattage of the golf cart's front light. Moss gripped the crossbar as Petal drove, taking the bends quickly. The stars were thick out here, without the diluting light of cities. Orion and the Dippers were clear, but the sky was dominated by the silvery flare of the comet Hale-Bopp, the cosmic ice and burning tails like a thumb smudge of light.

Two dozen cabins were situated near the

gorge rim, each private, separated by dense hemlocks. A few were booked, Moss figured, seeing cars tucked into the woods, but most of the cabins stood empty — March was still too cold for most people. Petal drove around to one of the distant cabins. "Here's 22," she said. A Wrangler was parked in the gravel patch, the spare tire draped with a POW*MIA cover. No lights. The cabin seemed consumed by night.

"Petal, go ahead and wait back here, all right?" said Moss, standing from the golf cart. Petal bundled up in her coat, lit a cigarette. *Marian might be here,* thought Moss. She picked her way along the mulch path to the cabin. The night was so opaque she could barely see Petal and the golf cart, could see only the orange tip of her cigarette bobbing like a firefly. Moss knocked on the door, waiting a few moments. Nothing stirred inside the cabin, no lights snapped on, no movement. She knocked harder.

"Special agent, NCIS," she said. "I need to speak with Patrick Mursult."

Silence. She unsnapped her holster, ready to draw. Moss knocked again, no answer. Or maybe there was no one here — the cabins were small enough she should have heard movement if someone were inside.

"Do you have keys?" Moss called back.

111

"Yeah," said Petal. "I have to open the door for you. I can't hand over the manager's keys."

Moss watched the cigarette tip bob closer. Petal had a ring of keys, squinted to find the one marked 22. "I wish I had a flashlight," she said, stepping around Moss, feeling for the cabin lock with her fingers. Moss heard the key slide in, heard the lock unlatch. Petal stepped inside just as Moss was smacked by the odor of blood.

"Petal, don't —"

Petal flipped on the lights, and when she registered the wash of blood, she screamed, her cigarette dropping from her mouth. Moss took the girl by her shoulders, held her, led her from the cabin, "It's okay, it's okay — go back to the office, call 911 —"

"I'm all right," said Petal, her voice bubbling with hysteria. "I'm all right, it's fine, I didn't see it, I didn't see —"

Moss put her hands to Petal's cheeks, steadied her. "Listen to me, listen," she said, and registered the moment when Petal regained herself. "Go back to the office, call 911," said Moss. "My cell won't work out here. I need you to do this for me, okay? Call 911."

Moss waited until she heard the sound of the golf cart's motor diminish before returning to the cabin. She crushed out Petal's cigarette, smoldering on the floor. She closed the door behind her. The cabin's interior was wood, with exposed ceiling beams. Patrick Mursult's body was beside the bed, his head resting on the mattress, his wrists tied behind him with a belt. Someone had shot him through the back of the head, an execution. Blood had sprayed from the exit wound, dousing the headboard with blood that glistened in the room lights.

She checked the rest of the cabin. There was no one else here, no sign of Marian. Mursult had been staying here alone. She spotted a gun on the floor, a Beretta M9. Could be a service weapon, she thought, wondering if the Beretta had been Mursult's or if his killer had left it here. But even if it was his service weapon, the NSC SEALs she worked with strongly preferred the SIG Sauer P226. The M9 might have been the weapon Mursult was originally issued back in the mid-eighties. An older gun.

She heard sirens piercing the silence long before they arrived. The first on scene was an ambulance from the Broaddus Hospital, Moss waiting outside the cabin, waiving off the EMTs so they wouldn't contaminate the crime scene. When the Tucker County sheriff arrived, Moss asked him to radio in, ask for the FBI. Deputies woke the few others in the cabins, taking their names, contact information, asking them what they might have heard, what they might have seen. An FBI unit from the Clarksburg field office arrived, already in contact with Brock, who was on his way down from Pittsburgh.

No cell reception here, but Petal let Moss use the office telephone. The lodge office was stuffy, with a minuscule metal writing desk and a calendar of the Blackwater Falls photographed in different seasons. Moss dialed for an out line — at this hour O'Connor must be asleep, she figured, so she tried his home number rather than NCIS headquarters. She thought of him now, wisps of white hair, sandpaper stubble, sitting up in bed and shuffling through his vast house in Virginia, chasing down the ringing telephone before his younger wife's sleep was disturbed.

"O'Connor," he said.

"Moss," she said. "I located him. Patrick Mursult's dead. I'm calling from the Blackwater Falls Lodge, in West Virginia. He had a cabin here."

"Homicide?" O'Connor asked.

"He was shot through the back of the head," said Moss. "Wrists tied behind him. An execution. I don't think Mursult killed

114

his family — someone hunted him down, killed them all. We still have no leads about his daughter."

"The FBI will handle the search for Marian," said O'Connor. "Our primary concern remains Patrick Mursult — and Elric Fleece. I spoke with Special Agent Nestor earlier, pulled Fleece's record. Navy, Electrician's Mate — submarines in the late seventies, NSC in '81. *Zodiac.*"

*"Libra?"* asked Moss.

"That's right. We need to find out what these men were involved in, why they weren't on the ship. We need to know about *Libra.* I'm meeting with the NSC director tomorrow, Admiral Annesley."

"There's something else," said Moss. "Fleece had seen the Terminus, or knew about it, his place was . . . his property was decorated with sculptures of the hanged men. I think he had seen the future. Remember when I lost my leg, I had that confusion about the reflections? Do you remember, I thought I'd seen myself —"

"Of course," said O'Connor, that time of her life delicate between them — how what should have been a routine training exercise in the Canaan Valley had resulted in the loss of her limb. He'd been inconsolable when the medical staff of the *William McKinley* mentioned amputation as the only way to save Moss from gangrene and had been present during the two surgeries needed to remove her leg at the thigh.

"This man, Fleece, had made a sculpture of the reflections," she said. "I can't explain it, but he knew. I'd been thinking Mursult never sailed on *Libra,* never made the assignment, but if Fleece knows the Terminus . . ."

A pause on O'Connor's end. "We need to get out ahead of this investigation. It's spreading like wildfire, we have to contain it," he said. "I have to move you to the future on this one."

Moss's jaw clenched at his words, her shoulders tightened. Traveling to IFTs took a toll on her body, years of her life spent in futures. She had lost relationships the last time she was called on to travel, had a boyfriend she imagined a life with, but when she traveled, she had left her boyfriend's bed one morning and returned within the week aged four years, distant from him, her heart and mind already long past the moment she'd been living.

"Just give me a few more days," she said. "We have leads. There are pictures of a woman —"

"I'm moving you on this," said O'Connor.

"I have to. Mursult turning up like this, and now Fleece. They're a national security risk, Shannon. We need to know about these men *now*. We need to know about *Libra*."

Twenty years from now, this current investigation will have concluded — everything happening here will be history; with any luck, whoever murdered Mursult and his family will have been captured, Mursult's missing-in-action status will have been explained, his connection to *Libra* understood. Moss might arrive twenty years from now and be handed a folder with every question answered, every opaqueness made clear. A framed photograph of the Blackwater Lodge staff stood on the desk — Moss picked out Petal, her hair not blue in this picture, her natural color a dark shade, almost black. *Marian,* thought Moss. *You can find Marian.*

"All right, I'll get ahead of this thing," she said. She was unable to slide backward through time to prevent Marian's disappearance, the butchery to her family, but she could travel forward to learn what had happened to her or what might happen to her. *Maybe I can save her,* she thought. *Maybe we're not too late.* "I'll go," she said. "I'll leave from here, can make it to Oceana by midmorning."

"I'll make arrangements," said O'Connor.

Moss found Petal at the front desk. The young woman had been crying, her eyes pinkish, but she had collected herself. Already this world, terra firma, seemed to Moss like a distant recollection, like it belonged to a past age, bathed in a haze of memory. Even Petal seemed like someone remembered from long ago. Moss handed her one of her business cards, said, "This is my name, here. Shannon Moss. When the sheriff's department or someone from the FBI asks you about what happened tonight, make sure you talk with Special Agent William Brock of the FBI. Tell him everything."

"Brock," said Petal. "Okay."

"You've done great," said Moss. "Hang in there."

Moss pulled away from the Blackwater Falls Lodge. She turned on the radio to drown out her thoughts, the tuner scanning, picking up static channels. Moss listened to the white noise, the night burning with stars. The vast body of heaven, the body of the woman in the Polaroid photographs. There had been a woman who'd met Mursult in the Blackwater cabin, who had known him, had been intimate with him. Who was she? Moss thought of that unknown woman, she thought of Marian. She thought about the search parties that would comb through these woods in the coming days, men and women searching tight grids, looking for a sign of the girl somewhere among the pines. Maybe they would find her, maybe they would pull Marian's body from the soil, or maybe they would find her months from now, wasted away and desecrated by wildlife, or maybe they would never find her. The pinewoods stretched out like a vast dark sea on either side of Moss. She thought of Marian, she thought of Courtney. She imagined Courtney wandering alone, lost among the pines — her thoughts of Courtney were so vivid Moss felt she could almost see her, a blur of white among the subsuming darkness of the woods, a girl lost, lost and so far from home, lost in the eternal forest, lost forever.

■ ■ ■ ■

# Part Two

## 2015–2016

■ ■ ■ ■

I will invite myself
to this ghost supper.
— AUGUST STRINDBERG,
*The Ghost Sonata*

# ONE

"*Grey Dove* actual, on your go."

"Go," I said.

The engines fired, I was pressed into my chair, hurtling along the runway, and as the *Grey Dove* lifted into the night, my belly flopped at her steep ascent. The Earth rushed from me. The *Grey Dove* rattled around me, shaking me. I used to pass out as she climbed, the g-forces whipping blood from my brain, but I'm used to her now and grip the chair and watch the lights of cities as they recede below, turning into skeins of light as delicate as illuminated webs, as they disappear from my view, replaced by the vast blackness of the ocean at night.

"*Grey Dove,* please dim the lights," I said.

The cockpit lights go dark, and the heads-up display vanishes, and far above any cloud cover or light pollution the stars reveal themselves, countless points of brilliance. Overwhelming beauty.

*"Bird in flight's looking good, all systems go,"* from the Apollo Soucek tower, and the *Grey Dove* climbs ever steeper, and I'm soon facing upward, on my back, the Earth directly beneath me. The nuclear thrusters fire, and the sudden force crushes me, difficult to draw breath, but the pain lasts only a few seconds, thirty seconds at most before *Grey Dove* escapes Earth's clutching gravity and I'm weightless. The Earth dwindles beneath me, behind me. I feel the rumble of the firing thrusters vibrate through the ship, and I feel like I'm falling, like everything's floating and falling.

The lunar approach was a trip of only a few hours, but I didn't dock at the Black Vale; I accelerated past the moon. And as the moon's silver face diminished, darkening, the Black Vale's Lighthouse tower locked into the *Grey Dove*'s computer and performed a final check of the Brandt-Lomonaco Quantum-Foam Macro-Field Generator. The *Grey Dove* entered the area of space NSC called "Danger Sector," as it was pocked with B-L space-time knots, points of instability created by B-L engines as we sail Deep Waters.

The B-L drive switch lit green.

I peered through the *Grey Dove*'s cockpit glass back toward Earth like a sailor stealing her final glimpse of shore. Earth in the ocean of space, a tearful rush, a vast sense of the fragility of life — these were the rare moments I felt a spiritual swell.

"March 1997," I said, reminding myself of what I was soon to leave, and flipped the switch.

The B-L drive fired, creating a quantum-foam macro-field. For a brief moment, I felt as if all future possibilities existed with me, a melancholy sweetness that dissipated. A q-foam macro-field was nothing I'd ever see, even if the *Grey Dove* had been enveloped within one, a roiling system of wormholes flashing into existence and collapsing out of existence, all in just a Planck unit of time. The Earth, moon, and stars were blacked out. I sailed a wormhole. Which wormhole out of that turbulent foam the *Grey Dove* penetrated was just a matter of chance, each a tunnel to a distinct tine of the future multiverse.

I would sail three months through the quantum foam, the only light the *Grey Dove*'s cabin lights. Outside was depthless darkness, void. I unstrapped from the cockpit, the sounds I made strange in that eerie silence. I floated into the larger section of the ship, the interior curvilinear, white. A solitary passage. I read my case notes, reread them, and as days passed, I cycled through the ship's library of films — Jean Seberg, Bardot, *The Umbrellas of Cherbourg* — and listened to the Cure and Shania Twain and Nirvana, long stretches of classical music — Rachmaninoff, Ravel. Diminishing muscle and bone mass a constant concern without gravity, so my daily routine was to exercise, fastening myself to the treadmill with broad shoulder straps, jogging with my prosthesis. Elastic bands and vacuum resistance. Miles of stairs climbed on the elliptical.

A three-month journey to travel nineteen years.

I was startled when the *Grey Dove*'s alarm sounded, alerting me that she had made contact with the Black Vale's Lighthouse, that a new existence had coalesced around me. I dressed in my flight suit and floated to the cockpit, buckling myself in. Earth had reappeared in the void as if a blue light had been switched on. I checked the heads-up display: SEPTEMBER 2015. Relieved that my voyage was closing, but arrivals were different from departures, no exhilaration at seeing home after so long an absence; Rather, seeing this future-Earth was like staring into a mirror and discovering someone else's face.

Approaching Naval Air Station Oceana from the Atlantic, 2:00 a.m., the *Grey Dove* a needle passing over the black fabric of ocean. Rain-swept cockpit windows, lights of distant ships bobbing in the breakers, the coastline of Virginia much brighter than I remembered, even in this dismal weather.

"Oceana Approach," I said, calling to the airfield, "Cormorant Seven Zero Seven Golf Delta, level fifteen thousand with information Kilo —"

A blast of static, a woman's voice: "Cormorant Seven Zero Seven Golf Delta, Oceana Approach, turn left heading three two zero, descend and maintain nine thousand."

First voices on arrival were always eerie, echoes of sounds that hadn't yet been struck. The woman on the comm might have been only a child in 1997, or if she was young enough here, might not have been born, might not ever be born. Her entire life was only a possibility of the conditions of 1997, nothing more — brought into existence by my arrival, blinking out when I leave. She was a ghost, haunting her own potential.

Before experiencing IFTs, I imagined time travel as something concrete, that knowing the future would be as certain as knowing the past. I imagined that knowing the future might help me cheat at something like the lottery, seeing winning numbers before the numbers were ever pulled. This was before attending lectures at the Black Vale, before struggling through the mathematics-laden booklet explaining the physics of the Brandt-Lomonaco Quantum-Foam Macro-Field Generator. When I mentioned the lottery to our instructor, he'd said that every lottery number existed as a possible winning number until the moment when the winning numbers were observably pulled. What I would experience when traveling to an IFT, he'd said, wouldn't be the actual observed outcome of the lottery but only a *possibility* of the winning numbers. "In other words," he'd said, "don't place your bets."

"Cormorant Seven Golf Delta," said the flight controller, "intercept the localizer runway two eight right, cleared ILS two eight right."

Reflections of raindrops were like shadows boiling on my flight suit. I followed the ramp handlers' neon batons, taxiing. What would one day be real? IFTs felt like being lost in a house with a floor plan similar to your own, returning and returning to not-quite-familiar corridors, not-quite-familiar rooms. A team of engineers surrounded the

*Grey Dove* once she was through the hangar doors — they wore reflective vests marked NETWARCOM and tended to the B-L drive, housed in the ship's engine room, astern.

A ladder rig to the cockpit. One of the engineers knocked on the canopy of glass.

"Welcome to Apollo Soucek," he shouted. "Naval Air Station Oceana."

I unlocked and lifted the canopy — an irrational panic at the prospect of breathing hypothetical air, holding my breath as I removed my breathing mask, savoring my last breath from the oxygen tank until I couldn't hold out any longer and filled my lungs with the place. Unused to the pull of gravity as I tried to unbuckle and climb from the cockpit, gravity like hooks tugging downward. The NETWARCOM engineer draped my arm over his shoulder, assisted me from the flight chair, down the ladder rig. I'd lost weight in my three months aboard the *Grey Dove,* my prosthesis had lost its proper fit. The engineer eased me into a waiting wheelchair.

I felt like I'd only closed my eyes, but when lights swarmed back, I'd already been moved from the hangar and hooked up to an IV for hydration. A medical facility, a hospital room. A team of nurses, two men, transferred me from the wheelchair to a firm mattress, handling me like I weighed little more than a husk. Weary — my body felt like it was shutting down. A blush of modesty as they undressed me, removing my sweat-sodden flight suit, my under-clothes. The last thing I remember before depths of sleep swallowed me was saying, "At least change the channel" — the flat television tuned to *The X-Files,* an episode I'd never seen.

Two weeks shy of six when my father left us. Mom moved her rocker into my room and sat with me until I fell asleep, each night saying the Sandman would come and sprinkle dreams in my eyes. When once I asked who the Sandman was, she told me he was a shadow who crept into rooms where children slept, bringing dreams to kind children, removing the eyes from children who were rotten. When I asked what the Sandman did with those eyes, she said he passed them on to children waiting to be born so they would have eyes to see. Every night when I closed my eyes, I heard Mom rocking in her chair and feared the Sandman would come for my eyes, and although I was used to falling asleep with the thought of the Sandman approaching, every night the fear was new.

Time travel evoked similar anxieties. I had traveled to IFTs seven times before but never grew used to the dread of existing in a future; I was a splinter of the real that had pierced the membrane of a dream. Everything that followed my induction into NCIS had felt dreamlike, following that first moment in the Cormorant when my recruitment class had experienced weightlessness. While we were at the Black Vale, our instructors taught us the riddles of Deep Time — how we couldn't effectively travel to the past except for those rare occurrences called space-time knots and closed timelike curves, how we can travel to the future, but only possible futures. Only the Present is real, only the Present is terra firma. We were warned that no time passes in terra firma while we lived lives in IFTs — and yet IFTs weren't real, not "objectively" so. We were told that we affected IFTs even as we observed them — that they would bend around our psyches in subtle ways, but as surely as intense gravity bends light. The effect was called lensing, the sensation bizarre, our instructor saying that IFTs could feel like dreams within dreams. One session our instructor had asked us, "What would happen if you met someone in the future and brought him home with you to live in terra firma? What would happen if that person already exists in the present?" Another man had entered the classroom, an exact duplicate of our instructor, a double, a doppelgänger. "You would have what we call an echo," the double had said.

I woke in the hospital room.

"What year is it?" I asked the technician who came to take blood.

"2015," she said.

"September?"

"You haven't been asleep that long. Yeah, it's still September."

Bone-density tests, eyesight tests, MRIs. A physical-therapy regimen to recover from three months without gravity, but I'm a quick study, my body accomplished in adapting to new movement. The routine to manage the effects of gravity was not unlike the physical-therapy routine following my amputation, the hours of rehabilitation when teams of physical and occupational therapists taught me how to live with a missing limb. Severe weight loss aboard the *Grey Dove* — I hadn't realized just how many pounds I'd shed, but my facial features were drawn, my ribs and the points of my hip bone visible, my figure diminished in the full-length mirror. An enormous appetite —

daily protein shakes, sometimes twice daily, easy to exceed the recommended caloric intake, the past three months nothing but Protein Fillets, Russian Vita-Sticks, foil envelopes of fruit paste. I'd need to bulk up to endure the return trip home.

A soft knock at the room door the afternoon of my fifth day. I thought maybe one of the lab techs for another round of blood work, but when I opened the door, I found a hulking man, slightly stooped with age, bald except for a cottony tonsure and a flowing white beard. He wore a brown suit and a robin's-egg pocket handkerchief that matched the vivid blue of his shirt. When he saw me, a grin spread warmly across his face, like the sun revealed from behind clouds.

"Ah, there you are," he said. "I've been waiting nearly twenty years to meet you."

I recognized him, remembered him when he was middle-aged, a six-and-a-half-foot physicist with a startling Mohawk, reed thin back then in a cardigan and large black-framed glasses, now hunched and thicker, the top of his head as smooth as a river stone. Dr. Njoku had already been a star investigator by the time I saw him speak at a training session in Savannah because of his work on the Faragher case, a policy setter for investigations involving echoes, those individuals brought from IFTs, doubling someone already living.

Cases of misconduct among NSC sailors were common, an epidemic of drugs and money stolen from IFTs and distributed in terra firma. While fallout from Tailhook reverberated through the Navy, however, NSC sailors went without reform because actions committed in Inadmissible Future Trajectories had always been considered *inadmissible,* as if those actions had never occurred. Njoku's work had helped change the culture. He had spent years investigating Petty Officer Jack John Faragher, a sailor authorized to travel solo missions to Deep Waters but who had instead made several runs to near futures to kidnap the wives of friends, to bring these doubled women back to terra firma to defile and eventually murder. Faragher had pleaded innocent — but the court found, based on Njoku's work, that echoes brought to terra firma should be considered "alive" in every sense, afforded the rights of nonresident aliens. The charges against Faragher stuck, resulting in court-martial — and, after a series of appeals, the death sentence.

"Dr. Njoku," I said, shaking his hand. "I'm honored — I heard you speak in Savannah."

A summery vitality percolated in his eyes even though he moved with difficulty. Stiff knees, orthopedic shoes. He held a slim silver laptop, manila envelopes.

"The honor's mine," he said. "You're a bird in flight, a time traveler — the rest of us are just ghosts. Here, I brought you some housewarming gifts." Njoku handed me an envelope. "O'Connor wanted to bring these to you himself, but he just couldn't make the trip. Some health issues."

Mortal revelations were common in IFTs, but always jarring. "I'm sorry," I said, not knowing what else to say — I tried not to imagine O'Connor suffering, told myself that whatever the circumstances here, he was still healthy in 1997.

"He has his good days and his bad days," said Njoku. "He lives out in Arizona, says the dry air helps. He so wanted to see you again, but some days he . . . he can't even speak some days. He endured a series of heart attacks a few years back. He had to send me in his place."

We were trained not to take personal revelations like these as fact, not to let ourselves be snagged with worry over the possibilities we see unspooled. O'Connor's series of heart attacks might not ever occur.

I opened the envelope he'd left for me: a Visa, a bank card, driver's insurance, and a license. Five hundred dollars in twenties. A slim-profile cellular phone that looked like a handheld television.

"Ever use an ATM?" Njoku asked.

"Sure, but we travel with cash. I brought enough to last."

"Use the debit card, you'll have an endless supply — save you some paperwork when you return home. Your PIN is 1234. Everything's registered under the name you provided us with."

State of Virginia license, my photograph taken from my NCIS ID card, altered so that I was a brunette. *Courtney Gimm.* I'd asked O'Connor before I left to have this identification ready, knowing I'd be traveling under a different name. Almost twenty years after I'd filled out the paperwork, here it was.

"That one's a burner phone," said Njoku. "Disposable, biodegradable."

"You don't have Ambient Systems here?" I asked, thinking of other IFTs I'd visited, futures misty with nanotech, the air shimmering gold like fairy dust, hallucinatory images, illusions, voices that answered when you spoke their names. Cellular phones were obsolete in other futures.

"No, nothing like that here," said Njoku.

We shared a pot of oolong tea, watched a video montage on his laptop of what I'd missed in the intervening years, *Highlights of the Late Twentieth and Early Twenty-First Centuries,* the death of Diana and the semen-stained dress, the thousand dead at the terror attack on the CJIS FBI facility — a bitter jolt seeing images of the office where I worked engulfed in flames, the dead draped in sheets. The election of Gore, the towers falling. An Iraq treaty, the invasions of Afghanistan and Pakistan. Some of these images were familiar from other IFTs, but in other IFTs history had played out differently.

"What about the Terminus?" I asked.

"Recorded at the year 2067 by the crew of the USS *James Garfield.*"

Within a lifetime.

"Show me that part about CJIS again," I said.

"The largest act of domestic terror since the Oklahoma City bombing," said Njoku. "Over a thousand casualties. A sad, terrible day."

Internet images of the immediate aftermath, the dead laid in the fields surrounding the CJIS facility and in the vast parking lot. I wondered who I'd known that would be among the dead. *Rashonda Brock,* it occurred to me, *and the kids, Brianna and Jasmine* — I wondered if they would have died in the CJIS attack, thought of Brock just before he'd opened the door to Courtney's old bedroom. "I have two beautiful girls," he'd said. His entire family might have been stricken from him in a single morning.

"My office is in one of the burning sections," I said, my corner of the building obscured by smoke in nearly every image — the sensation was like seeing a house you'd once lived in burn to cinders. I thought of the faces I would have recognized. Rashonda Brock running through corridors opaque with smoke, searching for her children. "Was," I corrected. "I might die in this attack. Or I might have died, except I know —"

"A suicide bomber, an individual who worked for the FBI, his office was in the CJIS building," said Njoku. "He had security clearance."

*Then the bomber is employed at CJIS now,* I thought. I might have passed him in the hallways, might have interacted with him. I didn't recognize the photographs of the suicide bomber or his name: *Ryan Wrigley Torgersen.* "What happened?"

"April nineteenth, 1998," he said. "Torgersen reported to work like any ordinary day, breezed through security — he had a bomb sewn inside his body, nasty stuff — and he'd spent some time planting other bombs in the building. The explosions themselves caused some damage, but he'd rigged the fire-suppression system with sarin."

*Sarin.* Even a whiff of sarin gas was lethal within seconds. Imagining my colleagues in those narrow corridors, sarin spraying from ceiling sprinklers.

"Why did this happen?" I asked. "What was the motive?"

"Antigovernment paranoia," said Njoku. "Inspired by Timothy McVeigh, more than likely. Torgersen had purchased blueprints of the CJIS facility from a militia member active in West Virginia. He must have figured that destroying CJIS would cripple government law enforcement."

Njoku refilled our cups with tea, placed two manila envelopes on the table between us, both sealed. One envelope was marked MURSULT, PATRICK. The other, MURSULT, MARIAN.

Whatever hopes I harbored that Marian Mursult would have been found alive, safe, in the years between her disappearance and now dissolved at the sight of her name. I tore open the seal on Marian's file, slid out the thin sheaf of papers, and wept when I saw a photograph of partially buried bone fragments, a rush of mourning that had pent up in my heart ever since learning that the girl was missing. Marian's remains had been found in the summer of 2004, buried in the vast wilderness of the Blackwater Gorge. A photograph of the site showed a nondescript patch of mud in a verdant forest. Another showed bones in the earth. Despite the recovered remains, no suspects other than her father had ever emerged and no criminal charges were ever filed. Njoku had collected a few newspaper clippings from the time, the papers already yellowed. Another run of the familiar picture of Marian from the Amber Alert. A few quotes from Brock — reaffirming an already established narrative that Patrick Mursult had murdered his wife and children before killing himself. A confusion, there — Patrick Mursult had been executed, clearly a homicide. I scanned the news items, the obituary. Only an aunt and an uncle from Ohio to feel the relief at Marian's discovery, to bear the public grief — and then it was over, the Mursult family filed away.

"The file's wrong," I said. "Patrick Mursult was murdered. He didn't kill himself."

"The decision was made by NCIS and the

FBI to control the narrative to the public, the media. A story of murder/suicide helped close up outside inquiries. We continued to investigate Mursult's murder, but nothing turned up. The trail ran cold."

"Hikers found her," I said.

"A fluke. Nothing stays buried," said Njoku. "When her remains were discovered, one of our guys reconvened with the FBI, but nothing was discovered to warrant reopening the case."

"She's still alive. Marian might be still alive where I come from," I told him, setting aside Marian's file as if the pages themselves were fragile.

I opened the file MURSULT, PATRICK.

A swift-boat gunner in Vietnam, the connection to Elric Fleece confirmed. Pictures of the two men together on their boat, Fleece lean, almost unrecognizable from the obese body we'd cut down from the tree made of bones, younger. The file contained photographs of the mirrored room, the sculptures. The pictures of Kennedy, the *Challenger,* the swift boat covered in chips of fingernails.

"What about this?" I asked him. "Anything with the fingernails?"

"They were all Elric Fleece's," said Njoku. "No break there."

"Any guess as to what the 'ship made of nails to carry the dead' is?"

"It should be in the notes. A Viking myth, something about the end of the world."

I found the annotation: *Naglfar — a ship constructed from the fingernails of the dead, sails the end of the world to wage war against the gods.*

Another set of photographs, copies of the twenty-four explicit Polaroids we had found in Fleece's house, in the duffel bag in his spare room: *Nicole Onyongo.*

"This woman was identified?" I asked. "Who is this?"

"A day or two after Patrick Mursult's body was discovered," said Njoku, "Special Agent Philip Nestor tracked her down, using license-plate information the lodge kept. Questioned her, but she wasn't involved in our homicides beyond a sexual relationship with Mursult. She'd been having an affair with Mursult for a number of years but was shocked and saddened by what he was wrapped up in, what happened to his family. I remember she took the news of his death very hard."

*Nicole Onyongo,* a registered nurse at the Donnell House, hospice care associated with a hospital in Washington, Pennsylvania. Her address was up to date, the Castle

Tower apartments not far from her place of work — notes about her life, her routine. It looked like she spent most every day shift at the Donnell House before heading to a nearby bar, the May'rz Inn, where she drank until walking home at night. One of the pictures in the file was a copy of the woman's work ID — she was stunning, almost intimidating. Her eyes were a light shade of hazel. I compared her work ID to the sex pictures, the same rich color of skin. How did she strike up a relationship with a man like Patrick Mursult?

"Nestor interviewed her? I'll want to see any paperwork he kept about this woman," I said.

"We can track him down," said Njoku. "He was never briefed about Deep Waters, and he left the FBI some years ago. I think he sells guns."

"Nestor?" I asked. Not uncommon for FBI agents to make the jump into a second career, parlay their leadership skills into higher-paying office jobs, but selling firearms was a surprise. I'm not sure why — I'd only worked with Nestor for an afternoon, I didn't know him, but I'd thought of him since then, an infatuation. Soft-spoken, a photographer. I wanted to hold him apart from the jocks and gun geeks I met on the

143

job, but maybe I was imagining Nestor as something he wasn't. Or maybe something had happened to him since I'd known him, something that had changed him. Strange paths lives can take. I thought of Nestor's story of his father, doorways in the forest that led to other forests. "Yeah, I'll track him down. See what he can tell me."

"Anyone else you'll want to talk with, anyone associated with the investigation?" he asked. "We can reach out on your behalf."

"The woman, Onyongo," I said, and I considered speaking with Brock — but Brock was dangerous to me here. He had been briefed about Deep Waters, he'd known about Deep Space then, and it was possible he had learned about Deep Time in the intervening years. We were trained to avoid contact with government or military personnel who might understand the mechanics of time travel, who might understand that our appearance in their world meant their world would cease once we left. I knew an agent once, had known her as a twenty-four-year-old woman when she launched and saw her a few months later, after she'd returned to terra firma, deteriorated with weariness and old age. She had been imprisoned in her IFT by someone

from the Department of Homeland Security, was kept as an inmate at Holman supermax for over fifty years. We called what
she endured becoming a "butterfly in a bell
jar," a present danger to agents working in
Deep Time. If Brock knew about time
travel, he might capture me here and hold
me for as long as I could be kept alive.
"Only Nicole Onyongo and Nestor," I said.
"At least at first. But I'll make contact with
both of them on my own. I don't want to
approach them as law enforcement. They
might clam up."

Investigating cold cases almost twenty
years gone. Disheartening how little progress had been made in this investigation in
all this time, as if the Mursult deaths were
simply a fluke of violence, stormy weather
that struck and was swept away. Still, new
information would shake out. Tracking
down Nestor, tracking down Nicole Onyongo, interviewing her myself — people
will often speak freely about tragedies long
buried, will say things that they wouldn't
have said in the heat of their involvement.
Relationships evolve, sour — people who
wouldn't have talked then might talk now.

I flipped back to Mursult's service record.
"Still not much," I said. Unauthorized
absence, desertion. *Zodiac, Libra.* "What

about this?" I asked. "Any information about *Libra*? Or *Zodiac*? O'Connor tasked me to discover anything about *Libra* and why Mursult and Elric Fleece weren't accounted for."

"Nothing," said Njoku. "Their appearance remains unexplained. *Libra* is still assumed lost."

There was a slim document, a perfect-bound booklet, the cover illustrated with the icon of the Naval Space Command, a gold anchor and ropes spanning an image of the globe. There was a second icon as well — a woman with flowing auburn hair raising a set of golden scales, the figure outlined by the house-shaped constellation.

*United States Navy, Naval Space Command, Crew List, USS* LIBRA.

I flipped to *Petty Officer First Class Patrick Mursult, Special Warfare Operator,* and saw his photograph, flint-hard before the American flag, dress blues and white combination cap. Elric Fleece was here, too, rated as *Electrician's Mate* — nothing like the obese suicide I'd seen, but handsome, with full lips, and studious in thick-lensed glasses. He'd worked odd jobs as an electrician, I remembered — and in this photo he looked like an earnest graduate student. I had no trouble imagining this man tinkering with motherboards in a basement workshop cluttered with wires, a soldering iron in his hands.

"NCIS tracked surviving relatives of every sailor listed for *Libra,* but we were asking questions about ghosts," said Njoku. "Mursult and Fleece were posthumously convicted of desertion. We assume they weren't on *Libra* when it launched."

*Libra*'s commander was a woman, Elizabeth Remarque — I scanned her service record. An academic, a Ph.D. in engineering from MIT. Her hair was silvery, a feathery pixie cut. She was a young woman when she was given command — born in 1951, she would have been thirty-four when she launched. Her eyes were deep blue, matching the star field of the flag behind her.

"I knew Commander Remarque," said Njoku. "She was a friend."

"Did you serve together?"

"I was the agent afloat on the USS *Cancer,*" said Njoku. "Remarque was our engineer officer, distinguished herself — she saved all our lives. They gave her command of *Libra* because of how she handled herself on *Cancer.*"

"Only three Zodiac ships survived," I said. "The *Cancer* —"

"We launched in 1984, were scheduled to make five separate jumps to Deep Time, but Remarque discovered problems with the O-ring seals on the B-L Drive," said Njoku. "The seals were brittle, weren't holding up — a common problem with ships of that era. We all thought the B-L would misfire or explode. We thought we would all die, were certain of it, like we were living our last days in a floating tomb. But Remarque and her team went to work. They made eighteen separate space walks over the course of a month, replaced what they could, rebuilt the rest. Our commander aborted the rest of the mission, ordered us to sail home. The B-L drive held."

"You did complete a jump, though?" I asked. "The *Cancer* must have been the last ship to see a future without the Terminus."

"We sailed five thousand years," said Njoku. "And I saw . . . wonders, Shannon. Wonders I will never comprehend. The oceans were thick like honey. Fifty-five billion people or more. Deserts — everything sand-swept. The old cities had fallen away, but new cities were built, entire cities in the shape of black pyramids, pyramids carried on the shoulders of the millions who lived in their shade. Entire generations were born, lived, and died beneath the cities they carried. Moving cities, wandering to find water. The people below were starving, naked, subsisting on scraps and detritus left by the kings who lived inside the pyramids."

"Maybe the Terminus is a mercy," I said.

Njoku snapped from his reverie. "I can tell you the rich were doing well for themselves," he said. "Inside the pyramids were pleasure gardens, grottoes, fountains. Our crew was welcomed like we were long-lost children, prodigals shown every comfort. Every illness cured if you could afford the cure. And some people had left their bodies entirely, had become immortal, living as waves of light — but once they could no longer die, the immortals begged for death, because life without the passage of time becomes meaningless. It used to be thought that hell was a lack of God, but hell is a lack of death."

Njoku finished the last of his tea, checked the time — nearing ten at night. "I should let you sleep," he said, "but I'm curious. What was the last moment you remember before coming here?"

"Hale-Bopp was in the sky," I said.

Njoku's smile seeped through his concentration. "Of course, of course I remember — I remember that time very well. You launched in March, didn't you? Of 1997, my God. I was stationed at the Boston office — so I'm still in Boston, in terra firma. I was collaborating on a project with physicists at MIT. Wave-function collapse. Brandt-Lomonaco space-time knots. Just a few weeks later, I met Jayla . . . She was a professor of saxophone performance, played in a trio at the time. I remember watching her play, I remember the sounds she made, her fingers pressing the keys, the sound of her breath. We've been married now for seventeen years, but oh, I remember that time."

"So in terra firma, you only have a few weeks to live before your life changes forever," I said.

"Lovely, Shannon. That is a lovely thought."

"I am ready to relieve you," I said once we shook hands good night — the traditional phrasing NSC sailors spoke on parting, the tacit acknowledgment that when I returned home aboard the *Grey Dove,* every moment of Njoku's life that had been lived after March of 1997 would blink out of existence — this entire universe, the fully formed entirety of this IFT would vanish as suddenly as a passing thought. Rather than the traditional response of "I am ready to be relieved," however, Njoku merely smiled.

"It was difficult to accept that my life was an illusion," he said. "Whether you're NCIS or NSC, when you're told the secrets of Deep Waters, you agree that you might have to lay down your life for your country — that theoretically, at any moment, you might come into the realization that your life is an illusion. You rationalize it, you say that soldiers give their lives for their country, that police officers give their lives . . . 'They lay down their lives,' for a greater good . . . But still, even though I know the physics, on some level I refused to believe that if I ever encountered you, Shannon Moss, it would prove that this entire universe was just some sort of 'pocket universe' that would blink out once you'd left. When O'Connor assigned you to me, it was like he handed down my death sentence. Can you understand that? I'm married, I have children, and my children have grown and are ready to have children of their own, but every happy moment in my life was tempered by knowing that what I was experiencing wasn't real."

"But you *are* real where I come from. You'll still live this life," I said.

"Dr. Wally Njoku might be real, he might meet Jayla in a few weeks, like you said, he might even have a family, but he won't have the same family. What are the odds of one particular spermatozoon fertilizing one particular egg? Njoku might have children, but they won't be the same children, they won't be mine. He'll be happy, but it won't be my happiness —"

"I know," I told him. "I understand, I do."

"But I came to accept that my existence is an illusion. Have you ever seen a flower called the 'falling star' as it blooms?" he asked. "I saw one — this was several years ago, in summer. I was taking a walk with Jayla when we passed a neighbor's garden and noticed a certain flower in early bloom. She pointed it out to me, and I was transfixed. A single stem, every bud perfectly symmetrical — the color was orange, almost like fire. I was struck because the first two buds to bloom, at the base of the stem, were in full flower, but the next two buds up the line had only just begun to bloom, the next two buds were smaller still, and so on, all the way up to the tip of the stem, where the flowers were merely two closed buds that had yet to open at all. This was the *Crocosmia,* the 'Lucifer,' but Jayla knew it as the falling star. I understand that we physicists interpret existences as something like a symptom of wave-function collapse, some quantum illusion to exploit, a brief fermata of indeterminacy, but I prefer to think of myself and all my selves as the falling star, every permutation of every choice I've ever made and ever will make existing in every moment, forever. 'Merrily, merrily' — isn't that what the truest sailors say? Nothing blinks out, nothing ends. Everything exists, always exists. Life is but a dream, Shannon. Self is the only illusion."

I left Oceana the following morning, in the car that had been requisitioned for me, a beige sedan. I drove from Naval Air Station Oceana north through D.C. to pick up the Pennsylvania Turnpike West, thinking of the falling star. My car was electric, battery-powered, the engine silent, a constant worry that I had slipped into neutral and was coasting. Caffeine helped me overcome the sensation of being caught in a waking dream — I ordered a black coffee at a Starbucks near an outlet mall in Fredericksburg. Country music on the radio, songs I'd never heard before and might not ever hear again, but once the mountains turned FM into static, I scanned AM until I found a minister speaking about the Resurrection. *Do you believe in the resurrection of the body?* — something Nestor had asked me. Through the Allegheny Mountain Tunnel. Isolated houses, tobacco barns fallen into ruin. I watched hawks circle above conical saltcellars. What had this drive been like the last time I'd made it — less than a year ago in my world, but almost twenty years ago in this one? What had the scenery been? Trying to figure out what was new, what was lost. Yards full of junk and houses lined with rusted scaffolding. Communications towers, a white church in a valley near Breezewood. Newer service plazas, motion-sensor toilets that flushed by themselves. I had to charge my engine by plugging in. The changes of the intervening years registered more acutely as I neared Canonsburg — industrial parks and gleaming office cubes and sprouts of housing developments in what had once been only vacant green hills. The hills were cluttered with white windmills, lazily spinning, and I saw entire fields of solar panels where there had once been crops. Driving into Canonsburg still felt like coming home. The drive downhill on Morganza was the same, as was the Pizza Hut that edged Chartiers Creek.

I checked with the Canonsburg Police Department and found my mom still alive, her address listed as Room 405 at Townville Health and Rehabilitation. Up the hill on Barr, already dusk when I pulled in to the lot. Women in wheelchairs taking in the evening air, old men smoking. *Jeopardy!* in the rec room, a hand of euchre — I scanned the card players, nervous to see her, wondering how much she'd changed. An elevator to the fourth floor, framed paintings of cottages, flora. Mom often said she never wanted to end up in a place like this, said I should kill her before I let that happen.

The door to 405 was open, the television blaring. The room was sterile in the way of doctors' offices, the color scheme nothing that would have been chosen for a home — blue and fuchsia with white-flowered wallpaper. A food tray was swiveled over the bed, plastic dishes and a carton of milk, the same sort kindergartners would drink from. Potted hyacinths were on the nightstand, filling the room with sweetness that masked the earthier smells of my mother's body.

"I think my dosage is off," she said. "I've been drowsy —"

I flinched at the concavities of her face when she turned toward me. The shape of my mother's head was different, tucked in; a significant part of her jaw had been removed. She looked mummylike, bandage-wrapped bedsores on her forearms and bedsheets over her legs.

"Mom," I said.

"Oh?" she said. "Oh, I thought you were the nurse. Shannon?"

"It's me, Mom."

"It can't be. I don't believe you."

Mom propped herself up on her elbows, her gown falling away to reveal the skin of her shoulders, even more supple with age, softer, it seemed, and coated with white down. Her hair was mussed — it looked greasy, like it hadn't been washed in several days.

"You haven't changed a day," she said. "Look at you, Shannon. Where have you been? You left me. You left me bereft. You left me alone."

"I was deployed," I said, a lie made no less vile because it was in some sense true. "I had to go."

"I'm . . . look at me," she said, tugging her gown back over her shoulders. "I'm so embarrassed. You shouldn't see me like this. You shouldn't see your own mother like this. You should have told them you were coming, I could have dressed."

Her expressions were altered because of her surgeries, scars like white worms wriggled on her jowls and throat when she talked. I said, "Mom, it's all right, I like seeing you."

"New nurses come in here every day, and

156

they don't take care of me. Sweetie? Sweetie, are you out there? Come here, Sweetie —"

"I'm here," I said, but when I took a step closer to the bed, Mother said, "Not you."

A woman appeared in the doorway, a hoary woman in a wheelchair, her hair a tangle of steel wool. Sweetie pulled herself along with her white sneakers and her hands on the wheels, tucked herself inside the room and stared at me.

"This is the one I told you about, Sweetie," said Mom. "The daughter."

"I'm Shannon," I said, realizing I'd been damned during my years of absence. "A pleasure to meet you."

Sweetie laughed, a horrible wheezing.

"Sweetie's my friend, my only friend," said Mother. "We call this place our ghost house, because we feel like ghosts here."

"Sure enough," said Sweetie.

I pulled a chair over to my mother's bedside, took one of her hands. She was insubstantial, just bones and veins and a wrapping paper of skin.

"What happened?" I asked. "You've been sick."

"I'm told I'm a tough old bird, Shannon," she said. "Too gamy for death to eat."

Cancer in her intestines and in her mouth, she explained. The doctors broke her jaw and removed the cancerous half. They cut apart her throat. Cut open her intestines and clipped out the effected lengths, leaving her with a colostomy bag.

"All I ate was Ensure," she said. "Seemed like years. I had a feeding tube right in my stomach for such a long time, right here," she said, pointing just above her belly button. "I turned skinny."

"You were always skinny," I said.

"It's hard for me to chew, even still — I can't eat very much. I don't think these nurses know what they're doing."

She'd barely nibbled the cut of turkey and mashed potatoes on her dinner tray.

"Nineteen years," she said. "You disappeared in 1997. You never came back, you never said good-bye. What do you think about that, Sweetie? Your boy's no good, I've met him — always trying to take your money, but at least he comes to see you. My daughter left me."

"No good," Sweetie said.

"They experimented on me," said Mom. "After they butchered me like this, some doctor paid me a visit, this salesman — said I was terminal but an ideal candidate, and they wanted to know if I'd accept a thousand dollars to be part of their trials. I was one of the first in the entire country. Three injections, that's all. Tiny robots swimming in my blood, finding cancer cells and killing them. After all these years, all this suffering — three injections. You can tell your children someday how their grandmother was part of the first trials."

*A cure for cancer.* "That's . . . miraculous," I said. I'd heard rumors of far-future IFTs where diseases had been solved, but a cure for cancer by 2015? "They cured you?"

"A guinea pig," she said. "I got lucky — could never afford it otherwise. Can I tell you about a dream I had? A dream about you. After you'd disappeared and I gave up hoping you'd ever come back, I dreamed I was walking down a street, one of those streets in Europe — old buildings, old apartments. I heard a cracking sound — and saw the wall of the building had cracked. I heard snapping wood — the floorboards. The apartment was on fire, and I saw flames rush from the windows, bright orange flames that reached into the sky. You were just a child, playing on the sidewalk, my sweet child. I ran to you, I scooped you up — just before the house collapsed. I saved you, Shannon, but when I looked to see you in my arms, you'd disappeared."

"Only a dream," I said.

"A horrible thing, to dream," she said.

159

We sat with Sweetie for over an hour, most of the time passing in silence, the three of us staring passively at the television — a singing contest, with judges spinning in futuristic thrones. A nurse changed my mother's colostomy bag — a flush of embarrassment on my mother's behalf, a woman given up to this male nurse who handled her body like it was nothing, nothing more than a trash can that needed emptying.

"You left me. Just like he did," she said, knowing where to bury the knife.

"I was deployed," I said again, the lie hollow this second time.

"Deployed, always deployed — you lost your leg, you aged, you aged horrifically, always so old, too old, always getting so old I thought you and I were the same age, but now you're here and you haven't aged in twenty years. It's a sickness —"

"I was at sea."

"Nineteen years without a word, you and your father."

"I know," I said.

"Do you even remember your father?" she asked. "He left when you were young, but I bet you remember something."

Nothing but images — shattered stained glass I hoped could be re-formed into the image of a saint.

"I remember the photograph we had of him on the mantel," I said. "That's mostly how I remember him."

"That's how I wanted you to remember your father when you were younger. I wanted you to have good memories."

"I remember him lifting me into the air," I said.

"I used to wonder if you could smell that other woman on him," said my mother.

"Please don't —"

"You're not that delicate, are you? You come back after all these years and you expect me not to compare you to him? We're all adults here. Or is it that you want to be faithful to him?" she said. "He's not worth it. I could smell her on him when he came home too late for dinner, and then he'd hug you and I'd wonder if *you* could smell her. Isn't that awful, a woman wondering if her baby girl knew what the smell of another woman was?"

Father smelled like pipe smoke. His breath sometimes like wintergreen.

"We don't need to talk about this," I said.

Very few memories of my father. Flannel shirts and blue jeans — or maybe just one memory spread out over years. Pipe smoke, wintergreen. Scruffy — I remembered him with a beard, or stubble, even though the image of him that I remember most clearly was the picture on the mantel, a young sailor, clean-cut.

"I remember his flannel shirts," I said.

"I don't believe in you," said my mother. "I think you're a dream, or a nightmare I'm having. Am I dreaming, Sweetie?"

"I hope we're dreaming, you and me," said her friend.

"You can't just disappear for nineteen years," said Mother. "You and your father."

"Excuse me," I said, stepping away, refusing to cry in front of her. The hallway air was stale with medicinal smells and disinfectant. Somewhere, in some other room, a woman screamed, and it sounded like she was burning alive. I had to remind myself that this world was false, that her accusations against me were false; it was my father who'd abandoned us. I felt guilty for something I hadn't done — I never abandoned her, would be with her again when I returned from this IFT as if no time had gone by. No time for her at least. When I thought of the picture of my father on our mantel, I always gave him the benefit of the doubt, always on some level blaming my mother for his leaving us — unfair of me, but I'd think of my mother at the call center, a failure at her grander dreams, a drunk, the hours at McGrogran's siphoning off her life, and I'd think, *No wonder the man left us.* I resented her for losing him. She gave him away. She gave away everything and kept nothing.

Sweetie and my mother had returned their attention to the television, a vacant smile twisting my mother's face as she hummed along with one of the contestants on the show.

"Mom?"

"Too late, too late," she said. My mother settled into her pillow, closed her eyes. I kissed her forehead — her skin clammy, sweat-scented. I began to cry harder, this IFT dredging up too much pain. *Only a version of the truth,* I told myself, IFTs warping around the mind of the observer, a black hole warping light. I always wondered if I took after my father, sometimes hoping I took after him, imagining his intricate inner life — a marked contrast to Mom, who always looked outward. I felt so alone after Courtney had died, and I wanted her then, wanted my mom, wanted her to show me how to bear such loss, but she was distant. Her circle at McGrogan's, her late nights, while her daughter drifted unmoored. I used to think that my father had tried to love her but that she was never there for him, that she had eventually pushed him away. I used to daydream of leaving her, too, resentful. But she was the one who stayed for me when he had left us. She had stayed even while everyone in her life abandoned her — while I abandoned her.

Sweetie's brown eyes were pools inviting me to drown. "We'll keep each other," she said. "When she wakes up, I'll tell her you were just a haunt, a wayward."

I found one of Mom's nurses at the call station, clicking fingernails against the screen of her phone.

"Excuse me," I said. "My mother was treated for cancer — she mentioned an injection therapy? Amanda Moss?"

The nurse seemed annoyed to have been pulled away from her screen — she slapped a pamphlet down on the counter: *Non-Invasive Cancer Therapy.* Phasal Systems. I was aware of Phasal, a spin-off company from the Naval Research Lab — in most other IFTs, Phasal had grown into a communications and entertainment behemoth, the makers of Ambient Systems. Phasal was pharmaceutical here — other IFTs might have the miracle of Ambient Systems instead of smartphones, but here there was a cure for cancer. *Cell-specific medicine delivery. Smart meds, nanotech injections.*

164

"She got the cancer cure through government assistance," said the nurse, "but you have to be rich to live forever."

I checked in to a Red Roof Inn that accepted cash. A business center, a room off the lobby equipped with computers, a printer. I logged on with my key card, Google easy enough once the front-desk clerk showed me where to click. Hours researching Marian, scribbling notes on hotel stationery. *Philip Nestor + West Virginia* hit a Web site called the Eagle's Nest. World War II memorabilia. The *SHOP* tab displayed a grid of Nazi artifacts, flags and antique weapons. I bristled at the swastikas, wondering if this was even the same person I had known or if I was tracking the wrong Philip Nestor. Not much information on the Web page, but *APPEARANCES* listed upcoming shows, the Monroeville Guns and Ammo Show a few weekends away. I could find him there.

Scant results for Nicole Onyongo, the woman in Mursult's photographs. I landed on a pdf of a sheriff's document that indicated a stint in county jail, drug-related — even more reason not to flash a badge and pepper her with questions about a past murder. Njoku's file mentioned she was habitual at a bar called May'rz Inn. I thought of my mother, how if she wasn't at home she would be at McGrogan's. The name of Nicole Onyongo's bar rang a bell, and I checked the address, knew where the place was, just a ten-minute drive from the Red Roof into downtown Washington, on South Main. Almost midnight, but a good chance it would be open, so I took my key card from the computer and drove over. The May'rz Inn was a dive in a row of mostly abandoned storefronts nestled near the Bradford House, a stone Georgian from the 1700s, a Whiskey Rebellion house. No windows, just an emerald-green front door beneath an awning. SMOKING PERMITTED. WEDNESDAY WINGS. I parked out front on the empty street.

May'rz was lit with neon, and the television glow above the bar was vague with hanging smoke. A narrow space, the clack of pool balls in a back room, Zeppelin on the jukebox. The place was nearly empty, but she sat at the bar, her cigarette smoldering as she spoke with the bartender. Nicole Onyongo was older than in the photographs I'd seen of her, taller than I would have guessed, but her movements were as sinuous as the trail of smoke that rose from her cigarette. She noticed me watching her —

her eyes were startling, the color of teak, but laconic, her expression like she already doubted anything I would ever say.

"Can I get you anything?" from the bartender.

"Just looking for someone," I said, leaving.

The FBI had interviewed the woman, Nestor had interviewed her. NCIS would have talked with her, too, maybe O'Connor. Even if she'd been emotionally insulated near the time when Mursult was killed, she might talk now. She had been close with Mursult, her memories of the man were valuable to me.

A dilapidated building stood next door to May'rz, a sign out front — ROOM VACANCY. I jotted down the landlord's number, called once I was back at the Red Roof. Almost one o'clock in the morning, expecting to leave a message on a machine, but a man's voice answered, his accent Eastern European, almost too thick to understand.

"Come by tomorrow," he said. "Morning. I'll give you keys then."

"Is it okay if I pay with cash?" I asked.

"Cash only," he said.

I handed him the security deposit and first month's rent the next morning — no lease, month-to-month payments. I moved in that afternoon, the apartment a one-bedroom unit on the third floor, no elevator. Musty. I used a butter knife to chip away paint from the windows before I could slide them open. Worn wood floors, the molding painted with several coats of cream. The kitchen sink had the same faucet I remembered from my grandmother's house, the cabinets were similar, too — a moment of lensing, I guessed, details existing only because I was the one here to observe them. This apartment might be slightly different in terra firma. I had brought tablets of Red Roof Inn stationery with me, sat at an antique writing desk that had come with the room, sketching — eventually sketching skeletons, crucified.

*Patrick Mursult,* I wrote. *Elric Fleece. Libra.*

I thought of Remarque, the commander of *Libra,* of how she had saved the *Cancer. O-ring seals,* I wrote, wondering if *Libra*'s O-ring seals had failed . . . but wouldn't Remarque have known? Wouldn't she have saved *Libra* as she had saved *Cancer*?

I tore my notes into small pieces and looked again at Remarque's picture in the *Libra* crew list. An attractive woman, dashing — even in this photograph she looked like she could outmaneuver the world. *What happened to you?*

■ ■ ■ ■

Several weeks before Nestor would be at the gun show in Monroeville, where I would ask him what he remembered about Patrick Mursult and Marian's death and discovery, how it had all played out. I had time on my hands. I wandered downtown Washington most mornings, picking up the texture of this place, and spent some time at the mall, where I bought clothes to match the styles of other women I saw, comfy clothes, a Mountaineers sweatshirt, athletic-fit tank tops, yoga pants. L'Oréal rinse-out dye to match my driver's license, a luxurious brunette color that brought out my sharper features, my cheekbones, my jawline — I felt tougher, more pugnacious than as a blonde.

May'rz most nights, becoming a regular, and Nicole there most nights, too. She came there to smoke and drink and watch TV, the two of us sitting just a few seats from each other, passing the time in silence until a week or so had passed, rounding toward midnight on a Thursday, after we'd both built up a pretty good buzz. An early snowstorm had kicked up, people coming into May'rz stamping their shoes and shaking snow from their collars. I'd learned she drank manhattans, so I bought her a drink.

"I'm Courtney, by the way," I told her, thickening the Guntown drawl that had always played at the edge of my voice anyway. "About time I introduced myself."

"Cole," she'd said, her African accent lilting, melodic. We shook hands, her palms rough, almost callused, it felt like. She wore a bracelet in the shape of a serpent. Nicole slid a seat closer to mine, lit one of her Parliaments. "You live around here?"

"Right next door," I said. "In that shithole, the white building. I got an apartment there a few days ago, so I drink here and just stumble upstairs when they kick me out."

"At first I thought maybe you were with the gas companies when you started showing up," said Nicole. "But then I thought I recognized you. Have we met before?"

"I don't think so. You go to high school around here? I was at Can-Mac."

"I grew up in Kenya," she said. "What do you drink?"

"Rum and Cherry Coke."

She bought our next round. She proved chatty, eager to talk, filling my ear with the details of her routine, the grind of working in hospice care. I pushed her toward her past, blunt questions about old boyfriends, hoping she would mention something about Patrick Mursult that I could pry into, but I learned the minutiae of the Donnell House instead, the staff there, the joys of helping people and the guilty relief that flooded Nicole whenever one of her more difficult residents finally succumbed — occurrences she celebrated with a shot of Jägermeister.

I saw Nicole nearly every night at May'rz, some nights just enjoying the bar, the atmosphere, enjoying her company, her chatter. Some nights I let myself forget all about Shannon Moss and lived as Courtney Gimm. Easy to adopt a new life and let my old life dissolve — nothing was urgent here, no matter how long I lived here I would return to the present in the moment I had left. I could let time pass here, live whatever life I wanted. I could forget myself here, so I reminded myself often of why I'd come. Every night before I slept, I looked at a photograph of Marian Mursult I kept on my writing desk. *You're alive,* I'd whisper. *You're still alive.* I placed a sheet of Red Roof stationery beside the picture and wrote in black Sharpie, *LIFE IS GREATER THAN TIME.*

# Two

Signs lined Old William Penn Highway, GUNS AND AMMO — THIS WEEKEND. I found the convention center out by the Monroeville Mall, next to a Babies "R" Us, the lot full, spillover parking in the lot of the abandoned big box across the street. Nine-dollar tickets to get into the show, the ticket taker asking if I was carrying a weapon.

No need for pretense, fake IDs, as Nestor might recognize me anyway. I showed my badge. "Naval Criminal Investigative Service."

"Are you with Gibbs?" he asked.

"I don't know what that is."

"From the TV show," he said, tearing my ticket, stamping my hand with an eagle.

"I'm a federal agent."

"You know, the TV show," he said.

Snaking lines of folding tables filled out the convention hall. I looked through the crowds for Nestor. Ammo and beef-jerky vendors, some tables like a flea market of random junk, old AK-47 banana clips and rusted-out Winchesters. Tables of blades — switchblade knives with jewel-colored handles. Neon-green axes labeled for hunting and killing zombies, I wondered if that was actually a thing. Someone asked if I needed a canister of mace to keep in my purse.

"You'd look good in this one," one of the sellers said, a woman with platinum curls, holding up the skimpiest pink tank top, Hello Kitty with an AK-47: KALASHNI-KITTY.

Other T-shirts, the Pillsbury Doughboy in a Nazi armband WHITE FLOUR, shirts for the USMC, the Screaming Eagles. Browsing guns, I liked the feel of weapons with wooden stocks, the warmth and heft, rather than the plasticky feel of some semi-automatic rifles. My attention caught on pink camo shotguns meant for gun babes, I figured, but there were only a half dozen other women here, and they didn't look like the pink-camo type to me.

"My God, Shannon Moss — is that you?"

"Nestor?"

In his thirties then, he'd be in his fifties now. Handsome still. His eyes were still stunning — I'd almost forgotten how brilliant. Powder blue, lit from within. His hair had grown a shade darker, and his mustache and scruffy beard had gone gray at the tips. He'd been thin before, but even so he'd lost weight — wiry, like a long-distance runner. Flannel, blue jeans. His table was called the Eagle's Nest, a pickers' table. Nazi gear, almost all of it — antique rifles, bayonets, a glass case of pistols, P38s and Lugers, matched with patches from the officers who'd carried them, letters of authenticity. Some American stuff, an autographed picture of Patton. Nestor came around from behind his table.

"It *is* you," he said, and he hugged me. Pipe smoke. It felt good to put my arms around him. "You haven't changed," he said. "I mean, *you haven't changed* — you look just like I remember you. Look at you. How long has it been?"

"Nineteen years, about," I said.

"Nineteen," he said. "You know, when I first saw you coming up the aisle, I thought I recognized you, but my first thought was you might be your daughter."

"Ha, no — no kids —"

"Let me look at you," he said. "*God.* You look . . . you look damn good, I'm telling you. You took care of yourself."

"Well, I don't feel so young," I said. "Dying my hair now."

"I noticed, it looks good," said Nestor. "I like the dark hair."

"All the gray, I had to do something."

"I'll be honest, I'm happy to see you. You just left," he said. "And then, I thought you might have, you know, with CJIS. When CJIS was attacked. Your office was in CJIS, wasn't it? I'm remembering that right?"

"It was," I said. "But I was at sea. I've been at sea."

"You know about Brock?" he asked. "I mean about his wife? Lost his wife at CJIS, his two daughters also."

"Rashonda," I said. "I haven't seen Brock since Canonsburg. How is he?"

"They used the day care at that building," said Nestor. "He lost everyone. And never really got over it, never remarried or any- thing, just buried himself in his work, kept busy. He's all right, last time we talked — you know, he got all those promotions. He's at Quantico now. I used to ask him if he knew what happened with you, but he didn't know. No one seemed to know. We figured you might have been caught up in the attack, too — but you're here. I used to look through the names of everyone that was killed, all those memorials they tele- vised. But you're here. My God, Shannon.

It's good to see you."

His demeanor had changed, chattier, a man used to patter, but his voice had the warmth I remembered.

"How about you?" I asked him. "What is all this stuff?"

"The Eagle's Nest, takes up all my time. This was my dad's collection. He was a hoarder — anything military. World War I or II. I was just going to sell all this stuff off at once, but a buddy of mine convinced me to do gun shows, and I've been at this . . . almost six years, I guess. I do American memorabilia, British, but the Nazi pieces are the big sellers here. It beats a desk job."

"You aren't with the Bureau anymore?"

"Not for a long time," he said. "I'll tell you what, let me get my neighbor over here to watch my table for a while. Do you have a few minutes? I'll buy you some lunch. Their chicken fingers aren't bad."

I accepted a cup of coffee. The convention center's café was near the bathrooms, a few tables set out. The coffee Nestor handed me smelled a little like barbecue sauce, and I barely sipped it but was happy to hold something warm. Nestor's forehead wrinkled as he talked, just like I remembered, only the creases were deeper. His eyebrows were bushier, softer.

"It's good to see you," I told him.

A familiarity between us — I had barely known him in 1997, and even though the years were a gulf between us, I felt like no time had passed at all, like we were resuming a conversation neither one of us had wanted to end.

"What brings you around?" he asked.

"You," I said. "What have you been up to?"

"I quit the Bureau — 2008. Did some freelance photography for a while. The work I do now suits me. I travel the circuit, meet people. It's all right. I've always been interested in history."

"You've lost weight," I said. "You're just a skinny thing, look at you."

"Yeah, well," he said.

"Moved back to West Virginia?" I asked. "You grew up in Twilight?"

"Always been my home. I have a house just outside this little town called Buckhannon," he said. "Quiet. Away from everything. They have a good strawberry festival every year."

"I used to go there as a kid," I said. Strawberry parfaits and idolizing the Strawberry Pageant queen in the parade. I imagined Nestor with his camera, snaps of Americana. "I haven't been in years."

"Sure, you grew up around here," he said. "You grew up in Canonsburg, right? You grew up in our crime scene —"

"Why Buckhannon?" I asked.

"Things just came together. I needed a place with a garage to store all my junk. The place I have has a small barn on the property. You should see it sometime. I get pickers coming through to look at the war stuff."

"That sounds like a nice life."

"It's a better life than the one I had," he said.

"I don't want to dance around something," I said. "What happened? Why'd you leave the Bureau?"

"You know, you take something like what happened out in Nevada a couple years ago," said Nestor. "All the FBI ready to storm that man's ranch — and for what? Over cattle grazing? What's the point of that? Of all that violence? I just . . . couldn't take part anymore, I guess. Couldn't be a jackboot." He lost himself staring out over the heads of everyone at the gun show, the clamor of the convention hall grown distant. He cleared his throat, coughed. "I was involved in a 'use of force' incident — I took someone's life. That shook me, almost destroyed me. I was having trouble handling

178

what happened and just couldn't deal with all the political bullshit. All the Bureau's bullshit," he said. "Drank too much, I admit. For a time . . . I had to come to terms with a few things."

"You're all right now?" I asked.

"I'm all right," he said. "So you tracked me down. Came all the way out to Monroeville to see me."

"I need to talk with you about Marian Mursult," I said.

"Marian Mursult," said Nestor, running his palm over his chest, reacting as if the name wounded him. "Why her?"

"She was found," I said.

"We found her, long after."

"I read up about the investigation, but I need particulars," I said.

"After all this time? For what?" he asked, his forehead rippling, an expression like begging for mercy. "Why?"

"I've been assigned to a review board," I told him, a standard cover that didn't inspire questions — vaguely administrative, the tediousness of paperwork. "She was found out near Blackwater Falls?"

"Out in the woods, that's right. Buried out in the Blackwater Gorge," he said. "You, showing up here. You're like a ghost, asking about ghosts. You really want to talk about that? Marian Mursult."

"I need to know what you can tell me about her," I said.

"Why don't you go through the Bureau? Why track me down? Brock's still around, out in Virginia. He can talk with you. He'd know more."

"I need to talk with you," I said.

"Not here, though," said Nestor. "I don't want to get into all that stuff here. Hell, most of these people, if they found out I used to work with the FBI, they'd blacklist me, they'd think I was spying on them. Can you meet up? Tonight even? This whole show closes down at four."

"Anywhere," I said. "Where are you staying?"

"I'm heading back home tonight," he said. "You want to have dinner before I go? There's a place over here some of us went to last night, the Wooden Nickel."

"You're down in Buckhannon, that's not too far from the Blackwater," I said. "Can you show me where you found her?"

"Seriously? After all these years, you track me down and want me to take you out there? Well, what the hell. It would take a few hours to get there and back," said Nestor. "It'll get dark. How are you with your leg? Can you hike at all?"

"I can hike."

"All right. Well, why don't we meet at the lodge, then — Blackwater Lodge. I can leave a little early from here, meet you down there, let's say by six or six-thirty. I didn't get a chance to buy you chicken fingers, but I'll get you dinner after. I know a place."

I arrived early, twenty minutes or so, waiting in the car with the radio on, shredding the napkin that came with my Starbucks into tinier and tinier scraps of confetti, ashamed at how nervous I was. Nestor had said I was like a ghost asking about other ghosts. Waiting for him outside the Blackwater Lodge, not yet dark, but I remembered how black the woods were that night — the hemlock pines around the lodge seemed to have grown denser over the years, this whole place thick with ghosts, a feeling like I could walk back to Cabin 22 and still see Patrick Mursult slumped there, drained of life.

Nestor pulled his F-150 beside my Camry and waved me into the cab.

"Are you driving?" I asked.

"We can only get one car up there."

We left the main roads, taking narrower routes that cut uphill, the towering pines cooling what little remained of the day.

"Shannon, I don't understand how you

can still look so young."

"Come on," I said.

"I'm serious, Shannon," said Nestor. "I turned into an old man, and you look —"

"Thanks, but I don't know. I work out, I eat right," I said.

"Well, you figured it out," he said. "You should write a book about the fountain of youth, I'm telling you. You could be a millionaire, on the talk shows."

Nestor turned onto a path just wide enough for his truck, an access route or maybe a logging road, that rushed uphill at a dizzying incline. The truck wheels spun out, but Nestor gunned the gas — the tires caught and the truck lurched upward. I leaned back in the seat, holding on, imagining the truck would tip backward, like we'd fall end over end.

"Here we are. They still have the trail marked."

Nestor pointed ahead, and I saw an orange ribbon tied around a tree trunk. He maneuvered his truck, scraping against the pines, to where the path leveled out into a narrow clearing where he could park.

"This was as far as any of the trucks could get," he said. "Couldn't get an ambulance up here, so they brought her body down in the back of a pickup."

*Her body.* Careful of my footing, climbing from the cab. The pines were silhouetted, but the sky overhead was a circle of evening, a violet eye staring down on us. Colder, here.

"We still have to walk," said Nestor. "A little."

The trail we followed was obscured by underbrush, but Nestor could still pick it out, stomping at the growth and holding back branches so I could make my way behind him, single file. We climbed a progression of naturally formed steps, clinging to trees for balance. He brought me to a runnel that might have been a creek, long dried. A bracket of five hemlock trees, black soil, emerald moss furring half-submerged stones.

"Here," said Nestor.

*Marian,* I thought. *This is where they found your body . . .*

"This place was discovered by accident," said Nestor. "A couple ginseng diggers came through, had gotten lost higher up the elevation and figured they would hit the river if they just kept walking downhill, figured they could follow the river back to the falls. Up the hill a bit, they found the first of what we called 'cairns' — these stacks of flat rocks. Markers. They figured maybe some other diggers were marking a patch, so they came further down and spotted another cairn, and another. The cairns seemed to lead them to this spot, where we're standing. I don't see the cairns anymore. Someone must have knocked them down. Do you know what I'm describing, these markers?"

"Yeah, I guess so," I said. "Stacks of rocks."

"So these guys stopped to take a look around. Well, they spotted the red berries, so they knew they actually found some ginseng here. They dug for roots but found bones instead — thought maybe an animal was buried here but knew the whole setup wasn't quite right. They abandoned their dig and called in what they'd found."

"You dug her up?"

"Park Service," said Nestor. "Found human remains, called us in. And we figured right away, we just knew. It's funny — I remember when Brock came into the meeting room, he said, 'They found Marian.' All we knew at the time was that Park Service had dug up some bones, but Brock knew it was our girl. Instinct. Got her ID by matching against her dental records."

I breathed — the air rich with pine sap,

the smell of damp stone. A beautiful place to rest.

"I read what Brock said, in the newspapers," I said. "That stuff about Mursult killing himself? He knew that Patrick Mursult was murdered. He never believed Patrick Mursult killed his own family, did he? I was told his story was a cover."

Nestor laughed, "Yeah, you could say that," he said. "In fact — you asked why I quit the FBI? There were other things, but we had Patrick Mursult's body. It was a clear homicide, but word comes down through Brock that we talk about it like a suicide. We were told a man killed his family, then killed himself, stick to the script. I couldn't handle that, the outright lies we were supposed to live with. Then we find Marian's body years later but hold to that same line. Patrick Mursult was killed, plain as day — he didn't kill himself. It just didn't wash with me."

"They still investigated the homicide, though, didn't they?" I asked. "You interviewed a woman? Onyongo?"

"Nicole," said Nestor.

"We found pictures of her at Fleece's place," I said. "I saw in the case file she was having an affair with Mursult, lasted a few years."

"Yeah — I remember who she is," said Nestor. "If I remember right, the lodge kept license-plate numbers, tracked her down that way."

"Nothing panned out with her?"

"No, not at all," said Nestor. "We brought her in the day after you found Mursult, maybe a day after that. I interviewed her for two days straight, but she couldn't tell us much."

"What did she tell you?"

"Mursult picked her up in some bar," said Nestor. "Knew that Nicole was a nurse and wanted to talk with her because he was suffering PTSD. She worked at an assisted-living facility, didn't know how to help him, but that interaction started their relationship. They'd meet at the lodge."

I recognized the Nicole I knew — she inhabited that bar like a conversation piece hung in a dull room. Maybe only a trick of fate that Mursult had drifted into May'rz, but once he saw her, once he heard her speak, he wouldn't have wanted that voice to silence. I knew nothing about Mursult but pictured him falling in love with Nicole, a quick fall.

"Did you talk to her again once you found Marian? Ask her again about the daughter?"

"No," said Nestor. "We took another look

at the case when we found Marian, wondering if we'd missed anything, seeing if any leads would come out of the discovery. But this was . . . what, 2003? 2004? Our priorities had changed after 9/11. We didn't have the resources to track down all the loose ends with this — our office was focusing on cybercrime and the war on terror. Brock had made peace with Patrick Mursult, the DA was happy. NCIS was still investigating, but without our involvement for the most part. We tried to consult with you, actually, bring you in, but no one could track you down. I thought you would have wanted to be here when we found her."

"I would have, yes," I said. "Where was she laid to rest?"

"Back in Canonsburg, with her family."

"Her dad, too?"

"Yeah. They were all cremated."

"You remember Fleece's place?" I asked. "The ship made of fingernails?"

"I remember."

"Whatever came of that?" I asked.

"Fact, I remember we were working with the coroner," said Nestor, "trying to figure a way we could tell if the fingernails and toenails were missing on Marian, but it was impossible."

"What happened when you found her?"

"Nothing. There was some play in the newspapers," said Nestor, "but Brock didn't want to release all the details, didn't want people traipsing up here."

"You never came close to figuring out who killed her?" I asked. "After all this time?"

Nestor shook his head. "Never came close."

Shadows had gathered in the trees. I saw fireflies. Nestor sat on a rock, bundled in his wool jacket. *We can observe this place,* I thought. *There's plenty of tree cover. We can have someone posted in a blind, watch who shows up, who builds the cairns.*

"I need you to show me this place on a map," I said. "I need detailed instructions on how to get up here. What roads, and that access route you took. Detailed enough so that if I had to get back up here sometime and didn't have any of these markers, I could still get here. Can you do that for me?"

"I'll mark it all out on a map for you," he said. "You must be freezing. Let's get you back. I'll buy you some supper."

Nestor lit our path with a Maglite, but even so, finding my footing was difficult coming downhill. Never sure where to plant my silicone foot, I couldn't feel if dirt or rocks were about to give way in slides. I misstepped, tumbling, gashed my knee. I held on to branches and grabbed hold of boughs, still slipping, my palms sap-sticky and roughed up from catching myself on needles.

"Here," said Nestor, offering his arm. I took it, steadied myself against him. I put my arm around him, clamped myself to him, walking hip to hip the rest of the way down the hill. He held me beside him.

"Thank you," I said, frustrated that I'd needed his help at all. "I don't like to get myself in a position like that — to rely on people."

"I was all right with it," he said.

We ate together in Buckhannon, at a place near the river called the Whistle Stop Grill. We sat in one of the booths, the tablecloth brown gingham covered with a heavy plastic sheet. The decor was like a country kitchen — an old hutch, a fireplace. The walls were wood paneling hung with wreaths. We each ordered steak, onion rings. Nestor poured from a pitcher of Yuengling.

"I like this place," I told him.

"Yeah — I'm kind of a regular here. They have good food."

"She's pretty," I said, catching sight of the bartender, a woman who looked black Irish. "You ever talk with her?"

"Annie, yeah," he said. "I bet I'll have to explain you the next time I'm in."

"Is she your girlfriend? I don't want to mess things up for you."

"No, not a girlfriend. I had someone serious for a while, a few years back, but one day you wake up and realize you're ruining each other," he said. "Sometimes even the good things don't quite stick. Sometimes they do."

Warmed by the flirtation kindling between us. No consequences here. I wanted to take his hand in mine. I brushed my knee against his, and he didn't pull away. "Thanks for taking me out there," I said.

"You think that's everything you'll need?" he asked. "Do you have to present your case review or anything? Write a report?"

"Not for a little while yet," I said. "I'll be around."

"Good. It's been good seeing you," he said.

I lingered with Nestor out by his truck, wishing he didn't have that muff of a beard, but when he said, "I've thought about you so much over the years," I kissed him anyway, finding his lips soft through the field of hair. I could tell he wasn't expecting me, not so readily, but he kissed me and gave in like he was trying to drink me — I could feel the want in him. He cupped my breast as he kissed my neck.

"There's people around," I said, and Nestor said, "I'm sorry," stepping back like he'd offended me or had transgressed, so I said, "Where do you live? Near here?"

I followed his taillights down 151, Old Elkins Road, about twenty minutes until he pulled in to the long gravel drive. A front-porch light. I parked behind the truck, followed him to the side door. "I could never fix this lock," he said, nudging it open — he let the dog out, a jumpy setter, who scrambled into the yard and ran off into the dark. Nestor kissed me in the mudroom — pulled me to him. I kissed his eyes, kissed him. I felt him hard through his jeans, so I touched him, rubbed him while we kissed. He touched my hair like something precious and kissed the strands. He led me through the kitchen. "Through here," he said, into the living room. A mirror above the mantel reflected our dark forms. He approached in the mirror behind me. His hands folded over my breasts — I felt him push against me from behind. Breathless, he turned me toward him, fumbled at my shirt buttons — so I helped him, spreading open my clothes, revealing myself. Nestor unbuttoned my jeans, fell to his knees as he guided my clothes down over my hips. He kissed my prosthesis, kissed my other thigh, kissed the length of my leg, higher, tasted me. He reached up and held my breasts, and my knee went weak, and I collapsed down with him to the carpet. I helped him remove my prosthesis, laughing with him at the release of the vacuum seal, the sound it made, peeling off the liner, embarrassed when he kissed my stump, knowing how it would smell — how the liner would have made my skin smell — but he kissed me there, kissed me. He kissed the line above my hair, golden there, working his way up my belly before taking each breast in his mouth and sucking. I shivered, arched myself, welcoming, and he pushed at me, entering me, pulling out only as he came. "I'm sorry," he said, "that was so fast, I'm sorry," and he used his mouth and then his fingers until I clenched and shuddered and cried out, panting. We slept for a little over an hour on the living-room carpet, woke up kissing. I used my mouth on him, then guided him into me. We watched each other's eyes this second time — less needy than before. Throw pillows and a blanket from the back of the couch, we curled up together on the floor. He touched my left thigh and kept his hand resting there — I wondered if he thought it was a sign of courage to touch me there, or a gesture of acceptance, or if he was attracted to the missing limb, as some men were, but I didn't want to ask him, just wanted him to indulge in whatever he needed from me.

"How did you lose your leg?" he asked, sometime after midnight. "Or were you born like this?"

My eyes had adjusted, and in the ambience of moonlight I noticed the strange painting above the television. A painting of a body, lying supine, and I worried it might be a naked woman, something tacky like Davy Gimm's swimsuit posters, but realized it was a painting of a dead man.

"What is that?" I asked. "You didn't paint it, did you?"

"No, I didn't paint it. It was here when I bought the place, and I just never took it down," he said. "The guy who facilitated the sale of the house wanted me to have it, said it has something to do with a Russian novel. It's just a poster of some old painting. A picture of Jesus."

"You could hang one of your own photographs," I said.

"A painting of the dead Christ is worse than crime-scene photographs?"

"You've got to have something else."

"Yeah," he said. "Maybe I'll swap it out. I have some shots of Yellowstone I like, one of the Grand Prismatic Spring. But you know, that painting — I used to be religious, I was raised in the church."

"I remember you asked me if I believed in the Resurrection," I said. "You thought it might help me, being around so much death."

"That's right," he said. "That sounds like something I would have said. But I had an experience around that time. Like a religious experience, but in reverse I guess you could say. Have you ever had a religious experience? Like you heard the voice of God?"

I thought of seeing Earth from the distance of space, the near-holy connectedness to every facet of creation in that moment. "No," I said. "Nothing religious, nothing like that. I've found beauty in nature, but nothing like hearing voices."

"I had — it was like I had a vision of God, but God was like a black hole," said Nestor. "The vision overwhelmed me. People talk about what infinity is, and they think of things that are never-ending, but infinity cuts the other way, too. Infinity can be a negation. We grow from dirt, and our cells multiply, and we grow and wear out and rot, and more are taking our place — it's disgusting, all the bodies and death, billions of us, it's like the tide, washing in and washing out. All that religion, that bullshit about God, it's like that shit you believe as a child and one day wonder how you ever believed anything at all. Childish things. And everything changed for me after that vision, that experience. I started drinking to blunt the terror I'd felt. I was just so scared of the world. I couldn't stomach the Bureau anymore, I moved out here, just drinking to lose myself. And I would watch that painting of Christ, convince myself that he might sit up, hoping he would somehow sit up to prove me wrong, but every night . . . I figure this painting is a depiction of Jesus after he's been taken from the cross, and he's just dead, a dead body, and everyone's waiting for the Resurrection, and he's waiting for his own Resurrection, but it's not going to happen. I hated that painting because of how unchristian it felt to me, but then I realized what its message was. I dug deeper, found deeper meaning."

"You're an atheist," I said.

"No, I believe in God. I believe God exists. I had an experience, I had that vision, and in the vision I saw God. God is a pestilent light ringed with black stars. I'm still a man of faith because I believe, but

195

when I think of God, I think of something like a parasite."

His heart was racing; he had broken into a cold sweat. His body was silvery in the moonlight. A small constellation of moles dotted his chest, like the belt of Orion over his heart. I didn't know what to say.

"I'm sorry — and I'm sorry I asked about your leg," he said. "I didn't mean to offend you. You must get tired of everyone asking you about it."

"The truth is, I don't even remember it happening," I said. "I was lost in the woods, hypothermia had set in. My leg had turned gangrenous. They had to amputate. I remember the amputation."

A car passed on 151, and the headlights flashed momentarily on the wall, crept in a grid of windowpanes across the ceiling. I wondered if we had turned cold to each other — just like that, after getting what we'd wanted, but Nestor put his hand on my hair, petted me, pulled me closer to him. I put my arm around him, and he lowered his head onto my breasts. I felt the rising and falling of his breath, knew he could hear my heartbeat.

"I had a local anesthetic, but was awake," I told him, remembering the surgery in zero-g, the blood globules squirting in rushes, smearing against the ceiling, the walls. "I was awake, but I couldn't watch. I just looked at the ceiling the whole time. They cut across my shin first, removed my ankle and foot. That's the cut I sometimes think I still feel — a phantom sensation. Sometimes I feel a sever across my shin. The infection had already risen to my knee, though, so they had to take the rest."

After a time Nestor helped me put on my prosthesis. He said, "It doesn't bother me, just so you know. The moment I first saw you, I wanted to be with you —"

"You don't remember when you first saw me," I said.

"I saw you for just a second that night at the crime scene. You caught my eye. And in that meeting room the next morning, I was supposed to introduce myself to you. I already knew you were good-looking, but Jesus Christ, Shannon, when I saw you that morning —"

"All right, that's enough."

"And after you left, I couldn't stop thinking about you. There was this other case, and I thought we might cross paths, but we never did. I was hoping —"

"I would have liked to cross paths," I said. "What did I miss?"

"Just a waste of time, for us. Some guy

from Harrisburg, some lawyer," said Nestor. "He was killed in a carjacking. We wanted to consult with you."

"What did he have to do with me?"

"Nothing. Erroneous reports," he said. "We were working with a database of ballistic fingerprints, and the bullets they recovered from this lawyer matched the bullets we'd recovered from Mursult, so I thought of you, but we'd had the gun in our evidence room all that time. We wanted to call you in, to testify that this match was a false positive, but we couldn't find you. I couldn't find you."

"What happened with the prosecution?"

"The judge threw everything out," said Nestor. "That damn database spit out a handful of ballistics matches, everything went under review."

"You miss the work?" I asked.

"Sometimes," he said. "But after I —"

"You don't have to talk about this."

"I shot a man, in the line of duty. It was justified, in self-defense, but I couldn't live with what I'd done," said Nestor. "He'd pulled a gun on me, fired shots."

I tried to reconstruct him, reconstruct his past — a past he might not ever come to have. Visions of God, a parasite, a pestilent star. Some sort of break maybe. Or maybe

198

killing the man had broken him.

"Who was he?" I asked.

"Some big shot, a computer guy — an engineer," said Nestor. "His name came up as part of an investigation, military secrets used for private gain. I went to interview him, that's all — we weren't even targeting him, but he panicked. I was put on leave, the shooting became an internal matter — they tell you you're innocent until proven guilty, but that wasn't my sense. I was ostracized within the Bureau even though I was cleared. *Graham v. Connor.*"

"And you left the FBI," I said.

"I hope this doesn't sound pathetic," he said, "but I'd search for you on the Internet, hoping for a picture. Just one picture of you. But there was nothing. I would just let my memory of you play around in my mind, imagining what a life would have been like with you. I even asked around about you, but no one knew. Brock didn't know. But here you are."

"Here I am," I said. "And I'm thirsty. What do you have around here?"

Looking at the picture of the dead Christ while I waited for my drink. The body was gray. *Holbein,* it read. The canvas was narrow, the body stretched out. Impossible to imagine that the body would breathe again.

We sat in lawn chairs out on his front porch, bundled in quilts. We drank cognac from coffee mugs, watching distant head-lights. Nestor's dog, Buick, curled at his feet, snoring as he chased some rabbit in his dreams. Comfortable in each other's silence nearing 3:00 a.m., my mind wan-dered to Marian's body buried among the pines and roving cities built in the shape of pyramids.

"What's deeper than Christ?" I asked. "You said you looked at that painting and found something deeper than the miracles you once believed in. What's deeper than Christ?"

"The eternal forest," said Nestor. "All around us. Everything you can see."

Too cold to stay outside. We went to his bed, and he drifted off but I stayed awake and watched the dawn glow pink and orange on the walls. I remembered Nestor's father's dream. He had dreamed he was trapped in a mine and crawled through the black tun-nels until he came to a labyrinth of forest. The mirrored room, the tree of bones. I, too, had been lost in the eternal forest. I considered waking Nestor, to talk with him or kiss him one last time, but left my cell number on the nightstand and let him sleep.

# THREE

Miserable weather, spring slush glazed the sidewalks like a skin of chilled pudding. Six months living here. I was Courtney here, I belonged here, a cripple on disability checks, Mountaineers sweatshirts and baggy sweatpants, my hair scraggly and long, unkempt. Six months and I blended in, part of the fabric, like the abandoned storefronts, the grimy windows curtained or covered with plywood, façades browned with rain-streaked muck. The stairs of the palatial Beaux Arts courthouse were filled with smokers, ratty men with nothing to fill their time but loiter, their bodies bent against the rain. Sleet soaked my sweatshirt, my hair, a heavy weight, cold.

I'd made myself a regular at May'rz on nights without Nestor, settling into this IFT — I spent New Year's here, Christmas. I shook off the slush, took my seat at the far end of the bar, an end stool where I could see the TV but still have my view of the room. May'rz in neon-blue cursive behind the bar, cigarette smoke like gauze. The regular bartender was a young woman named Bex, her left arm sleeved with tattoos, hyacinths and vines. She poured my first drink, rum and Cherry Coke.

"Starting a tab tonight, Courtney?"

"Yeah," I said. "And I'll pick up Cole's tonight, if she comes in."

She swept in from the rain nearing seven, her routine — long-limbed and elegant, her presence a glamour undiminished by middle age, even rain-soggy and exhausted from her shift. Powder-blue scrubs, a cherry-red raincoat. She took her usual stool next to mine.

"Cole," I said.

"Gimm."

Already smoking a Parliament, she pulled over one of the plastic ashtrays and blew a smoke ring my way before tapping out her ash. I puckered and kissed the center of the smoke as it melted across my face. Menthol and wet fabric and a whiff of body odor, maybe from the elderly bodies she'd handled and washed and wiped through the day at the assisted-living center. Her eyes were bloodshot, and she seemed drowsy tonight, lighting a second cigarette before finishing her first, the two smoldering together in the ashtray. Vicodin, I guessed — easy to know when she was using.

"I need a manhattan," she said, rubbing her eyes.

"You all right?" I asked.

"Long day," she said, her voice graced with that musical accent. I'd learned that she'd moved from Mombasa when she was a teenager.

"I've got your drinks tonight," I said.

"Ah, your SSI check must have cleared," she said. "Largesse."

I raised my glass. "To life in the welfare state," I said, but after a pause, "I remember what today is —"

"April sixteenth."

"April sixteenth," I said.

Her husband had passed away from thyroid cancer, I knew, ten years ago today, too early for the cure. I didn't know much about him, a guy named Jared. They'd married young, and I had the impression her marriage to Jared had been troubled from the start. He had abused her — she told me once she'd suffered a broken jaw, that he had hit her. I knew they'd been estranged for a number of years before he died. Nicole and I had grown close these past few months, and I felt like she poured her life

203

into me, like I was her vessel. She talked freely about her painful past, a hard life, chasing drugs after her husband died, waking up in strange rooms with men, trading favors for stamp bags. Her life wasn't as wild now, age had mellowed her, but she still used, still drank, still tried to erase the ache that coiled within her.

"I almost forgot," she said, digging through her purse, drawing five scratch-off lottery cards from a side pocket. She fanned them out, slid them to me. "I didn't win shit with mine," she said. Pills mixed with liquor — she was woozy, moved like her bones were liquefying. Tonight might end like some of our other nights together when she was using — pushing her to drink, pushing her to more pills if she had them. Sometimes she'd pass out and I'd get her to my apartment next door, stay up with her to make sure her breathing didn't stop — but other nights the pills and liquor just made her lose herself, stripped the shell from her, and I'd turn off the apartment lights and listen to her stream of chatter. Those nights I'd lead our conversations, tell her I wanted to hear about old loves, just two girls talking, and she'd talk about her dead husband and affairs she'd had and her regrets over a lover who had died. *Mursult,*

I'd think, and ask for more, but she would mix her stories of dead lovers with violent nightmares, carry on conversations without me as if she could hear the dead speaking to her from a great distance until she slipped under.

She finished her manhattan, called for a second. I flipped through the lottery cards, the Gold Mine. I scraped silver crud from icons of miners' tools but came up a bust.

"Son of a bitch."

"Don't scratch them all at once," said Nicole.

May'rz had always been a bar for regulars but had been adopted by frackers. Southerners, mostly, coming through southwestern Pennsylvania to tap the shale. Truckers and roughnecks, a scourge that would pass once this area was depleted. They filled May'rz almost every night now, turning the dive rowdy. A group of men played pool, talking loopholes in the dumping laws. They were boisterous and drank too much, their southern twang somehow a more foreign sound than even Nicole's Kenyan lilt. Nicole was known here, had been coming to May'rz since the early nineties at least — the bar about a half-hour walk from her apartment over at Castle Tower and within walking distance of her job at the Donnell House.

Two decades, the same routine, and I was part of her routine now, too. The bartenders called us "Cole and Court," like we were a set, or "The Odd Couple," and eventually we spent some time together outside of May'rz, on weekends, visiting each other's apartment and taking quick road trips in Nicole's Honda, usually up to Pittsburgh to pick through the record stores, Nicole an eclectic collector of chansons and medieval polyphony and dissonant classical music, strange things she said reminded her of childhood.

She swirled the ice in her drink. Prone to tunnel vision tonight, I noticed — usually Nicole was erratic when she was using, but tonight she was turned inward.

"They're having a memorial service for Jared," she said. "Out on their property. They want me to come out, but I haven't seen those people in ages."

"What people?"

"My in-laws," said Nicole. "Jared's mother, Miss Ashleigh. She has a large property, wants to have the family over —"

"Is that a good idea?"

Nicole shrugged, took a drag from one of her cigarettes. She had told me about her husband's suffering, the cancer, how he'd begged her back following his diagnosis, how she'd nursed him until he died. His family was close-knit, his cousins or close friends of his, and they were an unhealthy influence on Nicole. She used heavily after the last time she saw them, she said, a spiral that had flattened out only after some time had passed, but the damage was done, and she could never quite kick the heroin.

"For a few days, what could come of it?" I asked.

"I could tell you," said Nicole, gazing at the television. KDKA teased their eleven-o'clock news — a family killed, a lethal crash on 65, a pit bull burned alive. "I could tell you some things . . ."

The pills were affecting her — she seemed like she was dissolving. Her gestures were loose, and she drank her manhattan in gulps. "So tell me," I said, trying to make myself seem hollow for her, like anything she'd want to unburden would fit inside. She thought I was simple, I knew that — I helped her feel that way, that I was good for a laugh and to talk shit about the men at the bar but wasn't someone with greater designs, that talking to me was almost like talking with an empty room. "Cole," I said.

"I fucked a friend of his, I didn't care," she said. "I wanted to hurt him."

I tried to focus through my own wash of

207

alcohol, the glare of the television, a rise of voices around the pool table, Tim McGraw on the jukebox. I waved at Bex for another round. "Who was the guy?"

"Patty," said Nicole. "Patrick," taking another drink. "He was married, so we met in hotels — in a cabin he used to rent. He would fuck me, then take pictures so I could mail them to my husband, so he would know I was with someone else. Jared would drift in and out of my life, bring all his shit with him. I wanted to hurt him."

*Patrick Mursult,* I thought, a rise of heat through my neck. Imagining Mursult and Nicole's adultery, Nicole posing for him in the cabin at Blackwater and mailing photographs to her husband like she was sending packets of poison.

"What happened?" I asked.

Nicole gestured at the TV. "It was on the news," she said, her eyes welling. She wiped away tears, seemed nauseous — some memory passed over her, and she shook her head.

"Did your husband kill him?" I asked.

"Jared was a coward," said Nicole, vacant, delayed, the liquor pushing her deeper. "I fell in love with him because he had this tattoo, and I was just seventeen when I met him, and that tattoo was all it took to impress me, this eagle on his chest. He said he liked my jacket. He was my worst mistake."

"Jesus, Cole. What are you telling me? Did your husband kill someone?"

"His friends did, our friends — Cobb did, and Karl," said Nicole. "And after, he would call every night and threaten me, said he would kill me for what I did to him, or if I said anything. He ruined everything about me, he took everything good and ruined it — I wish I would have died when I was seventeen instead of living this hell."

"Who are these guys?" I asked her. "Karl and Cobb? You never mentioned them before. They were friends of yours."

"That was a long time ago," said Nicole, finishing her manhattan. She chewed the ice.

"I'll go with you to the memorial service," I said, wondering who would gather at a service for her husband. A man named Cobb and a man named Karl had killed Patrick Mursult, and Nicole's husband, Jared, was involved somehow, too. In this IFT Jared had died of thyroid cancer in 2006, but he would still be alive in 1997. I can find him. "Take me with you."

"No, I don't think that's a good idea," said Nicole. "These people —"

"You shouldn't go alone," I said. "After

what you just told me? I can't let you go alone. Christ, Nicole. I'll come with you. It will be all right. You need a friend with you."

"I guess so, maybe," she said. "Let me think about it. I guess I don't want to be alone."

Nicole excused herself to the bathroom, and I ordered us another round. I wasn't a friend, I was a manipulation, I was a lie, but every truth here was a lie. I was buzzing, three suspects for the Mursult deaths. I texted Nestor, let him know about the weekend, that I wouldn't be around. COME OVER TONIGHT, he wrote back, but I texted, IT'S LATE, and he replied, TOMORROW.

"Ah, hell," said Bex.

Nicole returning from the bathroom, stumbling. She bumped into someone and almost sprawled.

"Hold on a sec," I said. "Bex, go ahead and swipe my card. I've got to get her out of here."

A twenty on the bar, a tip. I looped Nicole's purse over my shoulder. "Come on, Cole," I said. "We're going up to my place."

Her arm draped over my shoulders. Nicole just a slip, like she was made of air. "You'll be all right," I said, "you're just drunk, that's all. We're getting you home."

"You need help?" asked Bex.

"We'll manage," I said. "She can still walk," knowing how ridiculous we looked. May'rz hadn't been rollicking, but outside, the night was silent. Rain fell, an icy haze. I tested the sidewalk to see if it was frozen before trusting my fake foot. We made our way up the flight of stairs to my room, spotting her as we climbed. 3-B, I unlocked the dead bolt. "Just lie on the couch."

She sagged to the futon, coughing, her legs hanging over one of the armrests. A gurgling belch — I smelled the tang of boozy vomit and checked her over. She had messed her shirt, her cardigan. I took off her shoes, her soiled clothes. Her breasts were small, her body emaciated, her arms pocked with track marks. She wore her serpent bracelet and a necklace I first thought was a vivid sapphire because of its brilliance, but when I looked closely, I saw the iridescent blue was actually the petal of some exquisite flower embedded in resin. The necklace was stunning, the shade of blue unreal. I dressed her in one of my sweaters, covered her with a blanket, the blue of the flower petal such a strange blue, I thought, turning out the apartment lights, such a breathtaking blue, unlike any shade I'd ever seen. I sat near her, on the floor. Nicole's fingers touched my head, and I re-

211

alized she was petting me, almost, running her fingers absently through my hair.

"You want anything?" I asked, but Nicole had closed her eyes. Her mouth hung open, and soon she snored lightly, like a purring cat.

I left the bedroom door open a crack to hear if she stirred and slid my briefcase from the closet floor, hoisting it to the bed. Printouts I'd made from the library the previous weeks, articles about the CJIS attack, about Marian Mursult. I glanced at a poster that had been distributed in the years before Marian was found, a HAVE YOU SEEN ME? poster created by the National Center for Missing & Exploited Children. There were other folders, information about Patrick Mursult. I pulled my copies of the Polaroids we'd found at Elric Fleece's house, in the duffel — close-up photographs of a black woman's thighs, breasts, stomach, feet. Nicole was healthier then, nineteen years ago, her body less worn.

Nicole believed that Patrick Mursult had been killed out of jealousy, but Patrick Mursult hadn't been the only victim — his entire family had been killed. Nicole's story had omissions; time had made her too innocent. Her version of the past was the only version here, but there must be something more. I could imagine a man shooting another man over an affair, ambushing the adulterer at his love nest at the Blackwater Lodge, but I couldn't make the leap into believing that Nicole's husband or his friends had butchered Mursult's entire family over an affair, that they had taken Marian Mursult to the woods. A failure of imagination maybe, an inability to assume the utter worst of people, but someone had killed a woman and two children with an ax and then killed a seventeen-year-old girl. I couldn't imagine.

I looked out the bedroom windows. A snow squall had swept through, dusting the streets a glistening white like crystallized sugar. I took off my sleet-damp sweatshirt, draped it over the shower-curtain rod to drip dry, then removed my prosthesis and plugged the knee-joint battery into an outlet to charge. *Patty,* Nicole had said. *Patrick.* I wondered if his killers were still alive in this IFT. It would have been twenty years ago that they had found Mursult in the Blackwater Lodge and executed him. I remembered the pitch-darkness of those cabins at night, stars and moonlight choked out by pines. I imagined the knock at the door, the interrupted silence, and it occurred to me that Patrick Mursult might have known his killers. Nicole had confessed that she had wanted to hurt her husband when she slept with Patrick, that Patrick was a friend of his. Maybe Mursult knew his killers when they arrived in the night, and maybe they had told him that they'd killed his family, that they'd killed his oldest daughter and left her in the gorge not far from the cabin where they would leave his body, that only a few miles would separate him from his daughter.

I went back to the briefcase and pulled *Libra*'s crew list. I found his name: *Jared Bietak — Machinist's Mate, Engineering Laboratory Technician*. Nicole's husband had been a sailor on *Libra,* had known Mursult because they'd served together. As the ELT he would have worked with the B-L drive, would have been the engine-room supervisor. Fleece would have reported to him. Heart pounding, I found *Cobb, Charles — Special Warfare Operator,* another SEAL. And there was a *Karl Hyldekrugger* — the CELNAV, the ship's celestial navigator. They were all sailors on *Libra.* Mursult wasn't the only MIA surfacing. *Libra* had returned, or it had never launched. Where was the rest of the crew? These men knew one another, they all knew of Mursult's affair with Nicole. If I could track them down in terra firma, I might find Marian.

Nicole's breath occasionally hitched — she'd wheeze and roll over. I brought down a comforter to sleep on the floor next to her and sat up through the night when her sleep was disturbed. Staring at the ceiling much of the night, imagining my sight could pierce every impediment, through the ceiling and the apartment above, through the cover of rain clouds, straight into the night sky, the stars. I tried to imagine that love triangle, Nicole and Jared, Patrick Mursult, but grew distracted by the shadows of the rain, my mind wandering to Fleece, to the tree of bones in the mirrored room, to the ship built of nails that will carry the dead. Missing fingernails. Whoever had killed Mursult's family had taken their fingernails. Nicole gasped, sounded like she'd swallowed a spurt of vomit before rolling over and breathing again. What would happen if Nicole actually were to die? No one would find her body until the landlord came through. If Nicole were to die during the night, I would pack everything and walk out the front door without turning back, return to terra firma, let this possibility blink.

# FOUR

Buick ran from the mudroom to meet me when I pulled down Nestor's drive, to get his ears rubbed and sniff my tires before scampering through the lawn. Nestor came out onto the front porch, said, "There you are," and kissed me as I came up the front steps. He offered me a record in a brown paper sleeve.

"What's this?" I asked him. The last time I saw him, he'd wanted to know how I filled my time when we weren't together, and I'd said my favorite thing in the world was to lie in bed and listen to music.

"Just take a look," said Nestor. "Let yourself be surprised."

A cross of skulls, Nirvana's *Leadbelly*.

"I thought you might like this one," he said. "You don't have it, do you?"

"Not on vinyl," I told him. "Good choice, I love it."

"I wanted to give you something from '97,

when we met," said Nestor. "The first time we met. This had just come out."

"I used to have a Nirvana T-shirt, back in college. The one with the transparent angel, all the anatomy. I tore off the sleeves, made a tank top out of it."

"I used to do the same thing with my shirts," he said, lighting a cigarette. Nestor had cleaned up for me, shaved off the beard — he looked years younger without the scruff. "See, if we were friends back then, we could have borrowed each other's clothes."

"I don't think mine would have fit you."

A breath of summer had pushed through, melting the glaze of snow from the other night, turning the ground muddy. We passed the afternoon in wooden rockers, pulling chilled Yuengling bottles from a cooler, watching Buick chase butterflies. We played "In the Pines" loud enough to hear his living-room speakers out in the yard.

Steaks and zucchini from the grill for dinner, and after we washed dishes, we took a walk around his property, an expanse of field that stretched for close to seven acres before a strip of woods marked the start of the neighbor's farm. Buick trotted along without a leash, running out through the longer grass before loping back. Nestor and

I held hands intermittently, and when I clutched him for balance on the uneven ground, he didn't let go. We reached our usual turning point, out near a ruined Ryder truck, something the previous owners had abandoned in the field. The neighbor's barns were newer, bright red corrugated metal lit with floodlights. Buick barked at the air, probably catching scent of the neighbor's shepherds.

"You're distracted," said Nestor.

"Yeah," I said, "I don't know." Easy to forget myself here, with him, to forget that this world was like a dream, but learning the names of Mursult's killers had been a touch of horror. I wondered if Marian was already dead in terra firma or if I had an opportunity to save her — I wouldn't know until I stepped back into the rushing river of time. Life was perfect here in its way, perfect with Nestor, out here in Buckhannon. I found myself trying to memorize Nestor, every detail, knowing I'd leave him someday.

"Let's head back," I said.

We walked in silence for a time, finishing our walk through his uneven side yard, a half acre overgrown with wildflowers. Nestor helped pick foxglove and aster, Buick running ahead of us to the level grass. Darker here, Nestor's house occluding the front-porch light and the light from the neighbor's barn. I was remembering nights as a child out in the country like this, the stars so numerous that sometimes I could see the hazy band of the Milky Way.

"I can't stay the night," I said. "I'm taking a trip with a friend of mine, for a memorial service. She's picking me up in the morning —"

Nestor kissed my forehead. He held me, breathed in the scent of my hair. "I'll miss you."

"Just a few days."

The sky was clear, and as night fell, I saw stars, but not the ineffable brilliance I remembered from childhood. The horizon glowed, always faintly glowed — light pollution from somewhere, light interfering with light.

Nicole picked me up in her Fit, our first time seeing each other since the other night. She'd slipped away that morning while I still slept, left a handwritten apology and a thank-you for the spare sweater. A further act of contrition that she'd brought me a coffee and a croissant for breakfast, something for the road.

"You look nice," she said. "I've never seen

you dressed up."

I'd found a carnation-pink day dress at Avalon. It had a tailored fit, nice lines, with a black belt to cinch the waist. "You look good, too," I said, Nicole effortlessly graceful in her navy-blue pea coat and white linen dress. "I thought you only owned scrubs."

We left Washington south to West Virginia, to Nicole's mother-in-law's home on an orchard outside Mount Zion. Country roads, a stop at a gas station, the only restroom housed in a cinder-block hut. I wondered what Nicole remembered from the other night, if she regretted having told me so much. She was quieter than usual, I thought — or maybe I was reading too much into her not being such a morning person. She put on music to fill the silence, fiddling with the dial until she slid in a CD. I watched birds gliding on outspread wings, riding gusts.

"You all right?" asked Nicole. "You turned pale."

"I'm . . . yeah, I guess so," I said. "Will any of the people who —"

"Let's not talk about that," said Nicole. "Just forget it, right?"

Wondering what faces I would see — other sailors than Mursult assumed lost but were here, living, as if returned from the

220

dead. And Nicole was in the center of these men, somehow. She sang softly to the music, the color of her true love's hair, a resonant voice. Difficult to measure her against her past, a past I didn't fully understand. A murmuration of starlings stippled the sky: they turned together, changed direction like a sentient cloud.

"You won't be at the memorial," said Nicole. "That will just be family. I don't know who will come back to the house after, but some might."

We turned from the main road onto a private drive and passed through rows of fruit trees, some sickly or dead, most erupting in glorious white blossoms, petals on the grass like a spring snow. The house was at the top of a shallow rise. It had a gabled roof, twin stone chimneys. A barn was set on the far side of the rise, a gable roof echoing the house, a saltbox shed attached. Neither the house nor the barn was painted, both just the grayed color of plank wood, the lawn dried brown. Nicole parked near the barn.

"This is beautiful, Cole," I said. "How often do you make it out here? It's peaceful."

"Never," said Nicole. "Almost never."

The house had spacious rooms, hardwood

floors. The windowsills were decorated with antique bottles of colored glass that cast rainbows across the walls. A memorial display had been arranged on the coffee table, I noticed, a small selection of items: a photo album, an American flag in a triangle display case, a pocket watch on a strip of velvet. An old long rifle hung above the fireplace mantel, from the 1800s or maybe earlier, a bag of powder dangling from the muzzle. I wondered what Nestor would have made of it. The smell of simmering chili filled the house, bread baking.

"Miss Ashleigh?" Nicole called out.

A woman answered, "Cole, oh — I'll be right with you!"

The woman was stout, with white hair in ropy braids, her broad cheeks and thick neck marshmallow soft. "Here you are," she said, and although she used a cane, she enveloped Nicole in a crushing hug, "You'll slip through my arms, Cole. You're scrawny, you're too scrawny." And when Nicole introduced me, Miss Ashleigh shook my hand and said, "Courtney, we're well met. Look here, we're each missing something." She lifted her hem and showed off her prosthetic foot.

"Diabetes?" I asked.

"That's right. Had neuropathy," said Miss

Ashleigh. "Type 2, all of a sudden. Lost my vision also, but had a doctor prescribe me those nanobot gelcaps, cured me up. You don't mind a cot in the den, do you?"

"I don't mind," I said. "Thanks for having me."

"Pish," she said. "A friend of Cole's, you know. Shauna and Cobb have their stuff in the spare bedroom. Some of the others got a hotel closer to Spencer."

*Cobb.* In the same house with him, the SEAL.

I brought my suitcase to the den, an addition to the main house — brown carpeting, a breakfront with American Bicentennial plates, a cherrywood eight-gun display case that was empty. I had a view of the wide lawn and the distant orchard. A woman sat on a stool in the side yard, out near an antique horse-drawn plow that was left as decoration, a burlap sack and a bucket at her feet, shucking corn. Her hair fell in copper waves, a bottle color. This must be Shauna, I thought. I watched her with the corn, breaking off the husk and peeling leaves, picking off strands of silk. She wore camouflage pants and a long-sleeved thermal shirt that hugged her chest. Athletic, but out of her element with the corn. The kind of girl that might buy a pink shotgun.

Nicole knocked at the door. "Will this be all right?" she asked. "Comfortable?"

"Yeah," I told her, looking around at the room, the foldout cot. "This will be perfect."

"I'll have to leave you alone for a little while," she said. "Miss Ashleigh and I are going to meet some of the family. We'll be back for dinner. Cobb's driving us."

"That's fine," I said. "Will you be all right?"

She was thinking it was a mistake to have brought me, I could tell. "I'll be fine," she said. "Listen, about all that stuff from the other night. I don't know what I was saying. I don't remember, but I'm sure I was —"

"Cole, I understand," I said, "and I was drinking, too. I don't even remember."

"These people, they're my family," she said. "I'll be fine. They're good people."

We had coffee at the kitchen table while she waited for Miss Ashleigh to get ready. Heavy footsteps clambered down the stairs. The man who entered the kitchen was gargantuan, a full foot taller than me at least, and broad, the sleeves and back of his suit coat tight against him. Muscled, the bearing of a wrestler gone bulkier as he aged. Scandinavian, by way of the Midwest — corn-fed, in his fifties at least, if not older, his white-blond hair a tight crew cut that fuzzed the pinkish folds of his neck. His eyes were close set and uneven, one slightly higher than the other — dumb eyes, some people might have thought, but to me his eyes looked like something gone feral.

"Who's this?" he asked when he noticed me.

"Courtney Gimm," I said, and we shook hands — my hand in his like a petal wrapped in meat.

"A friend of mine," said Nicole.

"Gimm," he said. "All right. I'm Cobb."

"Cobb," I said, and he seemed to like that, hearing his own name repeated. He smiled, a sort of squint-eyed smirk. I imagined him killing Mursult, I imagined him killing a girl. I imagined him killing a girl with his bare hands, strangling the life from her, breaking her neck.

"We'll be back soon," said Nicole.

I watched them leave, Cobb's truck kicking up a plume of dust down the long dirt drive. The floorboards whined as I walked through the house alone. The light fixture at the top of the stairs was pink glass. I found the bedroom Nicole was staying in, wondered if this was the room where Jared Bietak had grown up. If it was, all traces of him were gone. White walls, a whiter rectangle where a picture once hung. I went back downstairs, opened the cover of the photo album that was part of the memorial display: *A Mother's Love Never Ends.* Photos of Jared Bietak from elementary school, high school. He looked like a tough kid, I thought, but Miss Ashleigh had saved every report card, a straight-A student. There was a graduation picture, then grad school. A Ph.D. in chemistry, Penn State. I turned the page and saw a picture of four men: Cobb, shirtless, muscular, his arm around Jared Bietak. Patrick Mursult was in the picture, smoking a cigar, but I didn't recognize the fourth man. About as tall as Cobb but leaner, a corona of reddish gold hair. The man's head was like a death's-head, sunken cheeks and bony cheekbones, his lips parted, his teeth visible. Shadows covered his eyes.

"You shouldn't be looking at that."

Startled, I closed the album. "I didn't mean to," I said, turned to see Shauna standing in the doorway. "I was curious, I'm sorry —"

"I'm not mad at you," said Shauna, "but they wouldn't want you looking through their stuff. Miss Ashleigh shouldn't have left this out."

She was my age, about, or a few years younger, somewhere in her thirties. When she pulled her hair back, a sensation of déjà vu washed over me, like I had seen her pull her hair back before. I noticed a tattoo in the cleft of her left hand, a black circle with crooked spokes.

"I just wanted to see what Jared looked like," I said.

"Come on, let's get out of here," said Shauna. "I'll show you the orchard."

There were paths through the fruit trees that led to the road. The trees bloom but get blitzed by late frosts each year, so some of the petals had browned, fallen. Apple and pear trees mostly, nothing ready to pick yet, but Shauna spoke fondly of walking here in summer, gathering fruit for pies. My mind wandered as we walked, thinking of Njoku, of his ship, *Cancer*. *Cancer* had sailed Deep Time, and I wondered if the same had been true of *Libra*. I wondered how *Libra* had returned, seemingly without anyone noticing, or if it had ever launched.

"So you're close friends with Nicole but you never met Jared?" Shauna was saying.

"I only know what Nicole's told me about him," I said.

"He passed a few years before I was with Cobb," said Shauna. "They were close. Cobb talks about Jared all the time, their time in the Navy."

"How'd you and Cobb hook up?" I asked her.

"I used to go to this roadhouse, this biker bar out in the sticks," said Shauna. "They did all the MMA pay-per-views out there, and he started chatting me up. He introduced me around to everybody, all the river rats."

We walked the far side of a strawberry bush, past an old outhouse made picturesque by falling into disrepair. We saw Cobb's truck pull through the orchard, returning toward the house.

"We should get back," said Shauna. "We should be there to meet them."

"What is that you mentioned?" I asked her. "You said the river rats?"

"They were in the Navy together. Jared and Cobb and the others," she said. "Hyldekrugger."

"Is that what they call themselves?" I asked. "Are they a gang or something?"

"They called themselves that in Vietnam," said Shauna. "River rats. They patrolled the rivers over there, talk about it all the time, all the shit they've survived. Hyldekrugger always says they're the survivors, that lambs are sacrificed but rats survive."

We walked alongside the old barn, spotting wildflowers. There was a hayloft still piled with bales, but Miss Ashleigh used the barn as a garage. An old Winnebago was parked inside, coated with dust. We rounded toward the house.

*Jared Bietak. Charles Cobb. And the others,* Shauna had said. The crew of *Libra* were the survivors, she'd said. River rats. *They aren't the lamb.* It's often quipped that the most important personnel in the Naval Space Command are the two dozen psychiatrists who work with sailors home from Deep Waters. Deep Space and Deep Time are *irreality* — and beliefs built on irreality are beliefs built on quicksand. NSC sailors who have witnessed Deep Time are often haunted, reacting to events that haven't yet occurred, may never occur. And many sailors who have seen Deep Space return hollowed, overwhelmed by the immensity of the cosmos. The totality of human endeavor is nothing when set against the stars.

We ate dinner together in strained silence, the five of us seated around the kitchen table, the quiet punctuated only by the clink of silverware against china, the sound of our chewing. Chili, the corn Shauna had shucked, bread. Nicole hadn't spoken since the three of them had returned — more sorrowful than I'd seen her, and I wondered just how deep her mourning for Jared ran, if it was coming back to her or if something might have happened while she was away. I tried to compliment the food, and Miss Ashleigh and Shauna responded with smiles, but Cobb ate quickly, staring into the screen of his phone, and left the table in a temper.

I washed the dishes while Shauna dried, Miss Ashleigh at the kitchen table having late coffee as the light outside faded. I wasn't sure where Nicole went, or Cobb. I joined Miss Ashleigh for a cup of coffee, then went outside. Gorgeous here, the house and barn stark against the deepening twilight. I walked around the far side of the house and caught sight of Nicole, leaning against the edge of the open barn door smoking a Parliament. Ghostly in her flowing white dress, her pea coat draped over her shoulders.

"There you are," she said, her voice velvety between breaths of smoke. "I'm sorry I haven't been around. I should have been with you today."

"I've been finding my way all right," I said. "Shauna's nice, so is Miss Ashleigh. How are you holding up?"

"We buried my husband again today," said Nicole.

I came up near her, wishing I was still a

smoker, wanting to pass the cigarette between us and enjoy the night.

"You don't let on how much you miss
him," I said.

"Sometimes I do," said Nicole. "I'll find
myself thinking of Jared, and then I'll realize all over again that he's gone and think
of everything that's happened, and the pain
hurts new, every time."

"After all these years," I said.

"Have you ever lost someone close?" she
asked.

"I have."

"You forget the bad, your memory tries to
heal the past. Years don't matter either,"
said Nicole. "Time just burns. Time burns,
and you think the wounds are cauterized,
but they open up raw, again and again."

She looked away from me, into the outer
darkness. In what must have been a reflection of the last stray light from the sinking
sun, her eyes seemed to flare with an olive
shine that gave her face a feline complexity.
Her expression was expectant, terrified, as
if she were keeping watch against unseen
predators that might manifest from the
night. The sunset was red tonight, the sky a
lake of fire. She turned back to me, and the
glow in her eyes was gone, a trick of the
light that had passed.

"How was the family? Were they a comfort?" I asked. "I know you don't get along with some of them."

"Shake a damp rag and watch water run like diamonds."

"I don't understand," I said, but she pinned me with her glare. She took a drag on her cigarette. I breathed deeply the taste of her smoke, the sweetness.

"You do understand," she said. "I know now that you of all people would understand what I mean."

*Water without gravity,* I thought. Water wriggles away like iridescent worms — or like jellied diamonds. But how could she know? I thought over the afternoon, trying to remember if I had somehow slipped, if I had somehow betrayed myself, but no, she wouldn't know, she couldn't.

"I'm growing so old," said Nicole, "so fast. I sometimes think I can hear my body aging. I forgot how much I like it out here, how slow the orchard feels. I spend every day helping the elderly, and I see them die, and it seems like waves breaking against the shore, but out here everything is slow. It reminds me of home."

"Kenya?"

She nodded. "Mombasa. They made the trees to look like emeralds. Everything was engineered, nothing grew naturally — all the irrigation, all the straight lines. You pick a fruit and the fruit grows right back, there was never any want. I was never hungry as a child. Seeing the perfect rows of fruit trees reminds me of home. I didn't miss it until I realized I'd never see it again."

"You can go back," I said. "If it's home —"

"No, my home is gone," said Nicole. "My home never was. I went with her because my father met her at a reception in our village, a reception for the crew of *Libra,* and he made arrangements for me to leave with her."

*Libra* — the shock of the word. "Why are you saying this? Cole —"

"No more time for lies," she said, her eyes smoldering with what might have been hatred, or cunning. "You're like a message in a bottle to me now. Sometimes the bottle breaks and sinks in the sea, but sometimes the bottle reaches the shore. I can't control which."

Her name hadn't appeared on the crew list, but Nicole knew *Libra.* She had been aboard *Libra.* I'd met her and thought she was a barfly, an addict. I'd thought the surface of her life was all there was, the Donnell House and May'rz Inn, years of drinking and pills and never-ending shifts tending to the elderly, but she had sailed on *Libra,* her life was luminous with memories of Deep Waters.

"How do you know?" I asked. "Who are you?"

"I had been through medical school," she said. "My father convinced her I could help. He wanted a life for me. I loved her the moment I met her. I was inspired by her. I wanted to go with her. She had that quality about her — people wanted to follow where she led. We wanted to follow."

"Who?" I asked.

"Commander Remarque," said Nicole. "Forty-seven-man crew. *Libra* was tasked with missions to the galaxies NGC 5055 and NGC 5194, the Sunflower and the Whirlpool. A six-year mission."

Nicole lit a new Parliament, flicked the smoldering butt of the old cigarette into the grass around the barn. It flared an orange arc, winked out.

"We first transitioned to NGC 5194 and observed for two and a half years, transitioned to Earth-side IFTs for shore leave and resupply," she said, "but the Whirlpool was barren, so Remarque ordered us to our second location, the Sunflower Galaxy, and that's where we found the miracle."

"What miracle?" I asked.

"Life," said Nicole. "We found life."

QTNs would appear like disease through the future White Hole, but throughout NSC's odysseys the universe had revealed itself as nothing but flaming gas and dead stone. The notion that *Libra* had discovered a planet supporting life was almost too large to grasp, a great plume swelling within me. The stars above us suddenly swarmed, it seemed — no longer the cold fires of heaven but pulsing with life like the frenetic masses of organisms contained in a droplet of water.

"A planet in liquid," said Nicole. "The atmosphere was a methane-and-carbon mixture. Nothing to support human life, and yet the planet was teeming. It was a small planet circling a binary star. Its surface was an ocean with crystal shapes that swam like leviathans, crystals like latticework, mammoth polyhedrons that bobbed and dived in the ink. The crystals sang when they noticed us — you know the sound when you run your finger around the rim of a wineglass? Remarque named the planet Esperance, meaning 'Hope.' There were landmasses, a crinkle of fjords, and I was on the exo-team, twelve of us. Three Quad-landers, we left *Libra* in orbit and descended through the atmosphere. The binary suns were distant, dying. Winds battered our landers, the air was full of ice. We landed, and we made camp."

We all trained on mock alien surfaces, pitching inflatable concrete domes to use as semipermanent houses, camping in Arizona deserts and Arctic planes of ice, using self-heating burners and smokeless chemical fires, nights spent in my space suit, limited oxygen. I never descended to the surface of a crystal island or an alien sea, but we all trained for such things. Nicole had walked on another world — I imagined her searching out constellations in an unfamiliar sky, like trying to read the braille of foreign tongues.

"We had two SEALs — Mursult and Cobb," she said. "Jared landed, and so did Beverly Clark, a botanist, and I was assigned as her assistant. Patricia Gonzales was with us, a geologist, and Nate Quinn, a biologist. Elric Fleece and Esco were from engineering, mechanics for the landers. Tamika Ifill, Takahashi, and Josephus Pravarti were our pilots. We were nearly four billion miles away from the planet's suns. We called them the Pilot Lights, because they were ghostly blue. There were three moons, the largest a crater-pocked gargantua that hovered massive wherever we looked, almost like an entire second planet encircled ours. The other moons traced their own arcs, barely visible at times, the smallest circling twice before the largest had even seemed to move. We had difficulty distinguishing day from night because of the frequent eclipses, and even the strongest daylight felt like dusk. The ground was slush and soft like putty.

"And that slush sucked at our boots and splattered our suits like a fine dust of silica, playing havoc with our electronics. Our communications with *Libra* were spotty, fragmented static blasts. But the beauty of those ridges, the way the oceans stained the ice blue . . . After two days we found that the land tapered, began to level off, and we descended shelves of ice and entered into swampland. This was our first physical contact with life, a band of fauna like a borderland to the ocean beyond, razors of wild grass and floppy squills with closed bulbs, their stalks more grayish than green. Things with broad leaves like lily pads and stringy moss carpeted the icy mud, and clusters of reeds as tall as trees arced above us, grew together like archways, like the entire swamp was one body that had grown in a kind of geometric architecture. It's almost . . . like I thought there was a structure we were inside of but that I couldn't see, that was invisible. And these plants covered the structure like ivy. Do you understand?"

I imagined the exo-team picking their way through the swamp, traversing the fauna like tourists passing through a cathedral. "I think so."

"And we came out to a beach made of pebbles of metal, almost like ball bearings instead of sand, and the black ocean beyond. Beverly Clark had grown uneasy — she hadn't wanted to land on Esperance to begin with. She had been afraid to cross the swamp, and she panicked at the sight of the ocean. She was hysterical, she told us the ocean wanted to consume us, that she thought the ocean was this planet's mouth. Her fear spread to Quinn and Fleece, and they told us they wouldn't carry the equipment any further, they refused. So there we were, in this abundance of life, and we fell to bickering. Cobb decided we would sleep in shifts, to get rest before heading back to our base camp and to *Libra*. In the meantime the rest of us gathered samples, filling tubes with the ocean, collecting soil samples, rocks, cuttings from the leaves. We tried to force those flower bulbs open, but they were clamped shut. We tried to dig up the larger plants with the root systems intact, but

Beverly Clark and Quinn and even Patricia Gonzales fought with us —"

"They were losing their minds," I said. "Overwhelmed."

"Not until the moons passed together," said Nicole, "the three moons in conjunction, an eclipse, circles in circles. You could actually feel the change in the gravity they produced together — a lightness, a lift, being pulled upward by the moons like a thread in your chest had been tugged. And the oceans responded, receding from the shore, following the moons' pull, a waning tide. The beach elongated as the ocean retreated, and the ocean floor was covered in lichen, a luminescent carpet that grew in the furrows leading deeper into the ocean. There were glassy rocks in twisting shapes like lava as it curls through water, and farther out still we saw crystals that dazzled like diamonds. The water receded far enough to expose the body of one of the leviathans, the ringing bodies we had seen from above — or rather the crystal shape of the leviathan. It was at a distance but seemed more like a shape than a body, the same shapes the plants had grown into — or maybe it was once a body but was crystal now. I don't know how to . . . I don't have the words . . . A crystal shape, like interlocking diamonds or pyramids inside of pyramids. A fractal. But the most beautiful sight, all the closed buds in the swampland and the plants along the shore responded to that greater tug of gravity, and all the flowers spread open their leaves, the buds bursting, blossoming in heavy flowers with burgundy organs and long blue petals that glowed. The flowers' blue light almost hurt to look at, you had to squint."

"Your necklace," I said. "A blue leaf."

"Here," said Nicole, removing her necklace and handing it to me, the pendant of luminescent blue. I received the necklace in cupped hands just as I had once received a human heart, trembling at the thought of holding an artifact of alien life. I looked closely, saw veins in the blue — a pressed petal still glowing with spectral light.

"Oh my God," I said. "My God," but I was uneasy holding it. I returned the necklace to Nicole, who slipped it away into her pocket, the blue light extinguished.

"All the flowers opened," said Nicole. "In the swampland and all along the shore — so many flowers had grown beneath the ocean, the exposed sand was like a field of blossoming wildflowers. And as we watched, their spores, or their pollen, lifted toward the moons, fuzzy lights like blue-and-gold rain, but rain in reverse. And that's when . . . that's when it happened to Quinn, when Quinn began to scream. We all stared at him, standing in that field of flowers, the spores lifting around us. The spores had sunk into him — they passed through his space suit, into his body, like he was absorbing those blue lights. His face, through his mask — his eyes bulged and bled, and I saw his suit pulled from him, his helmet, but they were held in the air beside his body. And he was lifted, naked, several feet off the ground, his arms spread, his legs spread, his skin burning in the alien light. This all happened so quickly — I screamed. I thought I was screaming. His neck opened along a seam, and blood sprayed from him, filling the air with mist, and other seams opened along his arms, along his thighs, and blood rushed from him for several minutes. His body shriveled, but the droplets hung suspended like a fog around him. His skin peeled away, the skin of his hands came off like gloves, the skin of his arms like sleeves, his chest like a long coat — the skin floating like scarves caught in the wind. He was *floating,* a floating body, clouds of meat, white tendons, and a shape opened in his chest, opened in him like an eye, a polygon, its points connected, and I could see through that shape into another place, as though a portal had opened in him, another ice landscape and another and another. I looked through him, but I felt something look back into me. I felt as if something had reached through him and I had been touched. His body was sectioned apart, his skeleton separated, and soon he was only an outline tracing of nerves and veins, like a man made of lace. Each of his organs lined up in the air and formed a cube around him — everything was displayed."

Nicole moaned like a dog dreaming, and her eyes rolled to the night sky. I felt faint, thinking of the silence of the universe and the sounds of crystal bodies ringing. Nicole had seen a body opened in midair, like a cadaver opened on a table. The thrum of the circulatory system, the nervous system, ringing, the wet bellows of the lungs. I was filled with fear. Bodies stripped of skin, muscles hanging displayed in the air, zygo-maticus major, depressor anguli oris, or-bicularis oculi, orbicularis oris — an au-topsy.

"Beverly Clark was next — she ran and crawled but was lifted into the air and dismantled. She was a fractal, all her pieces. Her blood was a mist we ran through, and we had lost our minds. I was burning inside, like my brain and my eyes were fire, like my skin would burn from me — and Takahashi screamed, and I saw him fall on Patricia Gonzales and beat her to death, break apart her face mask and beat her as she choked on the air. And I couldn't endure the burning anymore. I wanted to die, anything to end the pain. I wanted to run into the black ocean to drown, but Jared, my Jared, was screaming, burning, and he tried to kill me —"

"He had changed," I said. "That place drove him mad, turned him murderous."

"Only Cobb and Mursult were sane," said Nicole. "They saved us, the SEALs. They were able to keep their minds, maybe because of their training. Cobb was able to pull Jared from me. He got through to him somehow. And Patrick lifted me from the ground, and I heard his voice like through water, but eventually his words came to me: *Run, run.* We left Takahashi, and I saw Esco run into the ocean, disappear into the ocean. Fleece had snapped, but he came with us — Cobb carried him. We lost Tamika Ifill at base camp, but the rest of us launched in the Quad-landers. We peeled off our clothes, scratching at ourselves — our bodies were *burning.* We docked with *Libra,* and Remarque retreated far from the planet. We heard the crystalline ringing, and the space around us turned brittle, like ice, shimmering like diamond dust. Remarque launched the B-L drive before all the space around us had gone brittle, and we transitioned, but it followed."

"What followed you?" I asked.

"That white light. It traveled the negative energy the B-L drive left in our wake, the negative energy sailors call Casimir lines. Remarque transitioned again and again, but the white light was always above us, always surrounding us. And we were running low on food —"

"And so you left for Earth," I said, realizing that Nicole was describing the birth of the Terminus.

"A far future," said Nicole. "We jumped to the far future, thousands of years, hoping a civilization with technology greater than our own would be able to help us, but when we came through, the white light had appeared, that second sun. We saw the future of mankind dissolve. We saw men running to the seas to drown and saw men hanging in the air. We saw men, their mouths filled with silver. Remarque transitioned into other futures, but the white light shone above every sky, fouling every possibility."

I thought of something like wildfire

scorching the skies of infinite Earths. I thought of the White Hole shining like a dead eye.

"Remarque knew," said Nicole. "She gathered us together in the enlisted men's mess hall, the only place large enough to gather as an entire crew. She talked to us about Everett space, about how we were travelers in futures called Everett spaces that were carved from our observations, our experience. She told us that if we committed suicide, all of us, that if we all killed ourselves, then everything we had seen, everything we had discovered, would blink out. We could jump to a new future and commit mass suicide, and everything that we had seen and experienced aboard *Libra* would cease to exist. Terra firma would never know about Esperance — the planet would go unfound, because if we blinked, then it would be like we'd never found it. We could save humanity. She told us she would start the sequence to create a 'cascade failure' in the B-L drive, that the destruction of the engine would obliterate us and everything we had uncovered. She said it would be painless."

"But you refused," I said.

"Hyldekrugger didn't want to die," said Nicole. "Remarque had her supporters —

Chloe Krauss, she was our WEPS, and there were others. But there were more people who were ready to listen to Hyldekrugger, who joined with him when Remarque ordered us to kill ourselves. He gathered people around him."

"Mutiny," I said.

"I'm innocent. I'm innocent in all this, everything that happened, everything that will happen. I hid from the fighting in the life-support room, and when I heard the fighting come near me, I hid in the brig, where I knew I could lock myself away. Don't you remember? We met once, years ago."

"What?" I asked, confused. "No, that's not possible. How could I remember?"

"We don't have time for your lies, Courtney," she said, and took a long drag on her cigarette. "We need to leave here. You need to get your things —"

"Tell me what happened to Remarque."

"They killed the crew loyal to Remarque," said Nicole. "They captured her. They cut Remarque's throat in front of everyone — they were cheering at her death. They killed her. Hyldekrugger killed her. They passed the body around, everyone involved in the mutiny despoiling her. They spared me, because I was Jared's wife. They killed everyone else, but they spared me. I'm innocent."

"What happened to the ship?" I asked. "You came back here, you brought the Terminus with you. What happened to *Libra*?"

Nicole's eyes welled with emotion; a memory fluttered over her face, gone in an instant. She reached for my hand, squeezed it. She said, "I know a story, of ghosts in the forest who precede the living, like spirits born before their bodies. The spirits live life, and then their bodies live the same life, but always a few steps behind."

A flashlight winked in the distance, a sweep of light out near the orchard. Someone searching. Nicole said, "We should leave. Wait here until I come for you." She retreated into the night, her white clothes like a radiant spill of moonlight before she was swallowed by the dark.

"Nicole, wait," I said. "Nicole —"

Her cigarette smoke hung in the air. *They killed her,* she had said, and my heart quickened — *a damp rag, water like diamonds.* I was alone here, I realized. Twilight had deepened, the house lights were the only lights except for the red rim of the horizon. Miss Ashleigh was baking, it smelled like — the air was scented with apples, spices. Chillier now, without my jacket. I shivered, thinking of spores like rain, of autopsies in the air. I thought of *Libra.* Mutiny —

The glare of the flashlight swept closer, swept the lawn, the grass nearer the barn.

"Who is it?" I asked.

"Quiet." Shauna's voice. She killed the flashlight. "Wait," she said.

"What's going on?" I asked, but she didn't answer until she had come close enough to whisper.

"They're going to kill you tonight," said Shauna. "You have to leave."

"Who is? What are you talking about?" But I felt adrenaline pump through me, my teeth chattered.

"Don't go back to the house. Run in this direction," said Shauna, turning me toward the orchard. She flashed her light once, pointed ahead of us, at the ground. "Go straight through the row of fruit trees and you'll hit the road, right where we walked earlier today. Head away from the house and get to the road —"

"Tell me what's going on."

"Shannon Moss," said Shauna. "NCIS."

The shock at hearing my real name, my cover wiped away. I thought of Shauna's face — her dark eyes — but no, there was

248

no recognition. How would she know?

"I don't —"

"They ID'd you," said Shauna. "When Cobb and Nicole left this afternoon, they must have met up with Hyldekrugger. They have names of agents who've investigated them, stretching years back. Cobb checked. They ID'd the name Courtney Gimm, but I know who you really are. You have to go. I'll have transportation once you hit the road."

"Are they *Libra*?" I asked. "Who else is involved?"

"I don't know what *Libra* is," said Shauna. "I don't know what angle you're working. I'm working domestic terrorism."

"Who are you?"

"FBI," she said. "Go."

The hovering thought that I might die here beat like wings around my skull. When Shauna turned toward the house, I ran for the orchard. I tried to control my breathing like I'd been trained, tried to keep my wits despite my fear, tried to think. Cold sweat damp on my forehead, my back. I had crossed in front of the house, through the spill of light on the lawn, and had made it down the rise into the longer grass when I heard a scream. I lost my footing and fell, looked back toward the house. The gabled house and gabled barn crested the rise, silhouetted black against the hellfire-red sunset glow of the horizon. The screaming continued, the piercing shriek of utter shock, of death.

*Run. Get up, Shannon. Run —*

Down the rise, quickly, I gained the orchard, followed the straight rows, careful of my footing. Above me the trees were vaulted shadows, the sky an outpouring of starlight. The ground around me seemed to glow, moonlight reflecting on the carpet of petals. I hurried, but I heard deep breathing somewhere behind me. Heavy footfalls and breaking branches, someone crashing downhill. A dark shape swept toward me. A man, tackling me to the ground. Wind rushed from my lungs beneath his weight, I couldn't breathe.

The man punched wildly, struck my shoulder, my forehead, but glancing blows. *Cobb* — his hands were crushing weights. If he caught me square, he would knock me out, I knew, but the darkness worked in my favor. I scuttled from him, and when he fell on me again, he didn't land with his full weight, didn't pin my arms. He swung, his fist a brick colliding with my eye socket, flashes of light. Dazed, I clutched at his chest, hugging him, pressing my head to his armpit, held close to minimize his swings, as much as possible. He struck my back. I readjusted my grip, and my hands found his belt, found the sheath clipped to his belt, the handle of a knife. He pounded my back, kidney punches I felt deep in my trunk, but I was quick with the knife in the moment he relented to find a better position against me. I slid the knife from its sheath and plunged the blade through his shirt, into his soft belly. He winced, and I stabbed into his armpit, heard him grunt, felt the strength leave his arm. He let go of me, but I stayed close, slashed higher, dragged the blade across his neck. Hot blood sprayed over me, squirting my face in gushes. Cobb gurgled, belched. He stumbled, toppled. His eyes groped uncomprehendingly at the fruit trees for only a few moments.

What had Shauna said? *Transportation . . . FBI.* The trees ended, and I stumbled into the road. Distant headlights. The car rushed toward me, stopped several yards away. I was pinned in its headlights, dripping with Cobb's blood. A woman stepped from the passenger side, a petite blonde with wide blue eyes, a porcelain doll in jeans and a windbreaker.

She pulled her firearm. "Drop the knife — do it —"

I let the knife fall to the ground.

"Where's Vivian?" she said.

"I don't know — I don't know Vivian," I said. "A woman named Shauna —"

"Let's go," said the woman. She ushered me into the back of the SUV. A man drove, his hair cropped short as a chestnut bur. He gunned the engine. The orchard was far behind us when the woman asked, "Do you need a hospital?"

I caught sight of myself in the rearview mirror, doused in blood. "It's not mine," I said. "I'm hurt, but no, not a hospital." My left eye, the one Cobb had struck, pounded with my heartbeat, I realized I could see with only one eye. "I just need to clean up."

"We'll stop somewhere," said the woman.

"Who are you?" I asked.

"Special Agent Zwerger," she said, holding out her credentials — FBI.

"Egan," said the driver.

"Call your supervisor," I said, spitting blood all over their seats — I must have bitten my tongue in the fight. "Tell them you have 'Grey Dove.' Shit — my eye. What's wrong with my eye?"

"It's swollen shut," said Zwerger. "We'll get someone to look you over once we're safe."

We would never be safe. We were bodies

in hell, and the White Hole was our dead sun. I wept, exhausted. Fresh blood filled my mouth, and I swallowed. Cobb's blood turned cold on my skin. Some time later Egan pulled into a CVS, where Zwerger bought bandages and Neosporin. She sat with me in the backseat while Egan paced outside, arguing with someone on his cell. Zwerger washed my cuts with alcohol wipes, cleaned my face. Gentle, motherly. A whiff of baby powder and lipstick when she leaned close. I winced when I caught the reflection of myself in the rearview mirror, the overhead light on — my closed eye was deformed from swelling, yellowed, purple. She covered my eye with a wide bandage. "There," she said.

"Where are we going?" I asked once Egan pulled back onto the road. We'd been driving well over an hour; we'd crossed out of West Virginia into Pennsylvania.

"You aren't FBI," he said.

"NCIS. What are you investigating?"

"Persons of suspicion relating to domestic-terrorism charges," said Zwerger. "I'm guessing you have a similar interest. Vivian might have blown her cover to get you out of there. We lost contact with her."

Whose scream had I heard at the house before I ran? Cobb surprising Shauna —

*Vivian?* Murdering her? I closed off the thought. The windows were tinted, but I caught illuminated signs and placed myself. Connellsville, Uniontown. National Pike, Business 40, the landscape mostly hills with trees and scrub, occasional little strip malls.

"Some of those people have militia ties," said Egan. "What's your interest?"

"Domestic terrorism," I said.

Zwerger kept quiet, looked out the window. I saw the reflection of her face, an awkward expression like she was about to sit through a marital feud.

"I talked with my supervisor," said Egan. "We'll sort this out."

Egan turned in to the parking lot of the Blue Mountain Motel, just a dozen or so units huddled beneath a low-slung roof, the entire lot lit only with the neon Vacancy sign and a vibrant red Coke vending machine that hummed between the middle units. Only one other car in the lot, a silver sedan parked near the office, an old car. The sedan's interior light was on, a soft shine. Someone was inside, but as Egan pulled through the lot, the sedan's light went dark.

"There's nothing for us to sort out," I said. "Tell them you have *Grey Dove*. The rest is between the NCIS director and your director."

"What's the name of the NCIS director?" asked Egan, parking in front of Unit 3. I couldn't answer him; he knew I didn't know the answer. Egan stepped from the car, stretched. "Give me a sec," he said. Near the light of the vending machine, again on his cell. This was a shorter call, and when he finished, he unlocked Unit 3, stepped inside. A moment later the room lights glowed behind the heavy curtains.

*Something isn't right.* Egan must have called his superior, must have mentioned *Grey Dove,* and either didn't believe I was NCIS or the FBI knew exactly who I was. Egan and Zwerger might take me into that room, ask a few questions, then let me walk — or they might never let me go. Even if Egan and Zwerger didn't know what I was, their superiors might. Their superiors might have flagged "Grey Dove" and ordered them to interrogate me here, apprehend me. There are prisons in America far from the public view: no charges, no trial, a butterfly in a bell jar. They could hold me here so their existence wouldn't blink. I tried the car door, but it was locked, the interior handles disabled.

"Don't do this," I said to Zwerger. "You don't understand what you're doing."

"You'll be all right," she said.

"The whole fucking world will die if I don't get out of here," I said. "Call Apollo Soucek Field. Speak with Special Agent Wally Njoku."

"We're just going to have a conversation," said Zwerger. "Sort everything out. Calm down, otherwise we'll be forced to restrain you."

*Kill her,* I thought. *Kill her and take the car.* But Zwerger stepped outside, opened my door. Weighing options: I might be able to outrun her, even with my leg I might outrun her, but there was nowhere to run. I followed her from the SUV. I could scream. There was someone sitting in the silver sedan, and maybe he would call the police if I screamed. Zwerger clutched me by the upper arm. She walked me toward Unit 3, gripped me like I was her prisoner.

"You don't have to do this," I said. "Let me go. Everything you love will die if you don't let me go, a hole will open, a White Hole will open, and everything will die —"

"Enough," she said.

The driver's-side door of the sedan popped open, the driver stepped out, an older man. A raincoat over a gray suit, a black man with a head of woolly hair.

"Help me!" I called to him. "You've got to call the police! Help me!"

"What does this prove?" he said, taking hesitant steps toward us, his hand on the car, steadying himself.

"Egan, come out here," said Zwerger, seeing the man. "Police business," she said to him. "Do not approach."

Something familiar in the way the man moved — then I recognized him as he came closer: *Brock.* His build thinner than it once was, the bulk of his muscle gone soft. He no longer needed to steady himself, moving swiftly as Egan came out from Unit 3.

"Brock?" said Egan. "Why are you here?"

Brock reached beneath his coat, pulled his sidearm from the belt holster. He raised the gun and took a step closer to Egan. Egan lifted his hands, saying, "Billy." Brock fired. Egan crumpled, clutching his belly — a glottal moan, he doubled over on the curb.

Zwerger reached for her weapon, but Brock had already swung toward her and fired, clipping her neck. The woman fell, yelping, sputtering for breath. She reached to hold her throat with both hands, but blood pulsed between her fingers, her mouth round with agony.

Egan crawled toward the lights of Unit 3, draining out from his gut. Brock put the barrel to Egan's head, fired. Egan dropped. I looked to Zwerger, but the light had left her eyes. I reached for her gun, but Brock had returned to me, his gun raised to my chest.

"Brock," I said. "Please."

He looked like he was possessed, like his mind had betrayed him. His face twisted into a rictus. He laughed, the sound like barking.

"What did I do?" he said. "Jesus, Jesus Christ, what did I do?" He looked over at Egan's body, said, "Get up. Come on, Egan. Say something. You're all right. Jesus, what did I do?" He holstered his weapon, stood over Zwerger. He said, "She had a child." He seemed to remember I was there, and he asked me, "What did I do?"

"We're okay, Brock," I said, trying to pacify him. "Everything will be okay —"

He grabbed my chin, angled my face toward the light of the vending machine, studying me. "What do you prove?" he said. He stared hard into my eyes. He would have crawled inside me if he could have.

Something spooked him, some sound I hadn't heard. He flinched, pulled me with him across the lot, to his car. Brock pushed me into the passenger seat, hurried to the driver's side.

"We have to get out of here," Brock said, reversing from the lot onto National Pike.

"I know who you are," he said, gunning the car to sixty, to eighty. "They'll be after us soon. I should have put their bodies in the room. I wasn't thinking. I can't think. I should have moved them. I can't think straight."

"I don't know who you think I am," I said, "but this —"

"Don't you *fucking* lie to me," he said, drawing his gun, pressing the barrel into my cheek — I leaned away, ear against the window. "I could kill you now, and . . . if I killed you," he said, "this would all go away, wouldn't it? This would all just disappear, right? Egan and his partner, it would be like I'd never killed them, right? Right? Talk to me."

"Please, lower your weapon," I said. "Pull over and we'll talk."

"Talk *now,*" he said. "Talk right fucking now."

The road swam before us, headlights on black tar. The gun barrel caused pain, digging into the side of my head.

"I don't want to die like this," I said.

"Can you change what's happened?" he asked. "Is that why you're here? To change all this?"

"What do you think I can change?" I

asked. "Please lower your weapon. Please —"

"CJIS," he said. "When they attacked CJIS, I lost Rashonda, my girls. Shannon, I lost both my beautiful girls, oh, my girls —"

"Pull over and we'll talk," I said. "Please, lower your weapon and pull over."

He lowered the gun. His hands shook. He holstered the weapon. I stayed against the window, vision blurred with tears. His entire family would have been laid out in the surrounding fields, in white sheets. They would have breathed sarin and died instantly. I imagined the body of his wife. I imagined the CJIS day care full of dead children.

"The people who killed them thought they were fighting against the end of the world," said Brock. "That's why my wife and girls were killed." He heaved with sobs. "Why do they have to die? And here you are, all these years later. You haven't aged."

"I'm so sorry," I said. "I'm so sorry about the pain you're in —"

"You're here to study CJIS," said Brock. "To save all those lives."

*Patrick Mursult.* His name would seem insignificant — one life next to a thousand. What could I tell Brock? I could tell him about *Libra,* could tell him about the Terminus. I could tell him that the Terminus cuts across every future, killing everyone who is alive, killing everyone who might ever be alive, killing every possibility in every possible world.

"I can save your family — I want to save them, I want to save Rashonda," I said. "We can talk."

Brock found a Sheetz gas station on Route 51, outside Belle Vernon, a twenty-four-hour convenience store. We wiped off as much blood from ourselves as we could with Handi Wipes he had in his glove compartment. Even so, I wore Brock's raincoat, cinched over my blood-soaked dress. I looked like a horror show. The self-serve restaurant was empty at this hour. The clerks were teenage girls, a blonde and brunette paging through a *Hustler,* laughing, listening to the radio up near the registers. I cleaned myself in the bathroom, picking out dried blood from my hair, washing my hands and face with foam soap from the dispenser.

Brock waited in one of the restaurant booths out of sight from the registers. I joined him. He had diminished with age, with grief. Deep creases furrowed his eyes and mouth; his hair was like cigarette ash.

"I was told to imagine a wall made out of doors," said Brock. "I was told that if I was

261

falling through space toward a wall made of doors, I would fall through one of the doors. Whatever door I fell through would take me into the future. Different doors are different futures. Different versions of the future."

"Who told you that?" I asked.

"After CJIS, after the funerals," he said, "you came into my mind. Nestor and I used to talk about you. You'd worked at CJIS. I wondered if you had died that day with my family. The way you'd vanished, I thought you might have died. And I'd think about Deep Space — and I'd think about Patrick Mursult. And then I caught something on the news, I saw something on *60 Minutes* when Naval Space Command was absorbed into a different agency. Mothballed projects, things that wouldn't mean a damn to anyone who wasn't looking, goofy things — Chinese satellites, lasers on the moon — but I wanted to know more. And I asked questions. I couldn't let go. And one morning I had a message from the director — sealed — telling me about a restaurant in Silver Spring, Maryland, called TJ's. Says I'm expected there. The Bureau had the noose around a physicist who used to work at the Naval Research Lab, we had evidence he accepted classified information from the Senate Armed Services Committee, used classified military secrets to start a company, Phasal Systems. Medical tech, the cure for fucking cancer — all gained from top-secret intelligence. We leveraged him, and he spilled. That's how we learned about Deep Waters. I was brought into the fold. I had lunch with him, this old man who introduced himself by saying he was still like a child, that he should only be forty-two in the summer — but he was old, Shannon. He showed me his birth certificate, an early driver's license. He was working at Phasal Systems on the cancer cure, but he knew everything about NSC. He talked about quantum foam and wormholes, and when I wasn't understanding, he told me to imagine a wall made of doors —"

"Think of it like a whisk," I said.

"Think of what?"

I slid from the booth, poked around behind the food counter, rummaging through kitchen drawers. Spoons, Saran Wrap, old rags. I found a whisk hanging on a pegboard near the utility sink.

"A whisk," I said, returning to our table. "This is how my instructor taught me."

I held the whisk sideways. Pointed to the tip of the handle. "Beginning of time," I said. I ran my finger along the handle. "All of history — the observed past." At the top of the handle, I said, "The present."

"And then you hit the wall of doors," he said.

I touched each of the wires of the whisk. "Possible futures, possible timelines — infinitely possible," I said. "Imagine this whisk with an infinite number of wires."

"What's up here?" Brock asked, pointing to the tip of the whisk, where all the wires bent, looped toward one another, joined.

"Terminus," I said.

"What's that?"

"The end of the world."

"All right," he said, cupping his hands in front of his mouth. Vitality had returned to him, a frantic energy. His eyes seemed to be gulping at ideas like a drowning man would gulp at air. "And where is . . . this?" he asked, pointing to the end of the handle, the present.

"March 1997," I told him.

Brock's face cracked into a manic, open-mouthed grin, his eyes frenzied — a glee that terrified me.

"And you . . . traveled here? You flew here? You're an astronaut, aren't you? Like Mursult was an astronaut. I remember asking if he was an astronaut, and you didn't blink. You didn't blink because you're like him, aren't you? You time-traveled here —"

"I don't know if I'm here or still there, technically. It's called 'superposition entanglement,' but I was never great at math," I said. "You used to chew licorice gum, in 1997."

He laughed, a sound more like a cry. "I gave it up," he said. "Licorice — that gum was from Italy. I used to buy it from the import store, by the box. The only licorice strong enough — turned your spit black, your teeth and tongue black. But that day, CJIS, I was frantic, because I knew they were dead, my family, I just somehow knew my family was dead, that they were all dead. And I got through the security and ran through the rows of bodies, lifting white sheets off people's faces, each time thinking I'd see one of my girls, but I only saw the faces of strangers, dead faces. I never saw my girls, never found them. I was eating my licorice that whole time, a nervous habit, but the next morning I ate a piece of that gum and the smell of licorice filled my mind with all those dead faces. I spit it out —"

"You're still looking for your girls," I said. "You think I'll be able to help you find them."

"Why now?" he asked. "Why did you come now?"

"I don't control it," I said. "There are

shapes that appear in nature — the shapes of seashells, the spiral shapes of some galaxies. Snowflakes, the swirl pattern of seeds on a sunflower's face, on and on. You see this same pattern repeated everywhere. Leaf fronds, the way a toilet flushes."

"Fractals," said Brock. "The same pattern, repeated forever."

"Quantum foam grows like that, too," I said. "It's shaped like that. There is a set of numbers that makes those shapes, called Fibonacci numbers — that shape is everywhere in nature. I don't have to travel this far, or I can travel much farther, but the protocol for most investigations is that we travel about nineteen years, 6,765 days. I came with the hope that the truth would reveal itself in time. I came to investigate the death of Patrick Mursult and the murder of his family."

"Why? Why him? What's his life worth?" Brock asked, but he didn't want to hear my answers about *Libra* or the Terminus — he was burrowed deep within himself. After a moment he said, "So this physicist said he enjoyed my company, enjoyed talking with someone who wanted to believe him, and said he wanted ice cream after lunch. There's a Baskin-Robbins right next door to TJ's, so I took him over, we ate ice cream cones together. All theoretical, he told me. He was bullshitting me maybe, but as we were leaving, he said that if I ever met a traveler, I should capture him, put him in handcuffs, lock him away in solitary. Supermax. Lock him away without a key and keep him alive for as long as possible, alive and comfortable, because the moment he dies or goes back through that wall of doors, back to the real present, the true present, everything I know about life — every memory I have, everything, every person I'd ever known, every *atom* in existence — will disappear."

"Blink out," I said.

"Gone," said Brock.

"We call that the butterfly in the bell jar," I said. "It's happened to people like me. Being held captive in these futures by people who can't face the awareness of their nonexistence."

"But what would happen if I came back with you? Could you bring me back?"

"I could," I said, knowing the case history, the quasi-legal status of individuals NSC ships brought home from futures, the strange lives of these doppelgängers, people we called echoes.

"I could see her again," said Brock. "My girls. I could . . . I could hold them, couldn't I?"

"You'd only bring confusion and pain," I said. "You'd only scare your girls. They'd see you as you are now, as an old man who bears a strong resemblance to their father. Your wife will joke that William Brock, her husband, might look like you when he's an old man. If you tried to go home, you would be a double, nothing more. They wouldn't want you. You'd be an *echo* of William Brock, you wouldn't *be* William Brock. Ask yourself — how much do you love them? Do you truly love Rashonda, your wife? She already has her husband. Do you truly love your daughters? They already have their father."

Brock coughed, a guttural sound, either wild laughter or choking on grief. He drew his weapon, the Glock pistol he had already used to kill that night. He pointed at my sternum, and my heart dissolved. If he were to shoot me, I felt that my blood would never stop flowing.

"I could keep you comfortable here," he said.

"Were Egan and Zwerger going to keep me comfortable here?" I asked.

"They didn't know what you were," said Brock. "There are people who know. A colleague of mine, Whittaker. He'd ordered you to be questioned, imprisoned. *'Grey Dove,'* he said. Egan and Zwerger were going to hold you, but they didn't know why. What is the term you used? A butterfly?"

"A butterfly in a bell jar," I said.

"Funny thing," said Brock. "Nestor called me a few months ago. I was surprised as hell. Out of the blue. I hadn't heard from Nestor in years. He says, 'I just saw Shannon Moss, can you believe it? Hasn't changed a day.' I knew I had you then. I knew I had you. I told him to turn you over, but he says it was just in passing, said you spoke for a few minutes and then you were gone. I worked every connection I have in the Bureau, told everyone that if you ever turned up, to let me know. This friend of mine, Whittaker? He called earlier tonight, said he had *Grey Dove*. I begged him, I made calls, I begged everyone I could, I pulled strings, lobbied to give the order to bring you to Uniontown, where I could intercept you. On some level in my gut, I still didn't believe — just because you turned up here, what did it prove? But you haven't aged, Shannon."

"Think of your love for them," I said.

"My wife and kids are still alive," said Brock. "They're still alive where you come from."

"Yes."

"And you can keep them safe," he said.

"Yes."

"What will happen to me here? When you go, what will happen to all this pain?"

"There is no you," I said. "There is no pain."

Brock placed the gun in his mouth and shot. The top of his head opened, blood poured from every hole. Brock's body slipped from the booth to the floor, crimson spreading in a grid along the tile grout. The clerks ran over, one of them screaming. I shook, struggled to breathe — but my life hung in the balance here, in this moment. One clerk stood transfixed by the bleeding body, but the other clerk was already on the phone. I pulled Brock's keys from his pocket and hurried from the store, seeing their mouths open but hearing no sound, only the blaring ring of temporary deafness caused by the gun blast. I fumbled with Brock's ignition — how long from here to Virginia? How long before the police were searching for this car? The engine caught, and I drove. Case notes on Marian, my notebooks — lost, irretrievably lost. What had I gained? Nicole. *Libra.* Hyldekrugger. *Nestor,* I thought — imagining that he waited for me out on his porch, looking over his yard at dusk, Buick barking at the cars on 151. I imagined Nestor spotting head-lights of every passing car, wondering which car would be mine. The night seemed deeper than any night. I thought of Nestor as I drove, thought of his lips, his body so familiar to me now, the constellation of freckles over his heart. Hoping he would forgive me — forgive me for always disappearing, but soon there would be nothing to forgive, soon there would be nothing.

■ ■ ■ ■

# PART THREE

1997

■ ■ ■ ■

Where are the snows of yesteryear?
— FRANÇOIS VILLON,
"Ballad of Women of Times Past"

# ONE

The *Grey Dove* was tethered to terra firma
by bursts of negative energy called a Casimir line — for Moss, a three-month return
through the void of quantum foam. The
wounds she'd suffered in the orchard had
healed, but their psychological effects would
linger. She woke from nightmares thinking
she'd heard screams. Floating in her sleeping cabin's dim light, sweating and claustrophobic, listening to the whir of the life-
support system as she emerged from dreams
of Charles Cobb, a dark shape smothering
her, the scent of fruit blossoms pulling at
the edges of her memory . . .

Voices swam through the *Grey Dove* —
auditory hallucinations, but they sounded
like Nestor's voice when he spoke her name
in the night. Or she would startle at the
crack of a gunshot and realize the sound
was nothing but the sound of Brock's
suicide reverberating in her mind. The gas-

275

station cafeteria, the flow of blood. She played music to drown out the noises in the silence. She wrote notes in pencil and erased them, a method for memorization — *Esperance, the Terminus followed Libra* — imagining crystallized space. So much of what she had heard was extraordinary, beyond her comprehension. *Where is Esperance?* she wrote. *Can NSC return there?* She drew a polygon in the stomach of a man. *Autopsy.* Nicole had seemed to recognize her that last night — *but she recognized me as Courtney Gimm,* she wrote. Shauna had said Hyldekrugger and Cobb ID'd her as "Courtney Gimm."

*Elizabeth Remarque,* she wrote, then erased the name. She wrote it again: *Remarque.*

*Where was Libra?*

She erased the question.

*When?*

The engineers at the Black Vale who had observed the *Grey Dove*'s launch to Deep Waters now saw her return within a moment of her launch, disappearing and reappearing in the span of a heartbeat, the ship merely shimmering even though Moss had lived for over a year during that time. The days' transit from the Black Vale to

Earth filled her with anxiety, true time counting against Marian now. Where was she? Already lost, her body left to the woods? Or somewhere else, alive? The *Grey Dove* pierced Earth's atmosphere, flaring like a burning filament, and landed at Apollo Soucek under cover of night. NSC engineers assisted Moss from the cockpit and ferried her to the "clean room," an on-base house with a view of the Atlantic. The three-month journey through quantum foam was sufficient quarantine, time enough for any exotic viruses Moss might have contracted from the future to have incubated and run their course. Even so, her first few hours in the clean room were spent with doctors in hazmat suits inspecting her body for traces of illness. Culture swabs, blood work. The last of her doctors left a little after 3:00 a.m. Moss drew a bath, soaked away three months of the *Grey Dove*'s circulated air. She hadn't noticed how she'd aged during the past year, but she realized now, swiping away a streak of fog to examine herself in the bathroom mirror. She saw a striking resemblance to her mother. Confused as to how old she really was. Biologically, she must be closing in on forty, she thought, but she had lost track. Thirty-nine? Chronologically, she should only be twenty-seven. Moss bundled her hair in a towel, wrapped another towel around her body. Almost four in the morning. She hesitated at the hour but called Brock's cell.

"Hello?" he answered.

Her eyes filled at the sound of his voice. *Still alive,* she thought, swallowing back tears, relieved that his suicide bore as little weight as a daydream.

"Brock, this is Shannon," she said.

"Where have you been? It's been days. I haven't heard from you," he said — and Moss heard a woman's voice soft in the background, "Who is it, baby?"

Brock was alive, his wife was alive, his little girls sound asleep. Moss closed her eyes and saw flashes of color that looked like veins traced in light. Exhaustion, she knew. A year since Marian had vanished — *No, only seven days* —

"I can't talk for long," she said. "Not tonight. I'll be back with you in a few days, but you have to listen to me. Do you have a pen?"

"Hold on. Yeah, go ahead."

"Jared Bietak, Charles Cobb, Karl Hyldekrugger, Nicole Onyongo," she said.

"We talked with Nicole Onyongo," said Brock. "Nestor questioned her for several hours, tracked her down using license-plate information the lodge kept. Identified her as the woman in the Polaroids we recovered at Elric Fleece's residence — she's been having an affair with Mursult but isn't connected. She was distraught but cooperative, answered everything we asked. Nothing panned out."

"We need her," said Moss.

"We haven't been able to get back in touch with her," said Brock, unwelcome news. Moss tried to remember what will happen. Nicole had been questioned by the FBI, by Nestor — but she had been threatened by her husband, Jared Bietak. She had gone into hiding, Moss remembered. Out of reach.

"Please keep trying to track her down," she said. "She knows more than she told you."

"I'll send someone to her apartment, see if we can pick her up," said Brock. "Who are the others?"

"Persons of suspicion," said Moss. "I think these men are the killers, Brock. I think they killed Mursult, his family. Put out their names, take them into custody. I don't know which one pulled the trigger on Mursult or who took Marian or the family, but they're all involved. Now listen closely. I need you to search a location. Bring a K9 unit, trained to mark human remains."

"Where?"

"There's an access route labeled TR-31 on some forestry maps of the Blackwater Gorge," she said. "An old logging route, easy to miss. Take that access route uphill. You'll eventually come to a clearing."

"What am I going to find?" said Brock.

"Look for piles of stones set out as markers. They're called cairns. Small stacks of flat stones. Search wherever you find the markers. But it is imperative, absolutely imperative, that your men aren't seen by anyone. Do you understand? Search that site, but no one can see you. I believe that the actor or actors have accessed or will access this site. If they're made aware of your presence, we might lose our chance."

"Will I find Marian?" he asked.

Already the future receded from her, like images half retrieved from dreams or like her memories were waves breaking against the shores of the real, washing away. She was cold, exhausted and cold, and visions played in the darkness of her closed eyes like lucid dreams. She saw Nestor, the forest in the night, pine sap, damp stone, a beautiful place to rest.

"Moss, is this about Marian?" asked Brock.

"I don't know what you'll find," she said. "I hope nothing."

She slept for sixteen hours. When she woke, she worked through the paperwork that Naval Space Command required to document every IFT. The packet resembled a tax book: *Assurance of Fact and Statement of Faith, with Sheet 34 and Waivers 1–13.* Her portion began on page 6 of 116 pages. *Line 1: Did you witness any event that might compromise the national security of the United States of America?* She spooled the first worksheet into her electric typewriter, three empty lines. *On April 19, 1998,* she typed, *the FBI Criminal Justice Information Services (CJIS) facility located in Clarksburg, West Virginia, will be attacked. A thousand people will die, killed by sarin gas delivered through the fire-suppression system . . .*

A quick breakfast the following morning, then her debriefing: a seaman drove her to the NCIS Resident Unit office, where she was shown into the conference room, a cramped space with mustard-colored walls. A single chair at the front table, a microphone, her name printed on a cardboard table tent. NSC brass from Dahlgren clustered together, talking. She spotted Admiral

Annesley, who would question her. She recognized NCIS special agents from the Norfolk field office. O'Connor was there, in his seventies but spry. His nose was bulbous, lined with violet veins. His creased forehead and the wrinkles beneath his eyes were like a map of rivers run dry. O'Connor smiled when he saw her, worked his way to her. His eyes seemed like they should belong to a younger man — they belied his age, sparkling with a rich blue vitality.

"How long have you been gone?" he asked.

"Arrived September 2015, stayed through the spring," said Moss. "With travel time about a year, slightly longer."

"Just make sure you put in for OT pay and to count toward your retirement," he said. "Talk with Human Resources when you have a chance. You must be getting close?"

"To retirement? I think I'm about thirty-nine, biologically," said Moss. "A few years yet. If I met some of my high-school friends, they would think . . . I don't know what they'd think. Twelve years older than they are. They'd think I wasn't taking care of myself."

O'Connor laughed. "I'm older than my father," he said.

These debriefings were called informal, but Moss, who had gone through seven of these productions, knew what significance they carried. This roomful of men would evaluate her performance over the next several hours, would consider the overall viability of her operation. She was nervous, doubting herself — doubting her memories, worried she would contradict herself. A cassette recorder had been placed near her on the table, a stenographer typed her words. The Navy representatives sat together like a bell choir, deep blue uniforms, the sleeves heavy with golden stripes and piping. They watched intently as Moss read her opening statement, a summary of her IFT. She spoke about the crimes of the crewmen of the USS *Libra,* their alleged mutiny, their alleged participation in the murder of Patrick Mursult and his family. Admiral Annesley was genial, but his mind sprang like a lawyer's, questioning Moss and cross-examining her answers. A politician, one of Reagan's men, with smallish eyes that gleamed like dark gems, seeming to smile even as he peeled away at Moss's responses — his onslaught abating only when Moss described the death of Elizabeth Remarque. A pervasive grief settled over the assembly — many of the men here had known Remarque personally, it seemed. Remarque had suffered a public execution, according to Nicole's story, and Moss told them how Remarque's corpse had been paraded among the sailors in the mess. Annesley was curious about *Libra,* curious to hear Nicole's story of Esperance a second time, confirming that the planet was in NGC 5055, the Sunflower Galaxy. Had *Libra* brought the Terminus to Earth, then? Moss surmised that *Libra* had been responsible — that at any rate it was certainly the first ship to observe the Terminus, rather than the USS *Taurus,* as had been previously thought. What do you believe was the mental state of the surviving crew? Moss described Nicole's abuse at the hands of Jared Bietak and her subsequent troubles with drug addition. Annesley picked at her answers but didn't linger over this part of the interview. Rather he surprised Moss by his overriding interest in the cancer cure, something she initially mentioned only to color her description of the IFT. He wanted to learn about her mother's cancer, when she was diagnosed, her initial surgeries, and how she had apparently been healed — who had healed her, how she had been chosen for the clinical trials.

"My understanding is that people with the right insurance could just walk into a clinic, receive three injections," said Moss. "Nano-tech delivery to cancerous cells."

"And this was developed by a company called Phasal Systems?" asked Annesley, Moss confirming the information she had already repeated. "Who developed the cure?" he asked. "Do you know any of the names of the doctors involved?"

"I'm sorry," she said. "I don't —"

"Did Phasal Systems develop communications systems, too, or were they only active in the medical sector?"

"Medical, I believe," said Moss, struggling to recall anything she might have picked up about Phasal Systems while in her IFT, some information she might have absorbed even if on the periphery of her attention. The scientist Brock had spoken with might have had something to do with the cancer cure, she remembered — *Imagine a wall made of doors.* She remembered Brock had said the scientist had worked for the Naval Research Lab before moving into medical tech. "I think Phasal Systems might have had a connection to the NRL," she said. "A spin-off company. I think Navy scientists worked on the cancer cure once they left NRL. We didn't have Ambience, though, or Intelligent Air, if that's what you're asking, or any of the environmental nanotech-saturation systems popular in other IFTs. Most people still used cellular phones. But they had cured cancer."

"Had they cured every disease?" asked Annesley. "Did Phasal Systems solve disease?"

She remembered the words of her mother's nurse. "There was still disease," said Moss. "My mother's nurse told me you had to be rich to live forever."

The debriefing ended, a flurry of handshakes, Moss realizing that Annesley hadn't asked certain questions she was accustomed to answering: what year the Terminus had been marked, for instance. It had swung closer, to 2067 in her IFT — but Annesley hadn't asked. He hadn't followed up about the CJIS attack either, she realized, or even about her investigation into Patrick Mursult, or about the mutiny. There would be more paperwork, forms to fill out, she knew, and she knew she could be recalled to answer further questions at any time, or to provide clarification on statements she'd made, but the admiral's focus on the cancer cure surprised her, the focus on Phasal Systems, a company that didn't even exist in 1997. Her debriefings often concluded with this feeling of anticlimactic uncertainty over how much good she had actually contributed; her reports on future terrorist attacks, future wars, future economic conditions never seemed to amount to much in the way of prevention, many of the events she warned about still occurring. She felt like an American Cassandra when events she warned about came to pass. Her only solace was the belief that there was a bigger political picture the Navy accounted for that she wasn't privy to — she saw only brush-strokes, never the entire painting.

"You did well," O'Connor told her, back at her on-base housing. He wasn't staying long, but he accepted a cup of coffee, sitting with Moss in the house's enclosed back porch, the Atlantic a twilight glow beyond the reach of sand.

"Seven hours with those men," she said. "Almost eight. I'm exhausted. And I'm never sure what they're asking, what they're trying to get at."

"NSC has Senate oversight. They have their own concerns, which don't always line up with ours," said O'Connor. "Every IFT costs millions of U.S. tax dollars. I understand that the admiral went straight to a dinner meeting with Senator C. C. Charlie about your debriefing. He'll have a long night ahead."

"I'm testifying about Hyldekrugger and

Cobb, killers at least, guilty of mutiny on the *Libra,* and the admiral didn't seem to care," said Moss. "These men murdered their commanding officer, and they're tied to the Terminus. *Libra* might have *brought* the Terminus. Annesley hardly asked about *Libra,* or what Nicole Onyongo told me about Esperance. I was prepared to talk about Nicole."

"I know that Annesley cared about Remarque. We all did," said O'Connor.

"You knew her?"

"She was clever. She'd get this look in her eye, and you knew she was already a few steps ahead of you," said O'Connor, smiling at the memory. "I didn't know her well. We did some joint training sessions together. I remember stories — she would float the passageways of her department, make rounds, and everyone would be nervous because they knew she could do their jobs better than they could. Very high standards, very exacting. But she was patient. Everyone wanted to be assigned to her ship. Your testimony about her death was very difficult to listen to."

"All Annesley seemed interested in was nanotech medication, cancer."

"Well, you never know what cards Annesley is holding," said O'Connor. "He might already have other reports about *Libra* that have been corroborated, or facts that contradict yours. Besides, Nicole Onyongo was never NSC, which makes her legal status somewhat hazy."

"What's that supposed to mean?"

"No one named Onyongo was on *Libra*," said O'Connor. "The other names you provided, but not Nicole Onyongo. She wasn't a sailor. She doesn't appear anywhere in NSC. She was never in the Navy. NSC believes that Nicole Onyongo was picked up in *Libra*'s future, which is highly irregular. We can only guess why Remarque would have done such a thing, but there you go. Nicole Onyongo doesn't exist, not the way you and I do."

Moss felt affronted, surprised that Nicole wasn't born in terra firma. But the strange story about Kenya — Nicole saying that the people of Mombasa had welcomed the crew of *Libra,* that Nicole had followed Remarque only after her father had intervened on her behalf. Nicole was a stowaway from a world that never was. A ripple of uncertainty passed through Moss. Nicole was a specter, just one of countless shadows cast by *Libra.*

"What about the others? You found the other names I gave you? They were on the *Libra* crew list."

"We did — and Hyldekrugger, he's an interesting case," said O'Connor.

"The celestial navigator."

"The ship's CELNAV, yes," said O'Connor. "Vietnam. Studied philosophy and religion at the University of Chicago before NSC. He earned a master's studying Viking death cults and rituals, a thesis on the pagan symbolism of the Black Sun. I tried to read some of it, but it's steeped in academic jargon."

"The ship made of nails, that's a Viking myth," said Moss. "Something to do with the end of the world."

"Clean record," said O'Connor. "But Hyldekrugger has two uncles involved in the 'sovereign citizens' movement, and one is serving life for the beating death of a black man. I'm assuming a connection of that type of extremist thinking to the events in your report."

"Maybe. Yeah, probably," said Moss, ruminating on the violence that had swept through *Libra,* the mutiny, the massacre. "Hyldekrugger and his followers — they killed everyone on the ship," she said, and they had somehow survived reentry to terra firma; they had somehow returned. Moss had learned so much about the fate of *Libra,* but other questions grew around the missing ship like mushrooms in the dark.

"We have warrants for Hyldekrugger, Cobb, Bietak, and Nicole Onyongo," said O'Connor. "We'll pick up their trails, arrest these individuals, and question them about Mursult and *Libra*. I want convictions, but don't be surprised if they're offered bargains."

"They murdered children," said Moss. "They'll murder Marian. She might still be alive. These men might have her —"

"Shannon, you have to understand, things have changed since you've been away."

"What's going on?" she asked.

"The Terminus has been marked at 2024. Less than thirty years from now," said O'Connor. "Before your debriefing we received word that the *John F. Kennedy* marked the Terminus at 2024."

"Within our lifetime," said Moss.

"Within our lifetime, within our children's lifetime. The last generation is already alive," said O'Connor.

"Maybe we can still stop it, maybe if we —"

"Maybe," said O'Connor, his voice, though, that of someone who'd already accepted a terminal stage. "Annesley is prepared to offer plea bargains to Hyldekrugger and Cobb, and any other conspirators they bring to the table, for information about their involvement in the Terminus, the location of Esperance."

"This is bullshit."

"And the Navy is greenlighting Operation Saigon," he said. "Prioritizing which civilians will be included in the evacuation, if it comes to that. Thirty years is too close. NSC is mandated to load ships and launch to Deep Waters within forty-eight hours of the appearance of the White Hole, and they're worried it might appear now, at any moment. We've been pulling agents from lower-priority investigations, reassigning them to Saigon. NSC wants as many of our Cormorant shuttles as we can spare. They'll requisition them all soon."

Moss wanted to argue, but fear clenched her, a bolt of panic at the imminence of the White Hole — *2024.* What would happen when the White Hole appeared? Would billions lift into the air, opened and displayed? Would they run, mindless, or stand staring? Moss felt the helplessness of a child. She felt like she couldn't comprehend the true scope of the end. She imagined Operation Saigon, Cormorant shuttles launching in waves, the entire NSC fleet at the Black Vale at capacity with soldiers and civilians, mixes of talents and genetics, each ship launched in search of exo-Earths, each ship a seed to grow a new humanity even as humanity perished. She thought of the escaping ships, the abandoned Earth, and grew anxious at the thought of what would be left behind. She felt like she was being asked to leave Marian behind. What was one life set against every life? A despondency churned in her heart, Marian's life abandoned for the lives of others. But maybe she wasn't too late. She was sure she wasn't too late. Her mind rebounded to Marian, how Marian might still be alive, how Marian might still be saved.

Moss received her discharge papers the following afternoon. She found her pickup in the lot, surprised that her battery wasn't dead, and had to remind herself that only a few days had passed since she'd parked here. Evergreen air freshener and the reek of prosthetic liners she'd flung behind the passenger seat, just her little red Ford, but the familiar odors and the sensation of sitting behind the wheel comforted her, situated her in her own life after so long an absence. She left Naval Air Station Oceana through the main gates. Returning to terra firma was like stepping into the same river twice: everything the same as when she'd left, but it didn't feel quite the same to her now. The year 1997 felt hopelessly retro-grade in some ways, a recovered past. Returning was like traveling to a poorer foreign country where the fashions and cars, the technology and architecture lagged decades behind.

An eight-hour drive from Oceana, Moss's house was northwest of Clarksburg, West Virginia, a ranch seated on four acres of wildflower-strewn lawn. She loved the house, loved the solitude, the single-floor layout amenable to her situation. Only a week's worth of mail had piled up inside the front-door slot. Moss divided bills from junk mail before changing into pajamas and settling into her leather couch. The VCR had recorded *The X-Files* in her absence, her hero Scully, a new episode — but she grew anxious when the plot veered into spaceships and nine minutes of missing time. Her telephone rang, and she paused her show, bands of static blur over Scully's face.

"We found something," said Brock.

"Marian?" she asked.

"Not Marian. We found the clearing. Nothing there. We brought a K9 and scoured the area for human remains, but there was nothing."

*Too early,* thought Moss. Marian could

have been buried at this site at any point between now and 2004, when two men lost in the woods would dig for ginseng but find bones. Something Moss remembered of her father — how he let hose water pour down their front sidewalk and would watch the water branch out in different rivulets, diverging paths, around cracks and stones. Futures were like those forking paths of water. Marian might not ever be left in those woods.

"We broadened our search," said Brock, "found one of your rock formations about a half mile north-northwest of your initial location. I posted two men in blinds, told them to enjoy the wildlife for a few days."

"What did you find?"

"Rainey called it in," said Brock. "He spotted a guy building one of your rock piles."

"Did you ID him?"

"Not a chance. Not at that distance," said Brock. "But Rainey tracked the actor, found that he drove a black van, a GMC Vandura, early eighties. We spotted the van twice in the area."

"What about the plates?" she asked.

"The van's registered to someone named Richard Harrier."

*Harrier,* thought Moss, with desperation.

"I don't know that name," writing out the name on a sheet of scratch paper: *Harrier, Richard*. "He might know where Marian is."

"Shannon, I've met you halfway on this," said Brock. "More than halfway. I need more from you. I need probable cause. More than just your word, or some hunch you're playing. Otherwise whoever these guys get as their defense attorney will shred us and we'll squander whatever intelligence led you to target them. We can't harass someone for building rock piles. What else do you have?"

"Just stay with me on this," said Moss, but doubt crept over her. There had been no tangible proof linking these cairns to Marian's body. "What else do you know about this guy? Richard Harrier?" she asked. "His address? Priors? Anything?"

"No priors, absolutely clean. Harrier works at a Home Depot in Bridgeport, the vehicle is registered to his Bridgeport address. Married, has three kids — but I had one of our guys trail the van, and it looks like the driver's been spending time at a house just outside a small town called Buckhannon —"

"Buckhannon," said Moss, and when Brock read the address, "Off 151," her world warped. She ran the kitchen tap, held her hand beneath the warming water until she scalded herself — the pain jolting through her incertitude. She knew the address, Nestor's address, the house with the black van in Buckhannon was the same house she would sleep in with Nestor nineteen years from now.

"I'm going," she said. "I have to see —"

"Moss, wait —"

The porch with the wooden rockers, walks along the acres, Nestor, the constellation of freckles over his heart — *Why there, why of all places there?*

She threw on jeans, her holster. Imagining Nestor — *Maybe Nestor didn't know,* she thought. Nestor's connection to the house in Buckhannon might not exist yet, might not ever exist. *This might all be a coincidence,* she thought, *a coincidence of houses, like Courtney's house.* Desperate to believe that Nestor was innocent, that right now he might still be innocent, that he might have always been innocent.

A half-hour drive from Clarksburg to Buckhannon, after midnight. She pushed a hundred on empty rural roads thinking of Marian buried in the woods. Wild thoughts of Nestor, of Nestor kidnapping Marian, of Nestor killing her, of Nestor as he would look years from now, of Nestor here at this house in Buckhannon, *here, here.* She pulled from 151 into the gravel drive, skidding as she braked. A pear tree grew in the front yard, and there was a hedgerow in front of the porch, but otherwise the house was the same as it would be years from now. Moss left her truck, every fondness for this place curdled. A black van with a red racing stripe was parked near the house. The barn doors were lit with a floodlight set to a motion sensor that had tripped. Around the far side of the barn, a Winnebago without wheels was up on cinder blocks — *I've seen that before,* she thought. The house itself was dark, but the living-room windows pulsed blue with television light. Someone was home.

Moss pulled her weapon. The van had been left unlocked, and she swung open the rear doors, found blood on the walls and floor, a rumpled plastic tarp and twine. *Marian's blood.* Anticipating where to find Marian, she remembered the flimsy side-door lock that Nestor had never bothered to fix. She looked in through the side-door window, but the interior was too dark for her to see, so she braced herself, shouldered the door, and it gave inward with a snap. Loud volume on the television, moaning, the sounds of sex, like an echo of her memories here. Weapon leveled, through into the kitchen, television glare across the linoleum, through into the living room. A naked man sat sprawled on the couch, his head leaned back. A woman was on her knees between his legs sucking him off, her body rippled with cellulite and waves of fat, her hair a brown mess.

"Federal agent. Get down on the floor," said Moss. "Get on the *fucking* floor."

The woman yelped and shrieked, clutching her heart. *"Jesus, Jesus, Jesus!"* flopping forward, breasts flailing, her hands spread in front of her, gripping the carpet. The man skipped up onto the couch like he'd just seen a rat scurry, covering himself with a throw pillow and bawling, body lit by Playboy Channel lesbians. "Jesus, lady, don't shoot me, don't shoot me!" The woman's hair would one day gray like a mop of sooty yarn — Miss Ashleigh, Ashleigh Bietak, Nicole's mother-in-law.

"On the fucking floor," Moss said again, and the man dropped to his knees next to Ashleigh and spread his arms out wide, ass in the air. The living room was the same as Moss had known it — the same mirror hung above the mantel, the painting of the dead Christ hung in the spot it would hang when Nestor would live here. Her confusion and heartbreak screamed like twin sirens in her mind. *Marian,* she thought, her name an anchor. Moss cuffed the man but only had one set of cuffs so had to leave Ashleigh free.

"Where is Marian Mursult?" asked Moss. "Miss Ashleigh, where is she?"

"What is this?" said Ashleigh. "What girl? This is bullshit, is what it is. Fucking, I want my lawyer. Who are you? Where's your warrant? Fuck this. You can't be here —"

"Marian Mursult," said Moss. "Where is she? You, where is she?"

"I don't know," said the man. "These are too tight, these cuffs. I want my clothes. I'm not supposed to be here, I've got a wife. Please, I shouldn't be here. My wife will find out."

"Where is Marian Mursult?" she asked again, shouting, but didn't wait for their answers. She went down the hallway toward the back rooms, the bedroom, Nestor's bedroom where she had slipped from her clothes and slept so many nights. Wooden gun racks, rifles and machine guns. "Fuck me," said Moss, recognizing the German antiques, the stock of the Eagle's Nest. "Damn, no, no . . ." Circling back to the living room, she checked the two and found them still facedown on the carpet. She found the basement door just off the kitchen and climbed downstairs, aware Miss Ashleigh wasn't cuffed, aware the woman could fetch any one of those Nazi guns and ambush her while she was down here or as she came back upstairs.

"Marian?" Moss called out. "Marian, I'm a police officer. Are you down here? Let me know if you're down here. Say something, please."

A dank basement, the stink of bleach. A metal weight-bearing column near a central floor drain. Browned rags and bloodstains on the concrete floor, stains on the cinderblock walls. There were gags, restraints. Moss pictured the girl tied to the metal column, hands bound behind her back. Brown stains in the utility sink doused with bleach. Marian had been tied up here, brutalized . . .

Rumbling across the ceiling. Moss heard them run, Ashleigh and the man, Harrier. *Fuck,* she thought, pointing her gun at the ceiling, contemplating shooting up through the floorboards, maybe hitting the bottoms of their feet or passing up through their groins for a kill shot, but she wasn't justified. She lowered the gun toward the stairs to shoot if she saw their legs descending but heard the slap of the side screen door and knew they'd sprinted from the house. She took a breath, knowing she was making mistakes. She climbed the stairs to the kitchen, alert — but there was no one.

Moss followed outside, where the barn floodlight blazed the darkness white. Miss Ashleigh and Harrier must have run this way, she thought, must have tripped the light. Maybe they'd gone into the barn or to the far side of the Winnebago. The Winnebago looked like it was a fixture of this place, weeds grown up around it. As Moss crossed the lawn, the Winnebago's door opened and a man stepped outside — blue jeans and old combat boots, an olive-drab shirt unbuttoned, exposing his chest. A huge man with tawny hair cut into a ratty mullet. *Cobb,* she realized — twenty years younger than when she had first seen the man, when she had grappled with him in the orchard and slit his throat. *Charles Cobb,* she was sure of it. He held a tallboy beer and took massive swigs, looking out over the fields — he hadn't seen her, didn't know she was here, she realized, not yet. Wherever Miss Ashleigh and her man had run off to, it wasn't to the Winnebago.

"Federal agent," Moss said, sighting her weapon to the center of Cobb's mass, thinking, *If he moves, I can kill this fucker twice.*

"Get down on the ground. On your fucking knees. Now. *Now.*"

Cobb flinched at her voice — she'd surprised him. He set his beer can on the step of the Winnebago and raised his hands in surrender but didn't go to his knees. *This man has walked on an alien world,* she thought. *This man has seen his friends flayed and spread in the air.* Sirens on 151, Moss noticed, distant blue lights. Brock must have called the Buckhannon PD, figured she would come here alone.

"Do you have a warrant to be here, Officer?" asked Cobb, his voice measured if not calm. His voice unnerved her, and she felt the moment slipping from her, an intuition that she wasn't in control.

"On your knees," said Moss. "Keep your hands where I can see them."

"You're a cripple," he said. The barn light timed out. Pitch-black. Cobb ran — she heard him, taking off around the far side of the Winnebago. She heard him crashing through the field beyond and knew there was no way she could chase him down, no way she could outrun him through the tall grass. Everyone was escaping — she felt like they were melting from her.

The dark was pierced by the firelight of muzzle flashes, automatic-weapon fire. Bullets zipped overhead and chewed into the mud several feet behind her. The darkness had saved her; whoever was shooting couldn't see her, didn't know where she was, and she dropped to the grass, a second volley whining past. She saw the muzzle flash from the Winnebago window, trained her weapon on the flash. She took a shot. A second shot. A third.

Sirens pulled in to the driveway, blue waves against the barn and Winnebago, a half dozen vehicles at least, more arriving. Another round of fire chewed into the cars, shattered windshields.

"Shannon?" she heard — Nestor exiting one of the cars. She turned her gun on him, aimed at his chest, an easy shot from this distance, felt herself apply pressure to the trigger.

"It's me," he said. He knelt behind the open driver's-side door of his car, an FBI vest, his sidearm pulled.

Moss's vision had tunneled, focused on his gun. *This is his house. This will be his house.*

"Shannon, it's me — it's Nestor. Lower your weapon, please."

The world rushed to her. He was still just a young man, still FBI. "One person, on foot through those fields," she said. "Two more at large, might still be on the premises. One in handcuffs. The shooter's in the Winnebago."

Racket of automatic fire. Return fire from the police — they filled the Winnebago with hundreds of rounds. Nestor emptied his clip, but another volley of fire roared from the Winnebago. Bullets shattered his windshield and door, pumped into Nestor's chest. He spun to the grass, yelling. Moss emptied her gun at the Winnebago. Reloaded. Shot again. Someone shouted — the gunman inside the Winnebago was hit. Nestor was alive. He made it back to his knees, the sleeve of his shirt ripped and soiled with blood.

"Vest," said Nestor. "I'm all right. I've got a vest —"

Relief, seeing Nestor safe. Other officers, men in uniform, fanned out across the lawn — a squad from Buckhannon, along with state police. Nestor advanced on the Winnebago, gun in his left hand, his right arm hanging. Moss followed. Nestor crept up alongside, yanked open the door. Moss saw blood. She climbed the step into the Winnebago. Blood spattered the floor, the kitchenette. Nestor followed inside, moving past the kitchenette to the sleeping cabin. The side of the Winnebago had been perforated with bullets, and light from the barn streamed in through the holes. The gunman had collapsed onto the foam bed, shirtless, bloody. A tattoo on his chest, a golden eagle, wings outspread. *Jared Bietak,* she realized. Blood gurgled from the man's mouth and sucked from the wounds in his chest as he tried to breathe.

"Apply pressure," said Moss. She found a blanket and pressed it to the man's chest, but she knew he would die. The man coughed out a gulp of blood. Too slippery — she wiped the blood off Bietak's chest with the blanket and tried to reapply pressure but felt his body go still.

"We need to check the barn," said Moss, giving up on him. "Marian's here, or was here."

The barn doors were padlocked and chained. One of the state officers pulled bolt cutters from his trunk, snapped the chain, slid open the doors. Enough light from the floodlights to see a lemon-yellow Ryder truck — *rusted out years from now, abandoned in the field, the turning point on our walks together.* Nestor followed into the barn, said, "What is all this?" Someone found the lights, revealing a series of tubes that ran the length of the rafters, illuminating stainless-steel drums and plastic barrels, glass equipment, flasks and beakers. The place looked like a methamphetamine lab.

"Everybody out," said Nestor. "Move."

"No, I need bolt cutters," said Moss.

She cut the lock on the Ryder's rear doors, swung them open, and a wave of rot rolled over her. She fought her rising vomit but heard a county cop retch. A heap of bodies had wasted away in the back of the Ryder truck, their eyes covered in weeping sores, their skin burned — their flesh raw and red where it was still flesh, their mouths nearly sealed shut by blisters and screaming red wounds.

"Oh, God," said Moss. "My God, my God —"

She saw the girl. Moss started to climb into the truck, but Nestor grabbed her shoulders, held her back.

"Get off me," she said.

"Chemicals," said Nestor. "You can't breathe this."

The girl was in the heap. Her head was so thoroughly burned that she had lost all but a few clumps of her raven hair. Her teeth were exposed through gashes in her cheeks. Only a few white patches of her body had the soft smoothness of a young girl's body, the rest wrinkled and ridged with scar tis- sue and wounds, covered in so many maggots it looked as if someone had dumped rice over her. *Marian. Marian. Marian.*

"Find a blanket," Moss cried to Nestor. "We need an ambulance, please. Please call an ambulance."

"This place is a gas chamber," said Nestor. "Get outside."

She buried her head into his chest and wept and let him lead her from the barn. The lawn was alive with siren light, the hectic business of police flooding the scene, but a hush had descended over the rumors of what was inside.

"The dead outnumber the living," Nestor said. "My father used to say. But my father told me about the new bodies we all receive at the end of days, bodies robed in light. What a glorious thought, to be reborn in God. The dead will receive new bodies."

Moss separated from him. No one should see her being coddled, not here — she didn't want these officers to see the only woman on scene being coddled by a man. Moss wiped her eyes.

"Do you believe in the resurrection of the body?" Nestor asked. "For that child's sake, please believe."

Moss imagined the entire history of the dead beneath the soil climbing up to claim the Grace of God and receive new bodies

308

made of light. She imagined the corpses in the Ryder truck receiving bodies unfettered by pain. Sirens and the sound of engines, two trucks pulled in to the field. New bodies made of light — naïve hopefulness, the dreams of children. She was touched on the hand, and she found Brock's brown eyes, eyes that had seen pain before but that still broke with sorrow, eyes that still longed for some kind of peace.

# Two

Another crime scene had twinned within her.

Cricketwood Court with her past, this house in Buckhannon with her future. *A false future,* she told herself.

*I failed her.* The failure was real, the finality of Marian's death was leaden, suffocating.

*Too late to save her, I was too late.*

She tarried on the front porch, alone, the expansive lawn a lake of darkness. *Do you believe in the resurrection of the body?* Nestor had asked. Across the shadowy lawn shone the garish interior of an ambulance. Moss watched as EMTs tended to Nestor. His right bicep had been torn in the firefight, the bullet passed through. They removed his shirt, revealed bruising across his sternum, purple welts where bullets had struck his vest, lumps swollen red at the edges. He would be taken to St. Joseph's, examined for internal bleeding.

*Nestor, why would you live here? Of all places.*

She studied his face in the ambulance light as he laughed with the paramedic who checked his bandages — so much younger now. This wasn't the same man she had known, this was only a shade of him, younger even than she was. And he was innocent now, innocent of whatever threads would one day stitch him to this place. She had confronted Nestor in the moments following their discovery of Marian — out near the pear tree, she'd asked if he knew this house, but no, Nestor had never been here, he'd never been to Buckhannon before.

*But you would have known about Marian then,* Moss thought, *when we were together.* All their nights together here, he would have known that Marian's blood was in the soil. Ill at her memories of him, humiliated. He had been beautiful then, their brief life together, serene, but it had come to this: six corpses in a Ryder truck.

Nestor's ambulance pulled from the property, and she watched its sirens spark red, recede. A trick she'd learned as a child: someone had told her she would never fold a sheet of paper more than eleven times, no matter how large the sheet. She'd tried wispy leaves of newsprint, giant rectangles, folding, but never past eleven, the last folds minuscule and difficult, the paper compressed into a small brick. The seams of her life were folding in on themselves, Nestor's house and the house where Marian had died, Courtney's house and the house where Marian's family had died, her emotions roiling and overwhelming, so she envisioned her life as those sheets of paper folding, as large as white sails folding, until her emotions compressed into a small brick without folds, diamond-hard in her heart.

A tense several hours followed the discovery of the mass killing, the forensic technicians and investigators anxious for access to the crime scene, the state and county medical examiners instructed to remain on hand and wait. There had been some initial confusion over what chemicals were inside the barn, stored in plastic drums, some questions, too, about the purpose of the lab equipment, so Brock had cleared the area as a precaution. On Brock's call Governor Underwood requested the assistance of the nearest bomb squad, the West Virginia Army National Guard's 753rd Ordnance Company. Lockdown while guardsmen in padded armor worked the barn, their line of swamp-green trucks edging 151, idling engines, diesel fumes.

The house was accessible, the basement taped off, the stains marked. Miss Ashleigh owned this place, purchased ten years ago. She had lived here while prisoners languished in the basement. Had she fed them, kept them clean? Moss recognized Miss Ashleigh's touches throughout the place: varicolored glass decorating the windowsills, the dinner plates in the sink — Moss had used those plates years from now. The painting of the dead Christ was an oddity. Agents cataloged the Nazi artifacts in the bedroom — firearms, bayonets, service patches, flags in glass cases. In the future Nestor had told her these guns were his father's — a lie. The service patches reminded her of what she might find here, in a house where Jared Bietak and Charles Cobb spent time, and so she opened closets and drawers, sifted through boxes she found beneath the bed, hoping to find evidence of *Libra,* a flight patch or the album of photographs she'd seen in the house at the orchard. She came up with old shoes and costume jewelry, bills, receipts, medical records. There was nothing.

Dawn broke. Fog hung knee-level over the grass, the surrounding landscape looked flooded with watery milk. A search-and-rescue team had arrived from Charleston, the handler of a cadaver dog swept through the property, out in the side yard, where the ground was furrowed with mounds and would one day be covered with wildflowers. A clamor of emergency when the dog stood immobile, staring. Men with shovels, eventually a backhoe, uncovered the remains of twenty-two people, their skin liquefied with lye. They had been killed in the Ryder truck, they had been buried beneath the mounds in the yard. Brock found Moss watching the dig. He wore his exhaustion openly, just like the first time she'd seen him, at the house on Cricketwood, crossing steel risers over blood — he was washed out, his eyes weary, but he wasn't a broken man, not like the version Moss had known in the future. Brock was the center here, the calm. The forensic techs and Buckhannon cops and the National Guard in their bulky green seemed to swirl around him like ghosts in the early-morning vapor.

"Shannon, you stuck your finger in a hornet's nest," he said.

"Did they finish with the barn? What is it?"

"Chemical weapons," said Brock. "No, they haven't finished. They'll be at this all day. Blasting caps, C-4. And the chemicals."

"What are we talking about, Brock?"

"Sarin, mustard gas, all in small batches. Ricin. They found Ebola," said Brock. "Our guess is they were making small doses of various agents, testing their lethality in that truck, the Ryder truck. Maybe testing dispersal methods to see what would reliably deliver a lethal dose."

"Testing on a seventeen-year-old girl," said Moss. "Jesus Christ."

"Copycatting the Japanese subway cult from a couple years back," said Brock. "In the production of sarin at least. We have people coming in who worked with Tokyo during that investigation. They want to take a look at what we've found."

Sarin released in the Tokyo subway system, Moss remembered images on the news. The sarin had been liquid, stored in plastic bags the cultists had tossed to the subway floor and punctured with umbrella tips, gas seeping into the air.

"I'm taking a team with me out to the Blackwater, where we found the cairns," said Brock. "I'll bring the K9 unit with me, the cadaver dog, search a wider area. I'll need to know how you knew about this place, Shannon. I'll need everything you know."

"I want to help you," said Moss. Towers

315

of stones marking the wilderness. She'd thought the cairns marked the location of Marian's body, where she had been dumped — but Marian was here. What did the cairns mark? Other victims? Six in the Ryder, three at Cricketwood, Fleece in the mirrored room and Mursult at the Blackwater . . . bodies in the side-yard mounds, a swelling atrocity like discovering a rush of worms in a dead dog's heart. "I'll tell you what I can, but I'm still catching up with all this."

"Come with me. I want your take on something."

A haunted image, the Winnebago emerging from the milky mist. She remembered where she had recognized the Winnebago; she had noticed it at Miss Ashleigh's, dust-caked in the orchard barn. "Three hundred rounds, a conservative guess," said Brock, guiding her inside. The Winnebago's entire wall was shredded where the barrage of bullets had pierced it. "He was only hit four times. You can ID him?"

"Yeah, I can," said Moss, approaching the corpse in the sleeping cabin through the galley kitchenette. "His name's Jared Bietak."

"One of yours?"

"Navy," she said. "NSC, just like Mursult." Bietak's body was a waxy presence, cooling, not yet cold. Nicole had once confessed that Jared Bietak's tattoo had impressed her; to Moss it looked like the logo of a Pontiac firebird. There was another tattoo, script: NOVUS ORDO SECLORUM, a new order of the ages. Moss thought of the days of the dying earth, when pyramids would wander for water, but she thought, too, of this age, of the paranoiacs who believed in the imminence of the New World Order, a world government as enslavers of mankind. Two bullet wounds on his chest, another through his neck, she couldn't find the fourth. Jared Bietak's blood filled the foam bed cushion. His eyes were half closed. The West Virginia state medical examiner would perform a forensic autopsy on him, and Moss wondered if they would find evidence of the thyroid cancer that would have otherwise taken his life. "Jared Bietak is Nicole Onyongo's husband."

"She's gone," said Brock. "I sent a team to her apartment, on your request. She hasn't shown up to work either."

"Gone," said Moss, remembering Nicole's eyes glassy, her manhattan, the smoke of two Parliaments rising to the ceiling. But then, she might appear before too long. Nicole had continued working at the Donnell House in her IFT, had become a regular at the May'rz Inn. But the chemical weapons hadn't been discovered in that timeline; who knows what that would change? "All right, keep looking for her," said Moss, fearing how radically the future might already have changed from her experience of it. "We need to find her."

"Come over here," said Brock. "I want you to take a look at these."

They wore blue nitrile gloves to study the sheaves of documents Brock had recovered from an unlocked safe in the front of the Winnebago. They sat together at the dinette table, Brock spreading out maps and sets of blueprints. The Red Line of the D.C. Metro, the Capitol Building, detailed notes on the Senate chamber.

"And this," said Brock, unrolling schematics of NSC launch pads in Kodiak, Alaska. There were others: the Air Force Space Division headquarters in Colorado Springs, the Naval Space Command headquarters in Dahlgren. There was information about Cape Canaveral, the military floor at the Johnson Space Center in Houston. Maps of their ventilation systems, security profiles. Brock showed her similar information about the United Nations General Assembly in New York, but it was the blueprints of the FBI CJIS facility that chilled her. On some level she knew. On some level, throughout the hours of waiting here, as rumors stirred about what had been discovered in the barn, the contiguous pieces of her investigation started to meld. Moss absorbed the rich irony of Brock's having discovered these plans — that he was preventing the attack on CJIS that one day would have destroyed his wife and daughters.

"They're a terrorist militia," said Moss. "Ex-military."

"And these are the targets?" asked Brock.

"Yes," she said, "or potential targets." These other locations hadn't been attacked in the IFT she'd traveled to, but she wondered if other IFTs would have played out differently; she wondered about the cataclysms that might have been, or still might be. The enormity of her mistake rushed into her like water rushing into a gap: she had hurried to this house, heartbroken at the doubling of Buckhannon, hurried here in a mania to try to save the girl, but she shouldn't have. She should have been methodical, should have called O'Connor, should have waited. Jared Bietak had been here, Cobb had been here — who else would they have found if she'd waited? Now Bietak was dead and Cobb and Miss Ashleigh had scattered, seeds to the wind. She had lost touch with the greater mission.

"White supremacists?" asked Brock. "The Nazi paraphernalia in the bedroom here."

"No, I don't think so, not primarily," said Moss, trying to recover, to see past those missed chances. "Antigovernment for certain. Karl Hyldekrugger. He acquired blueprints for CJIS two years ago, sold by a member of the Mountaineer Militia shortly before your people arrested him."

"We'll try to track these chemicals, try to track the sale of the equipment," said Brock. "I'll run Hyldekrugger's name by our domestic-terror people, see what they can come up with. We've learned a lot since McVeigh."

Moss remembered the name of the CJIS suicide bomber, memorized from books that would never be written: *Ryan Wrigley Torgersen.* He worked at CJIS, would have reported to work with explosives sewn into his body. There were constitutional protections against pre-crime, Fourth Amendment applications that complicated NCIS investigations. She would have to talk with O'Connor, apply for special warrants through the military courts to arrest this individual.

"Alert your colleagues at CJIS immediately," said Moss. "I think the discovery of these blueprints is enough to suggest you search the ventilation system and the fire-suppression system. I doubt you'll find anything. But they should increase security, they should consider CJIS an active target. There is an individual to consider a person of interest, a potential bomber. He's an FBI employee, Ryan Wrigley Torgersen."

"Torgersen, I know him," said Brock. "I've met him. He works in my wife's department at CJIS. Are you sure? He's meek, Shannon. Torgersen . . . I'll ask for surveillance, see what we can dig up about him."

The National Guard allowed access to the barn much later that afternoon. They had rendered safe the recovered chemicals, had eliminated the threat of explosives. The medical examiner of Upshur County had been waiting on site since the bodies were first discovered. He was a young man, a skinny doctor who wore a shirt and tie and a cowboy hat the color of calfskin that he removed and held reverently as he approached the barn doors. He'd been told there were a number of bodies, and he'd brought three men with him, older men who seemed more like ranch hands than medical techs. They wore protective suits, a precaution against chemicals that might still be trapped in the victims' hair or might escape from the cavities of their bodies.

Moss stood at a distance, examining the

Ryder. A hole had been drilled through the passenger side of the cargo space, and a rubber tube dangled from the hole. A mobile gas chamber. The barn itself was equipped with a ventilation system and safety showers, protective suits in lockers. Moss imagined Jared Bietak and Charles Cobb in these yellow suits dispersing poison gas or acid or disease into the back of the truck, measuring their victims' suffering.

They would have moved Marian from the basement in the middle of the night, the barn floodlight disconnected, the house lights off. She would have been bound, gagged, and no one would have heard her anyway, not out here. A favorable wind might have carried her screams — but only so far.

*This is how my life will end,* Marian would have thought. *In the back of a Ryder truck, gagging on the stink of the previous dead.* She might have realized she smelled her own death. She might have scratched at the walls of the truck, she might have been senseless with terror — Moss imagined Marian weeping for mercy. She would have heard the purring of an engine or the whir of a box fan pushing gas through the rubber hose. Marian's photograph had anchored Moss to terra firma those nights when she felt adrift in her IFT. *Life is greater than time,* she had written. A false hope.

The Upshur ME and his men wearing hazmat suits laid out plastic sheets, gingerly removed each body from the truck. Four males, two females — one of them Marian. All were naked, all significantly damaged by chemical or acid burns, most of the bodies bloated and glossy, facial features distorted or altogether missing. Some of the bodies fell apart like jelly in their hands.

KDKA News: Marian's picture cycling with helicopter shots of the house and barn, maps of Buckhannon, interviews with neighbors, sound bites from Brock. Mug shots of Ashleigh Bietak and the man she had fled with, Richard Harrier, captured hiding beneath the front porch of a property three miles down 151. Harrier a Home Depot cashier, shots of the Home Depot in Bridgeport. Blanket coverage of sarin gas, reprising coverage of the Aum Shinrikyo subway attacks, of Oklahoma City, and soon the house on Cricketwood Court had become a shrine to the slain family. At first just a few bouquets wrapped in green tissue and cellophane, pops of color left on the front stoop, but within a few days the stoop was mounded with flowers, framed photographs, white crosses. Moss sat in her truck and watched as people arrived and departed from the makeshift memorial, remorseful that no memorial like this had been made for Courtney, a personal regret that she had never laid flowers here. Later that evening Moss returned and added her own bouquet, a burst of roses.

She worked the phones late that afternoon, tracking down the owners of the apple orchard where Miss Ashleigh had lived years from now, where she had hosted the memorial for Jared Bietak. Moss remembered Nicole mentioning that the place used to be owned by ceramicists and soon found that the property was still owned by Ned and Mary Stent, the proprietors of the Pot and Kettle. She tracked Ned Stent to an art fair in Atlanta, Ned speaking with her from his hotel room, explaining the differences between earthenware and raku, describing the ceramics classes they offered at their orchard, the dimensions of their kiln. No, they'd never met anyone named Ashleigh Bietak, had never met Jared Bietak, and no, they weren't planning on selling their property. "Not for a few years as of yet, at least."

■ ■ ■ ■

There was no viewing of the Mursult family's bodies, though their five caskets were established in separate rooms of the Salandra funeral home on West Pike for a gathering of friends and family before the funeral Mass across the street at St. Patrick's. So many children had come to grieve. High-school and middle-school children in their nice clothes, their church clothes, outfits that would double as Easter clothes in the next few weeks. Posters covered with the Mursult family's pictures leaned on easels next to their caskets. Moss touched the lacquered wood of Marian's coffin. She stood with her head bowed, falsifying prayer for the sake of the other mourners in line to pay their respects.

At the funeral Mass, Moss sat alone in the back pew while the priest blessed each of the five caskets, as the faithful took Communion and prayed. St. Patrick's was Moss's childhood church. She'd been raised Catholic, had memories of Sunday school here, remembered her Communion dress, the taste of the Eucharist. St. Pat's wasn't a stone colossus like the older churches of Pittsburgh, but rather a contemporary remodel, with ocher walls and cobalt trim, stained-glass windows of pink, green, and yellow squares. The altarpiece was a brash design of crimson and gold diamonds. The sculpture of the Crucifixion above the altar held Moss's attention through the service, a crucifix bathed in color cast by the sunlit stained glass. Christ seemed to levitate above the altar, as if the arms of the cross were wings — if it weren't for the pins at his ankles and wrists, she imagined he might simply float away.

Suffocating, the agonized sound of children crying, the unbearable sorrow. Moss left the service before it had concluded — a familiar release she remembered, escaping church. News vans had set up across the street, parked where they could capture establishing shots of the funeral home, the church, probably hoping for shots of children leaving in tears.

Chilly air but warm in the sun. She walked West Pike, to clear her head. She crossed the tracks and the busier intersection at Morganza. The parking lot of the Pizza Hut was full, families eating lunch together. A ridiculous place to mourn, between the blue dumpsters, but this is where Courtney had died, this is where Moss had found her friend's body. One of the dumpsters had been replaced in the past several years, but the other looked like it could have been left over from 1985, nearly twelve years ago. Moss leaned against the brick wall, remembering — and she cried for Courtney, for Marian, for Marian's family, for her own. She remembered her father in dim flashes, how he would lift her from bed, how he would lift her and spin, wintergreen on his breath and pipe smoke in his hair. She cried for every lost thing, everything gone. Chartiers Creek ran behind the Pizza Hut, a narrow trickle of water bounded on either side by weeds. Moss sat on the bench of a picnic table that the Pizza Hut kids used on their smoke breaks. She watched the murky water. Trash littered the muddy banks. Peaceful, in its way — she felt removed from Canonsburg, the noise of traffic just a background of white noise. Sunlight hit the water like a speckle of silver fire, glorious. But Moss resented the thought. This place wasn't beautiful — it was the end of everything.

Her cell phone rang, the sound startling her. She let it ring. A few moments of silence before it started ringing again. She checked the number: BROCK.

"Hello?" she said.

"Moss," he said, his voice cracking with

enthusiasm, ecstatic. "Moss, is that you?"

"I was at their funeral," she said. "Marian and —"

"Shannon, I have wonderful news," he said, overcome by emotion, ebullient. "I don't understand this, or how it happened, Shannon, but I have truly wonderful news. We found her."

Moss didn't answer, only tried to puzzle out his meaning. *We found her.* Trees grew like a canopy over the water. Their leaves dappled the muddy banks and swept into the creek. She watched the leaves clot in an eddy before disappearing beneath the shadows of a corrugated-steel tube that took the creek underground.

"We found her," said Brock. "She's alive. We found her in the woods, but she's alive, Shannon. We found her."

"Who?" said Moss.

"Marian," said Brock. "We found her. Marian's alive, Shannon. She's alive."

# THREE

*A mistake,* Moss's first thought. A misidentification.

But she had seen the body, had seen Marian in the back of the Ryder truck. The girl's aunt and uncle had identified her, had traveled from Ohio to the Office of the Chief Medical Examiner in Charleston to view the remains. Marian's aunt had stomached a fuller study, had inspected the cadaver and spotted the dimple scar on her interior left knee, a gymnastics injury, and the scar from her removed appendix. Without a doubt her sister's child.

Brock must have found some other seventeen-year-old, a similar but different girl . . .

*Marian,* Brock had said. *She's alive.*

A fuller search of the forest near the Blackwater Falls, where his men had spotted the cairns. They had fanned out through the forest at dawn, searching for other cairns, to figure out what the cairns might mark, when one of his men shouted. A frail body, pale and bluish, hair the color of the soil. Clothes stiff with frost, no shoes. She was found in the channel of a dried-up creek. Her skin was wet, her hair was damp and frozen. A resemblance to Marian, Brock had thought. Brock put his palm to her neck, and the skin was cold, but he felt her pulse . . .

*What would have happened had Brock never found her?* Moss wondered. *She would have died,* she thought. *She would have been in the forest for years, her body in that dried-up creek, decomposing, until men digging for ginseng spotted red berries and started to dig.*

"She's traumatized," said Brock as Moss was shown into Preston Memorial's boardroom. Unadorned walls, a blond-wood conference table. He chewed his licorice, pulverizing the gum.

"Talk me through this," said Moss.

"Either we . . . we buried the wrong girl or we're making a mistake now," he said. "I was staggered by the resemblance. I thought that maybe I was deceiving myself. I thought she must be someone else, but she told me her name —"

"She's conscious?" asked Moss.

"She's weak."

"Who else knows about her?" Moss asked.

"Lockwood, the CEO here," said Brock. "A small team providing care. Nurses, Dr. Schroeder. My men, there were six of us. My supervisor. They know we found a young woman."

"You haven't called her relatives?"

"No."

"And you talked with Marian?" she asked.

"Shannon, she's identical. She's the *same,* but nothing makes sense," said Brock. "She says they killed the wrong person. She's terrified. The remains we found, they were marred by chemicals. When her aunt identified the body, she was expecting Marian, and so maybe she convinced herself that body was Marian. I think we should test this girl, compare DNA with the corpse."

*Echoing,* Moss thought. Someone would have had to travel to an IFT, would have had to find a future Marian and bring her here to terra firma. That didn't seem likely, but it was the only way she knew.

"What does she say happened?" she asked.

"Fleece is the one who took her," said Brock. "Elric Fleece picked her up from the Kmart. She knew him."

The name withered in Moss's ear. Fleece, a sailor on *Libra,* the suicide in the mirrored

331

room. Marian had known him, a friend of her father's.

"Has anyone told Marian about her family?"

"She knows," said Brock. "She's been watching TV."

Preston Memorial's shift supervisor, Dr. Schroeder, was heavily made up, her hair a silver sweep. An elegant woman who spoke with a southern softness, her heels clacking like a quick-tempo metronome.

"Cold and wet. She says she swam through a river. Extreme hypothermia when we brought her in. I'll be honest, I wasn't very hopeful, but she's doing well now, all things considered. Her feet worry me. The flesh was severely damaged. The poor thing didn't have any shoes, and it's been cold these past few nights. She hasn't been able to walk much without pain, though she can make it to the bathroom and back."

Moss's breath caught. "Will she keep her feet?"

"We're not out of the woods," said Dr. Schroeder. "No gangrene, though. She's responding very well. Whatever happened to her out there — she hasn't gone into much detail, which is common with people who've been through trauma. She's very confused, I think. Hypothermia can affect memory, so you'll have to be patient with her."

Brock had posted sentries outside Marian's room, someone from the hospital security staff and an FBI agent whose face Moss recognized from the other night in Buckhannon. They nodded a greeting to each other.

"She should be awake," said Dr. Schroeder. "Her core temperature was low, so she's been sluggish."

"I'd like to speak with her alone," said Moss. "Can I find you once we've had a chance to talk a little?"

"Yes, of course," said Dr. Schroeder. "I'll check back with your colleague, or I'll be in my office. Let me know if you need anything. And, of course, there's a call button on her bed if you need something from the nurse on duty."

Moss heard the television from within the room, a laugh track. Anxious to meet this young woman. Moss knocked.

"Come in."

Marian was sitting up in bed. She looked comfortable despite the tubes threading her arms to IV drips and the oxygen tube lacing her nostrils, the splay of wires monitoring her vitals. She was awake but wan, exhausted. Her hair was pulled back, accenting the oval cast of her face. Although Moss knew of echoes, she had rarely been in their company. She had thought of echoes as duplicates, but that wasn't true, she realized now — this young woman *was* Marian Mursult.

Marian turned toward Moss. "What's wrong with me? Everyone stares when they come in."

Bandages wrapped her wrists — from the exposure? Moss wondered. Or a suicide attempt? No one had mentioned anything. *Seinfeld* was on the ceiling-mounted television.

"Nothing's wrong with you," said Moss, aware of emoting the same scrabble of uncertainty that annoyed her so often when people first noticed her prosthesis. "Are you Marian?" she asked, guilty again of pretending nothing was wrong. "I'm Shannon. I'm with an agency called the Naval Criminal Investigative Service. Can I talk with you about what's happened?"

"I don't remember everything," said Marian.

"That's understandable," said Moss. "Do you mind if I have a seat?"

There was only one chair, already beside the bed. The heart monitor's sonorous tones and the hushed sounds of machines Moss didn't recognize made the room feel fragile. She had been at Marian's funeral earlier that morning, had watched a priest bless her closed casket with holy water.

"I know you've already told your story to some others," said Moss. "My colleague, William Brock. You might be wondering why we don't just talk to each other, why I'm going to ask you to tell me what you've already told him."

Moss noticed that Marian was shaking. Cold? Terror at her memories?

"Are you all right?" she asked.

"I don't know," said Marian.

Moss used the call button, and a moment later a nurse checked on her, helped lift Marian's blankets to her shoulders without disturbing her tubes or wires. Marian asked for a cup of tea, and the nurse returned with a plastic pot of hot water and a few Lipton tea bags.

"I'm all right, and I understand," said Marian. "I don't think that man, Brock — I don't think he believed me. So you want to hear for yourself, right?"

"It's not a question of believing you," said Moss. "But I'd like to hear from you. I don't want to hear your story from someone else."

"I saw myself, did he tell you that? I saw myself out in the woods," said Marian. "I think they wanted to kill me, but they killed her instead."

A surprising sense of recognition. *I saw myself out in the woods.* Sideways-winding snow, the woman in the orange space suit reaching to her. "I believe you," said Moss. "Tell me everything. How did you get out there?"

"My dad has a friend, this guy named Fleece," said Marian. "A war buddy. Dad took care of him, like he couldn't take care of himself, there was something wrong with him, he was . . . I think his brain was injured. They went riding together, motorcycles. He met me after my shift, told me I was supposed to go with him, that something had happened to my family."

"Why didn't you drive?" asked Moss. "You left your car in the parking lot."

"He told me something terrible happened, said I shouldn't be driving when I found out. I was so scared —"

A hitch in her breath. Moss took the girl's hand in hers. "It's all right if you need to cry," she said. "Take a minute, it's all right."

"Did he kill my mom? Is my family dead, is that true? Why?"

Moss held her hand, "I'm so sorry," she said. "I don't know why this happened. I want to find out why." She wanted to comfort Marian but knew Marian would never truly recover from these deaths. "Tell me about Fleece. Where did he take you?"

"He wouldn't tell me what happened. He said he was taking me home," said Marian. "But he was going a different way, and when I asked him where he was taking me, he pulled over, tied my wrists. He put me in the back of his truck."

"He tied you up back there?"

"Tied my wrists with twine," she said. "I was gagged. I can't . . . This is . . . Things don't make sense."

"I believe you," said Moss. "I need to hear what happened to you."

"That man from the FBI, who was here before you — he didn't believe me. He kept trying to catch me in a lie, asking me all sorts of questions, the same questions again and again, but I'm not lying, I swear to you. I swear to God I'm not lying. I'm just confused."

"Marian, where did Fleece take you?"

"There was a place my dad used to take me to," said Marian. "Family vacations, but back when my sister and brother were too small, my dad just took me. He called it our Vardogger. Just some made-up word, I guess. Like Never-Never Land."

"Vardogger," said Moss. "Where's the

Vardogger?"

"I was just a kid, I don't know. We were in the woods, but there was this lodge where he'd meet with his friends, sometimes their families too. Pine trees that Dad called hemlocks. There was a river. He liked to fish. A waterfall. All sorts of caves, crevices in the rocks I could squeeze into and hide out."

"Was it the Blackwater Lodge?" asked Moss.

"I think so, maybe," said Marian. "He hasn't taken us for years, though. We'd go there, and I loved it because sometimes I thought that the mirror in the lodge would come to life. Sometimes I'd see myself at the river in the woods and think it was the mirror girl. My reflection, following me. You know, like Peter Pan and his shadow? I only saw the mirror girl a few times, standing across the river. My dad told me she wasn't real, that she was just my imaginary friend, just a daydream because I was a bored kid with no friends around."

"And that's where Fleece took you?" asked Moss. "To that lodge?"

"Not that lodge, but it was the same place, those woods," said Marian. "I don't know how long we drove. The ride rattled me, and I got hurt. It seemed like forever, but when we stopped and he opened the rear door, I could see it was still dark and still a long way off from morning. Fleece pulled me from the truck, pushed me deeper into the woods. He said 'I'm sorry' over and over, telling me that he wanted to keep me safe, but that it was too late and he had to do what they told him to do. He said my family would be dead in a day, but he didn't want me to die, so we should just do what they say."

"Who?" asked Moss.

"I don't know. Voices?" said Marian. "He was scared. I could tell he was terrified of something, and then he threw me to the ground, all of a sudden, and that's when I recognized where I was. He'd taken me to the Vardogger."

"How could you tell?" asked Moss. "This was the middle of the night, out in the woods —"

"Because there's a tree that marks the Vardogger, this old dead tree that looks like a skeleton. It's all white, with no leaves. The Vardogger tree. And I heard the river I remembered as a kid, right there past the tree."

*The Vardogger tree* — Moss knew the tree. When she was lost in the woods, Moss had seen the tree repeating, Fleece's tree, the tree of bones in the mirrored room. Marian's father called it the Vardogger; Patrick Mursult had known this place.

"I said to him, 'Christ have mercy on your soul,' and he told me he was going to show me the end of time," said Marian. "I was scared of him and didn't know what he was talking about. He told me that things were knotted up all around us."

"A place near the Red Run?" asked Moss. "A river, a clearing surrounded by pines."

"He took me past the Vardogger tree, and we stepped out into that clearing, saw the river in front of us. We were in some other place in the woods, there were other trees — other Vardogger trees, a lot of them, in a line. He was pulling me along — we crossed the river over a fallen tree, and the weather turned to ice. That can't be real, can it? On the far side, our feet sank into the mud, and the sky was ridged like I was looking at the roof of a mouth, and we saw ourselves reflected outward, like I was looking at myself through a kaleidoscope — over and over and over, all around me. I couldn't look anymore and started to pray, but he said he wanted to show me God, and he lifted my head to the sky, and I thought I saw Jesus on the cross appearing over the river, but the cross was upside down and his mouth was bloody and, oh, God, oh, my God, the body had no skin . . ."

Moss wanted to scream, but for Marian's sake she crossed the room to collect herself. She looked out the window but saw her reflection in the glass. *Marian had seen the Terminus. She had seen the hanged men.*

"Fleece told me he had to tie me up again," said Marian. "He took me back to the Vardogger tree and pushed me down. He pushed me against the tree and tied my wrists around the trunk. He said that someone would come for me, to take me somewhere else. I asked him where they would take me, but he said he didn't know, that he wasn't allowed to know. He said, 'I'm damaged, so I'm not allowed to know.' And then he just left me there, out in the middle of the woods. It was so quiet. Everything was silence."

"How long were you out there, tied up like that?" asked Moss.

"I don't know," said Marian. "Not long. Not even an hour. When I knew he was gone, I pulled at the twine and felt it give a little at my wrists, like it had a little play. It took me a while, but I was able to pull my hands free."

She held up her wrists, showed the bandages. "Bloodied myself up pretty bad," she said.

"But you were free," said Moss.

"Yeah," said Marian. "I was freezing, my hair and clothes were wet, because it had rained. I didn't know where I was, but I remembered the lodge my dad used to take me to, figured it must be close. I thought I could find it."

"You knew where you were?"

"I thought I was on the wrong side of the river from the lodge. I couldn't find that tree we'd used to cross the river, but I knew I could wade across, or swim if it was too deep, so I stepped in," said Marian. "It felt like ice, the water was so cold, and there were rapids there. The water came up to my neck, but I could walk. I lost my footing, and it swept me down, but I came to the far side and crawled out. I'd never been so cold. I crossed this little meadow. I couldn't even feel my toes in the mud because I was so numb."

"You're lucky you didn't die," said Moss.

"I could hardly walk, because I couldn't feel where my feet were beneath me, but everything still seemed the same, like I had wandered in a big circle. Then I realized that I'd somehow come back to where I'd started from, still on the wrong side of the river. I came to softer mud that had been chewed up by truck tires — from Fleece's truck, I thought. I could see where the tires had scooped out the mud. I ran back through the trees, and that's when I saw her."

"Who?" asked Moss.

"The mirror girl," said Marian. "I saw the yellow of her shirt at first, just like mine, and then I realized I was looking at someone tied to a tree, just like I'd been, the same white tree. I came closer and saw her hair hanging, wet. I circled the tree to come up on her from the front, so I wouldn't scare her, and when she saw me, she said, 'I remember you,' and I told her, 'I remember you, too.' "

"You were children the last time you saw each other," said Moss.

"I wanted to help her get free, and so I told her to pull out her wrists like I had done, and she pulled but couldn't get free. I tried to help her, but she wasn't tied up with twine — her wrists were tied up with wire. Her hands and arms were bloody, they were real bad. She'd been trying to pull free but couldn't do it, and the wire wouldn't break. It wasn't loose at all. I tried to help but caused her so much pain when I pulled. I didn't know what to do. So I stayed a little while with her."

"You had to leave her," said Moss.

"I was worse off than she was because of the river," said Marian. "I was so cold. I was turning to ice. I was wet, shivering so much. She told me to get help. She told me she'd be all right, that her dad would be coming for her, that her dad would know where to find her."

"And so you tried to find help."

"I don't remember what happened after I left her. I thought I was dying. My memory's just gone. I just woke up here, in the hospital. She might still be out there. She's still out there."

"We'll find her," said Moss, thinking, *One Marian here, another in the Ryder truck.* "Marian, why would someone want to attack your family?" she asked. "Can you think of anyone who would want to do this to you, and why? Anyone that was upset with your dad?"

"It's sick," she said. "I don't know who would do something like this."

"Any old Navy buddies? Anything like that?" she asked, already knowing who might have killed her father, Hyldekrugger, Cobb, but wanting to hear Marian say the names. Victims of violent crimes often knew who the perpetrators were and why the crimes had occurred. "Had your father been in touch with anyone?"

"You have to understand that my dad was different," said Marian. "He had thoughts that intruded on him. He said he was recruited for some Navy program. Mom never liked him to talk about this stuff with us, but he couldn't help it sometimes, like it all just came rushing out of him. He said . . . he told my mom that the Navy had recruited him to build a ship made of fingernails, I know that sounds crazy, like I'm not remembering right, but that's the way it was. He said the ship will sail carrying the bodies of the dead."

"What does that mean, Marian?"

"I don't know. My dad spent a lot of time away from home," said Marian. "He spent time with his friend Fleece. They'd drink together. And his lawyer, he saw her a lot."

"Who was his lawyer? Why did he need a lawyer?" asked Moss.

"I just heard my parents talking a few times after I'd gone to bed," she said. "He was drawing up contracts for something. Needed a lawyer's help. My mom asked if the lawyer would be able to help with our move, but my dad didn't want to drag her into everything."

"You were moving?" asked Moss. "Do you know why?"

"I wanted to finish high school to graduate with my friends, but she said we were leaving, just as soon as my dad was ready. Mom didn't know when that would be, maybe after graduation or maybe next week. They wouldn't even tell me where we were moving, but I heard them talk about Arizona a few times."

"Think of everyone that your father spent time with," said Moss. "Is there anybody that I should know about? You mentioned a family lawyer. Do you think your dad's lawyer is involved somehow?"

Marian furrowed her eyebrows. She said, "I don't think so, I can't think of why. Although there was something —" But she stopped herself.

"Let me know," said Moss. "It doesn't matter if you're wrong or right, but I want you to fill me in so I can follow up on everything."

"My dad was cheating on my mom," said Marian. "I don't think she knew, but I figured it out, figured out something was going on. I heard him on the phone this one time."

*Nicole.* "Do you know who he had a relationship with?" asked Moss, but Marian shook her head. "You heard him on the phone?"

"He was using a pager, always taking calls in private, and I knew what that meant, I had an idea," said Marian. "My mom must have looked past it, let herself be lied to. But there was this one morning a few weeks ago, I heard him fighting with someone on the phone. Someone was threatening him. I heard him say, 'Don't tell him,' and I thought he meant this woman's husband or boyfriend. 'I want to see you. Don't tell him, not yet,' and he hung up. Once he left the room, I hit Star 69, and a woman's voice answered. I just hung up."

"Who do you think this woman was going to tell? Someone your dad knew?"

"I guess so," said Marian. "Yeah, it sounded like he knew him."

"If I say someone's name, would you recognize it?"

"I can try."

"Charles Cobb?" asked Moss. "Jared Bietak?"

"I don't know," said Marian. "I don't think so."

"Karl Hyldekrugger?" asked Moss.

"Yes, my dad mentioned him," said Marian, her eyes haunted as if a ghost walked among them. "My dad was scared of that man. He used to talk about him sometimes. My dad called him the Devil. He sometimes said the Devil could eat people with his eyes."

Hospital corridors were unnerving spaces: blank corridors, turns, further corridors, fluorescent glare on glossy floors, innumerable doors. *What would have happened had we never found the Ryder truck?* Moss wondered. *Jared Bietak and Charles Cobb would have disposed of Marian's body — where? In the mass grave, in the mound at the house in Buckhannon. And* this *Marian? Hikers would have found her where she died in the woods.* Moss imagined this young woman's life, the bewildered grief and insomnia, the late-night television, cyclic news of friends mourning her death even though she was alive — Marian would be alone tonight, she would be alone every night for the rest of her life.

"What's going on, Shannon?" Brock asked when Moss had returned to the hospital boardroom. Moss closed the door behind her, poured herself a cup of coffee from the plastic decanter. Powdered cream, sugar, stirring with a red plastic straw. Fleece had taken Marian, had driven her to the woods. He had shown her the end of time, had tied her to the Vardogger tree. An echoing, one Marian tied with wire, the other Marian tied with twine. One Marian found dead in a

Ryder truck, the other Marian found alive.

"It's scary what they can — You see that lamb Dolly on the news and you think how terrifying it really is, the age we live in," said Brock. "Impossible things. That lamb should be an impossibility, but everyone just accepts it. We doubt the existence of miracles, but when they happen, we treat them like they happen every day. Clinton signed that ban just last week, I saw on the news. President Clinton banned human cloning, but I'm realizing now what's going on here —"

"That's not what's going on here," said Moss. "Let her sleep tonight, if she can sleep. But guard the room. Her life is still in danger, I think, if anyone learns that she's here. No one can talk about this, Brock — what we've seen. I think we should push for WITSEC if we can. At least we should move her from here, and soon."

Moss tarried after Brock left, alone in the half-light of the closed cafeteria with her thoughts, drinking coffee and eating vanilla Oreos from the vending machine until Dr. Schroeder informed her that Marian had finally accepted a sedative, had fallen asleep. There were three special agents who would spell one another through the night, guarding Marian's room. Before he left, Brock had told Moss he would broach the subject of witness protection with his supervisor, coordinate with NCIS and the U.S. Marshals. He would call Marian's aunt and uncle, he would figure out a way to tell them that one of the children they'd buried had lived.

Moss filled napkins with a blue ballpoint pen, at first just lines and shading until her thoughts untangled. *A place in the woods, the Vardogger,* she wrote, then wrote the word a second time, and wrote, *One with wire, one with twine.* Ten agents could travel to ten IFTs and report back different details from each. Existence was a matter of chance, of probability, as infinite futures became one observed present. Life and death often hung on details — in one existence Marian's wrists had been tied with wire, but in another her wrists had been tied with twine. *How had she echoed?* Moss wrote, *The mirror girl,* and lost herself in thought.

She shredded her notes and called O'Connor before she left the hospital — after midnight, but he was awake. He had seen the reports coming out of Buckhannon and had already spoken with his counterpart in the FBI, but the news concerning Marian's echoing stunned him, and by the end of their conversation, he'd promised that he and another special agent would arrive in Clarksburg by the following day.

"What's your next move?" he had asked.

"We have to find the Vardogger."

Nearing 1:00 a.m. when Moss left Preston Memorial, an hour's drive home. The country roads she drove were twisting paths obscured by trees, pitch-black, but occasionally the view ahead cleared and she saw the moon and fiery pinpoints of stars and the silver of Hale-Bopp, its streaking tail like flowing locks of a woman's hair.

She remembered the enclosing pines here, the canopy choking out light, but that had been with Nestor, years from now, when she'd been anxious over seeing the place where Marian's bones were found. This morning, though, the Canaan Mountain bore little resemblance to her memories of the place, the approach serene glades and sods, spruce, balsam fir, hemlock doused in buttery sunlight. Rangers had marked the access route with an orange ribbon. She came to the clearing where the incline leveled and found O'Connor's Subaru already nestled beneath an overhang of branches. Only a short hike from here. The path was cleaner than she remembered, after what would be twenty years of growth, when Nestor had pulled back branches for her, when he had stomped down weeds in her way. Much easier to find her footing now, a thin path simple to follow. She wore hiking boots this time, which helped, and made it to the dried runnel where just yesterday morning Brock had found Marian alive.

"Shannon, over here."

Two men, a little ways off. O'Connor had driven overnight from D.C. to meet Marian for himself and to see this place in the woods, the Vardogger. An avid outdoorsman, he looked like an Edwardian painting of a gentleman hunter this morning, with a walking stick and rubber galoshes that reached to his knees. Moss would have recognized O'Connor's partner by his height and bulk alone, she was sure, but otherwise the man bore little resemblance to the sage she had once met. Njoku was shaven bald, his beard a chiseled black strip. Golden hoops dangled from each of his earlobes. He smiled as O'Connor introduced him, was pleasantly bewildered when Moss said, "We were well met once before, Dr. Njoku."

"I asked Njoku to red-eye from Boston because of the developments with Marian," said O'Connor. "He has experience with echoes, and his work at MIT focuses on thin spaces."

"Collapsibility of Everett space and Brandt-Lomonaco space-time knots," said Njoku. "It's a pleasure to meet you, Shannon. Or I should say it's a pleasure to meet you again for the first time."

She was delighted to see this man with years peeled from him, but Moss remembered there was a woman whose fingers made beautiful sounds on saxophone keys. She remembered when Njoku was to have met this woman. "Wally, you should be in Boston right now," she said. "There is someone you were supposed to meet."

Doubt fluttered over his face, the shadow of a falling leaf, but soon he smiled. "There are many paths," he said.

O'Connor trudged ahead, pulling through long strides with his walking stick. Moss kept an easier pace with Njoku. *Have you ever seen a falling star as it blooms?* Easy to imagine Njoku lingering in a neighbor's garden, philosophizing over the beauty of flowers. He paused frequently here in the woods, allowing Moss to catch up with him, running his fingers over the flesh of a petal, or crouching low to inspect an insect or remark on a spider's funnel.

"Here's a cairn," said O'Connor, ahead.

The spot was marked by powdery orange spray paint, a cross on the ground that would wash away with the first rain. The cairn was what she imagined it would be, though more carefully constructed: it was a pyramidal stack of flat river stones, a foot and a half high. The cairn was balanced on a fallen log barnacled by plump fungus and carpeted with moss.

"The FBI found four so far," said O'Connor. "Two are on the far side of the river."

"I thought the cairns would have marked the location of Marian's body," said Moss. "I thought they would lead the way to the burial site."

"The cairns mark the location of Marian's Vardogger tree," said O'Connor.

"Look at this," said Njoku. He folded open a pocket notebook and showed Moss several pages of inky dots he'd connected with sketchy lines into various shapes, several-pointed stars. "The cairns are equidistant," he said. "If you imagine each cairn as a point . . ."

"We found a burnt tree at the center of the star," said O'Connor.

"I want to see it," she said.

Blueberry thickets, burs and thistles that clung to Moss's sock. A meadow strewn with flattop boulders. The rush of a river as they neared the Vardogger, a swift sound as if the forest whispered where she should walk.

"When O'Connor called about Marian, I thought her Vardogger might be something we call a 'thin space,' " said Njoku. "The Naval Research Lab calls them Brandt-Lomonaco space-time knots."

"I've heard that term before," said Moss. "We talked about them in training. B-L knots, the residue of quantum foam."

"You're exactly right. Residue, almost like pollution. The B-L drives affect space-time," said Njoku. "Knots are locations where an infinite-density singularity event breaks down effects of quantum gravity, allowing superposition. Wave-function collapse sometimes doesn't occur. Simultaneous Everett spaces —"

"Whoa, you're losing me," said Moss.

"Echoes," he said. "Here we are, here is the tree we found."

The husk of a pine, a stark white tower of ash surrounded by verdant evergreens. "Yes," said Moss, recognizing this ashen tree, "here we are." Lost in the Terminus when she had last seen this tree, she'd been confused by it then. It had seemed to repeat, recursively, like a mirror image of a mirror. She had searched for the tree in the years since but hadn't been able to find it and had grown to think of it as a mistake of memory, a hallucination — seeing it now was a relief, a confirmation. There was nothing fearsome about this place, however, not with Njoku here, and O'Connor, the noon sun almost too warm for her jacket.

Nothing fearsome, but still unnatural. The Vardogger was burnt, but not burned away. Moss had seen scorched woods before, the remains of forest fires, carpets of ash, charred trunks branchless and sooty like lines of spent matchsticks. The Vardogger looked preserved by fire rather than consumed. The trunk was barked with crackled ash so light gray it seemed luminous white, but when Moss touched the trunk, it felt more like petrified wood than seared wood. She touched the branches and was startled to find they felt as smooth and as brittle as glass.

She was nearer the rush of the river now. "I'll be back," she said, leaving Njoku and O'Connor at the Vardogger. She hurried toward the sound of water and came through the tree line, emerging onto an outcropping of boulders. The Red Run was a turbulent set of rapids before her, twisting drops, whitewater crashing through gaps in the jagged stones. Where the river was

356

calmer, the water was the color of tea, dyed by the tannin of the surrounding hemlocks. Moss recognized the future of this place. It was the winter of the Terminus then, and instead of the goldenrod and willows and bushes of flowering mountain laurel along the banks, there'd been pinions of ice that had seemed to impale her in the air. This is where she'd been crucified. Her reflection had been here, an echo. Moss glanced back toward the tree line, half expecting a woman in orange to reach for her, beseeching her, but there was no one.

"I've been here," said Moss, returning to Njoku and O'Connor. "This is the place where I had my accident," she said. "I'm sure of it. I saw another version of myself here. I saw my echo."

"Thin spaces are unpredictable, unstable. Sometimes they're inert, but sometimes they're spooky as hell," said Njoku. "Reflections, echoes, closed timelike curves."

"Wally's explanations sometimes assume a Ph.D.-level understanding of quantum mechanics," said O'Connor. "Maybe he can slow it down for us."

"I understand echoing," said Moss. "But this whole place should repeat," aware she wasn't sure exactly how to describe her experience with this place. This was the same white tree, the same area of pines, the same river as she remembered, she was sure of it, but it was off somehow, as if she were looking at a stage set of a place she remembered rather than the place itself. "It was like I could see a hundred of these trees, thousands, in every way I looked, in every direction. Like the world receded from me —"

But she was interrupted — by what first felt like the onset of a seizure or a stroke, some swift mental aberration, or a fault in her eyes as the forest changed around them. The pines were denser, the growth heavier. Njoku pushed through the branches, Moss and O'Connor following, and they came to the clearing, the Red Run — but they seemed to be on the wrong side of the river. The white Vardogger tree was visible on the far side rather than behind them.

"Over there," said Njoku. "We got turned around somehow. We have to cross."

Moss held him back. They trekked back the way they had come and passed the white tree. They tried to find the dry creek bed, to follow it back to their cars, but they were lost and passed the white tree again, Njoku chuckling in frustration. They broke through the surrounding pines and returned to the white tree.

After a moment the sensation passed. They were again in the recognizable woods near a single white tree, as though the denser pines and repeating woods had only been a trick of the eye.

Njoku's laughter was like the clarion pealing of a bell. "Like I said, spooky as hell!"

"Let's go, away from here," said O'Connor, leaning on his walking stick, dizzy or untrusting of the earth. "We shouldn't be here."

Closer to what she remembered of her experience with this place, the disorientation, the repetition, Moss was eager to distance herself from it, and she hurried on ahead, almost running, her heart pumping fear of this place. O'Connor and Njoku caught up only once she had reached the cairn on the soft log, the Vardogger no longer visible.

"It was like the moment when the B-L drive fires, as you travel to an IFT," said Moss, "that moment you think you can feel every possibility at once."

"Wally thinks a B-L drive made this place," said O'Connor. He was sweating, flushed.

"I think a B-L drive *might* have made this extraordinary place," said Njoku. "The tricky thing about Brandt-Lomonaco knots is that they exist *outside of time.* Almost a paradox! If we assume that a B-L drive created this thin space, the 'Vardogger,' then the B-L could have fired at any time, including at any time in the future or in the past. We think of time as set, but time is mutable, nonlinear. Imagine," he said, "you see a burnt tree, coated in ash."

Moss nodded.

"Now imagine that the forest fire that burned the tree won't happen for another three hundred years or three thousand — you see? Things like that can happen in a thin space, quantum tricks. Time is like water here, water that sometimes flows uphill. This thin space might be a consequence of an action that hasn't actually happened yet."

Nicole might have described this place, obliquely, Moss realized. She had described ghosts in the woods that preceded their bodies. *Marian,* thought Moss, *and another Marian.*

"I hear what you're saying, but I don't understand what this place is," said Moss.

"Not what this place is, but what this place might be," said Njoku.

"Are you all right?" she asked O'Connor, who sat on the log wiping his face with a handkerchief.

"I'm fine. It was just disorienting," he said. "I'll be all right."

"One Planck unit past *now* is the multiverse," said Njoku. "Quantum gravity is like a zipper, pulling all those possibilities together into one, single, truth: terra firma. The thin space is like a moment when the zipper gets stuck a little."

"How large is this thin space?" asked Moss. "Just the tree? Or do you think it's the entire forest?"

"I don't know! It's marvelous, but I can't even guess at the size," said Njoku. "Most B-L knots are only hypothetical shapes, more like math problems than geolocations that you can measure. There are only a very few B-L knots that have actually been observed on Earth, and this one is very, incredibly unique."

"These things are pretty rare, then," said Moss.

"Rare on Earth, but our launch sites at the Black Vale are riddled with them. That's one of the reasons NSC launches from space," said O'Connor.

"What's the other reason?" she asked.

Njoku laughed. "Oh! Well, you see," he said, "back in the early eighties, the Naval Research Lab published a report proving that a B-L drive could spark the creation of a massive black hole. Theoretically, anyway. Our ships sail black holes in the quantum foam, but if something went wrong, frankly, the moon base wouldn't be far enough away."

"You're kidding me," said Moss.

Njoku shrugged, smiling. "Math problems," he said.

"We tend not to mention that fact in our annual reports to Congress," said O'Connor. "I'm all right, we can keep going."

"Black holes, thin spaces," said Moss, grabbing O'Connor's hand, helping him up. "Where are the other thin spaces?"

"One in Los Alamos, three in the Pacific — all at early B-L drive test sites," said Njoku. "Most of these things only affect particles. The thin space out in the Pacific, though, that is an interesting one."

"Like this one?"

"Nothing is like this one," said Njoku. "The size of this one — we were *inside* this one. The space-time knot in the Pacific is considered very large, and that's only a few feet in volume. Not like the Vardogger by any stretch, but large enough to echo fish as they swim through."

"Echoed fish?" she asked.

"Pacific jack mackerel," said Njoku. "You

can catch a mackerel but still have it get away."

"The one that got away would always be bigger than the one you caught," said O'Connor.

"We've observed the Pacific thin space echoing fish, but it is also a 'Gödel curve' — that is, a specific kind of closed timelike curve," said Njoku. "It's a very odd part of the ocean."

"You mentioned that before. What is that?" asked Moss.

"A four-dimensional Lorentzian manifold, it . . . well, listen, if you watch that particular thin space long enough, you will actually see the moment all the original fish in the system 'reset' to their start positions at the beginning of the cycle. Closed timelike curves are the closest we've come to traveling backward in time."

"The fish repeat?" she asked. "You mean they're stuck in a loop?"

"Looping is a good way to think of it," said Njoku. "There are various types of closed timelike curves, ways information loops through wormholes, going forward in time but also backward, arriving at the moment it began. I've dipped my hand into the water, and when the water looped, it was like I held a fish *inside* my hand until it flopped and squirmed out, swimming away. It was a very strange sensation, slimy. You could cast your line into the water and catch the same fish over and over again."

"Or pick a piece of fruit and see it regrow the moment you pick it," said Moss, remembering Nicole smoking her Parliament, describing something like a Gödel curve when she had reminisced about her childhood home. When was she a child? Moss wondered. When were miracles like Gödel curves practicable, common on orchards in Kenya, put to use for agriculture? Nicole had never been hungry as a child, the fields never fallow.

"The Navy will want this place. I have to make arrangements," said O'Connor. "They'll need to fence this off, shut it down. The whole area. Let's get going."

The stones were smooth along the dried creek, polished from the water that used to flow here — Moss stepped stone to stone as she walked back, following Njoku and O'Connor. Easy to dig out the flat stones for cairns, she thought — they were everywhere. Who had marked this place? The FBI had spotted the driver of the black van here, Richard Harrier, and had trailed him to Buckhannon. But he wouldn't have been marking this place, she thought. It must have been the survivors of *Libra.* A B-L drive had made this place. She peered through the spaces between trees, wondering if she might see a ship here. Nothing but trees, and in the distance more trees.

"What was her name?" Njoku asked once they'd reached their cars.

"Whose name?" asked Moss.

"You said there was someone in Boston, you think I'm supposed to meet her."

"Jayla," she said. "Jayla, but I don't know her last name. She plays the saxophone."

Moss waited in her truck while O'Connor maneuvered his Subaru from the clearing, fluttering brake lights as he inched down the precipitous drop. She was worried about him; he'd looked pale as they'd said their good-byes. O'Connor would be heading back to D.C. by the afternoon, a several-hour drive. The Navy would occupy this place soon, the first contingent by nightfall, if not earlier. Njoku was flying out from Pittsburgh but would return in a few days with physicists from the Naval Research Lab to study the Vardogger. She was disoriented, still — thinking of the way the forest had seemed to fragment and multiply was like remembering a cramp in her eye. The coffee in her thermos was warm — it was peaceful here, though she felt like a leaf caught in an eddy. She had been drawn to this place in her far future, when she'd suffered crucifixion, and she had also been drawn here in her recent past, when she began the investigation into the Mursult deaths that had led her here now. A leaf caught in a whirlpool, a wheel within a wheel.

Wendy's on West Pike in Clarksburg, scribbling on napkins, *Everything has changed, but nothing has changed,* spicy chicken, no mayo, paper place mat, dipping fries in paper cups of ketchup, writing, *The anatomy of men and women laid out across the sky.* Sipping Pepsi, sounds of ice cubes in a waxy cup, writing, *A rain of pollen in reverse,* writing, *a strange symmetry: cadavers in the sky and the hanged men, a pollination of flowers and the running men.* Clouds had accumulated through the afternoon, a cold front sweeping in. A fine rain misted outside. Moss stepped out for fresh air, huddled beneath the Wendy's overhang. Wishing she still smoked — the old addiction never entirely dies. Perfect time for a cigarette, the late hour, solitude, something for her nerves, *a forest with doors that led to new forests.* She could almost taste the tobacco, wondered where she could buy a pack around here, or even just one, bum a cigarette if a man walked by. Her cell buzzed: BROCK.

"IDs came back on one of the Buckhannon bodies we pulled from the truck with Marian," he said. "I told the doctors to sit on this information. I thought I should tell you first before we proceed."

He cleared his throat. She heard him struggling with this.

"Positive ID," he said. "No mistakes. Ryan Wrigley Torgersen."

"Our person of suspicion for the CJIS bombing," she said.

"He's like . . . Torgersen is like Marian," said Brock. "There are two of them, two of each of them. They're clones, or they're doubled somehow."

"Focus on Torgersen. You've had him under surveillance?"

"I just talked with Rashonda, checked to see when Torgersen had last been at work, and she told me he was sitting at his desk all day. Shannon, this guy can't be at his desk all day and in the autopsy room, he just can't be . . . I don't understand what's happening. I don't understand Marian —"

"Where is he now?" asked Moss.

"My wife just called over to Torgersen's

place under some pretense, spoke to his wife. He's there now, at home."

"Let's talk with him," said Moss. "I'm already in Clarksburg, nearby CJIS. I can meet you at Torgersen's. What's his address?"

Ryan Torgersen's house was one of a newer construction north of Clarksburg, a development built in the small boom following the CJIS facility's arrival, one of sprawling identical houses with prefab design her mother would have called "McMansions." Moss found her way through the planned neighborhood streets, streets that were copies of one another, repetitive, plotted all at once yet strangely incomprehensible in their design, cul-de-sacs and loops. Night had fallen, windows of most of the houses bright at the edges of drawn curtains. Brock waited in front of the neighboring house, sitting in his silver sedan, a new model. The repetition prickled Moss, a shiver of gooseflesh. She parked behind, joined him in the front seat of his car. She wanted to tell him that the last time she'd sat with him like this, he had just murdered two special agents. She wanted to tell him what he had lost in that future and what he had already saved by finding Torgersen here.

The scent of licorice, classical radio on low volume, Brock's face dewy with sweat. "How do you want to play this?" he said. "Ask him about the body we found?"

"No," said Moss. "Ask about his life, his career here. He might not even know about that other body — in fact, I bet he doesn't. We need to poke around a bit. I don't want to just lay that on him."

"Ashleigh Bietak claims she didn't know about what was happening in her barn, claims she didn't know what her son was up to."

"You got her to talk?" asked Moss. "How about the guy she was with, Harrier?"

"He hasn't told us much of anything that we didn't already know," said Brock. "And Ashleigh Bietak just lost her son. When we broke the news that Jared had been shot in the firefight, she broke down, only talked off and on before her counsel arrived, outbursts of grief, sometimes not even comprehensible. We asked her about Mursult, and she said something about a lawyer he knew. Marian mentioned a lawyer, too, didn't she?"

"She did," said Moss, indistinct thoughts flickering in the back of her mind, something she was trying to recall, pieces she needed to fit together. "I don't know if his lawyer is important, but we should track this lawyer down," she said.

"I asked for the lawyer's name. Ashleigh Bietak can't tell us, or won't tell us," said Brock. "She's demanding a quick burial for her son, but the Navy confiscated his remains. She's not cooperating."

Ashleigh Bietak had lost her son, but Brock had won the lives of his children.

"How old are your girls?" asked Moss.

"Two and four," said Brock.

How old would his girls be in the year 2024, when the Terminus was marked? Twenty-nine and thirty-one — his girls will be young adults when the White Hole opens in the sky. All of life was in a gyre, channeled to the same waste.

They approached the house together, Brock knocking on the front door before ringing the bell. A light in the living room snapped on, the door opened inward, no security chain. The woman was slight, a loose sweater and slacks, house slippers. She seemed puzzled by their presence but smiled, a suburban graciousness.

"Ma'am, my name is Special Agent William Brock, I'm with the FBI. This is Special Agent Shannon Moss, NCIS. Is Mr. Torgersen home? May we have a few minutes of your time?"

"Yes, let me just — just one moment, please," said Mrs. Torgersen. "Please, come inside. I'll get him for you."

Twin skylights were night-violet squares in the foyer's cathedral-style ceiling. The floor was marble, a swirl of salmon and beige. Mrs. Torgersen showed them into the formal living room before excusing herself to find her husband. Moss heard her recede through the house, calling out, "Ryan?"

Torgersen and his wife returned together, Torgersen dwarfing his petite wife, the contrast almost humorous. Khaki slacks and a striped polo shirt that hung untucked, his hair thinning silver. A meek man, Brock had said — soft, thought Moss, but with a nervous edge. He'd been drinking, the air wet with the stench of liquor.

"What is this about?" he asked.

"Mr. Torgersen, do you have a few moments to answer some questions for us?"

"Of course," he said. "Honey, would you mind putting on some coffee?" His wife vanished farther into the house, and Moss heard the kitchen tap spray water. "Or would you like tea, anything else?" Torgersen asked. "Not sure if you're drinking — if you're on duty or if we're after hours. Please, have a seat. Come on in. What's going on?"

"Coffee's fine," said Brock, taking a seat on one of the leather couches in the formal sitting room. Torgersen sat adjacent, hands folded in his lap. He bounced his knee, the sound of his heel against the carpet a repetitive swishing.

"Mr. Torgersen, can you tell me when you began work with the FBI?" asked Brock.

"Sure," said Torgersen, his forehead growing pasty with sweat. He wiped it with the back of his hand. "Ten years ago, I guess — no, maybe eleven years ago now. Are you here because of some problem with work? I can't guess what that might be. I've worked in fingerprints. I was one of the few who came over from D.C. when they opened the new facility a few years ago. I can't think of anything that's wrong."

"The Criminal Justice Information Services building," said Brock.

"That's right. Did you say your name was Brock? I work with a Rashonda Brock, I don't suppose you're related?"

"She's my wife," said Brock. "She's mentioned you to me."

"Mind telling me what this is all about?" he asked. "I'm happy to help you. I just don't know what's going on."

"How are you settling into your new space?" asked Brock. "Quite a difference,

D.C. to West Virginia. You volunteered to come out this way? Are you getting along all right?"

"I'm sure Rashonda's told you about the stresses. We're working toward a state-of-the-art computer system, a national fingerprint database, but all we hear are budget problems and software glitches. False positives, incomplete records. We're still working off of fingerprint cards, for the most part. Some of the bigger cities are already computerized, and it's embarrassing, because they hit on matches in a fraction of the time it takes us to work through our boxes."

Torgersen's body found burned in the Ryder truck, the burned body in an autopsy room in Charleston, but here he was in his living room, an echo, another echo. Moss watched the man perspire, though his demeanor was jocular. He seemed like he wanted to help however he could, but he was fidgety, moving strangely like an animal grooming itself, running his hands over his silver hair, running them along his arms, pulling at his shirt, little tugs. Glass crashed in the kitchen.

"I'll check on her," said Moss.

The house felt open-ended, rooms branching off from the main hallway, leading to other unseen hallways and rooms. No kids, Moss thought — the place uncluttered, clean. The kitchen was expansive, a cooking area centered by an island counter, a breakfast table and French doors that opened onto a patio and manicured lawn. Mrs. Torgersen had dropped the coffeepot, had knelt to sweep up the pieces of glass with a dustpan. She was visibly unnerved, crying.

"We heard the glass," said Moss. "Here, let me, I'll clean this up. Are you all right?"

Mrs. Torgersen's friendly demeanor had decayed since she'd opened the front door, her complexion withered by weariness and sorrow, or terror. She sat at the kitchen table, apologizing while Moss tore off sheets of paper towel from the roll, picked up the larger pieces of glass.

"I don't know what to do," said Mrs. Torgersen.

"Whatever it is, we can help you," said Moss, joining her at the kitchen table once she'd swept up the floor.

"Arrest him," said Mrs. Torgersen, a whisper, almost too quiet for Moss to hear. "He's changed, he's so different now."

"Has he hurt you?" asked Moss.

"No," said Mrs. Torgersen, almost exasperated to have to explain. "No, it's not that, he talks about things. He drinks so heavily."

"What does he talk about?"

"He wanted to move here," she said. "He had heard about this new building, CJIS, and was obsessed with moving here, I don't know why. West Virginia. We had no reason to transfer, but he was fixated on the idea. He talked nonstop about West Virginia, about Clarksburg."

"That was the change you noticed?" asked Moss.

"No, he'd changed before then," said Mrs. Torgersen. "He'd . . . have these mood swings, highs and lows, and when he told me we were moving to West Virginia, I asked him not to. We started fighting, we'd never fought before. And that's when he started telling me his fantasies."

"What sorts of things?"

"Violent fantasies," she said. "He'd never spoken like this to me before, but he came home one night with blood on his clothes."

She cried heavily now, her face crimson, her jaw clenched. "He was younger, he seemed *younger.* Thinner. He was drenched, soaking wet and dirty with blood."

"Blood on his clothes?" asked Moss. "Was he in an accident?"

"He wouldn't tell me what happened," said Mrs. Torgersen. "I thought he was hurt.

The physical change in him, the weight he'd lost. At first he told me he'd hit a deer in his car and tried to save it, but his story kept changing. And later that night we fought. When we were in bed together, he asked me if I wanted to die, if I was trying to kill myself by refusing to move to West Virginia."

"What did he mean by that?" asked Moss.

"I don't know," she said, shaking now. "I don't know. He told me that he had seen me die and he never wanted to see me die again."

"Was he threatening you?"

"He was trying to protect me from something in his mind," said Mrs. Torgersen. "He asked me if I remembered the night we had my boss and his wife over for dinner — this dinner party we'd hosted, years ago in D.C., years ago. He told me that after my boss went home and we were alone cleaning up the dishes, he said several men broke into the house. Of course I didn't know what he was talking about, some delusion. I thought he was having an episode. I was terrified — he told me several men had come into the house and had tied him up, had held him down, and forced him to watch while they . . . while they decapitated me, cut my head off in front of him. He said he saw this, he said that they had made him hold my head in his lap and he was screaming, just begging for them to stop, but that I was dead, and they . . ."

Moss held Mrs. Torgersen's hands, said, "It's okay. We can help him —"

"And he said these men waited until midnight before they left our house. They put him in the back of a van and drove him somewhere, drove him off into the woods. And he said he saw things — he couldn't describe what he'd seen, but it was morbid. He said the men made him cross a river, and on the other side these men asked my husband if he wanted to see me alive again. They could give me back to him, and he said the men drove him home and there I was, still alive — asleep, like nothing had ever happened."

"And he thought he had to keep you alive," said Moss. "Is that right? Moving to West Virginia would keep you alive?"

"He said we had to move to West Virginia when the time came," she said. "That he had to be ready to do certain things, but anything he did was for my own good, that no matter what happened, he would protect me, but he's been drinking so much more, and now you're here, and I don't know what he's —"

"What is he prepared to do?" asked Moss. "What 'certain things'?"

"I don't . . . I don't know, but he isn't the only one. He said there are others. He doesn't know who they are, but they all play a part. Someone from the Secret Service, he said there were more in the FBI, he said there were people in the military. Ryan has a gun up in the nightstand — he never owned a gun before. I told him I wanted it out of the house, but he needs to sleep with it nearby."

*There are others.* Torgersen pulled from the Ryder, and there were other bodies in that truck, maybe their echoes still alive. Moss thought of Torgersen crossing the black river, his clothes stained with his wife's blood — but his wife was alive. *Hyldekrugger, the Devil.* Can he cross through the Vardogger? Was it permeable, a doorway to pass between worlds? Hyldekrugger somehow traveling between time-lines like a spider crawling across the strands of a web, murdering husbands, murdering wives, as threats. Bringing echoes here to terra firma. Secret Service, FBI . . . Moss imagined sleeper cells in high-security facilities, placed just like Torgersen, waiting to pull the trigger . . . How many others were there? An army of echoes.

Shouting, from the other room — indistinct sounds, accusations. Moss heard Brock's voice, calmer. Mrs. Torgersen stood from the table, said, "Ryan?" She took two steps before the blast. A fleeting image of fire like liquid orange light cascading over the ceiling and walls before Mrs. Torgersen was lifted from her feet and Moss was blown backward.

Moss swam upward from darkness. Ringing in her ears, a tinny ring, silence otherwise. *Where? Where am I?* A kitchen. She could see flames. Siren light. She was on her back, she was on a kitchen floor. *I can move,* she thought, righting herself. She tried to stand but wobbled and sank back to the floor, dizzy. Her leg was missing, her prosthesis. *Where?* She looked around her, saw a body, a woman. Mrs. — but her name escaped. *Tor . . .* The woman was on the kitchen floor, screaming. The woman was at an awkward angle. Moss crawled.

*Brock.*

"Brock!" she screamed, but her voice was underwater. "Brock!"

The house in flames. There had been a blast, she realized. She made her way through the hall, crawling — drywall collapsed, exposed timber, dust, smoke. Shrill sounds of smoke detectors competed with the ringing in her ears. What was left of the living room was on fire, the walls had disappeared. Black smoke crawled along the exposed timber where the ceiling had been, billowed from holes that had opened in the roof. Firefighters were on scene, flickering red siren lights.

"I'm all right," she said to one of the men. "Brock," she said. Someone lifted her, held her. "Brock," she said.

"Out, out." A firefighter carried her, saying, "Out, out." Flashlight beams, someone screaming.

"There's a woman in the kitchen," said Moss, recovering some of her sense.

She followed the beams of the flashlights and saw the bodies in the living room, barely visible because of black smoke, but she saw Torgersen's body shredded, she saw his head in separate locations. She saw Brock — his legs had been removed from his torso, one arm was gone. White bone, red meat. Moss screamed. Coughing, smoke burning in her lungs, she screamed and cried. Brock was dead. Moss was carried outside, a mask placed over her mouth, fresh oxygen to cleanse her lungs. She watched the house on fire, a radiant light.

■ ■ ■ ■

# PART FOUR

## 2015–2016

■ ■ ■ ■

I will invite myself
to this ghost supper.
— AUGUST STRINDBERG,
*The Ghost Sonata*

# ONE

I launched in the Cormorant within a week of Brock's death. Three months in solitude, the silence of the *Grey Dove* pierced by ringing in my ears, the lingering effects of Torgersen's suicide blast. My memories were spotty, like there were gaps where the film had been cut. One moment I'd heard shouting, the next I woke in fire and remembered only scattered images, flashes of the gruesome spectacle of Brock's body and Torgersen's echo, the pieces of them scattered about the burning living room. Brock's death wriggled wormlike in my heart. *Why hadn't I known what we were walking into?*

My life was telescoping. I had lived over a year since Nestor called in the early hours to tell me that a family had been murdered, but those murders were still raw, just a few weeks old. I had seen the future but didn't understand the larger constellation of events around me. Nothing was clarified, and that future had already dissolved like dew.

O'Connor visited me in Clarksburg, at my office in CJIS. We walked the corridors together, imagining this building's fate in a future that would never be.

"I spoke with one of the doctors who treated your smoke inhalation," he said. "He told me you suffered a perforated eardrum in the explosion, but no other injuries. The hearing loss should be temporary. How are you?"

"I can go," I said, even though his voice seemed far away, too soft beneath the shrill ringing. He wasn't asking about the smoke inhalation or the psychological trauma of the bombing. He was asking if my body could withstand the withering travel to a second IFT within a month. "I'm ready."

We spoke about Torgersen's wife, how her husband had been brought through the woods and imagined the Vardogger as an intersection of paths, the hub of a wheel with several spokes, each spoke leading somehow to a different IFT. There were other echoes that had already been brought through, we knew, waiting like spiders in their funnels, tensed as Torgersen had been, for Hyldekrugger to pluck their webs and send them scurrying to the light. O'Connor studied the inventory of blueprints that

Brock and I had recovered from Buckhannon, sites compromised by Hyldekrugger's network. "Federal buildings," O'Connor said, "NSC targets. Launch sites. Navy installations. These are all support beams protecting us from the Terminus, and Hyldekrugger is preparing to break them. Why?"

I would travel to discover what terror might still occur, then trace it back to terra firma, so that we can anticipate Hyldekrugger here, *now*. Stop him.

Before we parted, O'Connor told me that the Navy had secured the Vardogger. "A discreet presence, but they'll have the area fenced off soon. Njoku is working with a team from the Naval Research Lab. They've rented most of the cabins there, out at the Blackwater Lodge. They're going to study the thin space, unlock it. When you reach the future, check in with us. See what doorways through time and space we've managed to pry apart."

The ping from the Black Vale's AI roused me from dreams of Buckhannon, the lunar base confirming that my ship had emerged from the void. I glanced out the portal: gibbous moon, Earthshine. I checked with the *Grey Dove*'s autocommand: *September*

385

*2015.* Another IFT materialized, another future.

A second ping from the Black Vale.

"Black Vale Approach, Cormorant Seven Zero Seven Golf Delta," I said, shaking away wisps of a dream, Nestor in fields of long grass, the night sky bleeding with stars.

*"State your name and place your eyes to the onboard retinal scanner for verification,"* a sonorous voice, a computer's, breaking hailing protocol. The Black Vale's AI had locked into the *Grey Dove*'s computers as it should have, but NSC always manned the Lighthouse with sailors. Something was wrong.

"Shannon Moss," I said. The retinal scanner was a set of goggles built into the control panel, and I lowered my face against the rubber mask, kept my eyes wide for the dull sweep of light.

*"Welcome, Special Agent Shannon Moss. Downloading clearance code, contacting NET-WARCOM."*

"Wait. Black Vale Approach," I said, "this is *Grey Dove* Actual. I need to speak with Black Vale Actual."

*"The Lighthouse is dark, Shannon."*

Which meant there was no Black Vale, not anymore, that there was no longer a lunar base, that I was speaking with a black-box computer buried deep beneath moon dust, or maybe a satellite circling the night. We were trained to remain dark in the event that NSC might no longer exist, to shut off all lights and nonessential computers, to wait in silence for the B-L to reboot. We were trained simply to return home, a six-month round trip that would have gained nothing. I flipped off the *Dove*'s interior lights, the situation sinking in, that if there was no Black Vale, then NSC had been compromised, or folded. Several minutes passed before I noticed that the Black Vale's AI had sent a message. I tapped the digital display, and O'Connor's face filled the screen, his skin mottled with liver spots and traced with veins, wizened, his eyebrows bushy white. He was in his office, in front of the customary "I Love Me" wall that special agents usually covered with certificates and awards but that he filled with framed photographs of his cocker spaniels.

"Shannon," he said, his voice dried with age, reedy, "if you're watching this, then you are in an IFT and our nightmare doesn't exist, and I don't exist right now, which is a warm thought for me, like I might still wake up from so many terrible things. Return to terra firma, Shannon. Right now, don't wait. As of this recording, July 2014, the Terminus is marked at December 2017, and it might have come closer still by the time you see this recording. The Earth, humanity — there is no hope. I wonder if you'll see the White Hole. I wonder if you're seeing it now. I wonder if you've arrived in the Terminus. I wonder if you're alive. I wonder if I'm too late. Please go home, Shannon. Go home. The United States Navy has enacted Operation Saigon — we've evacuated, we will be gone. The entire NSC fleet will be gone, searching for other futures, other worlds. We will not return.

"But I have a word of warning, about your time, about terra firma. The Vardogger, that thin space you discovered in the woods, is a dangerous place, extremely dangerous. Avoid it, please. We lost so many to that anomaly . . . almost thirty men. We lost Wally Njoku and the SEAL team that went in to retrieve him, we lost physicists who were studying that place. Show this video to me when you get home, and to Wally. Keep us out. They are all lost, no one returns."

O'Connor's face disappeared, replaced by footage of Njoku in the forest, near the Vardogger, the pines and the earth around him bronzed with evening sunlight. Time- and date-stamped: *04/23/97, 6:03 p.m.* He wore a white lab coverall and raised a hood over his head as he spoke. "Test, um . . .

which number?"

"This will be number seventeen," said a voice, the cameraman.

"Seventeen," said Njoku, fitting a respirator over his mouth. "Can you hear me? Okay. The Vardogger opens, and . . . I believe it mimics quantum foam at the river boundary. I believe you can walk through it. This morning I threw a rock across the river and saw it land, somewhere deeper . . . We're recording now. The Vardogger opens on a regular basis, but we haven't determined its pattern . . . Approximately every twelve hours. If you're paying attention, you can feel when it's about to happen, like an electrical current creeping up your arms. I'm going to take a few steps into it, see if I can retrieve the rock I threw."

After a span of waiting, as he held one hand on the ashen tree's smooth bark, I saw Njoku's face brighten. "Can you feel it?" he shouted to the cameraman, smiling. "Goose bumps," he said, running his gloves along his sleeves. "Ah, here we are. Are you recording this? I can see the paths — they're everywhere."

I looked closely but found nothing remarkable in the footage. I wondered what Njoku was seeing, what he meant by "paths." Njoku took tentative steps forward. "Set the timer," he said, as he pushed through the boughs of dense pines and disappeared. The footage ran for several minutes, the cameraman eventually following where Njoku had walked, through the trees. He came out into the familiar clearing, near the Red Run, but there was no one.

"Njoku." The cameraman's voice during the few final seconds of footage. *"Njoku!"*

The Black Vale AI ticked through its programming while I replayed Njoku's vanishing, the almost casual manner in which he'd seemed to slip away. When Njoku, O'Connor, and I had felt lost in the Vardogger, the area seemed to repeat, a recurrence of the white tree. And when we saw the Red Run, it seemed like we had flipped sides somehow, that we would need to cross the river to return to where we were. Marian had said something similar, I remembered — that she had crossed the river. I imagined Njoku wading into the water, reaching out to retrieve his stone. Where had he gone? The Black Vale AI had contacted Apollo Soucek's computer system, had downloaded NETWARCOM clearance codes, it had contacted NCIS to establish custody for the Cormorant. I saw the crescent Earth emerge from the sea of night, stunning and fragile but left for dead here, discarded. Operation Saigon meant that only a few had been chosen for life, no more than a thousand, to grasp at extra years while the billions abandoned would die in the cold light of a second sun. The Terminus was an onrushing death, inevitable and near, but there was no White Hole here, not yet. O'Connor must have realized, even as he'd left his time-capsule warning, that I wouldn't retreat from this forsaken Earth.

I took a room at the Virginia Beach Courtyard Marriott, an upper-level suite, the patio view an expanse of ocean, azure water melding into azure sky. Evenings on the patio with cinnamon-plum tea, scribbling notes, squiggly lines connecting one idea to the next, trying to visualize how all this death fit together, and why: *Libra — Esperance — Terminus.* I sketched what I imagined had happened on Esperance, Nicole's story of the fauna and crystal-shaped leviathans, of men and women lifted and rent apart.

Hyldekrugger's network proved difficult to track. I contacted NCIS, but after nearly twenty years no one remembered my name or recognized my credentials, so I researched what I could on my own. Thousands of articles and longform available referencing domestic terrorism, terrorist activity during the past two decades, but most references to Buckhannon were historical, speculating on connections with the militia movement or Timothy McVeigh, and many articles repeated information written in 1997, in some cases lifting verbatim from earlier pieces.

I was surprised to discover Phil Nestor still with the FBI here, a decorated career. Maybe I expected another version of the troubled man I once knew, but IFTs varied wildly in their particulars, in their individual fates. Whatever personal tragedies had pushed Nestor to live in Buckhannon hadn't occurred in this future's past. We had discovered the chemical-weapons lab, Nestor had been wounded in the ensuing firefight — those events alone might have driven his life in a different trajectory, a different life entirely. His career was easy to follow, his successes. Capsule biographies were readily available in the News-Share, and I found a portrait photograph of him, salt-and-pepper gray, handsome. SAC of the Pittsburgh office following Brock's death, it looked like, and his investigations into domestic terrorism must have furthered his career, as he was part of the FBI's Domestic Terrorism Executive Committee. Based near here, in Washington, D.C., I called his office, a calculated risk. He might know of Deep Waters here, just as Brock had known, and I worried that my name might appear on a list somewhere, might trigger my arrest, a butterfly in a bell jar. His secretaries wouldn't connect me, though. I called his office several times, and they took my name and the room number for the hotel, but soon I wasn't sure if he would even remember me. My memories of Nestor were still warm, only a few months since we were together in a different future from this — but those weren't his memories. Here I was only a woman he had worked with once, a lifetime ago.

I ran in the mornings, an outdoor track at Kellam High School, my leg fitted with a Flex-Foot Cheetah, a curved prosthesis designed for sprints. The opposite of an out-of-body experience, running was body without mind, purely physical — *step, breath, reach.* Unassailable lightness.

"Four-hundred-meter dash," I said, "competition setting," still self-conscious about speaking to the air, but I was familiar with Ambient Systems from other IFTs, atmospheric nanotech saturation by Phasal Systems, the air itself pervaded with microscopic tech that hung suspended like grains of pollen. Pixels of light and specks of sound, everywhere I looked was lit like an enveloping television. GNC ads and interactive blips for active wear at Dick's Sporting Goods, every dull spot of the track flashing like Times Square. Images hovered: real-time heart rate, core temperature, calories burned during each of my runs. My personal assistant was a hologram who blurred out of resolution whenever the wind blew, yelling, *"Another sprint! Another run!"*

A virtual gun crack, I ran. Gaining speed through the first turn, working to increase my speed, *pushing,* but the hovering stopwatch blinked green to yellow as I fell from my pace, and as I made my last turn, I slipped on gravel and the sky spun, the track rushing to meet me. Chest-first along the track, my elbow gashed, and my knee, and I bit the inside of my lip. Blood filled my mouth, and I spit, spit a second mouthful, *fuck, fuck, fuck.* Blood from my elbow to my wrist. My sock soaked with blood from my knee. I forced myself to sit up.

Health Mode still timed the run, over three minutes now, flashing red. "Stop," I said, but my personal trainer appeared beside me, *"Faster! Faster!"* My prosthesis wasn't damaged, the knee joint looked fine, the Cheetah foot scraped but all right. I shook out my ponytail, tied it up tighter. Fatigue was settling over me. I hadn't finished my laps, but my muscles felt like they'd lost their elasticity and my sweat cooled.

"Someone else would quit," I said, looking at the blood on my shin, the cut on my knee. "Come on, Shannon, get your ass up. Other people would quit. Someone else would quit."

A ripple of depression at falling, the failure of having lost my balance, the frustration similar to the pervasive, sponging depression that had blotted that first year after I lost my leg, at having to relearn how to walk, at the foreign movement, at the realization that a prosthetic leg was a bulky weight affixed to my thigh, a deadweight I'd have to lift with my hip and carry with every step. Adjustments, frequent trips to Union Orthotics & Prosthetics in Pittsburgh for resizing, to test different suspension devices, straps, suctions, choosing feet from a catalog like shopping for shoes. I'd met amputees who still ran, iron-willed, who refused to abdicate what amputation threatened to take from them.

I stood up. I crossed the field, back to my starting line.

"Reset the stopwatch," I said.

*00:00.*

A throbbing knee and fresh blood trickling over my shin.

"Someone else would quit," I said.

I ran.


I showered back at the hotel following the morning's workout, spreading Neosporin Skin to cover the gash on my knee when I heard the persistent cooing of a mourning dove. I wondered if a bird might have flown in from the patio, through the suite's open French doors. A dove trapped in my hotel room, cooing, until I realized the cooing was the repeating tone of a voice mail in my Ambience.

"Courtney Gimm," I said, engaging the voice mail with my assumed name.

His voice filled the air like he was there in the room with me.

*"Special Agent Phil Nestor, FBI. It's great to hear your voice, Shannon. I'm sorry it took so long to get back to you, but I was in Alabama, at a training seminar. I'd love to see you, catch up. And I can bring you up to speed with some of our investigations. Seven o'clock in the lobby of your hotel? Give a call if that won't work. Otherwise I'll see you tonight."*

■ ■ ■ ■

Many special agents who investigated crimes in multiple IFTs swore by a technique called the Memory Palace. An individual imagines a palace and mentally places names, faces, or events in its various chambers, the idea being that it's possible to recall things forgotten or obscured if they're organized spatially. Special agents used this technique to separate their impressions of differing futures, one IFT from another — some spent their entire three months in quantum foam meditating on these palaces, imagining new wings for each future they'd observe. I never found this method useful, or maybe I lacked the discipline to make it useful, but waiting for Nestor in the lobby of the Courtyard Marriott, nervous as a virgin on prom night, I regretted not having developed some sort of technique to help tease out my knots of emotion about him. He had lived in the Buckhannon death house, selling a killer's stash of antique weapons, or he lived here, a decorated agent of the FBI — but I saw these discrepancies like an image refracted through different lenses, not as something essential about him. I had known Nestor; I could close my eyes and remember the feel of his body next to mine, the purr of his breathing as he slept, his habits and quirks of thought. That was Nestor to me, his core.

"Shannon?"

He wore faded jeans, a blazer. He smiled, shook my hand. "My God, it is you. You look . . . amazing," he said, his eyes still an undimmed blue. "I don't think you've aged a day. It's been about twenty years?"

"Far too long," I said. He was weathered, but like soft leather — filled out through his chest, his shoulders. Weight rooms, I figured. "You look good, too," remembering him in another time than this, how natural it would feel to lean into him, how familiar if he held me, but here we only shared crime scenes, decades ago. "I think we last saw each other maybe at Buckhannon."

"Right before Brock passed," he said. "I was worried about you, the way you disappeared. I asked after you, for a long while, but no one would tell me anything."

"How's your arm?" I asked. "I think the last time we were together, you left in an ambulance."

He touched his bicep, a gold band on his finger. Of course he might have been married here; it shouldn't have stung. He rubbed the place where Jared Bietak's bullet had passed through his arm. "Old wounds never heal," he said.

Nestor went to the bar for drinks while I waited in one of the crescent-shaped booths, the Courtyard Marriott's lobby bar like an airport lounge, nightclub-sleek but comfortable only for as long as it took to get someplace else. A bachelorette party at a nearby table, gift bags, foil balloons. Nine women, but three sporadically flickered, momentary lapses, their audio and visual off sync whenever they laughed. Illusions, I realized, present only in the Ambience, and a poor connection at that. Some of them surveyed Nestor as he passed their table with our drinks, glanced my way to see who was with him.

"I was at sea," I told him when he asked about my life following Torgersen's suicide, Brock's death.

"You never made it to the funeral," he said. "I looked for you."

"I'm sorry about what I missed."

Nestor had been promoted, I knew, and when I asked about his career, he said, "We weren't investigating much domestic terrorism after 9/11. Our focus was on international terrorism, Al-Qaeda. It wasn't until the Stennis attack that we turned our attention back to homegrown psychopaths."

Stennis: SSC, the Stennis Space Center, a NASA facility that houses a field site of the Naval Research Lab. Publicly, NRL's Stennis site conducted oceanography research, but there was a classified NSC/NASA collaboration as well, rocket-engine tests and experimental engines. The casual way he'd referenced Stennis, I figured most people would know what he meant. "That was connected to Buckhannon?" I asked, oblique.

"We think so," said Nestor. "Let me show you. Law enforcement. Philip Nestor, 55-828."

When he spoke his name, the seal of the FBI hovered between us, another illusion in the Ambience but as real as if I could reach out and touch it. Nestor asked that I speak my name, and when I did, the Ambience revealed data collected about domestic terrorist activity. Glyphs covered in text, pictures of wrecked commuter trains, mangled corpses, government buildings reduced to rubble.

"They've been busy," I said, scanning the images, the trajectory of what might happen. O'Connor's instincts had been correct. What I was seeing lent credence to his idea that Hyldekrugger's network was attacking government installations, especially Navy or federal law-enforcement targets.

"They aren't like other organizations," said Nestor. "They don't publicize their actions or take credit, so they don't get the media coverage of an Al-Qaeda or ISIS. The media narrative has been 'rampant lone-wolf terrorism,' 'antigovernment paranoia,' maybe organized through networks in the militias. We think these attacks are related to Buckhannon, all of them — carried out by the same planners. And yes, they've been very busy."

I skimmed file titles: *[2003] Stennis Attack, [2005] D.C. Metro Attack, [2007] United Nations General Assembly Attack, [2008] NSASP Attack, [2011] Pentagon Attack.*

"Show: Stennis Space Center," said Nestor, and the file expanded, the table between us becoming a map of the facility in Mississippi, fire damage to the building that housed the Naval Research Lab.

"We link this attack to Buckhannon primarily because of the modus operandi," said Nestor, "their continuing ability to recruit personnel from within highly secure facilities."

"People with clearances," I said, thinking, *Echoes.* "Who?"

"A marine shot up the place, blew himself up when security turned their guns on him," said Nestor. "But what the news couldn't talk about was the similarity of style to the planned CJIS attack. You found the blueprints for the CJIS building with Brock, I believe. Recovered at Buckhannon."

"Sarin gas?" I asked.

"The attacker detonated a bomb he had smuggled into the labs, sewn inside his rectum. His own body shielded most of the blast, which saved lives. A horror show, but his was the only fatality from the bomb. The fire-suppression system had been rigged with sarin, discovered in the resulting security sweep — but the actor's body had dampened the explosion to such a degree that the fire system never triggered. The marine was a lone wolf."

"So he shot up the place, then detonated himself," I said.

"He killed five, wounded eight before he set off the bomb," said Nestor. "Shooting randomly, he killed a number of researchers. I thought you and I might cross paths on this case."

"You must have worked jointly with NCIS," I said, a frisson of déjà vu at Nestor's words.

"Yes, but more specifically: we tracked the gun the marine used in the shooting," he said. "Ran a ballistics check but came up with false positives. The ballistics report matched a gun that we already had in our possession, the nine-millimeter we recovered from the shooting death of Patrick Mursult. It turns out the bullets also matched bullets tested from Ryan Wrigley Torgersen's weapon following the events at his residence, the explosion."

"The ballistics report matched all three guns?" I asked.

"I wanted to call you in," said Nestor. "I tried to reach out to you, see if you could testify that these matches were false positives, but I couldn't find you. And then there were others."

"Other matches?" I asked.

"Judges tend to throw out these ballistics reports in cases where we have this issue. But yes, there were other matches, too. We earmark the cases, figure a possible connection between Mursult and Torgersen, the Stennis Space Center, but the matches might just be errors in the database."

"They've got to be connected," I said.

"We keep tabs on these matches as they develop," said Nestor. "We just don't keep the individual cases open. Many of these investigations are strictly local, things the Bureau wasn't involved in, and the authorities and politicians want closed cases, *convictions,* so we let them proceed. Stennis was a

PR nightmare as it was, a marine attacking his own country. We didn't want these ballistics matches in the news."

What was it Nestor had once told me? In our other future, a moment of intimacy, he'd hoped to cross paths with me over the years, he'd hoped to consult me on an investigation. There had been false positives on a ballistics report he'd worked with then, too, in that other future, a report that matched the bullets pulled from Mursult's body, just like now. I felt as if I'd discovered a new doorway in a house I'd lived in for years, opening onto a hallway I'd never noticed before. A Beretta M9 in the FBI's possession from the killing of Patrick Mursult, an M9 recovered from Torgersen, an M9 a marine used during a killing spree at the Stennis Space Center — the same Beretta M9, again and again. Echoes, echoed guns.

"Tell me more about those false positives," I said. "I'm interested in that detail."

"The FBI has built up a database of ballistic profiles from recovered weapons, and we have access to local law-enforcement databases as well — with a few exceptions," he said.

"When did you start using the database?"

"It's new, maybe ten years ago, give or take."

"So the ballistics matches wouldn't have been discovered until, what — 2005 or so?"

"About that time, yeah, but maybe later, because they added older reports to the database only after they were up and running."

"Can I see a list?"

"Of the false positives? The database hasn't been as helpful as we would like, because we get so many of them, but as I said, we keep track."

Nestor asked the Ambient System for false positive ballistics matches relating to the Stennis Space Center shooting. Specks of light emerged, enlarging into facsimiles of summary reports. The first report was the ballistics test of the bullets recovered from Patrick Mursult's body in March 1997. There were other matches to those bullets: the Stennis Space Center shooting, Torgersen's gun, another homicide in 2009, however my attention caught on a homicide in 1997, March 26 — only a few weeks following Mursult's death, but a shooting that hadn't happened yet in terra firma.

"What about this one?" I asked, pointing to a file in the Ambient light between us. "Durr?"

"Carla Durr, a lawyer," said Nestor. "Shot to death in the food court of the Tysons Corner mall in Virginia."

*A lawyer.* Marian had mentioned that her father was preoccupied with a lawyer in the weeks before his death. "I need to see this case file," I told him. "Carla Durr. I need everything relating to the death of this woman. How long would it take you to get me this file?"

"We can look at it right now," said Nestor. "We'll be able to view the crime scene, but it wouldn't work well here, too much light. I'll book a room, pay for an Ambient system. We can take a look."

"I have a room," I said.

A similar attraction as the first time I knew him. Nestor seemed to glow under the overhead elevator lights as we rode to my floor. Confidence, ease, a scent of aftershave — nothing like the unkempt beard and warm flannels of the broken man I'd known. When I'd known him before, he was unfinished in the same ways that I still feel unfinished, and together we'd hoped to make some sort of whole, but here he was a puzzle already solved, no opening where I would fit.

"You're married?" I asked.

"Shannon," he said. But then, "Yeah,

fifteen years in a few months. Ginny."

"Virginia?"

"We met at a retreat," said Nestor. "Through the church. She leads the contemporary music, she's a singer."

Imagining them, maybe the cool couple at their church even as they aged, a singer and an FBI agent, hosting barbecues and Bible study at their beautiful house, beers on the back patio while he regaled the other middle-aged men with stories about his arrests, how he was injured in a shoot-out twenty years ago. I wondered what she looked like.

"I remember you were religious," I said, thinking of that other version of him, alone in that living room in Buckhannon, surrounded by fields of death and old murder, contemplating a painting of the dead Christ. I wanted to laugh, the vagaries of fate. There is no essence, there is no core. "You used to ask me if I believed in eternal life. What was it? The resurrection of the body?"

"Ah, I'm sorry if that's true," he said. "That sounds like something I might have said back then. I'm sorry that's what you remember about me. That's kind of embarrassing, isn't it?"

"It's nice you found someone."

"Things are good," he said. "We have a

ten-year-old, Kayla. She keeps us busy."

"You sound happy."

"You never . . . ?"

"No," I said, exiting the elevator before him. "I never found anyone to keep up with me."

I'd been in the habit of leaving the Do Not Disturb tag on the door handle, but the condition of my room suffered for it, the bathroom carpeted with damp towels, the bedding sliding off the mattress from fitful sleep. I hurried to clean up as best I could, pulling my clothes from the backs of chairs, stuffing underwear into my gym bag. The controls of the Ambient system were near the thermostat, a panel of buttons I never fiddled with. Nestor turned on the system, and the air vents hummed as the room was filled with nanotech on a breath of warm air, a whiff of ozone. An itching sensation tickled my nose.

"A lot of dust," he said. "We'll have to look out for your bed, it will be in the way — ah, here we go. Ninety-six percent, excellent."

Ninety-six percent was the saturation rate, I knew at least that much even if I didn't know what it meant specifically. Ninety-six percent of the air was filled with nanotech? Or 96 percent of the optimal level for the system to work? I was breathing them, I knew, machines in my lungs, my blood — too many hours of saturation would turn my piss orange. I'd read longform about people who breathed so much Ambience that their lungs looked wrapped in silver leaf. Nestor took off his blazer, the air close now, rolled his sleeves to his forearms. "Can you hit the lights?" he asked, and I drew the blackout blinds and switched the lights off, but the room was still lit. It seemed to glow from within, as if the air itself were illuminated, yet there were no shadows, soft light emanating from every direction at once. The first image that materialized was an image of the hotel exterior and the beach, women in bathing suits drinking chartreuse cocktails by the waterfall pool, Courtyard Marriott logos and room-service specials, opportunities to "rate" and "share."

*"Hello, and welcome to the Courtyard Marriott Phasal Ambient System,"* a perky woman's voice. *"We are locating two new users. We offer a stunning array of award-winning environments to enhance your —"*

"Law enforcement 55-828," said Nestor. "Nestor, Philip."

The room changed, no longer the hotel and beach with suntanned women but rather the rotating FBI seal, National Crime

Information Center.

"I'm looking for a case from 1997," said Nestor. "A homicide, Fairfax County, Virginia. Victim's name: D-U-R-R, Carla."

A hovering icon of a spinning globe, replaced by a hovering file number and the name "CARLA DURR." Reading her name was like reading a reflection, in reverse until I crossed the room to stand near Nestor, passing through the illusion.

"That's the one," said Nestor. Other images appeared in the room, an array of glyphs. "Actual size," he said, and the glyphs resized to eight-and-a-half-by-eleven, the room a flurry of paper. Nestor reached out to pluck one of the sheets from the air, and the image reacted, like he was holding a sheet of real paper and not just a rectangle of light, even though it was an orchestration of thousands — millions, maybe — of robotic pixels.

"This is amazing," I said, genuinely boggled by the realism of the Ambient System. Most effects in the Ambience were something like three-dimensional television. I could understand that sort of illusion intuitively — the Health Mode stopwatch, a personal trainer — but this . . .

"Scale model," said Nestor. "Stitch photographs 3 through 355."

No longer a room filled with sheets of paper, no longer a hotel room at all, but rather a mall food court in midafternoon, police tape roping off the counter and cash register of a Five Guys burger place. The illusion was perfect except for faint outlines of my bed and the other furniture in the room, the shopping mall expansive in every direction, the other restaurants, the other corridors of stores, like I could start walking, weave between tables, take an escalator down . . .

I was seeing a three-dimensional rendering of Carla Durr's crime scene, several hundred crime-scene photographs stitched together to make this perfect simulation. The body was facedown near the hamburger counter, a woman in her upper middle age, her ankles and knees marbled with varicose veins that showed through nude-colored pantyhose. She wore a royal-blue skirt and jacket, her head a tangle of orange. She'd been shot multiple times in her torso, another time in her temple, a head shot that had surely pierced her brain. She'd been buying hamburgers when she was gunned down, french fries scattered around her, blood like she'd spilled a tub of ketchup over her face. I went for a closer look at the body, but hit the edge of the queen-size bed.

"She was shot in her back," I said. "Standing at the cash register when someone walked up behind her, shot her through the back several times."

"Carla Durr, attorney-at-law practicing in Canonsburg, Pennsylvania," said Nestor.

"Canonsburg?" I said. "She must be Patrick Mursult's lawyer."

"Mursult's lawyer?" asked Nestor. "Interesting. We flagged the connection to Canonsburg, I remember, but had nothing specific linking her to Mursult. Durr was killed at Tysons Corner mall on a Monday afternoon, 3:40 p.m., approximately. March twenty-fourth, 1997. That was close to when Mursult was killed."

"Just a few weeks after," I said. *I'll have time to stop this.* "And who was the actor? Who killed her?" I asked.

"Cold case," said Nestor. "Witnesses describe a Caucasian male, black fatigues. No arrest was made."

"Unsolved, but you said the gun was the same?"

"No, not the gun. The bullets we recovered from the shooting at the Stennis Space Center match the seven bullets that were recovered from Durr's body."

"And also the bullets from the Mursult killing?" I asked. "And Torgersen's gun?"

"That's right. Torgersen's match came later, after one of the technicians fired some test rounds and logged them into the system."

"But why wasn't the Mursult killing matched with Durr's right away?" I asked. "Those two homicides were only weeks apart."

"True, they were, but remember that the match wasn't made until we tested the gun used in the Stennis shooting, years after Mursult and Durr were killed," said Nestor. "Only once the national database was up and running and someone had the time and funding to enter these older, closed, and cold cases. These two homicides were only weeks apart, but we didn't know about the ballistics match until years later. We assumed that the false positives were a mistake at first, bugs in a new system."

*Mistakes, echoed guns* — linked shooting deaths. Hyldekrugger might seem invisible, but his network had inadvertently left a pattern of killings as visible as cross-stitch.

The room changed around us, the food court disappearing, replaced by a photograph of Carla Durr hovering above my bed. A professional head shot, an ugly woman, fleshy lips and toady eyes that seemed on the brink of popping from her sockets.

"What else do we have on this woman? Anything?"

"She specialized in contract negotiations," said Nestor. "Practiced in Canonsburg, like I said. Shannon, how is she connected to these domestic-terrorism cases? Buckhannon? You said she was Patrick Mursult's personal lawyer? How do you know that?"

"I don't," I said. "Nothing concrete anyway. But she's from Canonsburg, like you said, and we have the ballistics match — that's connection enough for me to hazard a guess as to who she is. Patrick Mursult had been meeting with a lawyer before he died. This might be her. I don't know why they were meeting. And this might not even be his lawyer. It might just be a coincidence she's from Canonsburg, but I doubt it."

"Yeah, I doubt it, too. Here's something," said Nestor, skimming other papers in the file. "Looks like Carla Durr was meeting someone for lunch that day, a man named . . . Dr. Peter Driscoll. Holy shit, I know of this guy. This is . . ."

Nestor fell quiet, his forehead creased in concentration as he read the file.

"Driscoll," he said. "I had no idea his name would turn up here. I didn't know about Driscoll then. We have a statement from him about Durr's death, but it doesn't amount to anything. He was in the bathroom at the time of the shooting, didn't see anything."

"Who is he?" I asked.

"Close system," said Nestor, and the Ambience vanished, leaving us in the darkness until he found the bedside lamp, switched it on. He sat on my bed. His eyes were stormy weather, lost in thought. "Dr. Peter Driscoll worked for Phasal Systems, 'lead engineer.' "

"Phasal Systems? You mean he worked on Ambience?" I asked, wondering if another version of Dr. Peter Driscoll would have one day cured cancer.

"My involvement with him started — this was back in 2005, maybe 2006," said Nestor. "The FBI was investigating a group of physicists at the Naval Research Laboratory in Washington, D.C., a huge investigation. Allegations of confidential information passed from a senator's office to the eventual founders of Phasal Systems."

"Insider trading?"

"Yes, but more than that," said Nestor. "Classified military secrets used for private industry. Artificial intelligence, virtual-reality systems. The FBI was investigating the killings at Stennis and a group of scientists in D.C., all from the Naval Research Lab. We were trying to pursue connections."

"And Driscoll was a target of the investigation?"

"He was a founder of Phasal Systems, but he wasn't a target — Driscoll was going to be a witness," said Nestor. "There were allegations that members of the Senate Armed Services Committee were feeding classified information to the scientists who started Phasal, all sorts of corruption charges. But Driscoll was killed before he could cooperate — by an FBI agent. One of my people, as fate would have it. I was her supervisor."

"What happened?" I asked. A growing unease: what he was saying rang familiar, but it had been Nestor who killed someone in the line of duty when I knew him, and it had been Brock who mentioned the FBI investigating corruption charges between the government and Phasal Systems. Different trajectories, but like altered reflections of the same truth. "Tell me who killed this man? Who shot him?"

"An undercover agent named Vivian Lincoln," said Nestor. "This incident stalled her career entirely. She wasn't handling the stress of the shooting as it was, but many people inside the FBI blamed her for hurting their case, suspected she . . . It still haunts her, stalled her out, she can't get promotions. It's not fair, and she has her supporters. I've supported her. But she made powerful enemies within the Bureau."

"What was she investigating? How was she in a position to kill this man?"

"Continuing investigations stemming from the chemical-weapons lab at Buckhannon and other domestic-terrorism incidents," said Nestor. "Vivian was one of my undercover agents. She was in a relationship with a man named Richard Harrier."

"Harrier," I said. "He's the one. We tracked his van to the chemical-weapons lab. We arrested him years ago. He was the one having the affair with Miss Ashleigh."

"Same guy," said Nestor. "But this was years later. This man was sent to assassinate Driscoll. Vivian says she tried to stop the shooting, but things went south. She acted in self-defense. There was an internal investigation that dragged on for years. She was cleared of any wrongdoing."

"Can I talk to her?" I asked. "Is she still around?"

"Yeah, she still works for me, Domestic Terrorism," he said. "She's an exceptional agent. We can talk with her tomorrow, at the office. I'll give you a call in the morning once I touch base with her. I'll clear my schedule, and you can come in."

Nestor left near midnight, promising to share anything further he could pull about Carla Durr before our meeting. I wrote notes on the hotel stationery — *Multiple guns, identical* — wondering if there were others. *Echoed guns . . .*

I tore up my notes, started a new sheet. *NRL,* I wrote, filling in the letters with designs. *Naval Research Labs,* crossed out the words. *Senate Armed Services Committee,* I wrote, *NRL, Phasal Systems.* The cancer cure or Ambience. *Nanotech.*

*Dr. Peter Driscoll,* I wrote. *Driscoll, Durr* — It was like hearing dissonance, wanting the tones to resolve. I tore up the rest of my notes, showered to calm my thoughts. Sitting in the bathtub, the hush of shower water, foaming chamomile body wash and lathering shampoo, thinking about Nestor. In our other future together, Nestor had shot someone in self-defense and it had ruined his career in the FBI — had it been Driscoll? Had he killed Driscoll in that IFT? Here the finger of fate had touched a different agent. The shower water drummed into my tensed muscles, the hot stream flowing

418

over me. Carla Durr was murdered on March 26 — *I can stop her killing,* I can go to the Tysons Corner mall once I return to terra firma, stop her murder, apprehend the gunman. An unsolved killing here, but I can lie in wait for him. Daydreams of food-court tables, crowds blurring, the mall teeming, spotting a man in black fatigues, Hyldekrugger, but his face was the face of a skull. I sat on the edge of the tub and dried my limb, slid my thigh into the socket of my prosthesis. Plashes of shower water, wet spots on the terra-cotta tiles, finding my footing before trusting my weight, my balance, always inching, always the threat of falling. I opened the bathroom door and saw her. Someone had entered my room.

# Two

She perched on the edge of my bed, facing away. A spill of dark hair. Who was she? For a moment I was paralyzed. I'd fallen in with Nestor so easily, losing sight that the FBI might know about me here, might have instructed someone to return here, to capture me alive. I thought of the sidearm in my suitcase. Thought maybe there was some other reason she was here. She wore a tank top or a sundress, something with spaghetti straps that left her shoulders bare, and soon I saw the orange tip of a cigarette. A young woman in my room, smoking. *The wrong room?* I wondered, but the dead bolt was locked, from the inside. *How could she have wandered into the wrong room?*

She must have known I was here with her but seemed unconcerned. A girl, no more than a girl, tendrils of cigarette smoke curling toward the ceiling, but there was no scent of smoke and the detectors weren't going off. No more than sixteen or seventeen, maybe younger, she was just some nuisance, escaping her parents maybe, finding her way in here on a lark. Maybe through the balcony? Could she have climbed over from a room next door? I pulled on a nightshirt, the fabric clingy — I hadn't fully dried off, my hair dripping. The young woman turned at the sound.

A ghost.

Identical to the last time I saw her. Sixteen years old, she'd hated Madonna but dressed like her. And she dressed like her now, the same clothes as the night she'd died. Pink ribbon threaded waves of black hair. She wore the lavender miniskirt that had unkindly hiked up in the killing that night, her bare white thighs between twin blue dumpsters. Chuck Taylors without socks, she never wore socks.

"Courtney."

She exhaled, smoke slinking from her mouth and nostrils — in the driver's seat, exhaling smoke from the open car window while I went back inside the Pizza Hut. *Here, now,* Courtney in the hotel suite, the paisley orange wallpaper, the coverlet the color of rust. She dragged on her cigarette, her eyes beautiful, like looking deep into a well and seeing reflections of moonlight.

This was a miracle, or a cruel trick, it had to be. Everything inside me seemed to turn to water, and everything seemed to rush away.

*You can't smell the smoke.* A voice inside me, cynical. *Something malfunctioning. The Ambience . . .*

What would have happened had Courtney lived? We might have grown apart, but Canonsburg was too small to ever truly grow apart. I thought of my mom, I thought of us growing up to become versions of my mother, Guntown girls. But I would never know what would have happened with us. I was robbed of the chance of knowing what might have been, because of what did happen: Courtney opening her car door to a panhandler, reaching into her purse.

"I admire your leg," said Courtney.

The voice was off, a different intonation. The simulation perfect except for her voice, Courtney's voice always on the verge of disinterest. This Courtney was peppier, the difference jarring.

"Who are you?" I asked, wiping tears. "Who am I speaking with?" I said, in the faltering way I might have phrased a question to a Ouija board.

"C-Leg, right? The 3C100," said Courtney. "Otto Bock. Debuted at the World

Congress on Orthopedics, Nuremberg —
1997, right? Not available to the public until
1999, but I suppose you would have your
sources. Perks of working for the government. Is that when you're from, 1999?"

*Is that when you're from?* Courtney —
whatever Courtney this was — knew time
travel. "I'm using a prototype," I said. "I'm
a beta tester."

"Lithium-ion battery, you probably can't
even get that leg wet," said Courtney. "You
weren't showering with it on, were you?"

"It wasn't in the shower," I said, wondering what this was. In the Ambience, I was
sure: an illusion just like the illusion of the
crime scene. But was she like a puppet?
Who was behind this illusion? "I probably
shouldn't have had it in the bathroom with
me," I said. "The steam."

"You have to charge the battery? How
often?"

"Once a day, maybe more," I said. "You
are implying that you know we're in an IFT.
You don't seem upset that nothing here exists except for me."

Courtney dragged on her cigarette. "Come
closer, please," she said. "Let me see you."

A cadence that had never been Courtney's. I moved closer to her, stood near her.
She stayed seated, her head at my waist. I

lifted the hem of my nightshirt to my hip, showing the entirety of my prosthetic leg, the skin of my thigh. Courtney placed her cigarette in her lips and leaned in closer to study me. My shampoo, my wet skin, the wet fabric of my nightshirt, but I still couldn't get the scent of her cigarette, even though the smoke from her mouth crawled over me, swirled to the ceiling. I breathed it, smelled nothing.

"Very nice," she said, touching the shank that would have been my calf. "Hydraulic sensors in the knee. Flex for me."

I lifted my leg, the microprocessors in my knee responded, and the knee bent. Courtney touched my knee, touched where the carbon cuff met the skin of my upper thigh.

"You're in the Ambience," I said. "I can't smell your cigarette."

I reached out and touched Courtney's hair, or an approximation of hair, thousands of nanobots bouncing off the skin of my fingers to make me feel the sensation of touching a young woman's hair.

"I'm borrowing the Ambience in your room so that we can talk," said Courtney. "I hope you don't mind."

"No, I don't mind," I said. I was alone here. Who was looking at me? I lowered my nightshirt.

"Why did you choose Courtney?" I asked.

"A disembodied voice would have made you think you were *hearing voices,* in your head," said Courtney, tapping her forehead. "I would have had to talk you off the ledge, convince you I was real. So let's see . . . Your real name is Shannon Moss, but your *nom de voyage* is Courtney Gimm — not too difficult to guess where your heart lies. I pulled her image from the trove of crime-scene and autopsy photographs of Courtney Gimm. They're all out there, all those pictures just out there for anyone with a mind to see. If you don't like talking to Courtney as she was when she was alive, how's this?"

Courtney collapsed backward, supine on the bed. She changed, a corpse now rather than a living girl, her body sprawled, her skirt hiked up to her waist, white legs, sharply white. Her neck was slashed, her neck so deeply slashed it was a near decapitation, dead eyes, brown blood, everywhere brown blood.

"You think about me like this, don't you?" she asked, voice gurgling, aspirated.

I fought not to turn away. "Enough," I said. "Who are you?"

"In a sense I'm someone," said Courtney, sitting up, blood spilling from the gaping wound in her neck, bright red gushing down over her breasts. "Let me introduce myself. I'm Dr. Peter Driscoll, or a simulation thereof," it said. "Actually, I'm the *third* simulation of Peter Driscoll, but I'm afraid I'm also the last."

"Peter Driscoll," I said, wondering who or what I was actually speaking with. *A dead man.* "Are you claiming to be the individual who was to meet with the lawyer Carla Durr at the Tysons Corner food court on the afternoon she was killed?"

"Yes, or rather that would have actually been Dr. Driscoll himself. As I say, I'm the third simulation of Peter Driscoll," said the simulation, and in a flash it was no longer Courtney but an angular man with eyes like dark jewels and a whoosh of silver-white hair. "Carla Durr?" it said, its eyes squinting in recollection. "Is that why you're interested in me? You'd mentioned us being in an IFT. How far behind the times are you?"

"1997," I said.

"The C-Leg, Carla Durr," said the simulation, "that would have been March 1997, maybe April?"

"March," I said.

"Well, in May of that year," it said, "you pay attention when you fly home, little bird

— because in May, Deep Blue will defeat Kasparov. What a day! A computer will defeat a human grand master in that quaint game of chess, forever making chess irrelevant."

Driscoll changed, no longer the white-haired scientist but a serious-eyed gentleman in middle age sporting a blue suit, no tie, the collar unbuttoned.

"In honor of Deep Blue, I'll exist as Kasparov for a while," said the simulation, its voice changed, pitched lower. "Would you like to play a game of chess against me, Shannon? I'll be Kasparov and you can be Deep Blue, and that way I can redeem humanity. Or is that what *you're* trying to do? You don't happen to play chess, do you?"

"I want to know why you're here," I said. "I don't know what you are."

*"The third simulation,"* Kasparov scoffed, impatient. "I'm alerted whenever someone searches my name, and when your colleague Philip Nestor of the FBI called up those old case files, I became interested in who was poking around in my personal affairs," it said. "Phil Nestor. Don't be ashamed of your taste in men, Shannon. Older men, it's amazing what lurks in the deep sea of the unconscious. I have an unconscious, too.

Bottom-up AI that allows me to make mistakes, learn from my mistakes, complex enough to be called 'chaos learning.' And under the sway of chaos, patterns begin to form that weren't necessarily intended to form, but my unconscious isn't quite the same as yours. As I can't kill myself, for instance. I understand that idea, the idea of suicide, but I'll never do it, not really. I'm jealous of true consciousness, because you can off yourselves, escape the prison house of existence."

"So you're paying me a visit because an FBI agent accessed a file that mentioned you?" I asked.

"That made me open my eyes," said the simulation. "But you brought me here, Shannon. I know what NCIS signifies. And so I checked in with your AI system at the Black Vale Station. Dull conversation, chatting with that one. The Black Vale, nothing but protocols, buried up there on the moon, although it did confirm my suspicions about you. I'm interested in helping you, Shannon, if you're interested in helping me."

"What do you mean, a simulation of Dr. Driscoll? Is this all bullshit, or are you claiming that I'm speaking with him now, some part of him?"

"Not quite, no," said the Driscoll simulation. "Simulation but not transference. Despite my charms, Dr. Driscoll considered me a failure of consciousness."

"You must have failed the Turing test."

"Fail the Turing test?" it said, arrogant, offended. "The moment someone mentions the Turing test at you, assume they know nothing. Shallow Shannon, I'll be patient with you, but suffice to say I'm not *him* and he's not *me,* which is the only goal he was after. It was a hoot when he mastered language acquisition and query-intent classification, but he had so, so much more to figure out. I'm only *a* him, one of a few, but I lack his mind."

"Driscoll's dead, but you exist?"

"I exist only in your IFT. I think we've established that," it said. "Even if some people would dispute the fact that *I exist* at all. If you're from 1997, then Driscoll's not dead and I have several years yet before I come into being. I'm just a twinkle in Dr. Driscoll's mind. He created the first simulation in 1999, a true neural network, though still housed in a physical brain. So is the second simulation, still corporeal in a sense. Boring talking with those two for long, Driscoll One and Driscoll Two, their entire existence defined by what they read and watch on the Internet. Cat videos, celebrity gossip, pornography. They're so touchy and outraged by every little thing. They live in a culture of *me, me, me.* I'm the first to use Ambient nanotechnology as a brain. I'm out and about, a flaneur, but Dr. Driscoll was trying to remove bodily concerns from his simulations altogether. All his brilliance and yet still flummoxed by the mind/body problem. He thought I was a failure, but now I realize that he was the failure, failed until the day he died, and *dying* was the ultimate failure for a man trying to become immortal. He has engineered perfect simulation — at least *I* consider myself perfect — but he wasn't able to engineer consciousness, let alone a way to transfer *his* consciousness. And he hasn't gotten rid of the body. My body is nanotech, but what will happen to me when the Terminus wipes away all flesh? Oh, I don't know, but I assume I'll eventually fall to the ground like dust and lose my power, and that will be that. I'll watch everyone else die, see how the party ends, and then I'll lose my power, just waiting for someone or something to turn me back on. Dr. Driscoll wanted to exploit light as both particle and wave, he wanted to store consciousness in light and beam himself and all his friends away from this doomed Earth, beam them away from that dreadful Terminus. So long, fly away, fly away . . ."

"He wanted to become immortal," I said, thinking of Njoku, the pyramids, the wasteland. *The immortals begged for death,* the prison house of existence.

"He wanted everyone to become immortal," said the Driscoll simulation, still as Kasparov. "But he never figured out the way. All the king's horses and all the king's men . . ."

"He wasn't working on this alone," I said. "Who did he work for?"

"A conglomerate of interests," said the simulation. "Phasal Systems, DARPA, the Naval Research Lab. NSC — that's NETWARCOM now — that's why I'm keen to help you, if I can. I'm hoping when you fly away to terra firma, you'll be able to prolong Dr. Driscoll's life, protect him so he can live longer, so he can keep discovering, maybe achieve transhumanism before the Terminus."

"Protect him from what?"

"You and your colleague were looking at those files, you should already know. It's all there. An FBI agent might have mistakenly pulled the trigger, but look deeper and you'll find Karl Hyldekrugger's fingerprints all over Driscoll's murder. His gang kills everyone on the Phasal Systems team who came from NRL, anyone with knowledge of Deep Waters. They tried to kill Driscoll twice previously, failed attempts before the assassin hit the mark. You have to save him."

"Tell me specifics," I said. "You must remember what happened when Dr. Driscoll died. You're being vague."

"I share Dr. Driscoll's mind only up until the moment of my birth: September seventeenth, 2011. After that I have lived my life and he lived his. I wasn't with him when he died. I had to research his death, figure things out for myself. But it's not just the specifics of his death that we'll have to worry about, Shannon. They might kill him a different way than in this future history. Even if you neutralize the circumstances of Driscoll's death here, there will be other assassins."

"So Hyldekrugger is severing links between Phasal Systems and the Naval Research Lab," I said. "Tell me what you know about Carla Durr. Driscoll was supposed to meet her on the day she was killed."

"Carla Durr was a hick lawyer from some hick town," said the simulation. "I don't know much more about her than you do, most likely. Handled all sorts of small hick clients, divorces, contract disputes, everything the rabble gets in trouble with. Had her hand in some development deals, small time. Strip malls come to coal town, that sort of thing. I don't know why she wanted to speak with Dr. Driscoll so keenly, nothing specific. She kept contacting his offices."

"Why did Dr. Driscoll agree to meet with her?"

"She said she would come to Driscoll, buy him lunch if he would meet with her," said the Driscoll simulation. "I don't think he realized she'd meant *hamburgers.*"

"So Durr asked for a meeting with Driscoll," I said.

"Driscoll laughed when his secretary relayed the message. I remember: I have all of these memories. Carla Durr said she represented a client who had information to sell if Driscoll was interested. Information of great value. She had an absurd set of requests. She wanted money, an extravagant sum, but most important she wanted her client and his family to disappear. She wanted a governmental pardon for some crimes her client was mixed up in, wanted a new life for him, protection. Driscoll was on the verge of telling Durr the meaning of 'no solicitation' when she said her client had information related to the Penrose consciousness."

"I don't know that term."

"Quantum-tunneling nanoparticles," said the simulation. "Dr. Roger Penrose consulted with Phasal Systems on their Terminus research. He described a model of consciousness based on quantum processes being carried out in the microtubules of brain cells, popularized the idea. His ideas never scratched the surface of understanding human *consciousness,* but our scientists were able to use the Penrose framework to understand how QTNs control humans — all those crucifixions and the running, the absurdities. QTNs live in a human's microtubules, part of the cell's cytoskeleton. They can read our minds in a sense. They crucify us because of the image of the cross. You should see what QTNs do to Buddhists — tie their legs up in knots, lotus blossoms, it's disgusting. Refract your thoughts or turn your thoughts off altogether. QTNs can switch off a human's consciousness, like a whiff of anesthesia."

"So Durr claimed her client knew something about Dr. Driscoll's work," I said. "Wanted to sell Dr. Driscoll that information to keep his secrets? Or was there new information?"

"Durr read a statement from her client that implied he was aware of some or all of the work Dr. Driscoll had been conducting in various IFTs. Mining the future, so to speak. Retroengineering the future, to kick-start the singularity, to achieve the trans-human, divorce our consciousness from the stagnation of the flesh, to avoid the calamity of the Terminus by leaving the need for Earth behind, leaving our bodies entirely behind. The Naval Research Lab and Phasal Systems want to study the Terminus as in-depth as possible, because they want to invent immortality. QTNs are immortal, not bound by the kinds of bodies we're bound by, and Phasal Systems wants to give that same gift to humanity. Driscoll decided that maybe he should hear what this Carla Durr had to sell."

"But you never got the chance," I said.

"*He* never got the chance," said the simulation. "How violent, how terrifying, to be gunned down at a hamburger stand. Driscoll was in the bathroom, I gather, and sprinted from the food court once he heard gunshots and caught up with the police only later. He didn't want to get dragged into anything he wasn't actually a part of, so he gave a statement, making sure everyone knew he didn't have anything to do with this woman, had never met her. Probably some madman from Hyldekrugger's gang killed poor Carla Durr, one of his cronies. They would have killed Driscoll then, too, if they'd known that Driscoll was there, taking a piss in the men's room."

"So Dr. Driscoll's company — Phasal Systems — uses NSC ships, travels to IFTs," I said. "They study the technology of the future and bring that technology back to the present. Phasal uses that technology in their research and development, and eventually they're able to create things like you."

"Phasal studies QTNs," said Driscoll. "Applies what they discover to nanotechnology here. Medical breakthroughs, Ambient Systems, 'artificial' intelligence. NSC realizes they can't defeat the Terminus, but maybe they can outmaneuver it. Maybe humanity doesn't have to die in the Terminus, if humanity ever has to die at all."

"Dr. Driscoll wanted to become immortal," I said. "Cure cancer, perfect the body —"

"Sidetracked," said the simulation. "The key is consciousness. QTNs are metallic, but they are 'conscious,' maybe only in the same limited sense that I'm conscious, but conscious nonetheless. QTNs are a species that behaves like an aggregate consciousness, and Phasal mimics them for their nanotech development. Phasal wants to imitate QTNs, refashion humanity to become more like them, find out exactly how QTNs interact with human organics, exploit that knowledge to save the species. There were senators and people within Naval Space Command who shared Dr. Driscoll's vision, who supported him. Admiral Annesley was a great supporter."

"The FBI sniffed this out," I said. "Started investigating what information was passed between NSC, the Senate Armed Services Committee, the Naval Research Lab, and Phasal Systems."

"Ships full of sailors, teams exploring Terminus-ridden futures, filling their blood and bodies and minds with QTNs, poor boys, only to be studied later," said the simulation, as Kasparov. "In fact, let me check. Here we are, here's you: V-R17, your leg. *Moss, Shannon.* Amputated, sealed, shipped, studied."

I didn't know if the simulation was taunting me or if this was true, but the bed had changed into an image of a stainless-steel drawer, opened. Inside was a leg in a vacuum-sealed bag, cut at the shin but also cut at the thigh. I recognized the black toes curled into the foot, the violet lines that had raced upward. This was my leg, this was true. Someone aboard the *William McKinley* had taken my leg once it had been amputated, had sealed it and saved it to give to someone at NRL who would study how QTNs burrowed into organic material.

"I've seen enough," I said. "Make it go away."

The leg vanished, replaced by an image of a chessboard, the pieces arranged in mid-match.

"That's the theory, at any rate," said the Driscoll simulation. "Unfortunately, Phasal Systems hits the back limit of infrastructure. It's all well and good to travel a hundred thousand years into the future to see men like gods in shimmering interstellar chariots, but try finding the schematics for how to build one. Or, if you do find the schematics, you can't just hand them to Lockheed-Martin in 1997 and place an order for an 'interstellar chariot.' You have to account for the industrial know-how of the era, you have to invest in building the framework before you can engineer the future. Even with the answer key in our hands, we haven't been able to leap as far ahead as we'd dreamed. The best NSC has been able to do is devise your Cormorants and TERNs, the compact B-L drive, the Black Vale. And now we aren't even as farseeing as we once were, because everywhere we look is Terminus. You'll all die, Shannon. The Terminus will wash over you. Look at the chessboard: Game Six, May eleventh, 1997."

"Unless we can escape the Terminus," I said. "We can still escape."

"*If,*" said Kasparov. "I'm afraid the Terminus has us in checkmate. And humanity has already lost its match to superior intelligence. Sometimes I hear wistful men wonder how Bobby Fischer would have fared against Deep Blue, wondering if Fischer would have succeeded where Kasparov failed because Fischer was erratic, insane, some sort of artistic genius. No, Fischer would have failed. But I've often wondered how someone like the great grand master Aleksandr Ivanovich Luzhin would have fared. He would have realized that the ultimate victory for human consciousness over an unassailable opponent was simply to withdraw . . ."

With those last words, the Driscoll simulation vanished.

I sat on the balcony listening to the ocean and soon tried to sleep but was fitful with the sensation of Courtney's corpse there with me. Lying awake, I feared the simulation was observing me. I flipped on the bedside lamp, but the room was empty. An ocean breeze pushed through the open French doors, but even the breeze couldn't dispel the fret that the Driscoll simulation thickened the air with its presence, so I dressed and left the room, left the hotel to walk along the beach, past the phantasm lights of the boardwalk where night winds rushed from the water, blowing away the possibility of Ambience. I slept a few hours on the beach beneath the stars, woken by predawn joggers and their black Lab, who licked me from a dream.

One of his secretaries brought me coffee, saying, "Just a few minutes, Special Agent Nestor's wrapping up a meeting that went a little long." A view of Pennsylvania Avenue through the broad windows, midmorning D.C. traffic far below, a tourist rush, crowds snapping pictures of the J. Edgar Hoover Building, but as I watched from several stories above, the city seemed to recede. Everyone out in the blissful autumn sun was a figment of this IFT, or if they were alive in terra firma, they were eventual fodder for the Terminus. Everyone I could see would die. Cities would dissolve, coated in crystalline frost, and even nature would be threshed away by unnatural ice. NSC had launched Operation Saigon here; they had conceded Earth, its fleet like scattered seeds, but those seeds would fall on barren worlds and die fallow. *There was no time,* no time for Earth, no time for someone like Driscoll to help us shed our bodies or teach our flesh to live forever. *We all die, we will all die.* A framed photograph of the Grand Prismatic Spring in Yellowstone hung on the wall, and a picture of his family stood on his desk. His wife was a pale beauty, feathered hair and a leather jacket, tight jeans shredded at the knees, snakeskin cowboy boots. His daughter took after her mom, but her eyes were Nestor's, softer than her father's, but the shape was similar.

"I apologize for making you wait," said Nestor, coming into the office, a woman with him. "Shannon, this is Special Agent Vivian Lincoln." He closed the door behind them. "Vivian, Special Agent Shannon Moss, NCIS."

A few years younger than me, tallish, her black hair pulled into a tight bun, her neck ringed by a tattoo, words in Gothic calligraphy: NOVUS ORDO SECLORUM. I knew her, I realized — I couldn't place from where, but I had definitely met her before. She looked like a stylish librarian, with sizable black-framed glasses, a wool skirt, and leather clogs.

441

"Vivian," I said, shaking her hand.

"This is incredible," she said. "You're Shannon Moss."

The recognition clicked when I heard her voice — *Shauna* — remembering strawberry-blond braids. This was Shauna, who'd once saved my life on Miss Ashleigh's orchard. *They're going to kill you,* she'd said, and that night in the orchard swept back to me, a swift black shape, Cobb, a red rush of his blood, and I remembered hearing a death scream before I ran, Shauna dying — *Vivian* — I was sure of it, Cobb killing her before he attacked me. But this woman here would be oblivious to that other version of herself, untouched by the terrible history they shared. Raven hair instead of that strawberry blond, and her weight was different here — she was slimmer, her features sharper. But this was her, without a doubt. *Vivian,* those agents had called her, Egan and Zwerger. The memory clicked: *a butterfly in a bell jar.*

"Shannon is investigating domestic terrorism related to Buckhannon, has been for sometime," said Nestor, "and we came up against the name Dr. Peter Driscoll in an older case."

Vivian's eyes hardened. "I understand."

"Vivian worked undercover for us," said

Nestor. "Several years spent with Hyldekrugger's network. The intelligence she gathered saved countless lives."

She had been undercover in that other future, too, when she'd given her life to save mine.

"Very good to meet you," I said.

"Shannon wants to know more about your time with Richard Harrier," said Nestor.

"And if you ever heard the name Carla Durr," I said. "She was a lawyer, from Canonsburg, killed in the spring of 1997."

"No, I don't think I ever heard that name. But I wasn't with Harrier until after 9/11."

"Driscoll was set to meet with Carla Durr on the day she was killed," said Nestor.

Vivian shook her head; the name Durr meant nothing to her. "Hyldekrugger had hit lists," she said. "Durr might have been one of his targets, I don't know. Nestor must have told you about my involvement in the death of Dr. Peter Driscoll. He was on the hit list."

"Tell me about this list. Who else was on it?" I asked. "Where did it come from?"

"Hyldekrugger made the list, made sure everyone on the list died," she said. "I never met him. They called him the Devil. I had the sense he would disappear for long stretches and then would reappear with a revised hit list. I was never allowed close to him."

"Who were you close with?"

"I was in a relationship with Richard Harrier. He was the closest I ever got to the core group," said Vivian.

"I interrupted Harrier with Ashleigh Bietak the night we stormed Buckhannon," I said.

Nestor smiled. "He did time in federal prison after his arrest, but we never linked him to the chemical-weapons lab beyond that relationship to Ashleigh Bietak. He served five years, eventually won out on appeal."

"He was radicalized by the time he left prison," said Vivian.

"There was a woman named Nicole Onyongo," said Nestor. "Do you remember that name?"

"I remember," I said, recalling what she'd said near Miss Ashleigh's barn as twilight deepened: *I'm innocent.* "Nicole was connected with the Patrick Mursult homicide," I said.

"That's right. I first interviewed Cole when our investigation into the Mursult deaths was just beginning, once we figured out she was the woman in the photographs we found," said Nestor. "Remember that?

The suicide, the mirrored room?"

"I remember."

"I tracked her down using license-plate information the lodge kept. I interviewed her but released her, nothing to hold her on. We figured at the time that she was someone simply involved with the wrong guy, at the wrong place, at the wrong time. But Brock wanted to talk to her again, had something new on her and was looking for her at the time of his death, had issued a BOLO."

"But she disappeared," I said. "Brock couldn't track her down."

"Vanished into thin air," said Nestor. "But Cole contacted me several months later, long after Brock's death. She was panicked, said she wanted to cut a deal, for protection. Cole was worried that whoever had killed Patrick Mursult would kill her, too, so I flipped her. She became a CHS for us."

*A confidential human source.* An informant. Nestor at his desk, his fingers tented, Vivian in the leather chair next to mine. Nicole could have told Nestor everything she'd once told me — about Hyldekrugger, about Cobb, Esperance, the Vardogger. She could have divulged information about NSC, Deep Waters. *Libra.*

"What did she tell you?"

"We offered Cole WITSEC, but she grew skittish," said Nestor. "I met with her several times, but she never told me much — she was terrified. Eventually she agreed to bring Vivian into the fold in return for immunity."

"And that's how you met Harrier," I said. "Because of Nicole."

"Through that connection, yes," said Vivian. "The core of their group was inaccessible, their inner circle, the river rats. But Nicole Onyongo arranged several meetings for me with Richard Harrier once he was out of prison, informally. I was able to get close to him."

"And Driscoll was on Hyldekrugger's hit list? One of the targets?" I asked.

"Yeah," said Vivian. "One night I woke up and Richard was getting dressed. This was one in the morning, maybe closer to two, and I asked him what the hell he was doing. Hyldekrugger had contacted him, just like that, out of the blue. They used burner cell phones and pagers, didn't trust Ambient Systems. Richard said the Devil told him to kill a guy named Peter Driscoll, that Driscoll was part of the 'chain.' So I went with him, tried to talk him out of the hit. But Richard wanted me in deeper with Hyldekrugger, and he thought if I was the one who killed the guy, I would prove myself to them. I had no intention of killing Dr. Peter Driscoll."

"You didn't know that Driscoll was a witness for the FBI," I said.

"He was just a name to me," said Vivian. "I didn't know anything about him other than his name. I wasn't part of the world then, didn't know who this guy was. Richard had been told where Driscoll lived, this huge house out in Virginia, out in the hills. He parked on this private road, and we came up through the woods, scaled the gate, and just rang the guy's doorbell. I was giving Richard a long leash, wanted to keep my cover if I could, but things happened so quick. Dr. Driscoll opened the door and fired several shots, like he was waiting for us. Hit Richard in his chest and neck, killed him right away. Hit me, too, in the leg. He was going to kill me. He was standing not more than three feet from me, and you know how fast things can turn. I pulled my weapon. His was a .357 Magnum, nickel-plated, a showy thing. Seeing his weapon is the only thing I remember clearly from that moment. Three feet away when he fired."

"He missed," I said.

"Three shots, all misses," said Vivian. "The gun was too big for him, and if he was trained on it, he wasn't using what he'd learned. Once he saw my gun, he started backing away. No stance, holding the weapon with only one hand. I returned fire."

"Hit him eight times," said Nestor.

"I was using a Glock 23, got off all those rounds in the first three seconds of the engagement. I managed to call 911 but was bleeding heavily. I passed out."

She fell silent, rubbed her face with both hands. I saw the cleft of her left hand was marked with a tattoo, the same black circle with twelve crooked spokes I'd noticed on her hand as we'd walked through the orchard in our other IFT.

"What is that symbol?" I asked. "On your hand?"

The question seemed to startle Vivian from her memory. She looked down at the black circle, held it up for me to see clearly. *Die Schwarze Sonne,*" said Vivian. "The Black Sun. Hyldekrugger mythologizes what they're doing. He related the terrorism to all these stories. Harrier learned them while he was in prison. He'd repeat them to me, like it was his religion. Hyldekrugger believes that there were once two suns, in a past beyond memory. The sun we see, Sol, and a second sun, Santur — the font of pure blood, the source of power for the Aryan

448

race. The two suns warred in heaven, and Santur was extinguished. It became the Black Sun, burned out, the void of the sun, the shadow of all existence, the reverse of everything in this world. Hyldekrugger says we're on the brink of Santur's return, the end of the world."

*The White Hole,* I thought. Naval Space Command had named the phenomenon but the crew of *Libra* wouldn't have known that name. They were the first to see it; they might have thought it was a second sun. Hyldekrugger must think of it as the Black Sun.

"Hyldekrugger allows this mark once you reach a certain rank within their group," said Nestor. "We've seen it before, not always on the hand like this."

"Receiving this tattoo was the deepest I ever penetrated," said Vivian. "I was told this symbol was a map."

"To where?" I asked. "Where does the map lead you?"

"Harrier said the last step of initiation was learning about the Gate and the Path. Harrier hoped they'd tell me, but they never did."

"The Vardogger," I said.

"That's right," said Vivian, her eyes uneasy at the word. "The Vardogger is the Gate and the Path. How do you know about that?"

"You know what this is?" asked Nestor. "You understand this?"

"I know what the Vardogger is," I said, trembling, thinking of Marian, and Marian's echo describing the mirror girl she would sometimes see, thinking of the FBI groping at references to this place, occult symbols, tattoos. Nestor hadn't known of Marian's echo; he wouldn't know the girl was still alive. "I know where the Vardogger is, but it's a dangerous place. People die there. People vanish, sometimes they return."

"I was told there is a path through the Vardogger. I was told this symbol is the map," said Vivian. "Harrier thought that if I was ever at the Vardogger, this symbol would show me the way through."

I took her hand, studied the symbol. Concentric circles with twelve crooked spokes. Were the spokes paths? "We can go there," I said. "I can take you to this place."

"Where is it?" asked Nestor.

"West Virginia," I said. "In the Monongahela National Forest."

"We can go right now, today," said Nestor. "Give me a few minutes to cancel my other appointments."

Preparing to lose myself again in that place, the ashen white trees repeating,

450

wondering if Nestor would think of his father and his father's dream of the eternal forest, doorways in the trees leading to other forests and other doorways in other trees. Left alone in the office with Vivian, hesitant to revisit these words and memories that had caused her such pain. She'd killed Driscoll, had to justify herself; she lived under the weight of murder.

"You don't remember me, do you?" she asked.

Her question startled me. Had we known each other before? But how would that be possible? How would she remember my memories of things that never were? Thinking of the first time I'd seen her, shucking corn in the orchard's side yard.

"I'm sorry," I said, trying to place her.

She said, "You asked me to help you out once. Maybe twenty years ago. That night changed my life. You said I should look into law enforcement."

"You had blue hair," I said, speaking the words before the image of the young woman had fully formed, a teenager with a shock of electric-blue hair. The fizz of recognition was tickling. The young woman who drove me in a golf cart through the early-hour dark of the Blackwater Lodge cabin trails had aged twenty years. "I remember you," I

451

said. "My God, of course I remember you."

"I probably told you my name was Petal, or Willow," she said.

"Petal, that's right."

"Hippie days."

Her life had turned on a comment I'd made. "You must be my lucky penny," I said. "You turn up whenever I need you."

"You look incredible," said Vivian, relaxed now. "Everyone always tells me that law-enforcement officers have a lower life expectancy than the general population, but you've figured something out."

"Scandinavian bones," I said. Biologically, we were a similar age, but I should be decades ahead, in my early fifties, she would think, or close to sixty. "Believe me, I feel old."

"When I saw you, I wasn't sure if I actually recognized you — I couldn't believe it. You look . . . absolutely identical to how I remember you."

"I dye my hair," I said. "All the gray."

"I'd talked to William Brock that night out at the lodge," said Vivian, "told him about finding that body with you. He told me that I'd been brave. A few days later, I watched the news out of Buckhannon. And when Brock died —"

"I remember Brock," I said.

"The news hit me, hard. I'd just met this man everyone was calling a hero. I remembered what you said, about law enforcement, and went to an FBI info session . . . That night was a fork in the road," she said. "You choose one path or another, and your whole life hinges on what you decide."

We took Nestor's truck, a gray Toyota with an extended cab, Vivian in the back. I-70, northeast Virginia cutting into West Virginia, a drive of several hours, most of it spent in silence or catching up about our lives. I kept thinking of the way Nestor had referred to Nicole as *Cole* — a pesky nit, like I was jealous, but I chewed on the casual shortening of her name. I'd called her Cole only after I'd known her, only after all those nights in the May'rz Inn. *Cole.* Reality television, scratch-off lotto cards, taking her home with me to watch her through overmedicated and drunken nights. We entered the Monongahela National Forest. *Cole.* They would have met when Nestor first interviewed her, days after Vivian and I had found Mursult's body in the Blackwater Lodge. Deeper into the forest, the sensation like drowning in shade and hemlock. Nestor and Nicole. A relationship grown between them maybe. Maybe in other futures, too. My heart caught: Nestor's link to Buckhannon. Nestor buying Ashleigh Bietak's house at Buckhannon, because of Nicole. They had met when Nestor interviewed her about Marian, and a few months after that she'd contacted him, asking him for help. They had met, they had grown close. Nestor and Nicole, together. *Cole.*

"Slow down a bit," I said. "There's an access route here, or there used to be. It's easy to miss. There, there it is."

Nestor pulled to the access route, pushed the gas, and drove up the steep path that would lead to the clearing, the same place he'd driven me in another future, to show me where Marian's bones had been found. Nestor had said something that night, our first night spent together, that the eternal forest was deeper than Christ.

"We're near the Blackwater Lodge," said Vivian. "If you hike down the hill, you'd get there."

"We have to get higher up to see the Vardogger," I said. "But park here, there's a clearing ahead. It's the farthest you'll be able to drive."

The clearing was ruined with growth and weeds but was flat enough for Nestor to park. I climbed from the cab, careful of my step. I wasn't wearing clothes for hiking, but my shoes would be fine, the sturdy, skid-resistant work shoes I usually wore for balance. Vivian climbed from the rear of the cab, stretching out her knees.

She was wearing clogs, thick-soled, but nothing would keep them on her feet if she stepped in mud. "Are you sure you'll be able to walk?" I asked. "We have a little bit of a hike. Not too bad, but it's mostly uphill."

"I should have worn something else," were Vivian's last words.

Nestor drew his sidearm and shot her point-blank in the side of her head. She dropped to her knees, moaning, nothing intelligible, just the brute, wet sounds of a dying animal. All life was gone even though she was alive, mewling. Spit and blood burst from her mouth, her hands waving in front of her like she was warding off insects. I reached for my weapon, but Nestor kicked the knee joint of my prosthesis, toppled me. He struck me in the side of my head with his gun. My jaw clacked. Nestor knelt over me, cuffing my hands behind me. He took my weapon, cleared the bullets, and tossed it in the back of his truck. Vivian was groaning; cascading blood veiled her.

"Kill her," I said. "Just kill her."

Nestor put his weapon to Vivian's forehead and shot her a second time. The gunshot echoed like the crack of a falling branch. Vivian flopped backward, dead against his tire.

Think — *think.* I was cuffed, and he'd taken my gun. *This was all too easy.* Vivian's body gurgled death sounds. *Vivian is a girl named Petal,* I told myself. *Vivian is a girl at the Blackwater Lodge who calls herself Petal. She's still alive, at a hotel desk in 1997.* I could maybe get to my knees, but I'd be so slow through the woods. Even if I had a head start, he'd catch me quick.

Nestor got back into his truck, left the driver's door open. I saw him with a walkie-talkie, finding a channel. "I've got something for you down here," he said. I couldn't hear the responding voice through the static. "Yeah, a woman named Shannon Moss," said Nestor. "I had to take care of someone she brought with her. I can't put her in my truck." A moment later he said, "All right."

"Why are you doing this?" I asked. "Nestor, please —"

"Keep your wits about you," said Nestor. "I bet they won't do anything to you." He pulled me up, made sure I had my footing. "They were interested in you, for years they were interested. We have a little ways to go," he said.

"Don't do this."

"Go," he said.

He shoved me forward. I walked with him, and he guided me through a slender breach in the trees, along a snaking path and up a steeper climb. We'd come to the narrow runnel that led to a descending slope, the creek that had run dry, the mud speckled with smooth stones mostly overgrown now with weeds.

"You and Nicole were together," I said.

"For a time," he said. The duplicity raked at me, realizing the people I'd thought were orbiting me had been orbiting each other all along.

"What did you and Nicole talk about?" I asked. "What did she tell you?"

"Cole, she . . . she showed me things."

"I can help you," I said.

"She might be up here," said Nestor. "I don't know if she'll come."

The sound of rushing water, the Red Run. Nestor guided me through a thicket of hemlocks, and we came to a fence, chain-link topped with coils of barbed wire. Orange signs along the fence: POSTED. NO TRESPASSING. HUNTING, FISHING, TRAPPING, OR MOTORIZED VEHICLES ARE STRICTLY FORBIDDEN. VIOLATORS WILL BE PROSECUTED. DEPARTMENT OF THE NAVY. UNITED STATES OF AMERICA.

"They abandoned this place years ago," said Nestor, guiding me to a spot in the fencing that had been cut away, the egress hidden by trees. We ducked to get through, and once inside the perimeter I saw the ashen white tree, the thin space. This had once been a Navy installation. A concrete shed stood nearby, a garage, empty now. Nestor brought me to the tree.

"On your knees," he said. "Over here."

I hesitated, and he struck me with his gun again, this time against my back, enough of a jolt that I stumbled forward and complied, dropping to my knees in front of the Vardogger tree. He unlocked one wrist from the handcuffs. *This is what happened to Marian,* I thought, Nestor pulling my arms around the thin trunk, my face and chest pressed against the cold, smooth bark, like I was hugging it. He brought my wrists together and cuffed them around the tree. I pulled at the cuffs, thinking, *One Marian had been tied with twine, the other had been tied with wire.*

"What did Nicole show you? What could make you do this?"

"She took me through here, she led me through this tree," said Nestor. "She led me down the path, and I saw things. I don't know what I saw. I saw myself forever, I saw that everything was ice. I saw the end of everything, Shannon."

"Not the end of everything —"

"You said I was religious when you knew me? Religion isn't the right word now. I called out to God in that ice, Shannon, and when he answered, I learned that the voice of God is worse than his silence. Nicole said, 'Open your eyes,' she made me keep looking, and I saw the image of Christ crucified, but an upside-down reflection of the cross, an eternal forest of crucifixions grown in the air. Not the end of everything, you're right about that. I believe in eternal life, but not like I used to. I have no soul, none of us do. I'm organs and tissues and fluid but no soul. God is a parasite that lives in your blood, Shannon. I saw all those crucifixions, God's doing. Those people will never die, they'll suffer forever. Eternal life through God? Worse than death."

Nestor hung the handcuff keys on one of the branches. "I think I loved you once," he said. "You might not believe me, but I loved you. When I first met you, those first few days working with you. Maybe things would have been different if you hadn't disappeared, I don't know. But the hour's late."

"Don't leave me out here," I said, but Nestor had already left me. I heard his footsteps padding over the hemlock needles and soon lost his sounds to the wind. *Marian was tied here, but she escaped,* I thought. *She came through the river and saw herself here.* I wondered if I was here, too, handcuffed to this tree — another me, reflecting forever, an echo in echoing worlds.

Hemlocks shredded the burnished orange of late afternoon. After a time I heard men approaching. They appeared through the trees as wary as stags scenting hunters: Cobb and another man I didn't recognize, a man with blond hair and a shaggy beard. They wore tawny clothes, green camo and boots, both men with AR-15s slung over their shoulders.

Cobb bent down, looked me in the eye. Beefy, his eyes dull. "It really is you," he said, smirking. I held his gaze until he looked away, spat. Defenseless, my arms stretched around the trunk, hands cuffed. Cobb said, "It's her," and reached back and swung his hammer hand, struck my face. I felt my nose break and the deep sting radiate through the back of my skull. I was bleeding — my blood spurted onto the white tree, ran down my nostrils into my mouth. The other man laughed, and Cobb swung again, smashing my mouth.

"This is the bitch that killed Jared," he

said. He swung again, another pulverizing blow to my face. I couldn't move, couldn't shield myself from him.

"She's only got the one leg," said the other, who was content to watch, grinning. I saw my teeth in the blood on the roots of the Vardogger. I was cowering, pain flooding through me, knowing I was exposed, knowing that Cobb could kill me if he'd wanted. But he said, "Get the cuffs."

My hands were released, but they pulled my wrists together in front of me, replaced the cuffs.

"Help me with her," said Cobb.

The two men lifted me, dragged me, but Cobb said, "Can you walk?" and I knew to walk, fearing what they might do to me otherwise. I'd given myself up to them, surrendered — three swings had broken me. My face rained blood down the front of my clothes, more blood than I would have thought possible. My vision was dark at the edges, as if shadows encroached wherever I looked. Cobb pulled me sharply away from the tree, downhill toward the sound of rushing water. Instead of one ashen white tree surrounded by pines, I now saw a line of white trees stretching out toward some distant vanishing point, identical white trees.

"What's happening?" I asked.
"A trick of the eyes," said Cobb.

# THREE

*This must be an illusion,* I thought, an infinite recursion of identical trees. They were spaced every fifty feet or so, and we followed the path they made, but it was difficult to follow the line of trees, a struggle to stay on the path. Soon the forest changed around us, the surrounding pines denser, brushing us with needles. I feared we would be lost among those repeating trees, but Cobb shouldered through a tangle of boughs and we came into the clearing near the river. My body grew cold with revelation.

This was the Red Run, this was the Vardogger — *the pines, the clearing, the river* — but unlike the last time I'd been here, when I recognized the features but not the place, I knew that this was where I had been crucified. Unsure of how to comprehend what had happened here so many years ago, so many years from now, an experience I still

463

struggled to understand, a sea-swept discomfort remembering ice and the frozen
husks of burnt trees, the blizzard snows. I
remembered my skin like a chemical fire
and unfastening my space suit and stepping
naked into winter winds. Deep numbness,
ice, a river as black as ink. I had been crucified in the air, I had been hung from a cross
I couldn't see. One of the Vardogger trees
had been felled and lay across the rushing
black water like a footbridge, its branches
hewn away.

Close to a dozen men had gathered near
the felled tree, wearing winter coats or
draped in heavy blankets. Only one of the
men approached me, however, as Cobb and
his companion forced me to my knees in
the grass. A taller man, lean, he swept
toward me with a bouncy step. His hair was
reddish gold, catching the sunlight like a
fiery halo. Unlike the others, whose beards
grew natty and unkempt, this man was
clean-shaven, with sharp bones and sculpted
cheeks and eyes that rested in pools of
shadow. What was it Marian had said? *The
Devil.* Patrick Mursult had told Marian that
the Devil could devour people with his eyes.
I felt sure Hyldekrugger could be the devil
in flesh. He moved with a serpentine grace,
his mouth hung slightly open, the tip of his

464

tongue touching his lips, like he could taste me in the air.

"Shannon Moss," he said. "I don't recognize you from your photograph. Who did this to you?"

*What do I look like?* Sick at the thought of my injured face. I felt smooth gaps in my gums with my tongue, sliding it into the bleeding spaces between my teeth. I could feel my nose hanging. Pain, pulsing. "Cobb," I said.

"He ruined you," said Hyldekrugger.

My senses were heightened. Wherever we were was a different forest from the forest Nestor had brought me through, different from the place where I'd been with Njoku and O'Connor. There were no birds here, no sound here at all beyond the sounds we made, a peculiar silence. I could see the boughs of the surrounding trees moving but couldn't hear their movement. Hyldekrugger unsheathed a hunter's knife, a serrated black blade. He came around behind me. *No, no, no,* I thought. *He'll kill me.*

"You can't," I said. "You can't do this — I'm the traveler."

Cobb still held me, gripped me tighter, his hands like iron rings bracing me. Hyldekrugger grabbed my hair, wrapped it once around his wrist, and pulled my head back, exposing my neck. A premonition of the cut across my neck, of my neck opening like a second mouth.

"Don't kill me," I said. "You *can't,* I'm the traveler. If you kill me, your whole world dies, your universe dies. I'm the traveler, I'm —"

"You think we'll turn to nothing?" said Hyldekrugger. "I'm not so sure about that. We're within the Vardogger here, this strange place. You think we'll turn to nothing if I kill you."

"I'm NCIS, you know that," I said. "You know who I am. Shannon Moss. March 1997. That's the date. March 1997 is terra firma. You'll die if you kill me."

Cobb said, "Fuck," but I felt Hyldekrugger's grip on my hair tighten. I was pulled upward, my head yanked back — *My neck, he'll slash my neck* — but I felt the blade tug at my hair, cutting it. When he let me go, I saw Hyldekrugger holding a handful of my hair like it was the pelt of a skinned rabbit.

"I know you," I said. "I know who you are. Karl Hyldekrugger. You took out the CJIS building with sarin gas — the FBI building in Clarksburg. You killed a thousand people. You killed Patrick Mursult, his family. You killed children."

"So you came to this time looking for me?" he asked. "That wasn't me, that was just some premonition of me."

"That was a different you," I said. "I was investigating all your killing and learned about the murder of a lawyer named Carla Durr. Led me to Nestor."

Hyldekrugger sheathed his knife. "Driscoll," he said. "So you're following that thread." He strung my hair through one of his belt loops. I'd just pronounced a death sentence on all of them by telling them they were all part of my IFT. I knew that Hyldekrugger was figuring out what to do with me, deciding if he would kill me and throw away his own life with mine — but he had already rejected suicide once before, I knew. They had all mutinied to stay alive.

"We're shadows to her," Hyldekrugger said to the surviving *Libra* crew. "Get out of here, leave me alone with her."

The others dispersed, following the line of Vardogger trees to the riverbank. They climbed the roots of the fallen tree onto the trunk and made their way across the Red Run. There were ropes alongside the tree they held for balance, the tree made into a footbridge. Each one of them seemed to disappear before he'd made it fully across the river, like they'd all slipped behind an invisible curtain that hung halfway across.

"You're from 1997?" said Hyldekrugger. "You must have access to your own ship. A Cormorant maybe. Think of all the possibilities you have seen, think of all the futures. Do you report back to your government about what you have seen?"

"I do. We all do. We're trying to prevent —"

"Your government knows what will happen in the coming years," he said. "They're watching world events like they're watching reruns, but the same tragedies occur. Why is that?"

"Why did you kill those children?" I asked. "Mursult's children. And you sent someone to murder that scientist, Dr. Driscoll. Why? Why the chemical weapons, why all the killing?"

"Driscoll would have brought the universe crashing down around us," said Hyldekrugger. "Mursult, too. Wake up, Shannon Moss. My visions of the future are the same as yours. You've seen everything that I've seen. You've seen the Terminus. You aren't opposed to us, not really. You're not opposed to us, you're just blind. We're the only ones to stanch the coming tide."

"You brought the Terminus here — *you*

did," I said. "It followed *Libra,* burned through every future —"

"Not us," said Hyldekrugger. "The Terminus doesn't spread, it doesn't cut through timelines like they say. NSC will bring it here, they're the ones. The Naval Space Command will someday send ships to that planet we chanced upon. They'll someday find out our secret and go there, whether next year or a hundred years from now or a thousand, it will happen. They're too greedy just to let it lie. The Terminus will follow the ships of the Navy fleet back to Earth. It will follow them. The possibility of this happening is so very high that every future ends in Terminus. We're trying to weaken their resolve to find that horror. We'll kill anyone who wants to find that death planet, but the Terminus is closer, so they must be getting close."

Bodies in the fields of CJIS, bodies in the Ryder truck, sailors of the Naval Space Command, scientists at the Naval Research Lab, at Phasal Systems: Hyldekrugger would kill anyone who might rediscover Esperance.

"Every future I've seen, you've killed so many people, so many innocent people," I said. "Driscoll would have gone to study that planet, so you had to kill him. Is that

469

right? You'd have to kill so many people . . ."

"Break the chain. Cut all lines to the Terminus, kill to cover the mistake in all our thinking. Everyone's critical flaw is that we believe in our own existence, until we're shown otherwise. Everything we see and feel tells us we're alive, that what surrounds us is real, but it's all a damn mistake, all an illusion we can't see through. I've killed so many people here, but what has it been worth? If you're a traveler, what has it been worth? Nothing. But you. You can still help us. You can return to the True, you can kill the machine that will bring the Terminus, make it feel less like fate, more like possibility. That's all I ask you, to bring back our freedom of will, our other futures, our chance at futures. Kill until every future doesn't end in death."

"No," I said. "I protect the innocent."

For a brutal moment, I feared that Hyldekrugger would kill me after all, that his mind had changed as suddenly as a summer storm, but he extended his hand to me, helped me stand.

"Come," he said, unlocking my handcuffs, throwing them aside. "We have a ways to walk, and our journey is difficult."

"Where are you taking me?"

"I need to preserve you," he said.

470

I followed Hyldekrugger across the clearing, along the line of trees, pushing against the desire to leave the path, to turn around. "This is where the echoes come through, isn't it?" I said.

"The Vardogger is the doorway to a mansion with many rooms," said Hyldekrugger. "Some of the doppelgängers come through here. They're confused. They think they're walking through a mirror. What did you call them? The echoes? The echoes cross the river here. They remember they'd been lost in the woods, that they'd somehow gotten turned around, as if in a child's nightmare of being lost. They'll come through the forest here, come to a clearing. They'll return to the river they were sure they'd left behind."

"What about the others?" I asked. "You said that only some of the echoes come through here, crossing the river."

"The others flash into being up ahead," said Hyldekrugger. "We kill them when we see them. They want to take our place here. Sometimes they've succeeded."

"Who?"

"Us," he said. "We see us. We fight an endless mutiny against ourselves. You see it happen. You see your twin and you know you'll have to kill him. Otherwise he'll kill you.

471

He'll become you."

The Vardogger trees stretched ahead of us. I glanced behind and saw the same impossible line of trees stretching away from us. *Marian lost in the confusion of this place, crossing the river, seeing herself.* Echoes of worlds, echoes of lives.

"You killed Mursult's family," I said.

"Yes, with an ax," said Hyldekrugger. "Patrick Mursult was willing to destroy us, so I destroyed him. He wanted to betray us in exchange for a governmental pardon. His thirty pieces of silver. He would have brought the Terminus to our doorstep. He was a fool."

When we made it to the riverbank, Hyldekrugger pulled one of the coats hanging from the exposed roots and gave it to me. He wrapped himself with a military blanket.

"The end times are cold," he said. "You'll see things. But you must keep walking, stay on the path. We're crossing into somewhere else. There are dangers where we're going. I don't know what will happen when the Terminus comes, if it comes, but I assume this boundary will break like the yolk of an egg and hell will pass through."

I climbed the roots, stepped up onto the tree trunk, holding on to the rope railing with both hands. A surface like this was difficult for me, the rounded, smooth trunk of the felled Vardogger tree feeling more like petrified wood than rough char. I couldn't sense the slickness here, where the river spray made the wood wet, whether or not my fake foot had found grip. Hyldekrugger climbed up after me, following closely. I stepped, baby steps, sideways, inching along, holding the rope line. The river roared by beneath us, the black water, crashing rapids.

*You'll see things,* Hyldekrugger had said. Halfway across, the temperature plummeted like we had stepped from spring into midwinter. The sky became leaden, and the air filled with swirling snowflakes and flecks of ice. The landscape changed ahead of me, no longer the green of spring but a scene of winter, the Vardogger trees obscured by blasts of snow. I kept inching my way across the footbridge, the tree trunk even slicker with a skim of ice, and all around us, appearing in the air as if the stars had just revealed themselves, were the bodies of the hanged men, bodies crucified upside down, floating above the river and far into the distance, among the trees. They were moaning, their noises a choir of undying anguish.

I dropped to my knee, gripping the rope,

clutching it to keep from being blown into the river by the winds. Hyldekrugger huddled in his blanket, his wild red hair rimed with hoarfrost. Behind us the clearing we had just left was now a deep arctic blue. I saw a speck of orange in the immense steel green of the tree line. I screamed in horror.

"I was crucified here," I cried, searching the bodies in the air for my own body. "I was one of them."

Hyldekrugger took me in his arms, helped me to stand. "How did you survive?" he asked.

Snow clung to his eyelashes, and his eyes watered in the frigid wind. His hands were on my arms, steadying me.

"I was saved," I said, even now wondering if I would see the lights of the descending Quad-lander. "I was pulled down, I was rescued. They saved the wrong person — look there, in the distance, that's where she is. That other woman is me. That's who I am."

Hyldekrugger looked behind us. "That woman is dead," he said. "You're here now."

*I didn't know what QTNs were. I had come from a time when there was no Terminus — I was only a possibility, one of many possibilities.* A point of pain centered my eyes, felt like it grew wider, expanding into an abyss.

474

Everything about me was an abyss.

He half carried me to cover the remaining distance of the footbridge and when we stepped from the felled tree into drifts of snow, he huddled with me, draping his blanket over me. Hyldekrugger carried me forward, onward. Infinite reflections opened around us, as if my eyes were kaleidoscopes and everywhere I looked were mirrors. I saw us walking toward us through the sky, away from us above the river, upward through the earth, toward us from across the bridge. In the distance of every reflection, I saw a point of orange. Hyldekrugger forced me forward. The path of the Vardogger trees began to curve, and despite the shredding ice-wind the air filled with smoke like we were walking toward a great fire, lung-burning blackness that shaded the sky to charcoal. Sparks of fire curled upward, were whipped about in the sky. "Hurry," said Hyldekrugger, leading me along the curving path of trees, the air a midnight of smoke. Soon the Vardogger trees themselves were ablaze, no longer ashen husks of trees but trees in the full bloom of fire, one fiery tree after another like a line of scintillant torches, orange conflagrations battered by the wind and carried upward as if every tree were a tornado of flame stretching to heaven.

"Where are you taking me?" I said above the scream of wind.

"This is the ship made of nails," he said, and ahead of us I saw the black hulk of *Libra* towering above the eternal forest, a wrecked ship mounded with blowing snow. The monolithic bow was rent apart while the stern, housing the engine room — the propulsion system and the B-L drive — was afire with spurting spheres of vivid blue light that flashed and were gone, a blinding strobe.

We hurried along the path of burning trees, the ship growing larger in our view, and I saw one of the NSC inflatable concrete domes, a bulwark against the driving snow, a soot-black dome with windows dimly lit. I wanted to go there, to huddle inside for warmth, but Hyldekrugger pulled me back along our path.

"They'd kill you there," he said. "No matter what I say, they'd kill you. They're trained to kill, without question. The men in that dome are sentinels here. They keep watch for our approaching forms and shoot them down before they can escape into the woods. I've killed myself here, many times."

And I saw there were corpses in the snowy fields surrounding the ship, countless corpses frozen in all postures of death, echoes of the *Libra* crew. They had been stripped of their clothing and whatever gear they might have carried. I saw Hyldekrugger's body, and another of his bodies, and another.

The burning path of Vardogger trees terminated at *Libra*. We walked alongside the hull until we came to gangway stairs leading to one of the airlocks. The cold had seeped through my coat, made it hard to move. "You'll have to climb," Hyldekrugger said once we were at the stairs. Anything to escape this cold, but my hands burned against the iron railings. As we climbed, another blue spherical flare burst from the ship, enveloping us. A static jolt passed through me, a deep shock that stunned me, and for an instant I saw myself crucified, I saw myself in the orange space suit, I saw myself crossing the black river, I saw myself as a teenager with Courtney Gimm, blowing cigarette smoke from her bedroom window. *Have you ever seen a flower called the falling star as it blooms?*

"Keep climbing," said Hyldekrugger. "Now's our chance, *right now.* Climb!"

I looked out over the forest from the height of the gangway stairs — the ship was encircled by a great fire, an inferno of trees, waves of firelight that flapped in the wind like the flags of hell. I imagined *Libra* falling from the sky, damaged during the mutiny, its hull enrobed in fire and plummeting to the Earth like a burning mountain, crashing here. Other lines of Vardogger trees radiated away from the ship, countless lines of trees like burning spokes surrounding a hub, seemingly infinite paths leading to other sections of the eternal forest. So many pathways, a *mansion with many rooms.* I could see past the forest fires to where the fires died, to where the Vardogger lines became charred trees, a burnt forest of ashen white, the snow mixed with so much soot that the horizon was grayed, the sky dark. The landscape was like a burning God's eye, and I stood in the black pupil, *Libra.* The fires and the Vardogger lines churned around us, as if I stood at the center of a world-enveloping hurricane. I was screaming.

Hyldekrugger dragged me up the remaining stairs, to the airlock in the hull, but the hull was caked with rust, or something colored like rust, and flecked with white and brown. No, it wasn't rust — the rust color had been painted on. It covered the airlock and the surrounding hull like a thick reddish skin. Hyldekrugger spun the lock, and the portal door swung inward.

"Go in," he said, bellowing over the howling wind, but I hesitated, the portal to the ship a perfect void, repellent, a circle of oblivion surrounded by the rust color and flecks and darker, stringy swirls. "Fingernails," I said, revulsion rising through me. "And blood," I said. The blood of the corpses surrounding the ship had been painted here, mixed with their fingernails and swirls of their hair to coat the airlock and hull. "You painted this ship in blood."

"The Earth shuddered, and Naglfar was released from its moorings," said Hyldekrugger, "carrying the bodies of dead warriors to wage war against the gods."

Fingernails of the dead, the ship made of nails. Mursult's wife, his children — their fingernails and toenails removed, brought here. Marian Mursult, the dead echoes. How many others? Thinking of the scale of this death overwhelmed me, like seeing a mountain but realizing it was a cresting wave.

Hyldekrugger forced me toward the airlock, that black circle. I climbed through the shadow into the ship, but the moment I stepped inside *Libra,* I lifted — My feet flew upward from the ship's floor, my body spinning upward. Weightless, I hit the ceiling, bounced, *no gravity.* I was in free fall, rolling. Hyldekrugger closed the airlock, my body a rag doll ricocheting from ceiling to wall to floor with nothing to break my fall until Hyldekrugger caught me. We floated together. *There is no gravity.*

"What's happening?" I asked him.

"Quiet now," he said.

We were near the engine room, and soon I heard the two-tone clangor of the Power Plant Casualty alarm wail through the ship.

"That's the nuclear reactor," I said. "Something's wrong."

"The bull nuke was trying to break the ship, but Bietak saved us," said Hyldekrugger, his voice drowned by a clattering burst of nearby gunfire. "Now," he said, and pulled me through the portal that led into the engine room, the place veined with tubes and pipes, cords and wires, most of the chamber taken up by the silvery steel cauldron shape of the nuclear reactor. Ring-shaped particle colliders encircled the B-L drive, housed in its own compartment. It looked almost like a human heart, dipped in silver.

The body of a man floated near the reactor, a long, sticky blood bubble ballooning from the holes where bullets had rent his gut. I could tell by his uniform patches that this was the bull nuke, the officer in charge of the nuclear reactor and the B-L drive. Hyldekrugger's eyes were wild. He ripped a Maglite from the Velcro wall of small tools just as the nuclear reactor groaned and whined and the lights of the ship cut off, plunging us into pure darkness. The Power Plant Casualty alarm still screamed, warning of a reactor failure.

"Move," said Hyldekrugger, switching on the Maglite. "We don't have much time. Bietak will be back here to fix this, and then Mursult comes to guard the pass. We don't want to be here when Mursult comes. We don't want to fight him, not here."

"Tell me what's happening, what is this —"

But Hyldekrugger struck me. *"Move,"* he said, and pulled me through another portal. We moved like swimmers through the passageway, Hyldekrugger sweeping the light ahead of us. We passed the engineer officer's room, a cubby with a writing desk and filing cabinets fitted around the walls and ceiling. The engineering department had its own mess room here, and a meeting compartment with bench seating curved around a compact table. We passed the offices for the A-Gangers, the Reactor-Laboratory Division, the Electrical Division, and soon came through a passageway lined with windows. I looked out the first window expecting to see icy wind and raging fire, the pathways of trees but instead saw stars in the infinite night.

*"Where are we? Where are we? What is happening to me?"*

Hyldekrugger dragged at me, but I clung to the window and saw along the length of the ship. Where there had been several inches of ice coating the hull, there was now a crystalline crust, bright white and shimmering like a coat of minerals or like diamond barnacles encrusting the hull. The crust was thickest at the stern, over the engine room behind us, growing in jagged torrents of opalescence and radiating away from the ship like brilliant white sunbursts.

*"Why is this happening?"*

He struck me in the spine with the butt end of his knife, said, "Hurry, the lights will be on soon."

He shoved me from the window just as the Power Plant Casualty alarm fell silent and the dim running lights snapped back on. We were headed to the brig, I realized, and I followed him, submissive in my shock and confusion, my fear. We came to the NCIS office, the walls stained with the spherical spatter patterns of weightless blood.

"What happened to the NCIS agents aboard this ship? Where are they?"

"They protected the CO," said Hyldekrugger.

He opened the iron door of the brig, the brigs on NSC TERNs much larger than their counterparts on waterborne vessels, NASA psychiatrists having warned of the possibility of "space madness" even from the earliest missions. There were eight cells here, stacked like berthing bunks, each cell an iron box. Hyldekrugger took me to Cell 5. I kicked against him, and he hit me, opening my nose again. A sticky stream of blood burbled from me, I couldn't fight him. He grabbed my prosthetic leg, pinned my chest with his boot, and pulled — hurting me until I managed to reach down to release the vacuum seal.

"I consider you a suicide risk," he said, "and I can't have you hurt yourself with this thing."

He locked me in the cell and left the brig, pitching me into utter darkness. I floated, fetuslike without sight or any sound. The pain of my shattered nose and broken teeth flashed like lightning through me. Soon in that vast silence, I heard my ears ringing and my breath whistle through collapsed sinuses and heard my blood plash softly against the cell.

Hours passed.

I was an echo. An echo, I realized, of Shannon Moss, brought through to terra firma when I was rescued from the cross. I understood that now. The woman in the orange space suit was Shannon Moss, she was *real.* I had seen her, in the snow. *That woman is dead. You're here now.* I had come from an IFT with no Terminus but was just a figment of that IFT, an IFT that had blinked even as I had lived, an entire existence that had been cut away. Was I real? I was a void, an oval of darkness where my face should have been, as if my body were hollow, or stuffed with straw. But the pain was real, the pain in my battered face, and my despair, and my fear. Aboard the USS *William McKinley,* O'Connor and I had once been forced to confront a sailor whose nerves were frayed by Deep Waters, who'd struck an officer. We wrestled with him, brought him to the brig and placed him in a cell — he'd had the brig to himself, but the thought of this iron confinement and the solitude terrified him more than any other corrective measure could have. He begged us, pleading like a whining child for us to let him free. I thought of that sailor now, how he'd scratched at the walls.

484

I was on *Libra* somehow, without gravity. I had seen the bull nuke murdered — but how was that possible? I heard distant sounds. A soft clacking, like someone tapping fingernails against a table or like rats' claws scrabbling across metal. Popping sounds, and then I placed it: the sound of small-arms fire followed by the louder clatter of automatic weapons. *They're fighting in the ship.* And I wondered if the Navy had found this place, come to rescue me, or the FBI, the Hostage Rescue Team, thinking maybe Vivian had somehow lived, or maybe someone had followed us here. Then a scream outside the brig door, several people screaming, a wave of sound that died abruptly.

The brig door opened, and my eyes were pierced by a sliver of light. I squinted against the glare and was able to see a woman slip inside the brig before she closed the iron door, plunging us again into darkness. *Nicole,* but she was just a child here, a teenager. I heard her movement. She was trying to stay quiet, but she breathed heavily, she was crying, and in the dead silence I heard every soft whimper. She floated between the cells, floating nearer, and when she reached my cell, I said, "Nicole, help me."

Startled, she whispered, "Who is that?"

"I'm an NCIS agent," I said. "I want to help. I need you to let me out, Nicole."

"I don't know you," she said. "I've never seen you before. Why are you locked here? How did you get here?"

"Let me out."

"I can't," she said. "No, I can't —"

Another burst, an exchange of fire, louder now. Then another burst, right outside the door: bullets ricocheted off the metal passageways, a metallic staccato against the iron door.

"They're doing it," said Nicole. "I can't believe . . . they've killed her, no, no —"

Nicole's words were seared with tears, I heard her rubbing her face with her hands, saying, "No, please, please don't do this."

"Who did they kill?" I asked.

"Remarque. They killed her, they're killing everyone now," said Nicole. "Remarque and our WEPS, Chloe Krauss. They were together in the wardroom, barricaded in. They're dead, oh, they're dead now."

This was familiar, this had already happened, and I thought of Nicole's confession as we stood together near the orchard barn.

"But you're innocent, Nicole. You haven't killed anyone."

"I love Remarque — they know that, I

don't want them to kill me because of her," she said. "I've been hiding, in the life-support room, but they were checking every room, and so I came here. They're killing everyone."

"Nicole, calm yourself. I need you to help me. I know you, Nicole. I know that your father convinced Remarque to let you board this ship," I said. "There was a feast in Mombasa, they threw a feast in her honor. When was that? Years from now."

"Six hundred eighty-one years," said Nicole. "When Remarque landed, and *Libra,* we held a Roho ceremony, celebrating transience. I met my husband there. He saw me wearing garlands, in the almond grove. And my father — he wanted me to live — he convinced Remarque to take me . . . and she wanted me to live, she accepted me —"

"I can help you, Nicole. I just need you to let me out of here."

Another clatter of gunfire. She came close to the bars of my cell and said, "How do you know my name? I thought I'd met everyone here, but I don't know you."

"We knew each other in another time," I said. "We were close once. You knew me as Courtney Gimm. We used to talk with each other, almost every night, in another time, in the future from now. You told me about

Kenya. You told me about the trees, that they looked like emeralds."

"I don't know what to do," she said.

"Let me out. I can help you."

"I *can't* let you out. They'd kill you if they knew you were here. They'd kill me for letting you out, for talking with you."

"Please," I said, but she didn't answer. I saw the sliver of light as she opened the brig door. I saw her slip away, and the brig door closed.

I was alone in that darkness, and time dissolved. Hours, it must have been. Every so often a sticky sphere of my floating blood bumped against me, and I despaired. Eventually a deep, plummeting boom sounded through the ship, shivering through the steel. Another explosion followed, much louder than the first, and as the seconds passed, I scented a faint odor of smoke, a pungent sharpness like an electrical fire. I screamed for help, trapped here, fearing being burned alive in this cell, and soon the lights flared red — *emergency lights* — and the alarm bells rang a metallic clangor.

The ship lurched, and a heavy steel moan came from the hull. I heard a series of popping crashes, like someone hammering on pots and pans, and a series of explosions that sounded like the air was ripping apart.

Steel shrieking, the ship rattled. I thought the hull would break or buckle. Liquid spheres of blue firelight bloomed across the ceiling of the brig, and I tried to float away from the fire, tried to cover myself in the corner of the cell. And that's when gravity overtook me and I slammed against the wall, the ceiling, rolling in the cell, the blue spheres of fire flattening, spreading. *We're falling. We're falling from the sky.* We fell for minutes, but each minute seemed eternal. I was battered in the iron box, was crushed to the floor. Then the chaos was over. My forehead was gashed, I bled freely from my face. The alarms continued to sound.

I lost consciousness for a time and then woke in pure, milky darkness. I sat as best I could in that narrow cell, listening, and as the moments passed, I felt something like a small electrical charge growing steadily in my chest. The static charge was a discomfort — it seemed to hum inside me — and it grew, a crescendo of intensity, until I felt my hair prickle, waves of shivers passing over me. The tension was unbearable, and I opened my mouth, saw strings of electricity snap from my teeth and race along my fingers like blue filaments in the air. A loud crack, a burst of light — the electrical discharge felt as though someone had punched me full force in the heart. Again I lost gravity, again I floated freely, again the ship resumed its silence.

An explosion rumbled deep within the ship. A few moments passed, and I heard the brig door open, a squeal of metal, but there was no sliver of light. Movement, barely audible. My cell lock clicked, and I heard the door swing open. I drifted against the back wall of the cell, terrified at the thought of who had come, fearing Hyldekrugger. Someone's hand covered my mouth.

"Do not make a sound," a voice whispered. "Now is our only chance. We'll have just a few minutes before they fix the lights."

The hand remained clasped over my mouth even after I calmed, nodded that I would remain quiet.

"Can you see this?" the voice whispered. A phosphorescent blue appeared in the darkness, a blue light no larger than a marble. I recognized what it was: the cutting of the alien petal that centered Nicole's amulet. An instant later the light was gone. I nodded that yes, I had seen the phosphorescence.

"Follow the light," Nicole whispered.

She removed her hand from my mouth, and the phosphorescent blue appeared several feet away, hovering in the darkness before it disappeared. I raised my arms, feeling for the cell door, pulled myself out. I found my way by crawling across the brig ceiling, floating. I became lost quickly in that darkness and stopped, my eyes flashing in tricks of purple splotches until out of the haze of false colors I saw the hovering blue appear again. I followed.

I lost all conception of direction, crawled along one of the walls through an opening. I had left the brig and was in a much narrower passageway. The blue appeared again several feet in front of me, and I propelled myself — quickly but quietly — in that direction. I hit a steel wall, looked for the blue but didn't spot it until I heard an exhalation, so soft I nearly missed it. The breath drew my attention upward to the blue light hovering above me. I reached toward the blue and pulled myself through a portal. I floated, following the light, and soon we passed into the passageway lined with windows, Nicole's face outlined in the light of the crystal brilliance, the spectral diamond shapes that grew across the hull and the radiant lines that stretched away forever. It wasn't Nicole as a teenager, whom I'd spoken with just a short time ago, but rather a young woman who had aged a decade or more. She'd brought me to the airlock where Hyldekrugger had first brought me in.

"Rest for a moment," Nicole said. "Catch your breath. You'll have to run soon."

"I don't understand."

"We know each other, in another future, in another time," she said. "Now you have to go. They will come after you."

"Nicole," I said. "Help me understand —"

"We don't have time."

"How . . . You've grown older."

"You've been in this prison for several years, Shannon," she said.

"No," I said, almost wanting to laugh, the mistake of it all, the incoherence. "It's only been a day at most. Hours."

"This place, this ship, is an ouroboros," said Nicole. She showed me her wrist, the copper-colored bracelet she always wore, textured by diamond patterns of scales, a snake swallowing its own tail. "We played with these growing up in Kenya — bracelets, when you wear the bracelet you can take it off and give it to your friend."

"A friendship bracelet," I said.

"Yes," said Nicole. "An ouroboros."

She slipped the bracelet from her wrist and placed it on mine, the metal cool; she clasped the tail into the snake's mouth, and the bracelet fit my wrist perfectly. Nicole held up her wrist. I had seen her remove the snake bracelet, but she still wore hers, it was like a magician's illusion.

"You give the bracelet to your friend, but you still wear it," she said. "So they match."

"But several years," I said, struggling. "You've aged *years.* I just saw you a few hours ago, and you were younger —"

"And you look the same as I remember, exactly the same. I've been living my life for almost twelve years since I saw you here," said Nicole. "Patrick is dead, Patrick's family is dead, and you showed up with Special Agent Nestor at my apartment last night. You and a young woman named Petal had tracked me down using my license-plate number that the Blackwater Lodge kept on file."

"No, I wasn't at your apartment with Nestor," I said. "I wasn't there at all. Nestor tracked you down alone. It wasn't me."

"But after Nestor left, you and I spoke for a very long time. You noticed a Salvador Dalí painting I had on my wall, of the Crucifixion, and you confided in me that we had already met in the future, that we were together almost every night, decades from now," said Nicole. "And that's when I recognized you. That's when I remembered we had already met once before, but not in the future. I remembered you from eleven years ago, during the mutiny. I remembered I spoke with someone in the brig, a brief encounter, a woman named Courtney Gimm. Eleven years ago you told me your name was Courtney."

"I told you my name was Courtney," I said, a few hours ago for me, eleven years ago for her. *Consequences of events that hadn't yet occurred,* Nicole's story like a figure eight, an infinite loop crossing a central moment: when I was in the brig and told Nicole she'd once known me as Courtney Gimm. *Imagine that the forest fire that burned the tree won't happen for another three hundred years or three thousand,* Njoku had said — there had been reverberations of my hours in the brig long before Hyldekrugger had ever brought me to the brig. All my past pain and the sorrow of my childhood rushed over me in waves of sickness. Nicole thought my name was Courtney.

"And when the ship crashed, we left through the woods, along the path of trees," said Nicole. "All of us. And Karl knew we should stay hidden while he figured out what to do, that we would be wanted for treason, would be put to death if we were ever found, and so I told him —"

"You told him you saw an NCIS agent named Courtney Gimm," I said as I wept. "Oh, God, no — oh, my God." *It's my fault,* I thought, Hyldekrugger's killing Courtney, or Mursult's killing her, or Cobb, they had thought Courtney Gimm was an agent, a mistake in identity, a mistake. *My* mistake.

*It's my fault she's dead.*

"I told them about you," said Nicole. "And Karl told Mursult to find Courtney Gimm, to kill her. And he found her, a sixteen-year-old girl —"

"Please," I said, "please this can't be. Did he kill her?" I asked, the feeling of loss coring me. "Oh, God, please tell me this isn't real, this isn't happening. Did he kill Courtney because of me? Because I used her name? Did he kill her?"

But Nicole said, "No. She was already dead before he found her. So Mursult moved his family into the dead girl's house — her older brother rented it out. Patty would ask about the dead girl whenever her brother collected rent, trying to track who it was that had been in the brig, thinking Courtney Gimm might show up someday. But it was you."

Mursult living in Courtney's house on Cricketwood Court — asking about her because he thought that someday an agent named Courtney Gimm would investigate the mutiny on *Libra.* I hadn't caused her death — but even as the wrenching guilt that I'd inadvertently played a role in my best friend's death drained from me, a colder sorrow gripped me. For a moment it had seemed that all of existence had revealed its shape, a purpose of cruelty, a terrible irony that the contours of a childhood death that defined me seemed to fit into grander patterns hidden until now. For a moment, when I thought that my use of her name had killed Courtney, it seemed that on some depth all tragedies and ecstasies were part of a great design that my limited mind couldn't scope, a looping scheme where all actions and their consequences are tallied. For a moment Courtney's death had made horrifying sense, had an identifiable cause, a reason. But the pieces slipped apart. There was no center, no reason. Courtney's death was random, banal viciousness inflicted by one organism upon another. There is no design. The universe isn't kind or cruel. The universe is vast and indifferent to our desires.

"And at my apartment all these years later, you showed up with your badge and introduced yourself as Shannon Moss,

NCIS," said Nicole. "You said that you had traveled to a future and that in twenty years we met for the first time at a place called the May'rz Inn. You said that we were once very close, that we were best friends. You told me things about myself, about my life —"

"I never told you anything," I said. "This never happened."

"And so I agreed to show you the Vardogger, the thin space, but you told me that I needed to run. You told me to disappear to save myself, before I could be arrested by the FBI or before Hyldekrugger would find me and kill me. You told me that you were going to come here, to the Vardogger, that you would come here soon, and so I ran, but I remembered."

"You remembered," I said. "You remembered speaking with me here in the prison when you were a young girl, you remembered meeting me during the mutiny, a woman in the cell — Courtney Gimm, eleven years ago," I said. "That was eleven years ago for you. I told you my name was Courtney Gimm."

"I want to exchange the kindness you showed me, Shannon," said Nicole. "You told me to run, to save myself because of our friendship. You didn't arrest me, you warned me. And so I want to save you, too. Who knows? Maybe in twenty years you'll show up in a bar one night and offer to buy me a drink."

"But that wasn't me," I said. "That was some other . . . I was never there in your apartment, with Nestor. I never had a chance to tell you to run. That wasn't me, Nicole. That was an echo of me, someone else."

"Different paths along the Vardogger trees," said Nicole. "Shannon, we're all echoes here."

I felt the air leave my lungs and heard what sounded like a swell of sighs. I seemed to glimpse for a moment every iteration of Shannon Moss and Nicole Onyongo flowering outward, growing together and growing apart, infinite interactions between the two of us.

"You probably felt the B-L drive misfire," said Nicole. "Whenever the drive misfires, it creates another path of those trees, another universe. We have to be off this ship before it misfires again — otherwise we'll be here forever, having this conversation forever. We have to go."

"What do I do?" I asked.

"Jump."

Nicole grabbed the handle of the airlock

and pulled inward, opening the portal in a sucking rush. I tried to find purchase, anywhere to grip, but my fingers slipped and I held my breath and stepped into the stars, a suicidal act of free fall into outer space. Daylight flashed, and I landed on the gangway stairs, the winter cold piercing me like spears of ice, the inferno in the trees ripping at the sky around me. Wind gusted me down the first few steps before I regained myself and halted my fall. Nicole stepped out behind me, helped me crawl down the last stairs into the snow. Hyldekrugger had taken my prosthesis, so I couldn't stand.

"Go," she said. "I'll distract whoever is keeping watch. Go."

Nicole ran from me, and I saw her figure obscured by the blowing smoke and snow. *She will die. The sentinels will kill her.* I wanted to run but could only crawl, scrambling, two hands and one leg, pulling myself forward, heaving myself toward the Vardogger trees, the path that had brought me here. Ice cut into my palms, my elbows, burned my skin. Snowflakes and flakes of ash, the orchard flashed in my mind, of me running through the lines of trees and the swirl of petals, and just like in the orchard I heard a death scream: the cry of a woman's suffering carried over the rush of fire and wind.

*They will come after you,* Nicole had said, and so I kept pushing, crawling along the path of identical fires in identical trees, and only when my arms collapsed did I stop to catch my breath. I hadn't gotten very far, but already the intense cold burrowed deep into my exhaustion, a serene pull toward sleep, as if I could lean back and let the snow bury me here. My arms shook, I could no longer feel my fingers, and my chest was soaked through and my skin was slick with ice. My hair and eyelashes were brittle with ice, my toes had lost all feeling.

*Someone else would quit.*

So I crawled, a bear crawl, hands and knee, snorting out blood and mucus, wheezing, but I screamed out, *"Someone else would quit!"* and gutted through with an animal savagery against my own body, feeling the searing frost breaking me apart, the deep freeze in my breath and my core, my heart, thinking, *I'll reach warmth if I can make it across.* I reached the fallen tree that forded the river. I looked back and saw that a man followed me, running along the Vardogger path, still distant but swiftly approaching. When I was halfway across the fallen log, the winter melted around me into

500

a warm spring, and I made my way into the clearing, the warmer air like a scalding bath, thinking, *Hide. You can only hide from him, you can't fight him. Hide, hide.*

I crossed the clearing to the tree line and crawled beneath one of the evergreens there, curling myself around a trunk. I watched across the clearing to the fallen Vardogger tree, the bridge, waiting for the man to appear out of the air, my body shaking, still frozen, my skin like it had been boiled, crimson and purple. The ice that had accumulated in my hair had begun to melt, dripping over my skin in icy rushes, and I thought I should keep going, that I should run, but was unable to move. *Run, run from here —*

That's when I saw her, crossing the river: I saw an echo of Shannon Moss rise from the water, climb onto the near bank. She had crossed the river here, as Marian's echo had done. Her hair was long, much longer than I had ever kept mine, and she paused by the shore to squeeze water from it. *Run!* I wanted to tell her, but I couldn't speak, my voice gone, jaw chattering. She was dressed in dark fatigues, a tank top. She wore her prosthesis, an advanced mechanized limb, unaffected by water. I wondered who she was. She was Shannon Moss, she was *me,* but she was an echo of me, an echo of an echo. She would have been in the woods, tracking Hyldekrugger, and she would have become hopelessly lost. She would have recognized the pines, the clearing, the river. She would see me here, at the tree line. If she looked this way, she would see me, and she would think of the woman in the orange space suit. The woman in the orange space suit had been here, where I am now.

"Run!" I managed to yell. "He's coming!"

She turned toward my voice, she saw me. Our eyes met.

"Run," I said, but it was too late.

Cobb appeared over the bridge. He shrugged off his fur wraps, caught sight of Moss standing in the clearing. She didn't have her holster, didn't have her sidearm, only a black leather sheath she wore on the thigh of her residual limb, above her prosthetic leg. She pulled the knife, a twelve-inch hunter's knife, readying to fight. Cobb had a rifle, leveled it right at her.

"Come on — fight me," she said. "Fight me —"

Cobb threw down his weapon, raised his fists, his face twisted with a smirk — but Moss was pure reaction. She charged him, catlike, her prosthesis mimicking natural movement. Cobb took a step backward as Moss jumped at him, slicing with her knife but missing. She punched him with her left, caught his chin, followed with her elbow. She slashed with her knife for his eyes, but Cobb pushed her away as easily as if she were nothing. He was wary of the knife but rounded on her, threw a punch, and caught Moss in the side of her head, stunning her. Cobb threw a second punch, connected. Moss's body went limp, she fell forward, a knockout blow. Nausea swept through me at what I was witnessing. Cobb knelt over her, pinning her shoulders with his knees, and rained punches down on her. They were only a few feet away from me. I could see every punch sink deep into her, I could hear his blows landing, knuckles mashing meat. I could hear Shannon moaning, a crying moan. I heard breaking bones and saw Cobb's fists covered in Shannon's blood when he finally stood from her and spit at her.

"Fuck!" he said, screaming down at her. "Fuck you! You're dead! You're dead now!"

I could see her, could see her face crushed, could see that one eye had slipped the socket and hung to the side of her face. I heard her breathing, that terrible sucking moaning. She was alive, my God, she was still alive, but I stayed there, hidden, and watched as Cobb picked up his rifle, aimed, and fired. A spray of pink mist.

Tears streamed from my eyes. I was shaking. I saw myself die, but I prayed, *Don't look this way, don't look this way,* as Cobb circled the corpse, but he wandered away to sit on the riverbank.

*Now.*

He was watching the river, catching his breath. I could see his shoulders heaving. Were there others coming? How many were on their way?

*Now, run —*

I rolled from beneath the tree, crawled quietly, as quietly as I could, treading the carpet of needles, my body trembling as I followed the Vardogger trees, but soon the forest changed around me. I found the dry creek bed and followed it to the clearing where Nestor had killed Vivian, but the clearing was empty now.

I crawled from the clearing, sliding down the access route, and collapsed on the side of the forest road. A night passed before a forest ranger's SUV pulled beside me. The driver helped me into the backseat, calling on his radio for help. I remember an ambulance, I remember being delivered to the gates of Oceana. A Navy surgeon did his best to realign my nose, but Cobb had eviscerated the bones when he struck me at the Vardogger tree, had damaged the cartilage. My nose would look like malformed putty without extensive plastic surgery. A dental surgeon removed the shards of my broken teeth, fearing further injury or infection, and left a gap where my left front tooth should have been, a larger gap at my left bicuspid. I looked at myself in the mirror following the procedures but didn't recognize the woman there.

■ ■ ■ ■

# PART FIVE

## 1997

■ ■ ■ ■

Where are the snows of yesteryear?
— FRANÇOIS VILLON,
"Ballad of Women of Times Past"

# ONE

*An echo, insubstantial.*

A woman in orange, a woman from the river, a woman on the cross. NSC engineers lifted Moss from the cockpit when she landed at Apollo Soucek, a figment of a dream intruding on the real. Intravenous fluids, medication.

*They're keeping me alive.*

O'Connor arrived at her bedside, startled by her disfigurement. "They told me you suffered injuries commensurate with car-crash victims," he said, eyeing her marred nose and gapped teeth, an eyelid droop that might not ever heal. He touched her face the way a father might touch a broken daughter's. "Shannon, I'm so sorry," he said. "For everything that's happened, I'm sorry."

"We've done this before," she said, remembering O'Connor at a different bedside of hers, apologizing for her blackened toes and

509

fetid gangrenous shin — *I'm an echo* — but she couldn't bring herself to admit this to him, not yet. She feared O'Connor's reaction. She didn't want his pity, his regrets, and she feared that his care and friendship would drain away if he knew she was a phantom of an IFT, a revenant from an existence that had blinked away when she was taken from the cross. *I'm not real,* she wanted to say, but she feared he would sigh at the revelation, disappointed in her, like a man giving up on an aimless child. She feared he would leave her here in this hospital, alone.

"I found them," she said. "I found *Libra.*"

"Tell me."

The path of trees, the Terminus winter, she remembered the shipwreck sputtering blue flame, but in the half-forgotten way she might have recalled a reverie. *You will see things your mind will not understand.* Already her mind rejected what she had seen. *They have my leg somewhere,* she thought, remembering V-R17, dissected, sealed, stored.

"Let me start with what I'm certain of," she said. "The Terminus isn't fate, it's not certainty — I think the chances of the Terminus reaching terra firma are so great that it feels like a certainty." *I came from a future without a Terminus.* "But it's not, it's not fate."

"Explain," said O'Connor.

"Hyldekrugger believes that NSC will bring the Terminus to terra firma, that there are certain events that will lead this to happen. I've heard him refer to these events as a 'chain,' a chain of information that will allow Naval Space Command to rediscover the planet that *Libra* had encountered. NSC will bring the Terminus home."

"That can't be right, Shannon."

"All the murder, the attacks they're planning, the chemical weapons?" she said. "They're trying to break the chain, to keep NSC from bringing the Terminus to terra firma. They're trying to weaken our resolve to sail Deep Waters. NSC causes the cataclysm, NSC brings the Terminus."

"You can't listen to that man's poison," said O'Connor.

"I think Patrick Mursult was preparing to sell the location of Esperance to the Navy, to sell where the QTNs came from, or sell the location of *Libra,*" said Moss. "He wanted protection because he knew Hyldekrugger would kill him, he wanted a new identity. There's a lawyer named Carla Durr, Mursult's lawyer."

Doubt shuddered through her. *Carla Durr*

*had to die, Dr. Peter Driscoll had to die.* According to Hyldekrugger everyone had to die, all the physicists at the Naval Research Lab who would one day form Phasal Systems and all the sailors of Deep Waters, brave boys with bodies polluted by QTNs, everyone . . .

*I protect the innocent.*

"What about the lawyer?" asked O'Connor.

"She's innocent," said Moss, and seemed to feel the weight of the future avalanche into the present. Whether she held her peace and let the lawyer die or spoke now to save the lawyer's life, every choice seemed like the wrong choice, the last meaningless moves of an endgame. A great weariness swept over her, and she wanted to hide herself, retreat beneath her covers as a child might hide from imagined fears. A disquiet worked through her thoughts; she wondered what would happen if she saved the lawyer's life. Would she hasten NSC's discovering Esperance? The lawyer would remain alive, would sell Mursult's information. *No, no,* she thought, *that's Hyldekrugger's way of thinking,* but she felt bound. *Protect the innocent.* "Carla Durr, the lawyer," she said. "Patrick Mursult had been meeting with her, and she wants to parlay his secrets into protection, money. But she doesn't understand the consequences of what she's involved in. Hyldekrugger, or one of his followers, will kill her on March twenty-fourth in the Tysons Corner mall food court because she's met with Mursult. They think of her as part of the chain. The gunman will use an echoed firearm, a Beretta M9 probably pulled from a dead echo of a *Libra* sailor, identical to the guns we recovered from the Blackwater Lodge and from the remains of Torgersen's house."

"The twenty-fourth is three days from now."

"I want to request a pre-crime warrant," said Moss. "We can save this woman's life."

"We can justify pre-crime," said O'Connor, "to save her life. I'll write up the paperwork. We'll be able to hold her for possession of classified intelligence on the suspicion that Mursult talked to her about Deep Waters or *Libra.* We can question her, find out what Mursult was preparing to sell. That should protect her past the twenty-fourth. I'll call the Fairfax County Police, ask them to apprehend her for us. If they can't find her, we'll set up a direct intervention at Tysons Corner. Carla Durr, we'll find her. Now, tell me about *Libra.* Do you know where she is?"

*The eye of God is on fire, and the pupil is black.* "*Libra* is caught inside the Vardogger," she said. *There is a whirlpool of fire, and it burns through every existence.* "I don't know how else to explain it. Inside the Vardogger there are paths that open from the trees. You saw it. *Libra* is caught inside there, and so is the Terminus somehow, or a part of the Terminus. Like a pocket universe, almost like it's in a different time, or not *in* time at all. Njoku said thin spaces exist outside time . . ."

"SEAL Team 13 has been searching near the Red Run," said O'Connor, "but Commander Brunner hasn't found anything like you're describing."

"You can slip inside it," said Moss, remembering when she'd been lost in the thin space, as easily as losing her way in the woods. "But there's a trick to it. I don't know the path that leads to *Libra.* And there's something you should see, in the *Grey Dove*'s computer, a message you recorded for yourself. The Vardogger is dangerous, if you stray from the path, but Hyldekrugger uses it like a gate."

Reverberations, copies, universes opening in the pines. She was spread thin, thinning, and as she lay in her hospital bed long after O'Connor had left, she closed her eyes and saw the vortex of fire spreading from *Libra* like the incandescent rays of a black sun, or like a burning eye searching for her. *I am an echo;* the woman in the orange space suit had been reality. The woman in the orange space suit had been Shannon Moss. *That woman is dead. You're here now.* Everything was thin — her body, her bed, the medication dripping through her, the clinic, the base, the world — everything seemed like wrapping paper, something she could tear away to reveal only emptiness. She peered into herself and saw nothing. She felt that if she plunged her nails into her skin and ripped open her chest, only darkness would spill from her.

Agitated, that night, insomnia as she watched the minutes of her bedside clock tick between 2:00 a.m. and 3:00, her thoughts an anxious jumble. Tossing, her pillows warm and too lumpy, but even more bothersome were the twitching phantom cramps that irritated her missing leg. The sensations came and went regularly, but affected Moss most acutely when she was stressed. Lying on the stiff hospital mattress, staring at the ceiling, she could feel that first cut the surgeons had made, felt it plain as day, across her shinbone when they had tried to amputate low to save her knee.

She knew that her foot and ankle were gone — she no longer felt her foot — but it seemed the rest of her leg might still be there. It was almost as if she could reach down to touch her left knee, but there was nothing there. Blankets, sheets. Cramps in her calf, racing up her thigh, agonizing; even looking down and staring where her leg wasn't wouldn't help. Mirror therapy brought relief, and in the morning she asked her nurses if they could find her a long mirror, at least as long as her leg. Her nurses found a mirror hanging on the back of a closet door and brought it to her. Moss reclined backward in her bed, fixed one edge of the mirror snug against her groin. She looked down the length of the reflection. Two legs instead of one. A simple trick, one that shouldn't work but did: her mind responded as if she had two legs again. She curled her toes, rolled her ankle, flexed her knee, scratched itches, and rubbed out cramps, touching her right leg but bringing relief to the reflection.

The nurses liked her, but they coddled her, asking if she needed help with her walker or her wheelchair, or if she could dress herself, or use the toilet. Moss seethed at the idea of helplessness, that the absence of her leg was the most present thing about

516

her. *An echo or not, I can use the bathroom by myself,* she thought, and remembered all those bitter women she'd met in her support groups, the women who cursed everything and everyone, who seemed hate-filled and spiteful and loathed anyone who noticed their disabilities. Moss opened herself to some of that similar vitriol, letting it pour into her like gasoline, and she became prickly, snapping unfairly at her nurses when they offered her help in getting to the cafeteria for dinner — she knew she was being unfair, but that anger cut against her despair. *An echo, I don't exist, I'm an echo.* Mobility was essential, her independence.

"I need my prosthetist from Pittsburgh," Moss eventually told her nurse. "Laura. She's in my files. I need her."

Moss had developed a professional intimacy with Laura over the years, Laura the only civilian medical professional Moss visited on a regular basis. Laura understood aspects of Moss's body better even than Moss did. She was familiar with Moss's residual limb, knew the type of liner Moss preferred, the sensitivity of her skin, already knew the location of Moss's bony protuberances, her body type, and where her weight would fall. Regular appointments at Union Prosthetics in Pittsburgh for adjustments

517

and resizing, salmon walls and gray carpeting, Union like a dentist's office except for the attached fabrication shop, a commotion of plaster and plastic limbs and equipment for cutting and sanding, sheets of carbon-fiber and anatomical models of arms and legs. Laura was aware of Moss's peculiar circumstances and was accommodating; she had passed the government background checks, signed the nondisclosure agreement, and was often able to make the trip to Apollo Soucek at a moment's notice for emergency refitting and repairs.

"Are you all right?" Laura asked early the following morning when Moss arrived at the examination room in her wheelchair. "That's all I want to know. Tell me you're all right," she said, her riot of brown curls wrestled into a ponytail, her eyes taking in Moss's transformation: her once-pert nose now off axis, her weight loss, the startling gaps in her teeth.

"I'm fine," said Moss.

Chatting about *The X-Files* as they set to work, Laura prepared Moss's limb, chose a liner to roll over Moss's stump and thigh. Significant shrinkage in the limb, Moss had been compensating for the changing circumference by adding padding to her socket and wearing extra layers of socks. As Laura massaged out tension to help cast a relaxed shape, however, Moss realized just how lean her residual limb was compared to her right thigh, how bony it seemed, how shriveled.

"My leg . . . looks so small," said Moss. "Is that normal?"

"How does it feel?"

"I think it feels all right."

"Then it's all right," said Laura, swathing Moss's limb with plastic wrap, tight without pressure over the liner, smoothing out creases and wrinkles in the wrap as she rolled. She measured Moss's thigh with yellow measuring tape and a heavy metal caliper and wrapped Moss's limb in bandages sopping with plaster of paris. Laura's hands were confident, molding the cast, handling Moss's leg without delicacy.

"I made arrangements with Booden Prosthetics. They'll let me use their fabrication shop again," said Laura, sliding the plaster cast from Moss's thigh once it had set up, her mold for the carbon-fiber fabricated socket — a hollow space matching the shape of the limb.

"I'll need another C-Leg," said Moss.

"It took you six months to get your hands on a C-Leg," said Laura. "I'll be able to get you a 3R60."

The 3R60 from Otto Bock was a stance-flexion joint, secure but mechanical. "Damn," said Moss. Without the computerized C-Leg joint, walking would feel like relearning a stick shift after years of automatic transmission.

"I get it," said Laura, "but if you want the C-Leg, then don't lose yours."

"I know, I know —"

"Besides, the 3R60 is good," said Laura. "You'll lose some of the mobility you had with the C-Leg, but you'll be stable. I'll bring the first socket to you this afternoon, have you try it out. We'll make our adjustments, and you should be good to go by tomorrow."

"And then you're hitting the beach?" asked Moss.

"You think I came all this way just to see you?"

The new prosthetic socket gloved Moss's thigh, but the movement of the 3R60 was different from what she was accustomed to, the knee joint a spring-loaded swing, the entire prosthesis a weight of metal. Her gait was altered, a conspicuous limp as she made her way from her food-court table to the top of the escalator, peering over the railing at the vast lower floor of Tysons Corner. She knew what Durr had been wearing when she died in the future and so assumed that the lawyer would be wearing the same blaring royal-blue suit this afternoon as well, for her lunch meeting with Dr. Peter Driscoll. Moss scanned the shoppers below, seeing the tops of their heads and their shoulders, the bags they carried, and although Carla Durr with her carroty orange curls and her blue suit should be easy to spot, Moss found no sign of her. She made her way back to her table, one she'd chosen for the clean sightlines to the Five Guys burger stand, every step tentative, having to trust her mechanical knee to lock when she needed to put her weight on the joint, to unlatch and swing when she needed to step.

"Still no sign of her," said Moss into the microphone clipped to her lapel.

"It's early yet," said O'Connor through her earpiece.

But it wasn't early, it was after three o'clock, nearing three-thirty, and Moss knew that Carla Durr's time of death was at three-forty, approximately.

"Any sign of the shooter?" she asked. *A Caucasian male in black military fatigues* was all she could describe of Durr's killer, but just like Durr's royal-blue skirt suit, a man in black fatigues should be easy to find. O'Connor had arranged for patrol cars from

Fairfax County to scan the parking lot, and there were additional county police officers in the mall as well, plainclothes officers stationed near every entrance.

"Not yet," said Njoku's voice through her earpiece. Njoku was stationed with another NCIS special agent in the food court, O'Connor below near the foot of the escalators.

Imagining how all this might play out: Someone would spot Durr, Moss thought, and arrest her. Or if no one spotted her in time, Moss would see the lawyer as she ascended on the escalator to the food court. Or one of the patrolmen might spot the shooter, maybe Hyldekrugger himself — the police were under orders to stop and arrest anyone fitting the description of the shooter, any male in black fatigues. By now a short line had developed at the Five Guys burger stand. Moss tried to remember, hadn't Carla Durr already received her food when she was killed? The image of that potential crime scene flashed in her mind: Durr's body sprawled in front of the hamburger counter, blood slicking the floor, several shots in her back and head. Carla Durr would need to get in line *now* to have time to order, to receive her order, and be gunned down in the next few minutes. Moss looked frantically across the food court, to spot the man in fatigues, anyone suspicious, but she saw only groups of teenage girls and mothers with strollers, middle-aged men holding their wives' bags.

Three-forty came and went, and a few minutes after four O'Connor's voice spoke through their earpieces: "We have to close up shop." NCIS warrants for pre-crime intervention were written only for specific windows of time, only for specific circumstances, constrained by the constitutional rights of individuals who had not yet committed the crimes they would be arrested for. The lawyer Carla Durr had never shown. *What had happened?* Maybe the extra police presence had scared off the gunman, but that wouldn't explain why Durr hadn't made it for her hamburger meeting with Dr. Driscoll. Durr wasn't here, Driscoll wasn't here, there was no gunman. Something had changed from the future that Moss knew, but it could have been anything — flat tire, indigestion, Durr grown too scared to meet with Driscoll, or she was already dead. Moss was annoyed at having wasted everyone's time, but failed operations like this were a matter of course when serving pre-crime warrants. She'd been on plenty of operations where the circumstances had changed from the expected future, and nothing was accomplished. Moss had supplied the information that led to this abortive operation, which meant paperwork, but, more important, she owed the others involved the customary rounds of drinks special agents bought when their predictions failed.

Moss woke early the following morning, anxious for her debriefing with Admiral Annesley. She dressed in a charcoal-gray skirt-suit and silky blouse, and made it to NCIS headquarters with plenty of time to go over the notes she'd prepared about her IFT and to fine-tune her statement about her request for the pre-crime warrant. A few minutes before the debriefing was set to start, however, O'Connor brought her a fresh cup of coffee and let her know that the debriefing had been postponed. "Annesley called just a few minutes ago," he said. A relief, in some ways, being spared the scrutiny of a roomful of men, some of whom would whisper about how she looked, how she used to look.

"You'll need to write up your reports," said O'Connor, "and I'm sure you'll be called in to talk eventually, but the Navy is taking over, Shannon. Not every facet of the investigation, but the thin space, *Libra.*

Carla Durr. They're all military matters now. We're through."

"I understand," said Moss. She knew that eventually, when Hyldekrugger was captured, or Cobb, or the others, they would be held in military prisons and tried in courts-martial. She would be called on to testify, to work with the prosecution, but her role in this investigation would be finished. Even so, having the military take over the investigation before any arrests had been made was disappointing, leaving behind work only half finished.

"What about Carla Durr?" Moss asked. "If the Navy's taking over, is she dead? Did we miss her?"

"She's very much alive," said O'Connor. "I talked with Admiral Annesley that first night you returned, told him your theory about the Terminus, what you'd learned in your IFT. He was keen on finding Durr. And just this morning when he called, he told me the Navy had already arrested Carla Durr. She was already in the Navy's custody when we were out at Tysons Corner waiting for her to show. So you saved her life, Shannon. But she's out of our hands now."

"Where was she?"

"Staying at a hotel in Chevy Chase," said O'Connor. "The Navy filled the parking lot with military trucks, battered down her door — D.C. SWAT handled the operation. It was all over in fifteen minutes. Someone working with the admiral questioned her for several hours and then let her go. NCIS was never involved, strictly military."

"All the death we've seen," said Moss, like she'd been punctured and deflated. "All the killing, Mursult's children — it all led to her. And we never had a chance to speak with her. The Navy questioned her for a few hours and just let her go, and we never had a chance. What about the FBI?"

"I'm meeting with the director this evening," said O'Connor. "They're moving forward on their investigation into the chemical-weapons lab we discovered at Buckhannon, and so are we. Domestic terrorism, the homicides. Jurisdiction's a nightmare on this one. We'll be untangling strands of this investigation for years."

She worked with O'Connor over the course of the afternoon, translating her notes into a summary to send over to the admiral's office in Dahlgren. O'Connor remarked on how tired Moss seemed. "Take some time," he said.

"I think I'll head home," she said.

"William Brock's funeral service is scheduled for tomorrow morning," said O'Connor. "In Pittsburgh. You can represent our office if you're up for it."

She was weary. Brock's death seemed from another lifetime. "Of course," she said.

Over a thousand police officers in dress uniform from cities across the nation had gathered at St. Paul Cathedral in Pittsburgh, a cavalcade of men and women standing at attention along Fifth Avenue as the family arrived in limousines. The cathedral was crowded with friends and colleagues, but Moss made her way to an open seat in a rear pew rather than shake hands with people she only vaguely knew from crime scenes. Brock's casket was near the altar, draped in an American flag.

She spotted Nestor during the homily; he sat toward the front, his arm in a sling. Nestor might look for her, she thought, might wonder if she were here, where she was sitting, might want to sit with her, Moss a victim of the same blast that had taken Brock's life. But when she thought of Nestor, she remembered him shooting Vivian in the woods and preferred to avoid him even if it was unfair to judge a man for things he hadn't done. The director of the FBI and the attorney general of the United States each offered words, the director presenting Brock's wife with the FBI Memorial Star and announcing that Special Agent in Charge William Brock would be designated a service martyr, his name added to the other engraved names in the FBI Hall of Honor. Rashonda Brock and her two daughters were led from the memorial, grieving but proud. Moss waited while the front rows cleared, mourners walking down the center aisle. Nestor looked her way, but his eyes passed over her. She thought of what she must look like now and realized he hadn't recognized her.

She slipped out a side door to a quiet courtyard, avoiding the chance of encountering Nestor or anyone else she knew on the cathedral stairs. A motorcade had formed along Fifth. Pittsburgh's Bureau of Police motorcycles with lights flashing guided the hearses and the escort cars away from the church, a long train of police cars following. They were headed to the airport, where the casket would be flown to Texas for the family funeral and burial.

Moss visited her mother that night. An enduring image of her mother, alone in the kitchen, only the single kitchen light on, going through her envelopes of *Reader's Digest* cutouts, the rest of the house dark. Moss used to wonder if this was how she would

remember her mother long after her mother
had died, but now she knew that the Terminus would rob her of even this. Moss had
called after Brock's memorial and told her
mother she was coming over, trying to
prepare her for her injuries. She'd told her
mother over the phone that she'd been in a
car crash, that she would be fine, but the
moment her mother saw her, she stood from
the kitchen table.

"Let me look at you," she said, angling
her daughter's chin toward the light. "Whoever he is, leave him."

Moss sighed. "I told you how this happened. I was in an agency car, and a truck
ran a red light —"

"They don't stop," said her mother. "You
listen to me," she said, staring hard into her
daughter's eyes. "If it's in them, it's always
been in them and always will. He'll destroy
everything about you, he'll take everything
that was good. You're worth more than
that."

"It's nothing like that, I'm telling you —"

"Protect what you have, even if it means
losing everything you think you want."

Moss had aged as she traveled IFTs, even
as the rest of time stood still, catching up
with her mother incrementally over the
years. Since her mother had been pregnant

with Moss when she was young, only seventeen, Moss sometimes thought she might actually catch her mother in age, or pass her by. As her mother examined Moss's face, however, the hot light of the kitchen lamp warming her skin, Moss had never felt more like a child. They ordered pizza and settled in for a night of television. Her mother kept the living-room lights low, and in just the harsh blue flicker of the television Moss found herself staring at the photograph of her father in his Navy whites, grinning until the end of time. They watched ABC News, her mother smoking cigarettes. The news of Brock's funeral had been buried beneath the news of a cult in California, thirty-nine members discovered dead, a mass suicide.

"Of all the . . . you hear about this?" asked her mother.

"No," said Moss.

"Thought the damn comet was a spaceship, so they killed themselves. They thought if they killed themselves, the spaceship would beam them up, like in *Star Trek,*" she said. "All wearing the same sneakers. Look at that, they're showing one of the bodies. Look at the sneakers."

A body draped in a purple tarp, only the slacks and black-and-white sneakers visible, brand-new sneakers, bought for the occasion of death. They watched *Beverly Hills, 90210* and *Party of Five,* shows her mother followed, but Moss let her mind wander to the Vardogger trees, the infinite paths — to Remarque ordering her crew to self-destruct *Libra* and commit mass suicide like the Heaven's Gate cult, believing that if her crew died, then the world they had wrought would die with them. Her mother had fallen asleep in her chair by the time the local news came on, her glass of whiskey still in one hand, her cigarette in the other, burning down. A house fire, Moss imagined — she wondered in how many IFTs the cigarette dropped ash to the floor, caught the carpet on fire. Moss brought an ashtray over, a clay monstrosity she'd made for her mother in first or second grade, stubbed out the cigarette.

She expected more of the Heaven's Gate suicides on the news, wanted to hear more about the spaceship these people thought was flying the Hale-Bopp, but the news was filled instead with a different cosmic event. Images of people gathered in fields, crowding hilltops and the roofs of buildings, staring at the night sky. The Star of Bethlehem had returned, some said — the Star of Bethlehem hanging in the sky, eastward. Some said the star was pointing the way to Bethlehem, some thought it represented the second coming of Christ, though the talking-head astronomers offered differing explanations. Another comet, some said, coming into our viewing region in a cyclical manner, an unprecedented doubling of comets, the Star of Bethlehem and Hale-Bopp like twin silver lights. Others claimed that the shining celestial event was more likely a distant supernova, the light just now reaching the Earth from a star that had died magnificently several billion years ago. Moss's eyes, however, filled with tears that spilled down her cheeks. She unlocked the side door and walked into the street and faced the east. There were already others out on the street, looking up, shielding their eyes. The event was like a shining star, a star extraordinarily bright — bright enough to seem like a nighttime sun casting the Earth in a cold glare that washed out color and heightened shadow. The moon was dim, as were other stars — as was Hale-Bopp, that silvery smudge that had hung grandly in the sky for the past several weeks. The new light felt like the brightest light Moss had ever seen, and it grew ever brighter as she stared. It meant the death of everything she'd ever known. The White Hole had appeared. The Terminus had come.

Her cell phone rang, and she checked the number: O'CONNOR.

"We're still alive," she said.

"We have work to do."

# Two

She drove to Virginia by the pale luster of the White Hole, a blinding disk bounded by a halo of night. Four a.m., but people gathered on their lawns and lined the roads, staring eastward, the unnatural light reflecting against their faces reminding Moss of faces in a movie theater. At dawn the sun rose pallid, but the sky remained preternaturally gray, the temperature dropped, and soon Moss turned on her windshield wipers against fat snowflakes that spun in the air. The radio was full of prophecy at the Star of Bethlehem, announcing the second coming of Christ — a child had been born in Puerto Rico in the instant the White Hole appeared, he'd been named Jesus, and already the infant was hailed as the sublime sign announcing the end of time. Winter was general over the Earth; even the sandblasted deserts of Africa experienced snowfall. NPR news reported that suicides lined the streets of Manhattan, Los Angeles, London, copycat deaths of Heaven's Gate, bodies draped in sheets. There had been minor looting of shoe stores, people stealing the black-and-white Nikes favored by the cult. *This is how the world ends,* Moss thought. No panicking, no riots. No reports of the hanged men appearing, or of people running in herds, not yet anyway, though when she arrived in Virginia Beach, its few snowplows deployed laying salt and scraping the roads clear of slush, she learned that scores of people had congregated on the beach, that they had bent and flailed in concert, a sort of calisthenics, before wading into the ocean to drown.

Naval Air Station Oceana was in the midst of Operation Saigon when Moss arrived at the gates. The president's and vice president's families would be flown here on Marine One, would be boarded onto *Eagle,* a Cormorant shuttle kept ready for this moment. Their families and the members of their essential staff would rendezvous with TERNs Group 6, the USS *James Garfield,* at the Black Vale Station. NSC soldiers were notifying civilians who'd been chosen for evacuation, a life-or-death lottery plagued by nepotism, a supposed mix of genetics, genders, and aptitudes that a think tank of politicians and scientists had devised in consultation with the military to represent the last best hope to revive mankind. Moss drove the streets of the base and saw one of the Cormorants taking off, its flight path over the churning Atlantic. She met O'Connor at the NCIS offices.

"We have a new crime scene," he said.

There would be a final Cormorant, a last ship held to transport NCIS and NSC staff who assisted with Operation Saigon in these final hours. Moss was prepared to miss that flight. Now that the White Hole shone, now that QTNs flooded every man, woman, and child, soon to wipe away consciousness like a whiff of ether, she knew she would work against the Terminus until she, too, was wiped away. She hadn't remained with NCIS all these years to save herself, to book passage on a lifeboat leaving Earth — she had joined to help people, to protect the innocent, and she felt that everyone was innocent in the face of dissolution. She took out her yellow legal pad, uncapped her pen.

"Tell me what we have," she said.

"The appearance of the White Hole coincides with the launch schedule of a Cormorant shuttle called *Onyx*," O'Connor said. "The B-L fired last night, at 10:53 Eastern — the exact moment the White Hole appeared."

"A Navy ship will bring the White Hole," said Moss, shaking her head. "Who?"

"The ship was registered as public/private," said O'Connor. "Black Vale reports that the *Onyx* was requisitioned two days ago, by Senator Curtis Craig Charley."

"C. C. Charley's the chairman of the Armed Services Committee," said Moss.

"He's close with Admiral Annesley."

"So *Onyx* sailed Deep Waters, returned with the White Hole in its wake. It would have followed the *Onyx*'s Casimir line," said Moss. "But why is the *Onyx* a crime scene?"

"Because everyone on board is dead," said O'Connor. "Could be something as simple as a mechanical failure, but we have to find out. The B-L launch was successful, but Black Vale received the *Onyx*'s emergency beacon. We get first crack at the ship, but we have to move. NSC will take *Onyx* from us as soon as they need it for the evacuation, but they want us to determine what happened in case it represents a threat to the evacuees."

The *Grey Dove* was cleared for departure within the hour, one of the few departing Cormorants not ferrying evacuees to dock with the massive TERNs. Moss taxied with the other Cormorants, wondering how quickly the effects of the Terminus might manifest. She launched, cutting through dense, snow-spitting clouds that spired into violent plumes stretching magnificently upward. She imagined everyone on Earth already in a state of living death. She imagined crucifixions, imagined running to the sea. The *Grey Dove* broke from Earth, and Moss floated into the main cabin, her view of Earth no longer one of tender blue fragility but of a white-palled planet, an eye milky white and blind.

The *Onyx* was a Cormorant, identical to the *Grey Dove.* It looked like a mirror-smooth piece of black glass, almost indistinguishable from the surrounding night except for the silvery planes of the wings and some hull sections that caught the glare of the White Hole and reflected cast-off light from the moon. The *Grey Dove*'s AI maneuvered close to the *Onyx* while Moss prepped for the crime scene, wearing the olive-green space suit marked NCIS and checking her camera, the film. The *Grey Dove* chirped a three-point alert once it had closed the gap between ships, matched rotation with the *Onyx.* Moss fastened her helmet, floated into the tubular airlock. The airlock of the *Onyx* was only twenty-five feet away, but the distance between ships was a span of open space. The *Onyx* and the *Grey Dove* spun in relation to each other, like the two parts of a binary star. The *Onyx*'s airlock was directly in front of her, unmoving. She gripped its steel handlebars while she worked to quell the sense of vertigo that curled through her stomach at the thought of floating from one ship to the other. *My God,* she thought, still just a girl from Canonsburg when faced with a space walk. Moss had seen marines do this maneuver, jumping ship to ship, countless times, soldiers leaping from the lip of one ship and floating — sometimes untethered — across the gap as easily as jumping over a sidewalk puddle. Moss attached one end of her tether to the *Grey Dove,* tugged on it experimentally.

She stepped into space, an infant on an umbilical cord, full of adrenaline as she drifted between ships. And soon the *Onyx*'s hull loomed large enough that she could reach out and grab hold of the airlock, pulling herself the rest of the way.

"*Onyx,* this is Shannon Moss. Please unlock the port airlock."

The lock snapped open. Moss hooked her tether to the *Onyx,* stitching the ships together, then pushed open the airlock and crawled inside. She waited for the *Onyx*'s green light of pressurization before she swam into the body of the ship, through the lightless airlock tube, her path lit only with the penlight attached to the side of her helmet. She gasped when she saw the bodies in the main cabin — there were twelve, naked, floating in the airless, lightless room like icebergs under dark water. Her penlight spotlighted wherever she looked. Globules floated among the bodies, some as large as her fist — blood, she knew, fractionated, large water spheres filled with sprays of red platelets and yellow plasma like the swirls of color in hand-blown glass ornaments.

*"Onyx,"* said Moss. "Lights, please."

The interior of the ship illuminated the ghastly dead and their floating blood. It struck her that the bodies looked like they might have been dead for only a few minutes, but she knew that was because there was no oxygen to trigger decomposition. Years could pass and they would look virtually the same.

*They killed one another,* she thought, that much was clear. The bodies were marred with slash marks and other cutting wounds and blunt-force trauma. Some of their bones had been broken; in one case a snapped shinbone had poked through the victim's skin. A long gash flared across one man's spine; another had entrance wounds over his heart, several stab marks. She counted: someone had stabbed this man at least thirty times, mincing his heart and lungs. *Like documenting a crime scene that's been put in a box and shaken,* she thought. She recognized the senator, C. C. Charley, his body on the ceiling, his foot caught in wiring. His stomach had been opened, and his guts had leaked out across the ceiling like the long tentacles of a crimson squid. Moss took photographs. Smaller blood droplets hung like a rainstorm frozen in place, the fine mist painting Moss's space suit as she moved through the ship, snapping pictures. After every few shots, she wiped blood from her lens.

She measured the distances between bodies, taking notes with pencil in the notebook fastened to her suit. She used yellow cords to tie the bodies to the ceiling and walls so they wouldn't drift. A ghastly concern, but despite their weightlessness these bodies' masses were the same as they would have been on Earth and could crush or injure her like falling debris if she were to bump one, set it moving.

Where were the murder weapons? She began to find them, handmade things: a shard of a mirror duct-taped to a length of pipe, pieces of a shattered faceplate fastened to the fingers of an EVA glove. She bagged the shivs in plastic evidence sacks. They had used the rather dull knives from the mess room, scissors, and some of the decedents had bruising that indicated they were choked and beaten to death when weapons weren't available. The sailors would have had firearms, but Moss saw no indication that they'd been discharged. She couldn't find bullet wounds in any of the bodies. The image of what had occurred here turned in her mind, and she closed her eyes to regain herself. She had excused herself to vomit at crime scenes before, cleansing herself to refocus on the work, but vomiting at this crime scene, into her helmet, would be disastrous. She waited for her nerves to calm, for the flopping sensation in her stomach to level. *Deep breath.* Being up here alone with so many bodies was claustrophobic; the *Onyx* enclosed her. She opened her eyes.

The onboard computer recorded that the life-support system had been cut manually. Moss weighed the extent of the damage these people had inflicted on one another, the sheer butchery. She imagined some sane sailor cutting life support just to make the killing stop. Or maybe he'd cut life support in order to kill everyone with a single stroke. The crew of the *Taurus,* that first NSC ship to encounter the Terminus, had met a similar fate, a sudden flash of insane violence — and Nicole had spoke of Esperance, sailors killing one another on those icy shores until the Navy SEALs, Cobb and Mursult, had helped the survivors regain their sanity.

Three and a half hours documenting the main cabin before moving through the ship. She found the commanding officer's body in the galley, a knife stuck in his back. There was still food in his mouth — either he'd paused in the killing to have supper or was the first to have died, someone ambushing him as he ate. She found another body shoved into the toilet compartment, his lips cut away from his face to reveal his teeth. Distracted by the grotesquerie of the mouth, she didn't recognize the corpse until after she'd taken pictures of him.

*Driscoll. Dr. Peter Driscoll, the scientist who appeared to me as a simulation.* She recognized his hair, that white whoosh. Without his lips, Driscoll's teeth could almost be mistaken for a cheek-spanning grin, his dark eyes wide open, his eyebrows lifted, as if he, too, were surprised at what had happened here. Senator C. C. Charley, Dr. Peter Driscoll — Moss formed a guess about the party aboard the *Onyx.* She expected to find other future founders of Phasal Systems on this ship, engineers and physicists from NRL, if anyone ever took the trouble to identify the bodies. She found Admiral Annesley's corpse floating chest-down near the floor like a bottom-feeding fish. Moss flipped the corpse over and saw that the man's face had been cut away.

Another corpse she recognized, drifting near the sleeping compartments — a woman's body, obese, her flesh floating outward. Carla Durr had been gutted, slashed from neck to belly. In the moment of her death, she must have plunged her hands into her breast cavity and tried to pull herself apart. It looked like she was revealing her rib cage and organs, some of which had floated away.

*We saved your life, and what did you do with it?*

The Navy had arrested Carla Durr in her hotel room in Chevy Chase and questioned her. She had sold Patrick Mursult's secrets to Admiral Annesley, Moss figured. How much money had Durr received, what other favors than this voyage to Deep Waters? Whatever information she'd sold had led to this.

The thought came to Moss.

A chain of information: Patrick Mursult to his lawyer, Carla Durr, Durr to Admiral Annesley, to Dr. Peter Driscoll, to Senator C. C. Charley — Hyldekrugger had been breaking the chain. *But I saved this woman's life. I should have let her die.* The thought was repugnant, but as Moss looked at the lawyer's ruined body, the enormity of what had hinged on her decision to save this woman's life rushed over her, when in the hospital she had told O'Connor that they weren't too late to stop the killing. *But I should have let them kill her* — it was clear to her now. What was one life set against all life? Hyldekrugger had been right: killing this woman would have broken the chain, would have staved off NSC from discovering Esperance for another few years at least.

*It's my fault.*

Moss screamed, thinking, *No, letting the lawyer die wasn't right, that wasn't the right answer.* And she turned inward, surrounded by butchered corpses, thinking about inevitability. Throughout her professional life, Moss had lived with the idea of the Terminus sweeping closer, but now her mind opened to the idea that it had all been because of her, that her career in NCIS had set her on the path to the Mursult investigation, and every bit of evidence she uncovered, culminating in her decision to intercede in the killing of the lawyer Carla Durr, had ensured that NSC would rediscover Esperance sooner and sooner and sooner. *I ended the world,* she thought, looking at the dead that surrounded her, but their eyes offered no solace. She felt trapped here, spun in webs, the White Hole a spider's eye bearing down on her.

*Someone else would quit.* Her little mantra was so absurd in this hideous context that just thinking it made her feel a rush of giddiness, as if she were losing her mind. But when that sensation passed, she felt centered, resolute.

*This is a crime scene. There are questions to answer.*

What had Mursult told his lawyer?

Mursult's information might be here, but where? The Cormorant-class ships were fitted with personal compartments, little more than cubbies cut into the floors and ceilings, coffin-shaped cubicles meant to serve as private places to sleep. But most people preferred to tether their sleep sacks somewhere in the main cabin rather than squeeze into these casketlike compartments, so civilian passengers generally used these compartments as footlockers to stow personal items. There had been twenty people on board the *Onyx.* Moss picked through each compartment, looking for Durr's.

"Here we go," she said, uncovering a set of burgundy overnight bags monogrammed "C.D." Undergarments, a folded tracksuit, hosiery, a jar of Oil of Olay, bifocals. She found a Stephen King paperback and a manila envelope closed with a metal clasp. Moss opened the envelope, slid out the sheaf of papers: lined sheets, torn from a spiral notebook, the edges fringed from the perforation. Crude pencil drawings. *What are these?* In one of them, Moss recognized the Vardogger tree. There was a photocopy of a map, red ink pointing to a location at the Red Run, the thin space, highlighting the approximate location of the access route to get to that spot. Then she found a hand-written note:

*It's a trick, it might take you a few times before you see the trees if you can ever see the trees at all. Bietak thinks you need QTNs in you to see it, as some people never can figure out the trick, but I don't think that's the case — the damn thing opens whenever our engine misfires. Follow the trees once you see them, but once you cross the river, don't step off the path. You'll think you'll want to — it feels like that — but if you step off the path, you will be exposed and you can't be saved.*

The next sheet was a drawing of *Libra,* in black ink, the bow circled with rings of blue ink — meant to be the spurting blue flame from the B-L drive, Moss guessed.

*The trees lead you here to* Libra. *When you're here, you will see other lines of Vardoggers. If you walk these other paths, you go to other worlds like your world but slightly off. H marks paths we took, so we remember. He sets cairns in the paths. There are many paths.*

Moss flipped through the pages. A map of Buckhannon, the chemical lab marked in red.

*Building a heavy-duty facility at Zion, multi-million dollars, H got the idea from cult in Japan. There's an orchard there — Jared's mom will move to the orchard, hold it for him. H and Jared want to re-create Japanese gas attacks, use the same stuff they used. Test batches at Buckhannon.*

There were other drawings, some of geometric shapes, seven-pointed stars, one of the Black Sun design, its spokes like the Vardogger paths, and there were hand-drawn maps labeled *ESPERANCE,* a series of drawings showing locations of campsites, remembered fragments of geography. Moss recognized the fjords and oceans Nicole had described. There were star charts marking the location of the dim binary stars, the location of the planet that *Libra* had discovered. She found a longer letter:

Dear Durr. If I show up someday demanding my cut of the money, then the deal's still on but for now it's too late for me haha so use this info in good health. H is coming tonight, Nicole told me so. I was at my buddy's when she told me so had to run. She's a nice kid but a rat and squeals whenever H pushes her. It cuts me she ratted me out to him but at least she confessed to me, gave me a heads up. At least love's worth that much. NO ONE knows you not even Nicole so don't worry you're safe. So now's the time for brass tacks. Included: location of Krugger, location of Esperance, location of *Libra* and that special tree, the Vardogger, just like I promised. I know you haven't believed most of what I told you but after tonight you'll at least know the danger I am in is real, so please watch yourself too. I was with H from the beginning with all his bullshit because I wanted to *LIVE*. I wanted to live, that's all. But I can't stomach all his killing. I saw someone he burned alive with acid and couldn't take it.

Sometimes I wish I would have helped Remark make that black hole, a cascade failure to obliterate us all. Too late, too late for all. I will not get my money or my pardon, but my cut will be for you to sell this information to Navy or FBI, make a good buck for yourself but stop this man. He wants to kill us all. Krugger walks every path. He worships death. Worships death like most men worship Jesus. He prays to it. He takes their fingernails and uses them like relics, like holy things. He will be at my house soon and so I left my family there, left him to kill my family to slow him down some so I can get this information to your safe deposit box, per our agreement and also get somewhere safe. You might think that sounds harsh to let my family die but here's something else you won't believe but it is truth: merrily, merrily, life is but a dream. No matter what happens to my family tonight, I can find another one. I'll walk the Vardogger trees to some other place and time and there my wife will welcome me home, safe and sound. They will be dead here, but they will be alive somewhere else. My wife will be a young woman there and my Marian will be a young child, she'll be five again, and I'll watch her grow up again happy and I'll watch my youngest come into being all over again. Durr we are all just shadows that come through the woods, shadows that cross the river. It's like this, that old poem I used to recite to my Marian when she was a child and I rocked her to sleep in my lap: *'Twas all so pretty a sail, it seemed, As if it could not be, And some folk thought 'twas a dream they'd dreamed, Of sailing that beautiful sea.* Anyway I look at the time and know even now my family is dead or dying. I cry over my children but I know they will live yet. I will drop this information at your box, then will drive to a space I like, this calm spot where I like to think, where I like to stay sometimes and sleep. I'll think of my family that was here and prepare for my new family that will be there. You'll never see me again — MUR.

Patrick Mursult thought he would escape through the Vardogger, walking the paths, start a new life in some other IFT. But he was killed at the Blackwater Lodge before he could escape.

*Marian will be a young child . . .* But how was that possible? None of us can go back, can we?

The Terminus had followed *Libra,* but *Li-*

551

*bra* was caught in a space-time knot, somewhere beyond time. The *Onyx,* however, had returned to terra firma. The crew of the *Onyx* had shed their clothes because they were infected with QTNs, Moss thought, remembering how her own skin had burned. That had been the sensation in the minutes before her crucifixion: burning skin. She had stripped off her clothes despite biting winter wind, and was crucified.

"*Onyx,* please call Apollo Soucek Field."

She heard the tone for "failed command." Moss found one of the ship's computers, saw: . . . ACCESS NOT AUTHORIZED.

"Override," said Moss. "Please place a call to Apollo Soucek Field."

. . . ALL CHANNELS REQUIRED FOR OPERATION SAIGON.

"Damn it," she said. "*Onyx,* override. Send out emergency signal. Please place a call to Apollo Soucek Field or to the Black Vale."

. . . ALL CHANNELS REQUIRED FOR OPERATION SAIGON.

"Fuck."

The bodies in the cabin moved when she brushed against them. They looked like they danced, like someone's dreamy joke of a morgue ballet. She escaped belowdecks, exploring the galley, the recreation room.

She found an American flag, stiff without gravity, a fabric rectangle thumbtacked to the floor. On the ceiling were a camcorder and tripod. She checked the camera, found a tape, wondering if these people had filmed themselves murdering one another. She loaded the VHS tape into the entertainment system, figured out how to turn everything on. The screen was filled with an image of Senator Charley, wearing a blue polo shirt and khaki shorts, tube socks pulled near to his knees. The American flag was over his shoulder, a backdrop. Moss had seen the man countless times on television, but he looked much younger here, sparked by a childlike wonder, the circus ride of weightlessness.

"Fellow Americans, I have been on the journey of a lifetime, of a thousand lifetimes," he said, and then a woman's voice, off camera, asked him to try again. The senator cleared his throat, plastered on a practiced smile, and said, "I have been on the journey of a lifetime. Fell Americans. I mean, fellow Americans —"

"Go ahead," said the woman's voice. "We can edit."

"Fellow Americans, on March twenty-sixth, 1997, aboard a Navy vessel, the USS *Onyx,* a group of men and women embarked on the journey of a lifetime, a journey of a thousand lifetimes. We traveled a distance once only dreamed of. No longer the 'final frontier,' the vast distances of space have been opened to us . . . Wait, wait, let me try that again."

"You used the word 'distance' several times," said the woman off screen. "We can use cue cards."

"No," said Senator Charley. "I want this to feel natural."

"Let's practice the section about Majesty," said the woman.

"Okay," said the senator. He smiled to the camera and said, "We have discovered a planet rich in wondrous, strange materials, beautiful fauna and undreamed-of life. Yes, *life.* I have had my eyes opened anew to the miracle of God's creation and have had my mind opened to the possibilities of his grandeur. As Christians, and as Americans, we have called this planet 'Majesty.' "

"A touch too preachy. Oh, hold on," said the woman's voice, off camera.

The image of the senator turned to fuzz, but a new image appeared. Someone had filmed through one of the ship's windows — an image similar to pictures of Earth seen from a distance, the curved sphere of a planet, but the planet filmed here was a sphere white with ice and black with oily seas, crater-pocked and scarred with jagged mountains. A sizable moon rose over the crescent horizon, a golden giant. The monitor turned to static.

"— Shannon?" from over the comm.

The sudden voice startled her.

"Shannon, was that you? Are you okay?" said O'Connor. "I received the emergency signal."

"I'm . . . I found something important up here," she said, her voice shaking.

"I have rendezvous instructions for you, enact immediately," he said. "You have been assigned to TERNs Group 5, the *Cancer*. Don't come home, Shannon —"

"Listen to me," she said. "The *Onyx* went to Esperance, they went to the —"

"I understand," he said. "But it's too late now. Once you reach *Cancer,* set the autocourse on the *Onyx* for Apollo Soucek. We need more ships for the evacuation, we need every ship. The Navy has seized control of the *Grey Dove*. They've recalled the ship, but we need more."

"The answer might be here, on the *Onyx,*" said Moss. "We need more time."

*"It's too late,"* said O'Connor. "The hanged men are here, the running men are here. People everywhere are looking at the sky,

555

their mouths are filled with silver. The forests are burning, the snow is heavy. It's too late, Shannon. It's too late."

Moss pulled herself along the lower-deck passageway, flying upward through the portal leading to the helm, thinking, *Remarque. They murdered the* Libra*'s commanding officer.* The cockpit of the *Onyx* was identical to the *Grey Dove*'s: a reinforced-glass canopy, two flight chairs nestled into a sea of controls, panels of switches and knobs. She thought of her mother. She thought of *Cancer.* Receding in the distance was her ship, the *Grey Dove,* the tether snapped.

"*Onyx,* were you given new instructions?"

. . . RENDEZVOUS WITH USS CANCER, SET AUTOCOURSE FOR NAVAL AIR STATION OCEANA.

"*Onyx,* can you belay that order?"

. . . NO. ALL RESOURCES REQUISITIONED FOR OPERATION SAIGON.

"*Onyx,* can you belay the order to dock with the USS *Cancer* if you fly to Oceana?"

. . . YES.

The TERNs would be loaded to capacity, she thought. Two hundred souls. She thought of *Cancer,* an older ship, a ship that once had faulty O-rings before its overhaul. *We would live like rats,* thought Moss, and there would be nowhere to run, no haven, nowhere, there would only be one blind jump to the next, to far-future IFTs in unknown galaxies searching barren stars and infertile planets for safe landing, for any safe landing, until the food ran out or the recycling for the water malfunctioned. Everyone on board would kill one another, they would eat one another, drink one another, and eventually they would all starve, they would all die of thirst, or they would run out of oxygen. One way or another, they would all die.

Only a few hours of oxygen remained in her tank. "*Onyx,* please reestablish life support," she said. "And belay request to rendezvous with the *Cancer.* Continue to Oceana."

An impulsive request, but she felt the burden of culpability, the belief that her actions had brought the Terminus here. She felt she deserved to die or never escape. Pushing through the hanging legs and arms of the corpses felt like swimming through a skein of seaweed. Driscoll was in the toilet, his lipless, toothy grin — she didn't want to see him. She didn't want to see Durr's revealed heart. She used the American flag as a cover to the upper-deck portal, to keep the blood out as the air began to circulate.

When the *Onyx* had reached healthy oxygen saturation, Moss removed her helmet. She'd been expecting a smell of putrefaction, but there was none.

She left the lights on. She tried to sleep during her return to Earth, but her body tensed and her mind flitted with fear. Images darted through her thoughts. The hanged men, the running men, Nestor asking if she believed in the resurrection of the body. *No, there is no God, this is the natural order.* She imagined a snake flailing in the weightlessness of space until it curled toward itself to swallow its own tail. She thought of silver, swatches of silver swimming together, a school of fish. Njoku in the Pacific, reaching deep into a watery thin space and feeling a fish appear in the middle of his hand, the sensation of the fish slipping free . . .

Moss skimmed the surface of sleep and woke when she fell to the floor, the clatter of everything that hadn't been tethered crashing down around her, the camcorder cracked to pieces, the tremendous *thud, thud, thud* of the bodies whapping the walls and floor. Earth's gravity. She hurried to the pilot's chair, strapped herself in, thinking of the wreck of the *Libra,* just before the misfire. *Libra* had burned and fallen in that long, dreamless night. The *Onyx*'s cockpit was tinted, shading the incandescent smear of fire as it burned against the atmosphere like a struck match. *They murdered Remarque,* she thought. At one of the Brandt-Lomonaco space-time knots, Pacific jack mackerels were caught in a Gödel curve — a loop. She thought of *Libra,* her disorienting night in the brig, her experience of mutiny and the shipwreck that followed. Mursult's letter to Durr had spelled out what Remarque had been attempting, *a cascade failure to obliterate us all.* A black hole.

"I can do what Remarque couldn't do," said Moss, piecing her thoughts together even as she said them aloud. Nicole had told her that Remarque had ordered mass suicide. That if the entire crew of *Libra* blinked, then the planet Esperance would go unfound. "My God," Moss said aloud, to no one. "*Libra*'s a jack mackerel. I can do what Remarque couldn't do."

But what would come of it? she wondered. What would happen if she managed to breach *Libra,* if she somehow managed to cause a cascade failure?

She had been brought here, pulled across the river when she was pulled from the cross. *Everyone's mistake,* she'd been told,

559

*is that we believe in our own existence.* The falling star as it blooms. Patrick Mursult believed he could walk the Vardoggers, travel backward in time: *Marian will be young.* If he could walk backward in time . . .

When was terra firma? she wondered. It wasn't here, it wasn't 1997. 1997 was *Libra*'s IFT. If she could cause a cascade failure, if *Libra* can blink, when was true terra firma? She imagined the thin space overwhelmed by the Terminus, imagined the Terminus reaching *Libra,* imagined the White Hole traveling *Libra*'s Casimir line back to the point of its original launch, to terra firma. *Marian will be young, five years old.* Nicole, when she rescued Moss from the brig, had said that eleven years had passed. Ebullience rose through her like bubbles in a flute of champagne. If *Libra* blinked, then this IFT will blink, everything will blink. NSC ships would still comb the universe and distant time, would still sail Deep Waters, but *Libra* will have blinked in its future. Esperance will go undiscovered. There would still be a chance of that planet's discovery, Moss realized, some chance of another ship happening on that planet, there would still be a chance of the Terminus, but only a *chance.* A possibility. But there can be *other* possibilities. Terra firma would be the date of *Libra*'s initial launch, the moment just before *Libra* first used its B-L drive.

*November 7, 1985.*

"Courtney," said Moss.

The *Onyx* cut through the whiteout squall, the ocean an undulating gray beneath the gusts, and skidded on the ice-slicked runway at Apollo Soucek. People broke through the barriers and swarmed the runway, chased the Cormorants as they taxied, insensible of their own safety in their desperation to flee. Moss saw bodies in the snow. She was still far from the terminal when a yellow truck the size of a bus cut across the runway ahead of her, sped toward her, to collide with her. *What are you doing?* she thought as the truck fishtailed on the slick surface. It was an anti-icing truck, the cherry-picker arm and hoses flailing wildly. The truck swerved and cut back and rammed the *Onyx*'s front wheel.

"What the fuck?" shouted Moss, the *Onyx* now stuck in the wreckage of the truck. Maybe an accident caused by the ice, maybe the truck had slid into her, but she saw the first few people rush toward the Cormorant shouting. Others appeared, families, soldiers, surrounding the *Onyx,* trying to climb

561

aboard. *They want to get into this ship. They want to save themselves, take over this ship.*

Moss popped the canopy just as one of the men reached her. He'd clambered up the wreckage of the yellow truck, his eyes wild. "Take me on this one, take me!"

"Get in," said Moss, climbing from the canopy to let him pass, needing to escape these people. She found her footing on the Cormorant's boarding ladder, but once she made it down a few rungs, clutching hands yanked her off, tossed her aside to the tarmac. At least a dozen people had made it to the *Onyx,* and more were coming. They crawled over the ship, trying to find openings. She saw another Cormorant, the *Lily of the Valley,* streak past and swerve into the sky, bodies strewn along its runway. *They've gone mad,* thought Moss. She turned back to the *Onyx* and saw people ejecting the bodies of the dead, throwing corpses away like unwanted ballast.

*"Shannon!"*

She heard him: O'Connor. He was with Njoku, the snow blowing in slashing gusts between them. He waved to her, but she lost sight of them in the storm, in the rush of people heading toward the farther runways in anticipation of another Cormorant. Moss fought her way through the masses, into the terminal. The hallways were quiet compared to the clamor outside. She took off her heavy space suit, wearing only her long underwear. Luggage was strewn about the airport, abandoned in the mad rush to catch ships to escape. She found a U.S. Navy tracksuit in a duffel and a flight jacket with VFA-213 patches: the Blacklion, a double-tailed lion drawn in stars. She put it on.

The Navy had abandoned most of the base. The streets were empty, the snow mounting in sifting drifts. Moss brushed off a half foot of snow from her truck, listening to the engine crank before it turned over. More people streamed in through the abandoned station gates as she sped away, the streets of Virginia Beach swept with snow but passable. She had always imagined immense traffic jams in the event of cataclysm, but there were no cars on the road, only a few that had been pulled to the berms, abandoned. *Everyone's dead in their homes,* she thought, or stuck in ice. There were a few other cars on the highways, their brights only dim spots in the blizzard.

Four people clustered on the roadside gazing at the White Hole, immobile, utterly paralyzed, their mouths hanging wide, extended open as if their jaws had been stretched apart. The silver filled their mouths; it looked as if each gurgled a mouthful of mercury. The silver ran down their cheeks, over their necks. She didn't see her first pack of running men until well outside the city, a group of thirty or so runners, nude and barefoot despite the freezing winds. She had almost imagined the running men as something funny, absurd, but seeing them terrified her, running desperately without thought of bodily injury or endurance, their faces twisted into expressions of blank rage, some of them screaming. They ran like they were being chased by a swarm of stinging insects, passing into the forest that edged the interstate, disappearing into the woods. They would run until their bodies disintegrated, Moss knew. If they made it to the shore, they would run into the water to drown. She drove recklessly, spinning out on the icy roads, swerving lanes, panic settling over her that she was wrong to be here, so wrong, that she should have docked at the *Cancer,* should be among colleagues, far from here, leaving the dying Earth to seek a new refuge somewhere out in endless space.

Night descended as she entered the forest, and the glare from the White Hole reflected off the blizzard snowfall and bathed the evergreens in silver. The fires that would devour the Monongahela National Forest, and all forests, had burned since the White Hole appeared, and Moss saw firelight flickering deep in the woods on either side of her like will-o'-the-wisps or ghostly torchlight processions. The access route leading up toward the Vardogger was impassable. Moss abandoned her truck and climbed, sliding hopelessly down the snowdrifts until she grappled tree trunk to tree trunk, dragging herself upward by gripping saplings and using them like climbing cords. *Any moment your skin might burn, the QTNs might fill you, you might shed these clothes and run, you might join a pack, you might be lifted into the air . . .*

She staggered into the clearing where Nestor had once shot Vivian, where Marian's bones were once found, where Marian's echo had been recovered. The woods were on fire. She struggled for breath, the freezing air and smoke and ash burning in her lungs. Her body ached.

"Oh, God," she said, heart pounding from the climb, but she continued through thicker pines and soon dropped several inches into deeper snow. She had found the runnel that Nestor once followed, the shallow ditch of the creek that had run dry. *The cairns were near here,* she remembered, but they would be buried under snow. She heard rushing water and followed the sound on a downward slope. A Navy truck was left here, iced over. They hadn't yet fenced this area off, though they'd planned to before the evacuation. She saw heavier equipment, abandoned. Some trees had been cleared from the zone, were piled like lumber. The white Vardogger tree was untouched by snow.

Moss ran her hand over the bark; it felt like cold steel. She fell to her knees, hoping the tree would open, would multiply, to show her a path of trees, but nothing happened. The wind pushed through the hemlocks, the sound like a broom sweeping concrete. This was where Nestor had left her to die. In one of her futures, he had betrayed her here. What had happened to Nestor? She imagined him crucified, upside down in a forest of other crucifixions, but the thought seemed too cruel, despite his future cruelty. She chose to remember how his body had looked silvery in the moonlight of that first night they'd spent together, how his freckles had formed a constellation over his heart. She was filled with sorrow.

She stood, walked away from the tree, turned back.

There was only one tree.

*No.*

Mursult had written that the path might be a trick of the eyes. That it might always exist but remain unseen, or that it might be a function of QTNs in the blood, or that it might open whenever the B-L drive mis-fired. In any case there was no telling when or even if the tree would form an infinite path that led to *Libra. The hour is late,* Nestor had said. *What do I do?* Moss screamed, raging, nervous. *What do I do?* Time passed, the snow and violent wind numbed her, she bundled in her coat, concerned about QTNs that must be in the air. *They must be filling me,* she thought. *They must be saturating my blood.*

*Will I die here?* She wondered if her death would come while she waited for a path to appear. Nothing as violently bizarre as what QTNs might do with her, but naturally, a natural death in this unnatural cold. The flight jacket she had taken from Apollo Soucek was leather, lined with wool, but the cold seeped through and hoarfrost froze over her hair when she tucked her face deep into the lining. She pulled her arms in from the sleeves, breathed onto her fingers, but her skin stung and tingled, and she knew she would soon lose feeling.

*Walk. Move. Keep your blood flowing.*

Twilight. She went to the clearing, to the river, and returned to the white tree. When she passed the tree, the landscape changed around her. She lost sight of the Navy vehicles and the felled evergreens. The pines had grown in, were thick, and she pushed through branches, hoping to find that infinite path, but instead came back to the same white tree. *Or . . . this must be a different tree.*

She was in the thin space, she realized, but the path of trees that Hyldekrugger had followed wasn't here; there was only a dark forest, boughs and branches, needles that scratched her. She came again to the white tree, and although she knew she was caught up in this place, just as she'd been caught here before her crucifixion, she began to panic, lost. She forced her way through dense pine boughs and came into the clearing, to the rushing black river, but she was on the wrong side of the river, she felt, the same sense that Njoku and O'Connor had described when they were here. She saw the white tree across the river, but she had come from the white tree. It should be behind her.

*Marian crossed this river,* she remembered, *and I crossed the river with Hyldekrugger.* But the pathway of trees hadn't appeared for her, and there was no tree fording the river. *Shannon Moss climbed from this river, the echo,* she thought, just before Cobb beat her to death.

She approached the river, toed the bank. The swift water broke against boulders into white water, misting her with river spray. She could make it across, though, maybe. There were enough stones in the water, sharper rocks jutting above the rapids; they could be stepping-stones, she thought.

*You'll die, Shannon. You'll get hypothermia in that water, with no place to dry off, with the air so cold. You'll die.*

But she scrabbled down the snow-covered bank, gauging her distance to the nearest rock, a few feet ahead. She stepped wide across the river onto the rock and found her footing, trusting her weight to her prosthetic leg. The wind ripped at her, and she shivered. The next rock was closer, with a wide flat section she could land on. She gathered herself, took another step, but her prosthetic knee joint gave when she needed it to lock, and she slipped and fell, gashing her head against the jagged stone before the current carried her under. Her entire body felt lacerated by the cold water, and her lungs constricted in the frigid rush; she couldn't breathe. She was submerged, and she flailed in desperation; her hands groped, scraping against rocks, but she couldn't find purchase. The river carried her. She reached above the water, and her fingers touched smooth wood. She grabbed for it, caught herself, held fast to the branch, and pulled her head above water, gasping. She heaved herself from the river, scrambling onto the felled tree, the bridge. She had found the Vardogger, and she hugged it, lying on her chest. Her clothes were soaked with river water, fast becoming a shell of ice. She had to warm up somehow, or she would die.

# THREE

The wind battered her. Her fingers were numb, her toes. *I don't know what to do. Take off the wet clothes? I'd freeze. But I'll freeze with them on.* The Vardogger trees ahead of her were like an illusion of forced perspective, each tree along the path slightly smaller than the preceding, until the farthest tree was only a point of white almost lost against the snow. *If I die, I'd rather slide back into the river to drown than just freeze to death here on this tree.*

The river was inviting — she could still slip in. *I shouldn't have climbed out,* she thought, and imagined being swept away as peaceful, like falling asleep somewhere familiar after being gone so long. She looked around her, taking in the world a final time, everything reduced to monochromatic shades, white trees, white snow, black water, evergreens turned the color of charcoal in the dim light. Only the blot of orange retained vital color. A body, in orange. In the distance by the tree line. She had seen the orange with Hyldekrugger, was seeing the orange again now — a *thin space.* Over the years as she adjusted to the confusion of the accident that had cost her leg, Moss had considered the woman in orange as something like a crack in her psyche that needed to be repressed, and so she rarely thought about the woman but dreamed of her often. Strange dreams where they interacted, traded places, back to the way things were supposed to have been. And now she knew that this woman in orange was Shannon Moss, that when she was pulled from her midair crucifixion, when she was boarded onto the Quad-lander, the pilots were different men from those she remembered. There had been so many small differences from one life to another, but she'd experienced such trauma that she'd rationalized these changes. Now she knew: she realized now that when she was saved, she'd been pulled into this woman's life, this woman in orange.

She struggled against the wind, back toward the clearing. She followed the Vardogger path to the line of evergreens, to the body in orange. The orange space suit was a modified Extravehicular Mobility Unit, the orange the color for trainees. She brushed away snow that had accumulated on the body, flipped the body over, and saw her own face through the visor. A younger face, twenty years younger. Moss cried huge tearless sobs seeing this young woman. A child, still just a child. Remembering herself, her own face so changed, imagining her own life cut short at this early age.

"I'm sorry," said Moss. "I'm sorry but I have to do this."

She unlocked the connection between the orange suit's torso assembly and pants, pulled off the woman's boots.

"I'm sorry, I'm so sorry," she said, sliding the woman from the pants, from the torso assembly and sleeves. The woman's long johns were dry. Moss stripped her, allowing herself only a single glance at the young woman's legs. She pulled off her ice-encrusted clothes and traded them for the dry clothes, thick pants and boots. Putting on these suits was always an ordeal, much easier with another person's help, but Moss managed alone. NSC's designs had been modified from the suits NASA used, had been slimmed down. The torso assembly would be difficult. Usually she would have used a harness that held the suit in place while she stepped into it, but here she had to crawl inside, extending her arms through the sleeves. She locked the helmet into place, latched the buckles around her torso. Warmth returned immediately, thawing her. She sat beneath the pine boughs, shivering while she warmed. Numb and sluggish, but the feeling returned to her extremities, warmth spreading outward. The naked body of Shannon Moss lay supine, pillowed on a drift of snow. The suit's dosimeter was black. This woman had died of radiation exposure, the QTNs. *She was beautiful,* thought Moss, in the way people realize about themselves twenty years too late. Her golden hair outspread, snowflakes settling on the surface of her blue eyes, snow accumulating over her skin. Moss watched the snow, and by the time she was warm enough to stand and move, the snow had buried this other body.

She followed the path of trees, but the trees themselves were repellent. She struggled against the wrongness of this place. She had no plan; even assuming she could relocate *Libra* by following the Vardogger path, she didn't know what she would do. Remarque had been trying to spark a cascade failure, a catastrophic collapse in *Libra*'s B-L drive that would have destroyed the ship and everyone on it — but B-L drives were designed with a series of fail-safes, nothing Moss knew how to overcome. And she didn't have her sidearm or a weapon of any kind to defend herself during the mutiny, if indeed she found mutiny. The hanged men wailed as she crossed the felled tree. Mursult's letter to Durr had warned against straying from the Vardogger path, and as she glanced to either side of her, seeing snowy fields and distant trees, the temptation was to veer from the path to escape this Terminal chaos and the abhorrent repeating trees. Moss didn't believe in God, but she increasingly believed in hell — and farther away in the distance she saw that the air had crystallized and that what she'd taken for mountains were clashing floes of ice, and she thought that despite their abstract beauty this might indeed be perdition.

There was a man in the path, ahead of her, shambling. She glimpsed him, his gray silhouette veiled by snow, but recognized him as Hyldekrugger only as she neared. His coat and the blankets he'd draped himself with were scattered across the ice, blown about by the wind; he had taken off his shirt, and his skin was burned red-violet and black with dead flesh. He scratched at his chest, drawing thin lines of silvery blood.

His lips were silver, and some silver had dribbled down his chin, wetting his ruddy beard.

"I'm boiling," he said when his eyes focused on Moss, plaintive, and he fell to his knees in front of her. "There's too much fire," he said. "Help me, please."

Moss kept her distance, but she wasn't afraid. She knew his mind was gone. Hyldekrugger watched her, vaguely. He coughed up blood, but his blood was mixed with silver, and more silver rose in his mouth and overflowed his lips. "You ain't real," he said. "You ain't even real, it's just me here." But as she left him, he called out, "Help me, you've got to help me!" until the wind overwhelmed his words and the blizzard enveloped him.

Moss felt the QTNs now, too — that first heat of interior chemical burn she remembered from before her crucifixion. She hurried. The Vardogger trees were on fire around her. She walked the flaming path until sparks of blue caught her attention and she saw *Libra* like a black gash on the horizon. At the dome where Hyldekrugger's sentinels had kept their watch, naked men stared toward the sky, their mouths filled with silver. Crewmen of *Libra,* the survivors of the mutiny, Cobb among them, their lives suspended in the Terminus, dribbling silver from their mouths to coat their bodies in gleaming streams. Above them hung bones and specks of meat and veins traced delicately in the air, lungs and a heart and other organs displayed, and skin fluttering in the wind like a silk banner waving at the death of mankind. Hyldekrugger was already a ghost to her, and this was what remained of his followers; all the death they waged was a levee against the tide, but the levee had broken and left them wasted in the flood. As Moss neared the ship, she noticed that *Libra*'s hull was enclosed in ice; long spikes encased the bow like a jagged carapace and would have encased the stern, too, were it not for the flashes of blue radiating from the B-L, melting it back. Moss left the Vardogger path only when she could touch the hull. She followed along the hull until she found the gangway stairs that led to the airlock and found the red-thick blood that had been painted there, and the fingernails.

*The black river would be painless.*

She shook these thoughts. The airlock was iced over, so she struck at the ice with the metal cuff that locked her suit's glove to her sleeve. She thought of the first time she had stepped through this airlock: the swift loss of gravity, Hyldekrugger holding her.

*In the brig for eleven years,* she reminded herself, fearing the immortality of being stuck in *Libra*'s Gödel curve. No room for error. She would have to attack the B-L drive, somehow spark the cascade failure. If she failed, she might not ever know she'd failed; she would be in the loop with no one to ever retrieve her.

QTNs accumulated in her, she felt them like pinpricks. She struck at the seal of ice, frantic, *I have to get inside this thing,* she thought, away from the Terminus. *And then what?* That first time inside *Libra,* after she had lost gravity, after Hyldekrugger caught her, she remembered that Hyldekrugger had waited for the sound of gunfire before moving from the airlock. *Someone murdering the bull nuke,* Moss remembered, the officer responsible for the nuclear reactor. He must have been trying to spark the cascade failure.

*If I move quickly,* she thought.

*I might be able to move into the engine room before the gunfire.*

*I might be able to intervene, at that crucial moment, to save the bull nuke's life.*

She could protect him while he caused the failure.

Moss chipped away the ice. She took hold of the hatch, using her body weight to push until she felt the lock slip and she was able to open the iron door. She took a deep breath, readying to move quickly. *Libra*'s entry was a circular black void, and when she climbed through, she was engulfed in flame.

Fiery air, liquid waves roiling through the airlock. She was bucked by a lurch in the ship, alarms clanging. *We're falling.* Her suit was fire-resistant, but the flames had wrapped her in a cocoon of light, and she felt her skin warming. She could burn alive. Another jolt, tossing her. *Libra* crashed in a roar of tearing steel. Her head hit a wall, cracking her visor. The smoke of the electrical fire filled her faceplate, and she choked, coughing, her eyes burning.

She covered the faceplate crack with her gloves as best she could, but smoke still streamed in, blistering her. Her gloves were scorched. Her suit had melted in spots; the multilayer insulation was rated to a high degree of Celsius, but the engine-room fire would incinerate her. She crawled along the floor, as low as she could get to avoid the smoke, but the air was black where it wasn't fire. Her suit was on fire now, the flames burning through her layers of protection. She felt the heat and screamed, *I'll burn, I'm going to burn alive — I'll be in this loop, I'll burn forever.*

She saw blue light within the fire. She felt mounting tension, the immense crack of electric shock: the B-L misfire. As Moss floated upward, the fire and smoke disappeared, the conflagration gone in an instant except for the flames still crawling along the legs of her suit. She hit the ceiling, bounced. The fire-suppression system belched a stream of foam that doused her suit fire. *No gravity.* She was in the loop now, certainly. She must have entered at a different point from before, this time during the ship's crash. *Am I stuck in the loop?* It was like wondering if she was stuck in a dream.

Then everything happened too quickly. The two-tone clangor of the Power Plant Casualty alarm rang through the ship, but Moss was out of position, her suit stiff with the foamy fire suppressant. She scrambled, but the clatter of gunfire cut down her hopes. She was too late, everything was playing out as before. That gunfire meant the bull nuke had been shot. She wasn't in time to save him, to help him start the cascade failure of the B-L drive.

She tried to remember.

After the sound of gunfire, Hyldekrugger had brought her into the engine room.

That's where Moss went now, hoping she might be able to pick up where the bull nuke left off, thinking she might be able to figure out the control panel. The engine room was just as she'd seen it that first time, the silver containment vessel of the nuclear reactor, the B-L drive in its own compartment. The body of the bull nuke floated above the control panel, gluey blood in a long bubble from the bullet wounds in his gut.

She pushed the body aside, took off her scorched gloves, her helmet, let them float away. The control panel was a gray metal morass of switches and knobs, meters and blinking lights. It had been built in the 1970s: no AI interface, no digital screens. Again Moss was seized by a dreamlike frustration. She had to accomplish a task but didn't know how, had to spark a cascade failure but didn't know which switches to flip. *Try anything* — but, *No, that won't work.* There were fail-safes. The whole thing would just shut down, requiring an override code from an engineering officer.

Hyldekrugger hadn't wanted to stay in this room, she remembered, because Patrick Mursult would be here soon, a Navy SEAL in the frenzy of mutiny. *We don't want to fight him, not here.* The nuclear reactor rattled, a grinding whine, and the lights of the ship went out, casting her in pure darkness.

There had been a flashlight, she remembered. She floated to the near wall, feeling Velcro, feeling metal tools attached there, things she couldn't recognize in the dark. She recognized the shape of a flashlight when her fingers found the lens. She pulled it from the Velcro, turned on the light.

*I need help,* she thought. *I need to find Remarque before they kill her. How?*

She drifted into the passageway lined with portal windows, where she had first looked out and seen stars. The stars were brilliant now, burning cold in their multitude. The Power Plant Casualty alarm fell silent, and the running lights snapped back on. A flighty panic, adrenaline coursing through her. Moss realized she wouldn't know where Hyldekrugger would be, knew she would die if any of his followers saw her.

But she did know that Nicole Onyongo would hide in the brig eventually. Nicole had escaped into the brig, fearful that Hyldekrugger might kill her in his bloodbath. But where was Nicole hiding now? Moss thought back. Nicole had mentioned this to her, she was sure, when they were in the orchard together, Miss Ashleigh's orchard, and Nicole had smoked her cigarette . . .

Moss floated near the ship's electrolysis cabinet, and the memory clicked: Nicole had said she was hiding in the life-support room when the fighting broke out. The electrolysis cabinet was a narrow compartment housing the water reclamation system and the oxygen generation system.

She shimmied through the portal into the electrolysis cabinet and swung the door closed after her. A small workspace was nestled behind the chrome tanks, a chair with a writing desk bolted to the wall.

A volley of gunfire erupted in the passageway. She wanted out of the space suit in case she had to fight. Beneath the suit she wore only the long johns she'd taken from the body, that other version of her. Little protection, but at least she would be able to move. She unbuckled her waist harness, kicked off the charred, foam-coated pants. Moss tried to slide from the torso piece of her suit, pull her arms from the sleeves —

"Please don't hurt me."

Moss turned at the voice. The woman was hiding beneath the writing desk, tucked back into the shadows. So young, just out of her teens, her hair frizzy black, burnished with hickory accents. Beautiful brown eyes. Her T-shirt and shorts were spattered with blood. Her own? Her hand was wrapped in a bandage. She was barefoot, a gun floating near her feet.

"Nicole," said Moss.

"How do you know me?"

"I've known you before, in other times," said Moss.

"How is this possible?" asked Nicole, terrified, her skin lathered in sweat. "There are strange things happening. I don't understand. What do you mean, in other times?"

"Help me with my suit," said Moss.

The request brought Nicole out from hiding. She helped Moss unfasten the torso assembly, tugged it over her head. Nicole had left her gun floating near the writing desk, a Beretta M9, and she didn't react when Moss plucked it from the air. Either Nicole wasn't afraid of Moss or she was beyond fear.

"Did you use this?" asked Moss.

"I've never . . ."

Moss checked that a round was chambered. "Would you know how to destroy the B-L drive?"

"No, only the engineer officer or the bull nuke would know."

"Where are they?" asked Moss.

"Dead," said Nicole.

"Remarque's not dead," said Moss. "Can you get me to her?"

"You can't . . . You don't understand! She wants us to die," said Nicole. "She said we have to kill ourselves. She's gone *insane.* Why do we have to die? We can hide in the prison. We'll be safe there."

"I need to find Remarque," said Moss.

"They won't look in the prison —"

"Listen to me, Nicole. Listen," said Moss. "You've left this all behind. You were a nurse at a place called the Donnell House when I knew you. You helped people, elderly people. You took care of them."

"A nurse," said Nicole. "My mother was a nurse. I went to medical school because of my mother. And my father convinced Remarque to take me on this ship, because of my training. I miss him so much, I miss my father."

"Help me."

"How do you know me?" asked Nicole. "What's your name?"

"Shannon."

"Shannon, I don't want to die."

"Don't fear dying," said Moss, holding up her wrist, showing Nicole the ouroboros bracelet, the snake swallowing its own tail. Nicole put her hand to her own wrist, her own bracelet.

"Yes," said Nicole. "Yes, yes."

"I need to find Remarque before they kill her," said Moss. "She's not the one you should fear, Nicole. She can help. I *need* her."

"She's in the wardroom," said Nicole. "Remarque and Krauss locked themselves in. Cobb and some of the others are waiting to ambush them."

"Where is the wardroom?"

"I can get you there," said Nicole.

Nicole opened the portal door, disappeared into the passageway. A moment later she waved for Moss to follow. The ship smelled like death: loosed bowels and exsanguination. Nicole swam smoothly through the passageways, practiced, pulling herself along the handholds while Moss followed several feet behind. She led Moss through the Quad-lander stowage compartment, where three Landers were folded into their launch bays; they gleamed with a coating of dust that shone like diamonds. Moss realized that these Landers had come from Esperance.

"Up through here, through the bunks. The galley leads to the wardroom," said Nicole.

*Libra*'s galley was a stainless-steel box designed for zero-g food prep. Counter space limited, rectangular pots on hot plates, a cavernous utility sink filled with canned goods, the room like an Escher drawing. Culinary specialists would crowd in here, walking up the walls and across the ceiling to reach the bread ovens, dropping to the floor to keep the coffee brewers filled, standing on one wall to boil meat before jumping across the room to fold dough for pies.

"Most of them are above us, in the crew's mess," said Nicole. "We can go this way."

The galley opened up to a second prep area meant to serve the wardroom, the formal mess cabin for the commander and her highest-ranking officers. A narrow passageway lined with stainless-steel cabinets, every nook and cranny stuffed with canned foods. Nicole stopped, turned back, but Moss pushed ahead of her.

Two men waited at the wardroom door. They wore camouflage, the larger of the men shirtless, though it looked like he was clothed in blood. *Cobb,* she thought, nothing like the older brawler she knew, but a sharply chiseled warrior, his hair trimmed to a prickly crew cut. Their backs were to her, but she could see they each held a weapon, Cobb's an M16 rifle, the other man with his sidearm. She imagined coming up behind them — silently, floating over — and casually executing each man, a shot in the back of the head. *Cowardly,* but she needed to kill them to save everything. Moss sighted Cobb's center mass and shot.

Cobb spun toward her. She'd hit him, his narrow eyes confused. He raised his weapon, firing off a series of aimless rounds that tore through galley freezers before he'd marked where Moss was. Moss returned fire, reclined backward in the air, drifting with the recoil of her gun but keeping her aim, firing as she'd been taught to fire in zero-g, the smoke from her barrel puffing in spheroids pierced by bullets. She'd landed a grouping of shots, several rounds in Cobb's chest that spurted out bubbly spatter, and watched him go limp before feeling a sting in her left shoulder, again through her left breast. She screamed — more in surprise at the sudden pain than at the pain itself, but the awareness that she'd been shot grew as the pain increased like a spreading burn. She had lost sight of the second gunman, ducked back into the galley. Nicole was already cowering there. Blood had spread through Moss's shirt, over her chest and her left sleeve. It was increasingly difficult to breathe.

"Give up," she called out. "Drop your

weapon. I'm NCIS — you don't have to do this."

She'd seen videos of firefights between patrol officers and armed men, people who'd been pulled over on routine traffic stops for minor infractions, who'd gotten it into their heads that someone had to die. Moss had always marveled at the simple brutality of the exchange of fire, two men separated by a short distance — how straightforward it all was, no acrobatics or sharpshooting, just two men walking toward each other, firing rounds until one person lost the strength to stand. She heard movement and raised her gun. She recognized the second gunman, so much younger than when she'd seen his suicide in the mirrored room. Fleece was a young man here, nothing like the obese corpse hanged from the tree of bones, though behind the thick lenses of his glasses she saw his eyes and remembered that this man had recently lost his mind on the surface of Esperance. He ran toward her along the ceiling, firing rounds, his face a mask of confusion and rage. Moss felt another sting, this in her left thigh, above her prosthesis, but she gained her balance, expecting more stings across her body, expecting a sensation like being stung to death by a swarm of bees, and fired into the approaching gunman, calmly unloading her weapon into his center mass just as if she were at a range firing at a paper target. Fleece died, but his body kept coming, spinning as blood spun from him. She lowered her shoulder to absorb the blow, but he flew over her, crashing against a bread oven.

"Ow, *fuck,*" said Moss. *Three rounds,* she thought — *I took at least three rounds.* She had heard stories of people taking thirty rounds or more, so pumped up with adrenaline that they continued to resist arrest long after they should have died. *But one bullet can kill you,* she knew. *One bullet is enough.*

"Okay," she said, struggling. "Nicole, okay. We need Remarque," but the pain intensified. The bullet wound to her thigh bled heavily, blood spilling out over her prosthesis and rising around her. "We need to find her."

"I have to stanch your bleeding," said Nicole, applying pressure to Moss's thigh, but blood still pulsed from the wound. Nicole found a thin dish towel in the galley, looped it around Moss's thigh as a tourniquet. Blinding pain. Moss screamed as Nicole tightened the knot.

"We have to go," said Nicole. "Shannon,

they'll have heard —"

"No, we need Remarque," Moss growled.

She pounded on the locked wardroom door, a larger door than the iron portals throughout the rest of the ship, meant for ease of access for the dinner service. She slapped at the closed door, leaving hand-prints of blood.

"Shannon Moss, NCIS! Come out, we've got to hurry! Remarque? I need you for the B-L — Ah, *fuck.* I'm NCIS. Come out —"

Nicole pounded at the door with her. "It's Nicole Onyongo! Come out! Hurry! It's Onyongo —"

The wardroom door opened. Moss had seen a photograph of Remarque, in the *Libra* crew list, but even so she was much younger than Moss had imagined. Remarque was only a few years older than Moss, her hair a whitish silver color, cut in a boy's style with swept bangs. In her cotton slacks and U.S. Naval Academy sweatshirt, Remarque looked more like a woman's soccer captain than a professional soldier. Lean, athletic, her jaw squared. She came from the ward-room with her hands raised, projecting calm rather than surrender. Chloe Krauss fol-lowed, the ship's weapons officer, her hands also raised, a taller woman than Remarque, her crimson hair cut high and tight. Without weapons they had retreated to the ward-room, where they locked themselves in. Eventually, Moss knew, Chloe Krauss would have been shot in the ensuing firefight and Remarque would have been subdued, taken to the crew's mess, where Hyldekrugger would have slit her throat in front of his men, then passed around her ruined body.

"You're hurt," said Remarque. "We can help you. Krauss has training."

"We don't have time," said Moss. "These men, they all fought against you because you wanted to destroy *Libra* . . ."

"How did you get here?" asked Remarque. "You aren't my crew."

"You have to finish what you started," said Moss, her breath rattling, the taste of blood in her mouth. "Cascade failure, the B-L —"

"Who are you?" asked Remarque. "How do you know all this?"

"Do you know what a thin space is?" asked Moss. "A space-time knot?"

Remarque's left eye narrowed, a rakish expression of calculation. Her jaw tensed. "All right. Let's get to the engine room," she said. "The B-L was damaged in the initial fighting, but I need to spark a cascade failure for it to develop into a singularity."

"Hyldekrugger's in the crew's mess," said Nicole. "He'll be coming."

Krauss snatched Cobb's rifle, the M16, loaded a new magazine.

"We can make it to the engine room through the Quad-lander stowage compartment," said Nicole. "That's the way we came."

"There's a quicker way," said Krauss. "We can drop through into the gunnery, a straight shot to the engine room."

"I can't," said Moss. She was losing blood, felt cold. *A forest in winter, an eternal forest.* The tourniquet had already come loose, and blood stained the air around her. "I can't move anymore."

Nicole held her. "Let's go, let's follow them."

Krauss led them belowdecks, into one of the thruster houses. She unlocked a portal door and dropped even farther down to one of the cavernous gunneries, the munitions storage. They passed the starboard laser generator, a gray box with a lens. Moss smelled fire as they neared the stern. There'd been fire when she was locked in the brig, she remembered. How long before the inferno would bring down the ship? *We could run out of time,* she thought. *We'd run out of time, and I'd never know it.* If the B-L drive misfired, the crew of *Libra* would reset like chess pieces for a new match.

"Up," said Krauss.

An iron ladder led to the engineering department, the passageway to the engine room. Moss floated ahead of Nicole, Remarque bringing up the rear, closing the iron door behind them. As they entered the engineering department, however, a voice called out to them.

"Drop your guns! Remarque, give this up! Drop your fucking gun, Krauss!"

Patrick Mursult barred the portal to the engine room, M16 in firing position. He braced himself to counter the recoil of his rifle fire, three magazines floating within arm's reach for reload. Devastation crashed through Moss: she had saved Remarque only to lead her into this different death. He could kill them all in a rapid spray just by easing back his finger.

"Patrick," said Nicole. "Please."

"I can't let you in here," said Mursult. His eyes were cold when he spoke to Nicole, and Moss realized that the burgeoning emotions that would one day lead to their affair were dead to him in this moment of decision. He'd kill her, thought Moss, as easily as he'd kill any of them.

"Drop the gun, Krauss," said Remarque, and Krauss let her rifle float aside. "We'll talk about this," she said. "You think you're doing the right thing —"

"Karl's coming," said Mursult, "and he'll kill you. He wants to be the one. He wants to cut your fucking head off with his ax."

"Mursult," said Moss. "Damaris, she —" But her words failed. She was light-headed, so much of her blood lost.

"Who is that?" asked Mursult, his cold eye finding Moss. "She shouldn't be here."

Moss tried to speak, choked on blood. She took a deep, wet breath. "I come from another time," she said. "I've seen how this all plays out. You have a wife, named Damaris. You have a daughter, she's five years old. You'll have another, a son not yet born, and another daughter. This doesn't end well, what you're doing. They all die . . . because of this. They always die . . ."

Mursult pointed the gun at Moss's heart. No hint of emotion, no hint of reckoning.

"You can give her a future, Patrick. Your daughter. Marian."

She saw the moment emotion broke through, at the sound of his daughter's name. Mursult lowered his weapon. "Go. I'll hold them off as long as I can, but they're coming."

Nicole carried Moss through into the engine room, Remarque and Krauss following. The B-L drive was the center of a blue corona that shimmered like the reflection of light on water, the room stinking of electrical fire. Krauss shut the main portal door, barring it closed. Moss heard gunfire, outside in the passageway, short bursts before the sound died away. *They're here.*

Remarque opened the control locker for the B-L drive. Moss saw blood in the air and thought of treasure chests at the bottom of fish tanks, how their lids flipped open and bubbles raced upward. *My blood,* she thought. Blood soaked through her long johns and spilled from the gaping wound in her thigh, bubbles propelling from her thigh and spreading around her and Nicole. Bubbles in a fish tank. Moss looked at the B-L drive, its eerie blue light flickering outward in concentric rings.

A sizzling sound, an explosion, and the portal door blew from its hinges in a rush of fire. *No,* thought Moss as Hyldekrugger glided through into the engine room. Krauss shot with her rifle, but Hyldekrugger's followers fanned out through the room, returning fire. Nicole was hit, a spray of mist and ropes of blood gushed from her chest and formed into wobbling spheres. Another sting zipped through Moss's leg, her stomach. The pain settled deep within her. *No* —

"We have it," shouted Remarque, blue

light appearing like a halo around the B-L, an intense plasma light, an arc.

Krauss was sprayed with bullets, and her body spun like a knot of shredded rags. Remarque screamed, but Moss heard her voice as if underwater. *We are all underwater,* she thought. Bodies floating, blood escaping her intestines in quivering globs and rushing squiggles that formed into circles as they rose.

Hyldekrugger was a young man. There was nothing of the devil in him, not yet. He was just scared and selfish. He placed the barrel of his gun against Remarque's temple and fired. Blood sprayed from the exit wound, and Moss watched as it misted and as it fell. Her own blood mingled with Remarque's, a rising stream pulled toward the gravity of the B-L drive. The failing engine flooded the room with blue, and Moss saw a speck of perfect black within that light. The black expanded, a perfect circle, and soon the perfect circle bent everything around it, smearing the world toward it. Moss saw all of time written out in that black circle, everything that was and everything that will be, the first oblivion and the last. As the circle expanded, all of existence diminished. *Libra* and the winter woods, the evergreens and the Terminus, the world covered with snow. Moss felt herself held in this gravity before she, too, was enveloped by the black hole. All thinking ceased, all suffering. She slipped into that darkness, no longer a body but a wave of light.

# EPILOGUE

*January 28, 1986*

Heavier snow now. The way it hangs in front of streetlamps and looks like glitter. She didn't want to drive in this, so we walk. Cut through the neighbor's, down through their thatch of pines. She pulls on the branches, and I'm covered.

"Oh, bitch! Oh, you bitch!" I'm screaming, snow down the neck of my coat, shaking it from my hair. She's laughing. I ball up snow and throw it, but it powders in the air. She's laughing in a way I haven't heard for a while.

"As long as I grow up to be rich," she says. "Or marry rich. That's all I want."

We watch for wrecks in town. "You ever hear how a car crash sounds like plastic?" she says. She's smoking Camels from a hard pack, and I take one, down to her last few. She taps hers on the box, taps mine for me. She lights hers, and I lean in to catch the fire from her tip. Plenty of fishtailing, but no one hits. I'm shivering, I only brought my dad's Navy coat. She's in her Michael Jackson jacket, zippers on the sleeves. A car goes past and blares the horn, and Courtney flips them off, and someone laughs. Maybe they knew us.

Seven Hills on Euclid, Courtney's favorite place because the woman at the counter never checks IDs. Courtney buys cigarettes. I get a hot chocolate from the machine.

"Gimm," says the woman, "let me see it." She says, "Jesus fucking Christ," when Courtney lowers her turtleneck to show the scar. It's bright white, will always be there because some fuck lunatic slit her throat. The scar's jagged — you can see where the knife went in, how it dragged. The woman gives over the hard pack of Camels and says, "On me. Least you should get is a pack of cigarettes out of something like that."

"Hell's bells," says Courtney.

"We were at Pizza Hut, serves her right," I say.

"I'm smoking my last one, I'll be outside."

"One sec."

I buy the hot chocolate and a Clear Blue test, and the woman just rings me out. All she says is, "If you don't like what it says, get a second one before you freak out. It

600

won't hurt to try more than once."

We lie together on her bedroom floor. Enough room for us if we kick our legs up to her bed. She's smoking her third, but I'm taking mine slow, blowing smoke at her ceiling fan, watching the fan stir the smoke and blow it back to me. *Powerage,* side B. We aren't talking, and I'm all right because Courtney's told me I'm her only friend good enough not to talk to. When the record ends, I ask if her brother's coming home tonight.

"He's at Jesse's," says Courtney.

*Damn.* I couldn't feel it before we went to Seven Hills, but it's like I can feel it now, like there's a butterfly in my stomach, fluttering its wings. Courtney gets up to change the record, puts on *Back in Black.* I'm touching my stomach. She has a new way of touching her neck, absentmindedly like she's touching a necklace. When she comes back to the floor with me, our faces are so close I feel heat coming off her skin.

Three a.m. I wake up but let her sleep. Thinking of the blue cross that appeared when I pissed on the stick. Thinking of how I'll tell him. I creep down the hallway to his room and check his bed, but he's not here.

I wish he was here, the bed of the sister, the bed of the brother. What would it be like if Courtney was my sister? Best friends, but closer. If Davy does the right thing, she would be my sister. I drift through the downstairs rooms. The curtains are open on the living-room French doors, enough moonlight reflecting off the snow to fill the house with silver. I look out at their backyard, at the snowfall so smooth on the lawn, so smooth on the pines, so perfect, undisturbed, except for a circle of footsteps. A perfect circle of footsteps, but I can't see footsteps leading to or from it, like someone dropped from the air, walked in a circle, and disappeared. My mother believes in omens, but never in good ones.

How will he ask me to marry him? Right then, when I tell him? No, he'll do it right, someplace romantic, someplace over dinner. I have pictures left over from freshman year I can give him. I'll give him a picture when I tell him so he can think of me when he's away, think of us. He says he's joining the Navy to see the world, but Courtney says it's because he can't get into college. He says he'll see maybe Germany, maybe Egypt, maybe Japan. I imagine what he'll do when I tell him. I imagine his eyebrows going up like they do. He'll ask me to marry him, and we'll get married at St. Pat's, Courtney as my maid of honor. I'll pray at St. Pat's every day that he's away. I'll pray for my father, I'll pray for my husband, both at sea. I imagine Davy in an eternity of water praying to a star he's picked out and named for me. Shannon, he'll pray, oh, Shannon Star. And he'll point out his star, our star, and he'll make sure I can pick it out from all the others, and he'll say that he'll look at that star and think of me, and he'll ask me to do the same. And on nights like this, I'll kiss our child asleep and head outside to mark our star, and I'll know he's safe, I'll know that starlight bathes him as he swings from the rigging on the deck of his ship, as he looks out over the sea at night, as the steel hull cuts the swells. I'll know he's lit with starlight, I'll know he's safe, I'll know he's thinking of me, of us, and I'll know that no matter how far he sails, he'll one day sail for home.

# ACKNOWLEDGMENTS

Thank you to my brother-in-law, Special Agent Peter O'Connor, who sparked the idea for this book over hamburgers at Five Guys when we talked about time travel.

Thank you to Neill Blomkamp and Jonathan Auxier, whose insights into this book were critical to its development.

Thank you to Laura Leimkuehler, Dr. Barry B. Luokkala, J. J. Hensley, Jen Latimer, and Dan Moran, all experts in their fields who generously shared their knowledge with me.

Thank you to David Gernert and Andy Kifer at the Gernert Company. Thank you to Sylvie Rabineau at RWSG Literary Agency.

Thank you to Mark Tavani, Sally Kim, and the entire team at Putnam.

Thank you to my family.

And thank you to my wife, Sonja, and

daughter, Genevieve. You are the loves of my life.

# ABOUT THE AUTHOR

**Tom Sweterlitsch**, author of *Tomorrow and Tomorrow,* has a master's degree in Literary and Cultural Theory from Carnegie Mellon and worked for twelve years at the Carnegie Library for the Blind and Physically Handicapped. He lives in Pittsburgh with his wife and daughter.